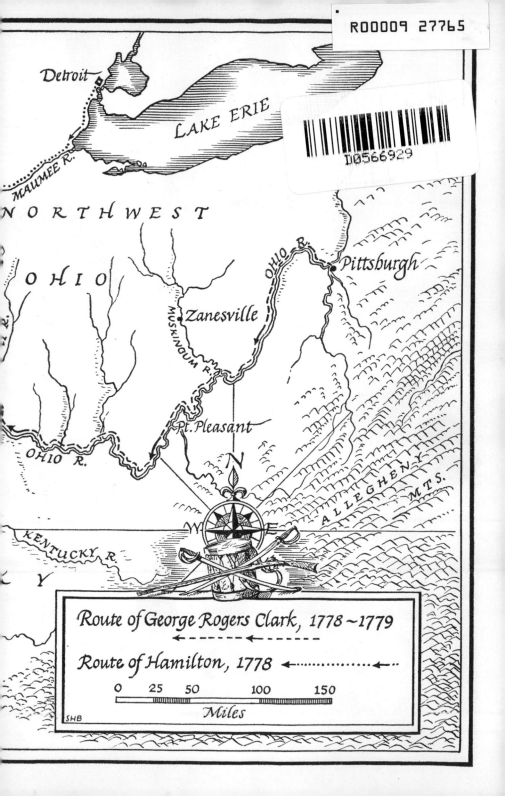

Detroit

LAKE ERIE

MAUMEE R.

N O R T H W E S T

O H I O

OHIO R.

Pittsburgh

MUSKINGUM R.

Zanesville

Pt. Pleasant

OHIO R.

KENTUCKY R.

K Y

A L L E G H E N Y   M T S.

N

W E

Route of George Rogers Clark, 1778~1779
← - - - - - - ← - - - - - -

Route of Hamilton, 1778 ← ·········· ← ··

0   25   50   100   150
Miles

SHB

Books by Bruce Lancaster

THE WIDE SLEEVE OF KWANNON

GUNS OF BURGOYNE

BRIDE OF A THOUSAND CEDARS

(*In collaboration with Lowell Brentano*)

FOR US, THE LIVING

BRIGHT TO THE WANDERER

TRUMPET TO ARMS

THE SCARLET PATCH

NO BUGLES TONIGHT

PHANTOM FORTRESS

VENTURE IN THE EAST

THE SECRET ROAD

BLIND JOURNEY

FROM LEXINGTON TO LIBERTY

(*A narrative history of the Revolution*)

ROLL, SHENANDOAH

NIGHT MARCH

THE AMERICAN HERITAGE BOOK OF THE REVOLUTION

THE BIG KNIVES

Juvenile

GUNS IN THE FOREST

(*The Story of Burgoyne's Campaign*)

THE AMERICAN REVOLUTION

TICONDEROGA

(*The Story of a Fort*)

THE
BIG
KNIVES

THE
BIG
KNIVES

BRUCE LANCASTER

With a Historical Epilogue by
EDWARD P. HAMILTON

An Atlantic Monthly Press Book

LITTLE, BROWN AND COMPANY · BOSTON · TORONTO

ATLANTIC–LITTLE, BROWN BOOKS
ARE PUBLISHED BY
LITTLE, BROWN AND COMPANY
IN ASSOCIATION WITH
THE ATLANTIC MONTHLY PRESS

Published simultaneously in Canada
by Little, Brown & Company (Canada) Limited

PRINTED IN THE UNITED STATES OF AMERICA

Now more than ever
for my wife
Jessie Payne Lancaster
and for
Southworth and Margaret Lancaster

Contents

Contents

THE
BIG
KNIVES

I

From Atlantic Sails to Mississippi Keeler

A STRONG April sun beat against the slatted shutters of Oliver Pollock's counting-house while the church, convent and garrison bells of New Orleans pealed out ten o'clock. Markham Cape, his eyes not yet adjusted to the softened light of the long room, walked carefully on past high, slant-topped desks where clerks stood hunched over ledgers and letter-books. Ahead of him the old chief clerk bobbed along, a neat queue swinging across thin shoulders. At a heavy door the old man stopped, rapped with an odd, jerky rhythm, slipped inside and closed it after him.

Markham stood in tightly controlled impatience as though waiting out an unavoidable delay. He seemed utterly unconcerned by the battered straw hat in his bronzed hand, by the skimpy white suit whose rough seams were strained by the spread of his shoulders and the bulge of thick arm and leg muscles. His straw sandals were too small for him but he was no more aware of them than of the tar-smear on one trouser-leg. Behind him the clerks whispered, broke into muffled snickers. Markham turned slowly and the clerks bent over their work again, stilled by the deeply tanned fresh-shaven face, the solid chin and the piercing dark eyes that looked coldly at them from under black brows.

Minutes passed. The door opened and the chief clerk bowed almost obsequiously. "If the Señor will be pleased to enter," he announced.

Markham thanked him and stepped into the owner's office. The light was better here and he saw a stocky man of about forty rising from a carved table. At first he felt a sharp twinge of disappointment. Despite gleaming linen and carefully dressed gingery hair

Oliver Pollock seemed almost commonplace, ineffectual. Then he noted the level hazel eyes, the sweep of the forehead, the firm mouth and his impression changed. "Your servant, Mr. Pollock," he said with a bow.

The merchant smiled noncommittally. "Yours, Mr. Cape. Sit down and tell me what I can do for a fellow American." He seated himself again in his carved, high-backed chair.

Markham drew another massive chair to the table and indicated the papers that Pollock held in his rather plump hand. "I see you've already opened the dossier that I gave your head clerk. I drew it up on the voyage from Havana. You might glance at it before we begin. It may save you questions and me answers later."

"I ran my eye over the first pages when Garcia brought it in." Pollock glanced quizzically at him. "He seemed impressed by you. I might even say a little frightened."

"I don't enjoy frightening people. But I was anxious to see you." Markham's mouth set as though biting back an impatient, "Let's get on with it."

Pollock riffled through the sheets. "H'm. Boston Latin School. That accounts for your clear hand." His eyes moved along the script.

Markham sat braced in his chair, determined to keep his foot from tapping on the polished floor. To avoid staring at the merchant, who read on impassively, he turned his eyes to the tall windows at his right. The sun had bleached the blue from the great U bend of the Mississippi and ships showed hard against a silver stream that was almost level with the second story of the counting-house. Along the restraining levee where willows held trailing boughs motionless in the still air a few oxcarts lumbered. Down-stream, crumbling palisades traced out the limits of the city on the left bank and ended with the jut of Fort St. Charles topped by the bold red and yellow flag of Spain. His mind took in and stored away details automatically, details of just one more port that he was seeing here in the spring of 1778 — just one more port, one more stage of a journey that had begun nearly two years ago when

— His attention returned abruptly as Pollock began shuffling the sheets of the dossier.

"Yes, Mr. Cape. I find this most interesting, unusual, in fact." He propped his elbows on the table, rested his chin on his linked hands. "Let's see if it's all clear in my mind. You belong to a Boston shipping family. In 1769 you were given a berth in Murchison's of Liverpool. I know the house. Old. Solid. How did this happen?"

"We'd had close ties with Murchison's since my grandfather's day. During the French Wars, my father was able to help Murchison's at a bad time. Later, this offer was made. I had two elder brothers ahead of me at home, so we accepted."

"You were sixteen then. Good age to start. You went to Murchison's branch at Cadiz in Spain, then after a time to Funchal in Madeira. That seems like steady progress in an exacting house."

"They kept me on, anyway," said Markham dryly.

"Now comes '74, and you are sent to Genoa, virtually in charge." He looked reflectively at Markham. "And 1775 coming closer all the time, then bursting out in full force. You must have found it hard to follow events over here, Genoa being off the beaten track. You'd have been in far closer touch at Funchal or Cadiz."

"Very little news, always late," said Markham tersely. "Bales of rumors, always wrong. I couldn't make out who was fighting whom, or if anyone was really fighting anyone. I knew that something was wrong because I stopped hearing from home in late '75. And I'm sure that what I had heard up till then was noncommittal, since my mail came to me via Murchison's in Liverpool and could have been read there. I still don't know whether my family stood by the Crown or by the States. It's possible, too, that Murchison's tried to keep me in the dark about American affairs."

"That's reasonable to suppose," observed Pollock, pursing his full lips. "You were an investment of time and money."

"Which they liquidated rather suddenly," said Markham. "Just the same, I can hardly blame them."

"You're able to look at it like that?" asked Pollock quickly.

"How else? A Cape master turns privateer and snaps up two Murchison ships out in the Atlantic. When that news finally reaches the elder Murchison, he isn't going to take that lying down. He strikes out at the nearest available Cape, who happens to be myself in Genoa. I'm just a symbol, of course, but a symbol who ends up on the beach with almost no money."

Pollock flicked through the sheets. "I note that your tendency is usually toward direct action, which is sometimes a good trait. In this case you struck out for home at once. Your course was a roundabout one, as it had to be, you having no capital." He began to read off the names of ships and ports once familiar in his trade reports.

But those ships and ports and days and weeks and months were distinctly vivid in Markham's mind. He had served as deckhand, as mate, as stowaway on xebecs and feluccas and sloops and tartanes. He had shuttled back and forth across the Mediterranean, had known Elba and Corsica and the Balearics. He had seen sunrises over Africa at Sfax and Tunis and Tangier. Larger craft had carried him out into the Atlantic, raising the Canaries and the Azores. He had gone west, west again, only to double back into the Mediterranean or nose up the coast of Portugal. There had been killing stretches ashore when, ragged and famished, he had combed odd waterfronts for a ship, *any* ship that might advance him a stage, even a half-stage on his way. At last, at Oporto, there was a Baltic brig, Havana-bound and shorthanded. That brig —

Pollock was speaking again. "Just why, Mr. Cape, did you think it worth your while to come to me in Spanish New Orleans, which is rather farther west than you wanted to be?"

Markham studied the merchant's face, but read curiosity, not suspicion in it. "There was no chance of getting north from Havana. Everyone said that British cruisers were far too thick. I happened to meet a *Guarda Costa* officer, Cadiz-born. We talked about his home and finally got onto my own wanderings. He told me that, as an American, I should come to New Orleans and see you. I didn't have any other ideas, so he got me a working berth on *Espiritu Santo,* a foul little raft. We anchored off the levee this morning."

Pollock's eyes were on the high ceiling. "As always, direct action. You hear of a supposed American in New Orleans who may further your travels in some unspecified way and — here you are. It's all in the pattern." His gaze sought Markham's. "You've had wide experience in trade. Garcia says your Spanish is excellent. You claim a smattering of French and Italian. You studied navigation ashore and put it into practice at sea. You've survived as a member of cutthroat crews and you've handled such gentry as mate. You've gone with and fought off boarding parties. You've used swivel guns and some heavy ones."

Markham raised his eyebrows. "Aren't you building up a first-class reference as pirate for me?"

"Not at all, though I've heard it said that the only difference between a seagoing merchant and a pirate is that a pirate is so careless." He picked up a quill pen and ran the plume reflectively between his lips. "I can take direct action myself at times. I'm not going to bother to look up the master of the *Espiritu Santo.* He could only account for you from Havana here. Anyway, I like to make up my own mind about people. I'm going to make a suggestion to you."

Markham braced himself inwardly against a word that might tell him that his trip from Havana had been in vain, that he was still a wanderer. "And that is?" he managed to say steadily.

"That you work here with me. You say at once that you've no capital. I say that you have — your experience and what I make of your character."

Markham paled under his tan. Did he dare risk antagonizing Oliver Pollock? He lowered his head like a boxer expecting a heavy blow. "That's an unusual expression of confidence, sir. There's no need for us to fence. I'm holding my course for home and whatever I may find there. Then I want a place, any place, in our Army. I may not have known much about what was going on when I was in Genoa. I've learned a good deal since."

Pollock's heavy eyebrows contracted in a frown and his eyes

darkened. "You're confoundedly obstinate for a man in your position, Mr. Cape." Then a slow smile spread over his face. "As obstinate as I hope I should have been at twenty-five. Very well. I'll help you get home, and to the Army, if that's what you want."

Markham leaned forward quickly. "*You will?*" he said hoarsely.

"Yes. What you heard in Havana is correct. The cards are stacked against a run up the east coast. And they won't always be dealt in your favor on the only other route."

Markham sprang to his feet. "I'm used to playing the cards that are dealt me. What's my route and when do I start?"

"One thing at a time. Let's clear you with the Spanish authorities first. Governor Galvez won't be at the Cabildo today, but his deputy, Galarmendi, can look after you. H'm, your present kit is hardly appropriate for a ceremonial call. Let's find something better." He rose, led the way into a smaller room and opened a big armoire. "I keep a few assorted changes here to outfit a few assorted people. Come back to the office when you've found something that suits you."

Markham ripped off his frayed suit and plunged his hands among the coats and breeches and pantaloons and shirts that hung so neatly on their oak pegs. A gold-braided waistcoat slipped from his over-eager fingers and a packet of neck-cloths flapped after it. "Slack off!" he muttered. "We're not on our way yet. How do we know that Pollock can clear us with the Dons? After all, he's only an American merchant on foreign soil."

Fifteen minutes later he came into the office, fingering a fresh neck-cloth as he worked his shoulders into a linen coat. Pollock nodded approval. "A good choice, Mr. Cape. We're having an unusually hot April and velvet or broadcloth would have been too much. Are those shoes all right?"

Markham looked down at the silver buckles gleaming against black leather. "I'm no judge, sir. These are the first real shoes I've had on since the fall of '77. To me, they're perfect."

Pollock smiled understandingly. "There's something heartening about the feel of good shoe-leather." He handed Markham a broad hat of finely woven straw. "Clap this on your black head against the sun. And take this silver-headed stick. Carrying one lends an idiotic sort of prestige here." He opened the door and led the way into the counting-room.

The clerks rose as though a string had been pulled, bowed deeply to their employer and to Markham. On the gallery outside Pollock pointed to wide stairs that led to the street a good ten feet below. "We'll go up the Rue Conti. I'll take the lead. The *banquettes*, the sidewalks that is, aren't really wide enough for two abreast."

At the foot of the stairs Markham seemed to move into a soft glow as the sun struck on bricks that were a pale red, almost orange, a shade that was repeated over and over by the thick pillars that lifted each building high off the ground. The spaces between the pillars were bricked up or filled by cypress planks set on end. Markham wondered about this type of construction until he remembered the high levee holding back the waters of the Mississippi whose crest must have been a good ten feet above street level.

Pollock swung along ahead of him, tossing occasional remarks over his shoulder. "An odd town, Mr. Cape. Half West Indian village, half frontier settlement. We're growing, though. Well over three thousand people here right now and —" He broke off as an oxcart laden with sugar sacks sent up a nerve-wracking screech from its ungreased axles on its way to the waterfront. Two more followed, heavy with cypress planks and bundles of shingles, their axle-voices even shriller than the first.

Markham followed along, dark eyes alert and lips compressed as he took in the flavor of this new port. He was continually stepping aside or pressing close to the buildings as passers-by headed for the levee. There were obvious Spaniards, mostly minor officials or clerks, equally obvious Frenchmen who strolled by superciliously in clothes cut to the pattern of a bygone Parisian generation. A swarthy captain of the Louisiana Battalion, Colonial Line Infantry, marched determinedly on in his white uniform, sure that junior officers, privates and civilians would make way for him. Two Ursuline nuns pattered along, eyes on the ground, while in the street a train of pack-mules, bulky with bales of hides and furs, trotted after their belled leader.

Inwardly Markham fumed at the slow progress. "Let's get on and see what the Dons will do for us!" he thought. Some of the eagerness left him. Do for us? Maybe they would do nothing. Why should they, for a waif sponsored by an American merchant who, unless Spanish trade-laws had changed utterly, could only exist here under tolerance? Pollock was calling, "We turn right here, down the Rue de Chartres. Takes us into the Place d'Armes. That two-story affair's the Cabildo, beside the Church of St. Louis." There were more pack mules to be dodged, a huddle of blanket-wrapped Houma Indians to be skirted before the Cabildo was reached.

Two guards, deep blue collars and cuffs sharp against their gray-white jackets, crossed their bayoneted muskets in a crisp one-two-three movement before the wide door. Then they came to order arms, each raising a hand to his red-pomponed cocked hat and stepping aside. Pollock smiled, touched his hat-brim with his stick and entered. "At least he stands well with the garrison," thought Markham. "Now what?"

An ancient usher stepped out of the shadows on a peg-leg whose din smothered all lesser sounds. He peered nearsightedly at Pollock and shook his head. A chill struck Markham and a nagging, inner voice insisted, "We're going to be turned away!" The usher peered again and recognition sent him bowing nearly double, unloosed a flood of Spanish. But of course Don Julio Galarmendi would be honored to receive Don Oliveros Pollock and his guest! Another official, braided and bearing a ball-topped staff, was summoned, stalked regally down a wide corridor that reeked of strong Louisiana tobacco, and flung open a door. The official's voice boomed like a church bell. "Señor the Commercial Agent of the Honorable Congress of the United States of America and his distinguished guest!"

Markham followed Pollock blindly into the room muttering, "I'll be damned! 'Of the Congress of the United States'! He could at least have given me a hint."

A tall, white-faced man with the prominent eyes of an astonished rabbit sprang up from behind a wide table, ran forward with hands outstretched. "But my dear friend!" Galarmendi's voice erupted from the depths of his paunch. "There is no need to be alarmed, no need to honor my poor office with your presence so quickly!"

Pollock's hat made a magnificent sweep. "Time ever drags between my visits to His Excellency, Deputy Governor Don Julio Galarmendi, and races far too swiftly when I am with him. May I beg the honor to present a young American friend, Señor Markham Cape? With the consent of the Spanish Crown, he may find it advisable to proceed north up the river someday."

Markham and Galarmendi exchanged deep bows, announced themselves each overwhelmed by the honor of such a presentation. Then Galarmendi turned to Pollock. His face set in an official frown that gave way to judicial profundity. Then all features were flooded with an expression of enlightenment in which even the tips of his ears seemed to join. "Ah!" Both hands flew high. "He goes north up our river! But he will speed like the car of Phoebus with the good will of Don Oliveros Pollock guiding him. Only — not that it is at all necessary, but if I might be permitted — a *pasaporte* — I should hold it a privilege — signed by me over the Royal Arms of Spain for the friend of my friend. Let him go as far as New Madrid, as St. Louis, even up the reaches of the wild Missouri, and every servant of the Crown will be honored to further Señor Cape in all his enterprises!"

Dazed by Pollock's obvious standing with officialdom, Markham managed to murmur, bowing, that he could not aspire to the honor of bearing such a document, but Galarmendi plunged across the room, volleying orders through an open door. Pollock gave a discreet cough. "You *ought* to stay here with me! Decidedly, you have a way with these people." Galarmendi charged back, mopping his face with a crimson handkerchief. Pollock bowed again. "You were good enough when we came in to speak of my being alarmed. I trust no affair of mine has been so mismanaged as to give concern to those who serve His Catholic Majesty."

Galarmendi stared at him. Then again enlightenment flooded every visible feature. "Ah! Then you have *not* seen Don Eliphalet Haskins of the Rue Royale? Don Eliphalet has *not* given you my message? Then it is I —" he thumped his broad chest "— who must tell you! Be seated, Señores." Pollock and Markham took high-backed chairs while Galarmendi whipped out a sheet of stiff paper and rapped it with his knuckles. "This came today, and by rights I should have had the man flogged for his insolence in bringing it. It is from the British *Comandante* of all West Florida. He, in terms that I now brand before the world as harsh, presumptuous, unchivalrous, overbearing, even, I may say, lacking in courtesy, demands once again that you be seized and delivered to him as a rebel against the British Crown."

He handed the paper to Pollock who read it, frowning a little, and then passed it back. "Thank you, Señor Deputy Governor. It reads much like that earlier demand."

"You understand, of course, how our Governor Don Bernardo de Galvez will treat it? He will fling it to the floor as I do —" the paper fluttered down "— and he will stamp upon it as I do!" The room rang as a large, flat foot whacked across the sheet.

Pollock looked troubled. "I am a simple tradesman, Señor, and there is much that I may not understand when nations deal with nations. No doubt your own wide experience throws clear sunlight on the reason for this demand. It occurs to me that recent doings at Natchez —"

Galarmendi's hands flew up. "Ah! And at the British plantations below!"

"Your confirmation of my own unskilled reasoning honors me. And there was also —"

Markham was soon lost in the torrent of talk from which strange place-names gushed and spouted. There was Natchez again and Manchac, Baton Rouge and Lake Pontchartrain and Lake Maurepas. Galarmendi spoke of Arkansas Post and Pollock countered with Mobile and Pensacola. The Spaniard's voice dropped as he mentioned a place called Fort Pitt and a river known as the Ohio.

To Markham, the pair might have been reading from a mysterious map of a long-lost continent.

Matters became clearer as Galarmendi almost whispered, "And those thirty thousand pounds sterling of Spanish military supplies which our Governor sent north up the Mississippi to the posts on the west bank. A careless word might have told those English —" he checked himself with a sidelong glance at Markham.

"Señor Cape has my confidence," said Pollock stiffly. "It is my hope that he may be honored with yours."

Galarmendi's arms flew wide. "I abase myself before Señor Cape. I am humbled by my clumsy failure to make it clear that I in no way question Señor Cape's integrity or his discretion."

Markham inclined his head. "Thank you, Señor." And it seemed to him that Galarmendi was pleased by that simple, unadorned statement.

"As I said," Galarmendi went on, "the unintentional indiscretion of a Cabildo clerk might have made known that those supplies are actually charged to the account of Señor Don Oliveros Pollock, Commercial Agent for the Congress of the United States."

Pollock shook his head. "Such indiscretions do not occur in the Cabildo where a Galvez and a Galarmendi preside. I shall pursue inquiries in other quarters. May I be permitted to transmit whatever I may learn to you and to Don Bernardo de Galvez?"

"Your least whisper commands the instant attention of all the Cabildo, Señor. And now we attend to the matter of the *pasaporte*."

Outside the Cabildo, Markham studied the parchment that Galarmendi had given him. "This seems to cover me. '*Concedo libre y seguro pasaporte a Señor Don Markham Cape para que pase de la Nueva Orleans por San Luís. Pido y encargo se le pongo embarazo,*' and so on. That ought to launch me. Mr. Pollock, you've placed me deeply in your debt."

The merchant waved a hand. "It's been a pleasant experience

for me, though I'm regretting more than ever that you won't stay. You were capital with Galarmendi."

"Good of you to say so. But all this has convinced me that I'm right. I couldn't follow your talk with him. I never heard of a lot of the places you two mentioned like Natchez, Fort Pitt and the Ohio River. And what was all that about trouble with the British upriver?"

Pollock frowned. "Something that could have helped us but which unfortunately had the opposite effect. It's a long story, but it won't touch you since you're leaving. Now we have our next move to consider and that is sitting in the shade of my courtyard and watching plates, heavily loaded plates, being brought out from my kitchens."

The New Orleans streets were still clamorous with the voices of axles, wheels and hoofs but over the din a single phrase rang in Markham's mind: "I'm heading home! I'm heading home!"

Turning into the Rue Conti he touched Pollock's elbow. "Who, or rather what the devil is that?" He nodded toward a tall, lean man who moved on with an odd, gliding gait. He was heavily bearded under a broad hat that had once been white. A full-skirted soft leather shirt dangled from bony shoulders and long fringes fluttered from hems and sleeves, were repeated on the breeches that clung to flat-muscled legs. A lumpy haversack flopped against his right hip and a long-barreled firearm was slung across his back.

"Careful," said Pollock. "Those people have ears like wolves and they're apt to act unpredictably if they think they're offended." They were abreast of the man, who turned a hawk-nose and hard eyes on them. Pollock touched the brim of his hat with an amiable "Howdy, friend."

The other nodded and answered, "Howdy," in a sleepy drawl as his gliding step carried him out of earshot.

Markham whistled softly. "That weapon of his. I swear that its bore was rifled, not smooth."

"You've a quick eye, Mr. Cape. Yes, that rifle's a sort of trademark. He's either from Western Virginia or Kentucky, very likely the latter to judge by the white hat. In a few weeks his type won't strike you as odd. Here we are at home. There'll be a bisque of shrimp, pompano with mushrooms and truffles, a gombo aux herbes and a grillade of venison. We'll have Xerez wine in memory of your days in Cadiz and Madeira for Funchal. I trust you've a stout appetite, Mr. Cape."

Late afternoon sun, its glare broken by split-reed screens, was filtering into Oliver Pollock's office as Markham entered. The merchant looked up from a thick letter-book. "Your siesta seems to have done you good, Mr. Cape."

"No siesta, sir. Too restless, now that the last stage of traveling seems to be in sight."

Pollock slammed his book shut. "Yes, it's time to think about that last stage."

"Overland, I suppose?"

"There *is* land to go over. But without a strong escort you *might* last as much as a week on it, though I doubt it. There are Indians who would not be interested in your wish to get home. We'll take a surer way, though I warn you that your Pilgrim's Progress may hold more hazards than John Bunyan invented for his hero."

Markham gave a tight smile. "That will be no novelty."

"That is just why I start you off with reasonable confidence that you'll arrive in good condition." He rose, crossed the room and unrolled a huge hanging map. "This isn't too accurate nor to scale, but it'll give you a rough bird's-eye view of your route. A wandering Frenchman, half surveyor, half artist, did it for me some time ago."

Markham stepped closer, eyes on the flowing black lines. "So that's how the Mississippi runs. Hello, here's that Ohio River coming out of the mountains way to the east to join it."

Pollock picked up a long brass ruler and ran one end north from the hachured spot marked "Nouvelle Orleans." "This isn't a true map of the river. There's never been one, never will be one. It's always shifting its course, throwing out a new loop, quitting

an old one, blocking the mouth of a tributary or digging an out-
let to an inland lake. Just when you'll start I can't say. It might
be within two hours or two weeks."

"I've never done any river navigation," said Markham.

"You won't do much here. Your sea-lore won't help you a jot.
It's a treacherous, dangerous river and you'll go as a working passenger under men who are interested in keeping alive and who'll
have no patience with people who might, through ignorance or
unhandiness, interfere with that understandable objective. Remember that you'll be a green hand."

"That's sound advice."

"Your craft will be a keelboat, moving by oar and pole and sail.
The work is killing. There are excellent chances that you'll be am-
bushed, unsuccessfully, I trust, by Indians from either bank. Most
men survive the trip by being tougher than the river and as tough
as those they travel with."

Markham's chin set. "I've not been with many parsons or
schoolmasters lately." He drew down his neck-cloth to show a purple scar that zigzagged out of sight below his collarbone.

"Such was my impression. Now your keelboat will turn east into
the Ohio River. By that time you ought to be able to plot your
own course. You can land at the Kentucky settlements and go
overland into Virginia. I've drafted a letter for you to Governor
Patrick Henry at Williamsburg. Or you can keep on right up to
Fort Pitt here where the Monongahela and Allegheny join to
form the Ohio. You'll have a letter to General Edward Hand
there. He'll send you on east."

"You're going to a great deal of trouble for me, sir. I hope that
someday I'll be able to cancel out the debt."

Pollock seemed to have forgotten him for the moment as the
brass ruler circled over the vast spaces west of the Alleghenies.
"Look at all that territory," he said as though to himself. "Who's
going to hold it? Those mountains are no true boundary for us, but
the Mississippi might be. If the British control all that land —" he
broke off, frowning.

Markham, still mentally pushing east from Fort Pitt, remarked absently, "How can they? I hear they're having trouble keeping their armies along the seaboard."

Pollock shook his head impatiently. "They can *control* without occupying, just by keeping their Indians raiding down to the Ohio and far across it. At the end of last year there weren't more than a dozen American families in all the Kentucky country. The rest had given up and gone east into Virginia. If that keeps on it'll mean that our country's penned up for good between the Alleghenies and the sea." He rapped the ruler against his palm. "*But* if we can secure the Mississippi as our west boundary — why, what's on the far bank facing us? A few French settlements run by a handful of Spanish officials who aren't too interested in staying there. Maybe the Mississippi itself isn't our true boundary. It may lie hundreds, thousands of miles west of it. Put a few score sturdy, pushing American families north of the Ohio and there's no telling where they may spread to."

"Interesting," said Markham. "But it's all too new to me. Now to get back to realities, can you show me any map of the country east of Fort Pitt?"

Before Pollock could answer, Garcia's staccato rap sounded, the gray chief clerk sidled in, closed the door after him and gave the merchant what looked like a strip of white bark. The latter read out, " 'Lieutenant Philip Brady, late Virginia Line.' Did he say what he wants? I'm rather busy."

The door swung silently on its hinges and in the opening, leaning on his long rifle, stood the buckskinned man. His eyes narrowed in quick recognition and he glided into the room. "Could have saved time if I'd known who you were back yonder. Sorry to bust in like this, but I'm in trouble and in a hurry, both at once."

Garcia left the room resignedly as Pollock said evenly, "Hurry and trouble are apt to go together. What part of Virginia are you from? What's your regiment?"

"My home's on the north fork of the Shenandoah. I served two years with the 3rd Virginia, Colonel George Weedon. Now I'm attached to an independent company at Fort Pitt. What I want is —"

Pollock cut in, "You know Captain George Gibson, 1st Virginia?"

"Yes, sir. Only he's Colonel now, State Troops, not Line." Brady hesitated, then went on, "I hear he loves gunpowder so much that in '76 he went clear from Fort Pitt to New Orleans to look at some. They say he liked it so much that he brought close onto two tons to Fort Pitt. Got an idea that's not news to you, sir."

"Not entirely. By the way, this is Mr. Markham Cape, a fellow-American. Sit down and tell me about your troubles and your hurry."

Brady acknowledged the introduction and seated himself beside Markham. He dropped his voice. "I've *got* to find Captain James Willing, United States Navy."

Markham saw Pollock's mouth tighten. "Better tell me why."

Brady's eyes snapped. "Official business," he answered shortly.

"Which the Commercial Agent for Congress ought to know if he's to help." Pollock's tone was crisp.

"I'm not accustomed —" began Brady. Then he met Pollock's keen glance and he flushed under his thick beard. "Yes. Of course, sir. I was sent here to find Willing. No one can — or will — tell me where he is. Two boatloads of supplies under Captain James O'Hara are going to start down the Ohio before too long and Willing's supposed to rendezvous with him at Arkansas Post and take over the supplies and O'Hara's men. Don't know what happens then. There was talk of his clearing all British sympathizers from the east bank of the Mississippi and then going on to take Mobile and maybe Pensacola. But all I'm to do is tell him about O'Hara's party." His buckskin fringes rustled as he swept a sleeve across his forehead.

Markham bit back a yawn. Here was more and more about places he did not know, more talk of war moves that seemed to have no connection with the war toward which he was aiming.

He started as Pollock, who had been listening with half-closed

eyes, thumped a freckled fist on the table. "Too late! Oh, *too late!*
Damnation! No fault of yours, Mr. Brady. But Willing — he came
downriver with his party under orders to win over the people,
mostly French, from Natchez and Baton Rouge south. The whole
thing turned into a freebooting expedition. He raided, burned,
looted pretty widely down the east bank. Now he's somewhere below New Orleans, doing the same thing. About all that can be said
for him is that he's confined himself pretty well to actual British
and British sympathizers."

"Where's the harm there, sir?" asked Markham, and Brady
echoed, "Yes, where's the harm? They hit us whenever they can."

Pollock rubbed his forehead. "He's antagonized a lot of people
who might have sided with us or at least stayed neutral. As it is,
he's chased them right over to the British cause. Worse than that,
he's stirred up the British West Florida command. They've got
armed boats on the river above us. They're garrisoning Manchac
and Baton Rouge and Natchez. Willing would be slaughtered if
he tried to get to Arkansas Post now. I rather wonder how you
were able to get down here safely."

"I came with French traders under the Spanish flag. Anyway,
I'm here. How about getting me to Willing?"

"No. I'm afraid not," said Pollock with a slow shake of his head.
"I'm in charge here. What you've got to do is to hit back for the
Ohio and intercept O'Hara. He can't be starting for some weeks
yet, so you ought to be able to do it. Tell him to make for Arkansas Post and wait for orders from me. If matters don't mend, he'll
have to go back up the Ohio. Fort Pitt can always use his men and
supplies."

Brady sprang to his feet. "You're abandoning Willing!"

"Willing will be helped to the utmost extent that he'll allow
himself to be helped — which is precious little. Well, let's look at
the immediate problem, one that you share with Mr. Cape — that
of getting up the Ohio."

Brady threw himself back in his chair, scowling. Then he said
resignedly, "If those are orders, I've no choice. I'm out of funds,
though."

"You won't be. Do you know anything about keelboats?"

"I've poled a good many miles."

"You'll pole a great many more. My people are watching the river for the next departure."

Brady's deep-set eyes studied Markham carefully, taking in his freshly dressed black hair, spotless linen and silver-buckled shoes. "I'm to travel with Mr. Cape? Does he know river work? It's killing. There'll be days of cordelling and —"

"Cordelling?" asked Markham, returning Brady's stare.

"Mr. Cape's a novice at river travel, but don't let that trouble you," observed Pollock quietly.

"Sorry, sir, but it does. He looks big, but that's not enough." Brady rose, held out his hands. "Give me a grip, Mr. Cape."

Markham got to his feet, started as the Virginian's hands clamped about his like blocks of wood. Numbness crept toward his wrists. He set his jaw, trying to force more pressure into his hands, aware that Brady's hard eyes were probing his. Suddenly the other's grip eased.

"I'm surprised, Mr. Cape. You're deceptive. Now how would you counter this?" Brady's right hand flicked over the fringed shirt-front and a long-bladed knife seemed to leap into it.

Markham's left hand shot out as though to catch Brady's wrist, but his right darted past it, caught the other's knife-hand while his left forearm jammed against Brady's throat. The knife came up easily for a few inches, then stopped. The two men stayed locked while Pollock watched calmly, turning his brass ruler between his fingers. Suddenly the knife clattered to the floor. Markham stepped on it, then picked it up and laid it on the table.

Brady, staring, muttered, "Where the devil did you learn that trick?"

"It's an old one. I twisted your sleeve against your wrist until it cut off the flow of blood and numbed the tendons. I couldn't have done it if your sleeve had been rolled up."

"How would you have handled that?"

"Roll up your sleeve, if you want to find out."

Brady glared at him. Then a growing respect came into his eyes. "That's wise of you. There's just a chance you'll do, after all."

Pollock spoke gently. "Mr. Cape has been in a good many odd corners and among a good many odd people. In my opinion he'll do very well indeed. Ah — you've something for me, Garcia?" The chief clerk slipped in, laid a piece of paper on the table. Pollock stared at it. Then he left the office abruptly, saying, "If you gentlemen will pardon me for a few minutes —"

Markham and Brady eyed each other with silent, covert appraisal. Finally Markham picked up the horn-handled blade from the table. "This is well balanced. Looks like a honed-down carving knife."

"Just what it is." Brady's manner warmed a little. "I got it out in the Kentucky country. People don't have much there except what they toted in themselves. When Indian scares came, the man of the house grabbed up his rifle and the first cutting tool that came to hand, usually from the kitchen-truck by the hearth. A good knife, used proper, has meant life to a lot of men who'd have ended up in the torture-fire otherwise. The Indians are more scared of a blade than of a rifle even. Matter of fact, that's what they've come to call all Americans west of the Alleghenies — The Big Knives. They even say —"

Pollock hurried back into the office. "I was overpessimistic, gentlemen, when I spoke of a long wait for a boat. The keeler *Poitou*, Maître Onesime Charcot. You'll be on board in one hour. Mr. Cape, we'll fit you out with buckskins, moccasins and a rifle. I'll see that you both have funds. You've a long journey ahead of you."

"How long?" asked Markham, springing to his feet and peeling off his linen jacket.

"With luck, a little over two months. With bad luck, more than three."

"Three *months*?" exclaimed Markham. "Why, yes, I suppose it might come to that. I've a lot of land to cover after I leave Fort Pitt."

"Oh, you misunderstand me, Mr. Cape." Pollock raised a cautioning hand. "The time I mentioned will see you only partway into the Ohio."

"The Ohio!" Markham's eyes darted to the map with its tangle of black lines. "Why, that's only —" He paused, then ripped off his neck-cloth. "It's 'only' nothing! By God, I'm on my way. How about those buckskins?"

II

Cordelle, Oar and Pole

COBBLERS, tinsmiths, fishmongers were scrambling about the *banquette*, putting up heavy wooden shutters against the oncoming night as Markham followed Pollock and Brady down Rue St. Louis to the high levee. There was a heady aroma of fresh-ground coffee and lights began to wink in second-story windows as shopkeepers and artisans moved from their workrooms to the living quarters above. Snatches of French and Spanish drifted down to the narrow street, men's voices, women's, affectionate, strident, angry, morose. Laughter laced up into the dimming air and Markham knew a sharp pang of loneliness as the river-city prepared for a night that walled him out as he had been walled out from countless other nights and cities in the past. A man soon became accustomed to being a waif, except in this one hour of the day when people withdrew into their homes, indifferent to those who had none of their own.

Not all people were indifferent. From an open window a girl, with the dusk of evening on her, leaned lazily out, masses of dark hair falling down each shoulder from under a dark mantilla. Elbows and forearms were white against the sill and the mantilla's folds parted slowly to show a swelling expanse of white below the throat. A heavy-petaled flower spatted at his feet and a husky voice called softly, "'Allo, Beeg Knaife, Beeg Knaife!"

Markham hitched at the long rifle slung between his shoulders, and the fringes of his new buckskins swished as he picked up the blossom. He tossed it back, kissed his hand to the window. "My heart breaks, *querida mia,* but the river calls me." Port-girls were port-girls the world over but he was somehow grateful to this one voice that called to him, however hollowly, from the withdrawn twilight world of a strange city. As he glided on in his new moccasins he thought, "Guess the Indians aren't the only ones who know what 'Big Knife' means." He quickened his pace to overtake his companions as they mounted the slanting steps built into the levee.

On the broad summit where willow trees marched endlessly into the gloom, he halted. In the west the sun was dropping behind a blackening expanse of wooded flatlands where swamps and backwaters of the far shore glowed blood-red to the last touch of the day. There was the river itself, a good mile and more across, with its far-wandering curves reflecting in the dusk-light so many points of the compass. It flowed to the south of him, to the north, to the northwest and the southwest and the southeast, weaving far and near the sinister labyrinth of its course, sweeping a dozen miles into the country before gaining half a mile on its journey to the sea, far below New Orleans. There were strange craft moored to stakes driven into the man-made levee. He saw pirogues, arrow-shaped forty- and fifty-footers with interiors burned laboriously from the trunks of vast cypress or cottonwood trees. There were bateaux, sharp at bow and stern, with stumpy masts and roofed decks. Here and there a radeau, square and raftlike, rocked clumsily to the river's touch. The Mississippi and its boats seemed alien, almost hostile to him. He shook himself. "Hell and death!" he muttered. "It's just water, and shipping that'll float on it. I'm on my way."

Someone lit a torch up ahead and he saw Pollock and Brady standing at the foot of a wharf. "Changed your mind about coming?" Brady's voice was sharp.

Markham broke into a trot, haversack and rifle flopping against side and back. "Just getting my bearings," he called as he neared them.

"Sound practice," observed Pollock. "Mr. Cape, I take leave of you now." He held out his hand. "Since your intention is east, it is not likely that we'll meet again. My good wishes go with you. It will be a pleasure to hear from you during your voyage and at the successful completion of it."

Markham returned his grip. "I can never clear the debt I owe —"

"Never mind it!" said Pollock quickly. "You've already thanked me. We're all working toward the same end, you and Mr. Brady and I. You've your money and letters to Governor Henry and General Hand and — and — I don't believe there's another thing I can tell you." He turned and walked rapidly along the levee where more torches were flaring.

Markham watched the stocky merchant striding away, now almost lost in the thickening gloom, now thrown into sharp relief by torchlight, the silver head of his stick twinkling. Pollock's earlier words flashed into Markham's mind, "You ought to stay here," and he had a sudden impulse to run after him. Then Brady called impatiently, "Come *on!*" and Markham joined him on the wharf, eyes on the half-seen bulk of the keelboat that seemed to stretch away into the very center of the broad river. In the pointed bow a cresset burned smokily and he made out an open space with a half-dozen rowers' benches and neatly stacked oars. Aft of the benches a pitch-roofed deckhouse, pierced by a stumpy mast, loomed up a good ten feet. Along the outer edge of the craft a walkway, studded with two-foot cleats, stretched off into the darkness. "Fifty feet, stem to stern, if she's an inch," guessed Markham.

"Seventy!" snapped Brady. "Get aboard!"

The two went down a swaying passerelle to the deck where a narrow bar of dim light fell from a partly closed door. Brady pointed to it. "Our quarters. We've got berths five and seven. Gear Pollock gave you's been stowed there by his men. That's home. Roof, walls and seven by four foot worth of plank to lie on. If you're too fine for such quarters, now's the time to say so."

Markham unslung his rifle and leaned on it. "It seems to me, Mr. Brady, that you're beginning to feel that I may be in the way."

"Don't be so damned jumpy," said Brady harshly. "If I had any real doubts about you I'd not have agreed to travel with you for fifty gold guineas. It's just that I know something about river travel, about this river and the Ohio. Known things I can beat — or I have so far. It's uncertainties that scare me. Mr. Pollock told me a lot about you while you were getting into buckskins back there. It didn't sound too bad. But that's all in the past. For the present and future, you're an uncertainty until I'm shown different."

Markham's chin came forward. "You're an uncertainty to me too. I don't like not being sure any more than you do. I suggest a solution to our mutual problem. We'll stack our rifles right here. This part of the deck's clear and we can grapple without bothering anyone. The first one to hit the water stays there — or gets ashore if he can."

Brady ducked out of his rifle-sling and Markham could catch a cold glint in his eye as he leaned the long barrel against the deckhouse. Then he picked it up again. "I'd like to." Brady's voice was almost a whisper. "By Jesus, I'd like to. But we've both got a journey to make. Let's leave the grappling to the end of it. In the meantime, I say you'll do — so far."

"And you — so far. Shake on it?"

"Suits me," said Brady.

Close by, hands beat softly and a girl's voice cried, *"Magnifique!"*

Markham's foot whirled out, kicked the deckhouse door wider and light flowed over a dark head bound in a bright red scarf, dancing eyes and teeth that glowed between full red lips. The girl cried again, *"Magnifique, Monsieur le Bastonnais!"* as she sat huddled under a worn blanket by the low gunwale.

Markham reached out quickly, jerked the blanket away from her, gave it a quick shake before dropping it onto the deck. *"Qui êtes-vous? Parlez!"* he snapped.

Not at all disconcerted, she tucked moccasined feet under her skirts and smiled up at him. *"Mais je ne suis qu'habitante. Je remonts a —"* Her words were drowned in a slamming of boots on the deckhouse roof. A short, very broad man jumped to the deck, arms waving. *"Sacré* goddam! *Nom d'un petit* hell! Mam'zelle Rose-Claire! A *la hutte des femmes!* Vite! Vite!" He made sweeping motions like a man chasing chickens.

She rose with a calm *"Toute a l'heure!"* Markham handed her the blanket, bowing. She took it with a regally gracious smile and swept aft, chin high, followed by the squat man.

Philip Brady exhaled softly. "Just why did you flick that blanket?"

"Habit. You can snake a knife out from under one slick as grease."

"Who'd want to use a knife on us here?" asked Brady scornfully.

"Anyone who knew we came from Pollock could figure we weren't beggars." His fingers touched his ribs, met the welt of an old knife-slash under the buckskin. "It's happened on other ships in other ports. I'd like to have talked to her a little more. Why did that hammered-down Frenchie run her off so fast?"

Brady leaned against the deckhouse, studying Markham. "You sure do move quick and positive when you take an idea to. As for the *sous-maître,* all women are supposed to stay in that cabin abaft the cargo space, the men forward. Let's duck inside and get settled."

The crew's quarters were long and narrow, about twenty feet by eight, Markham judged in the light of the flickering lantern at the door. Triple-tiered bunks, considerably less than the four-foot width of which Brady had spoken, ran along all sides, broken only by two doors leading to the deck and the walkway. Occasional glints from the shallow caverns of the bunks told of ports or windows. The air was heavy, smelling of forgotten cargoes of hides and furs, and along the far side two rank candles, set in their own grease, struggled against the murk. By one of them a man carefully counted through a pack of limp playing cards. At the other, a lined face bent over a fiddle while a lean forefinger anxiously tested a bass-string.

"Here's home," said Brady. "See where the '5' and '7' are painted on the posts? There's your gear from Pollock stowed in '7.' All right?"

Markham unslung his haversack and rifle and sat on the edge of his berth. "Any place afloat where I can stand up without banging my head's a palace to me."

"Huh! Wait till we get caught in a whirlpool and a hundred-foot oak tree tries to climb in through a porthole and see how you feel about your palace." Brady yawned and stretched. "Jesus, I'm glad to get out of that town. Towns always give me cramps."

Markham smoothed his black hair. "I haven't got room for cramps. I'm too full of wonders."

"Like what?"

"Well, did little Rose-Claire get chased aft because she didn't belong for'd, or because Monsieur Stumpy was anxious for her not to talk to us — or us to her?"

"She was chased. I know about Charcot. He runs a strict boat. Not like some masters who have floating stews."

"Maybe. But I've got another wonder. Someone got word to that girl quick as hell that I was from Boston."

"Faddle! That just shows that her people came from Canada originally. Up there they call anyone from the States 'Bastonnais,' because so many expeditions against Quebec and Louisbourg started from there in the old wars. She could have meant either of us. Got any more wonders?"

"Yes. Oliver Pollock. A bale of wonders, but they can wait. The one that's popping out of my cargo-hatch right now is this: we're supposed to cast off any minute. Where's the crew? Where's the master?"

"They're up on the levee with Charcot. That man can smell a wind coming half an hour before it knows it's going to blow. The first sniff he gets, he and his men'll come down here all a-helling and —"

Suddenly the wharf, the deck outside and the roof were loud with the thump of feet, the beat of voices. The card-player hastily stowed away his pack, the fiddler caught up his instrument and the pair ducked out of the low door. A bull-bellow crashed out, "*Les voiles! Hissez les voiles!*"

"Charcot," said Brady. "The crew'll cast off, set sails and back off into the stream hoping that the wind'll move faster than the current."

"If it doesn't?"

"You and I and every man on board'll take pole or oar and try to make up the difference. If it does blow good, we'll loll on deck and watch the shoreline whizz past — at maybe twenty miles a day. Let's get outside. Charcot knows you're on board and he can tell in the fullest dark if there's a pole or an oar or a line unmanned. Then he starts bearing down right and left with a club until he's clipped every soul in reach."

The din above went on undiminished. Then Markham felt life in the planks under his feet and knew that the *Poitou* was pushing into the stream. He followed Brady out on deck where half-seen men were manning the port side, balancing twenty-foot poles in their hands. Forward, a squarish ugly sail showed on the stumpy mast. The keelboat began to turn, pointing its stern downstream. All at once life went out of the seventy-foot craft and it hung motionless. "God damn!" snapped Brady. "We're — we're slipping backwards."

Markham faced starboard but there was nothing to see save the rising black mass of the levee and the dim glow behind it that marked the city of New Orleans. Then wood and water and wind began to talk to him. He felt a barely perceptible tremor underfoot, caught the faintest rustle of the river against the side of the boat, knew a slow-growing coolness at the back of his neck.

An exultant roar beat its way forward. "*Ça marche!*" bellowed Charcot. The polemen relaxed. Oarlocks began to moan, port and starboard. Perched cross-legged on the forward end of the deckhouse roof, the fiddler sent a ripple of swift notes toward the stars. A deep voice burst out:

C'était un vieux sauvage —

Others joined in:

Tout noir, tout barbouilla,
Ouich'ka!
Avec sa vielle couverte
Et son sac à tabac!
Ouich'ka.

The whole crew burst out in a final, shattering:

Ah, ah! Tenouich' tenaga,
Tenouich' tenaga!
OUICH'KA!

The following wind died, sprang up, died or was canceled out by weird twists and bends in the river that brought in full or quartering on the bow of the *Poitou,* joining with the eternal push and butt of the current to halt the boat or drive it back downstream. Through wracking days and nights, Markham's world shrank to the cleated walkway or *passe-avant.* The sun burned down on him. Rain rode stinging on high winds to drench him, to turn his long, ash-wood pole into a thing of greasy torment that bit water-soaked skin from his palms, to coat the walkway with a slimy film where moccasined feet skidded.

Aft by the stern oar, Maître Charcot bellowed, "A *bas les perches! Fort!*" With his five fellows, Markham drove his pole down until it jarred against river-bottom, settled the ball-end against the thick pad strapped over the hollow of his shoulder, pushed with all his strength and tramped aft until Charcot roared, "*Levez les perches!*" Then all six polemen, like their six fellows to starboard, whipped up their poles, turned as one man and ran to the bow, faced aft and plunged their poles into the water again at the next "A *bas les perches! Fort!*"

Tramping blindly along the walkway, lying in the crew cabin in the off-watches while the unbroken rhythm of feet outside and the swish of poles underscored Charcot's great voice, Markham knew an exhaustion beyond all previous experience. Feet and hands burned. His chest ached and his shoulder was alternately numb or throbbing from the thrust of the pole. He knew what it was like to meet deep, soft mud where he had expected to find sand or rock bottom. He tasted the sickening frustration when bad footing or poor timing brought the polemen to the bow just too late to catch the momentum of their last shove, to see the current nudge the bow around. The people on the boat became impersonal machines. He could jostle a fellow poleman and neither know nor care if the man were Philip Brady or a nameless *habitant* from upriver. He could shake his hair from his eyes with an oxlike wag of his head when, at the aft end of the walkway, bonnet-framed faces turned up to him. Rose-Claire, the McKinney girl, the dumpy, yearningly hopeful Belliveau twins, St. Louis-bound, meant even less to him than his companions at the poles since the former contributed nothing toward pushing the boat on. And always there dinned in his ears the endless "A bas —" "Levez —"

The very fiddler on the roof, though exempt from poling, seemed to have caught the universal exhaustion. No longer did his "Ouich'ka!" go soaring up. Instead his bow drew out mournful notes while a few of the hardier crewmen found voice to sing with him:

> *Battu de tous les vents —*
> *Ah! Je vous dis, mes frères,*
> *Personne sur la terre*
> *Endure tant de misère.*

There were worse times, when the channel was too deep or the bottom too soft for poling. Yells of "A la cordelle!" set the crew boiling in angry activity. Men swarmed up the mast, made fast a thousand-foot line to the very peak while others rove the free end through a rope bridle in the bow. The rest of the crew swam or waded ashore, carrying the tough line in endless coils on their shoulders. With them, Markham floundered along swampy banks, toiled up sand hills, scaled rock faces, his heavy stick flailing at bushes to beat off snakes or to free the towline that ran along the thin column of men. He bruised his feet, twisted his ankles and only noticed the blood on his hands when whining flies and mosquitoes settled on raw flesh. No one sang, no one talked. The only sounds were of trampling feet and labored breathing.

On fairly lucky days, Petion, the towline chief, shouted, *"Ici!"* from the head of the column. The line was passed around a big cypress close by the river while quick axes hacked away a ring of bark from the trunk. The whole crew lurched on downstream, step by heavy step, the tough hemp cutting into their shoulders, until sap oozed from the axe-wounds on the tree to form a natural lubricant between wood and rope. Then the going became a little easier, relatively. On such occasions Markham could look to the river through sweat-blurred eyes and see the *Poitou* apparently motionless while its oars churned the water frantically to battle a strong current or eddy. Yet always it moved, and when its bow came abreast of the tree where the line was looped, all hands ashore turned, beat their way upstream again until another suitable bole was found.

On bad days when only swamp or open meadows showed, the cordelliers strained like oxen, step by floundering step through the shallows until the current eased or the wind shifted or a vast new bend of the river dictated a change in tactics. When shallows, firm banks and trees all failed, lines were loaded into two skiffs that fought the current upstream. When the leading craft found a sunken tree solid enough for its purpose, a line was made fast to the derelict trunk and heaving men in the bow of the *Poitou* hauled the keelboat on, hand over hand, until the makeshift mooring was reached. Meanwhile, the second skiff was working on still farther upstream, looking for a similar grounded oak or cypress or pine. Twice, just as the arm- and lung-cracking tugging was ended, a following wind sprang up, seeming to jeer at Markham and his fellows for their now useless efforts that would have been unnecessary had the air come to life two hours, one hour earlier.

On board, men off duty stumbled from deck or walkway, crawled into the cabin too spent to talk or even sleep. When the cook, Aubain, whanged an iron spoon against a kettle, they struggled aft where the galley fire burned in its bed of sand, held out bowls for sloppy rice, hard bread and salt beef or pork. Inky coffee splashed into their mugs, heavily laced with taffia, a rank, powerful rumlike drink. They ate mechanically and lurched back to their quarters. Beef-barrels became waterlogged, throwing off an unholy smell. Charcot had them jettisoned and sent hunters ashore, lithe, silent men who ranged far inland. Sometimes they could be seen waiting by a bend, a gutted deer and a heap of wildfowl at their feet, or a flayed carcass might dangle untended from a high tree by the water, mute evidence of their work.

April faded into May and Markham began unconsciously to catch the rhythm of keelboat life. He learned to pace himself with pole or oar, to keep his body poised so the bite of the cordelle was tolerable, even on the roughest ground. His mind woke gradually and he found himself studying Charcot's river navigation. The Frenchman never seemed to leave the great stern oar, standing by it as his eyes and ears and nose interpreted the vast Mississippi to him. Now he would hold the *Poitou* close under the east bank, running easily through water that looked just like the rest of the river to Markham but which actually was almost currentless. Then he would bellow, send the boat lumbering into midstream where deep ripples told of sunken rocks and ledges and where the air hung inert. But always there seemed to be just enough water under the keel, always a breeze sprang up and the *Poitou* trundled on upstream. Markham could only marvel, shaking his head as he admitted the wisdom of Oliver Pollock's remark back there in New Orleans, now hundreds of miles astern. A lifetime spent at sea would not carry a man a mile up the awesome Mississippi.

His crewmates slowly lost the anonymity that had masked them and became individuals, to have pasts and futures as well as present existences. There were wizened, runty little men, red-sashed and red-stocking-capped like their fellows, who always seemed on the point of exhaustion and yet who kept to pole, oar and cordelle when bigger men gave out. They told Markham that they were *coureurs de bois* and that when they reached the town of St. Louis on the west bank, they would throw their packs into canoes and head far, far up a river they called the Missouri for a winter or more of trading with Indian tribes. A few men, who looked as though river-mud and river-spray had replaced the blood in their veins, had spent most of their lives shuttling back and forth between St. Louis and New Orleans and looked forward to nothing better unless a succession of lucky voyages gave them a keelboat of their own.

Most, however, stockier, more voluble than the rivermen or the *coureurs de bois*, had farms in the St. Louis area or near villages like Kaskaskia or Cahokia or Prairie du Rocher on the east bank, the Illinois country as they called it. They told Markham of the long, narrow strips of land, worked by wife, brothers or sons during their absence. In the fall, they would drop downriver again to sell their wheat at New Orleans, might winter there or at Arkansas Post and work back to the Illinois lands next spring.

Odd lives, those of the *coureurs de bois*, the rivermen and the farmers, Markham reflected, but no odder than many that he had encountered before such as Mediterranean sponge-divers, or men who lived by raising ransom money to buy back Christians seized by Barbary pirates, or ship-masters who preyed on Mecca-bound pilgrims. He stored away countless details of these lives in his mind almost unconsciously, as a man might pick up bits of knowledge while leafing through books in some great library through which he would never again pass. What mattered now was that they seemed to accept him as a fellow-crewman who did his share of the work and who could be counted on to bear a hand in difficult times.

The only man to hold back was Philip Brady, who seemed to resent Markham's reasonably quick adaptation to the river world. Straining at oar or pole or cordelle he grunted, "Got a hell of a long way to go yet, Cape. Haven't rightly even started," or "Why don't you go back to sea? You could drop off at Arkansas Post and the Dons will send you back to Pollock." If Markham answered at all, it was a curt, "I'm making do." But Brady's sardonic eye was always on him. "He's waiting for me to crack," Markham thought. "He's too late — years too late."

Charcot's discipline never slackened so far as the half-dozen women and girls, isolated by the thick bulkhead aft, were con-

cerned. Except for a hasty glance when poling brought him to the
far end of the walkway, Markham rarely caught sight of them. A
stern, square matron in a vast cape always bore down on the effer-
vescent Rose-Claire if the latter attempted an " 'Allo, Monsieur le
Bastonnais!" or fluttered a small hand at him. "If you're hanging
around on account of her, forget it," jeered Brady. "Take one step
aft and Charcot'll throw her in irons and you overboard." "No
keelboat Venus will ever trip me," growled Markham. "I'm heading home!"

  "So you've said — and you're a hell of a long way from it."

  "So you've said. Get moving. It's our turn at the oars."

  Twenty miles a day, fifteen miles a day, thirty miles a day the
keelboat worked up the bends and twists of the vast river. Storms
burst suddenly, turning the stream into an onslaught of water that
beat furiously against the Poitou. Gouts and spurts of water shot
high in air. Immense tangles of branches broke surface, vanished,
rose again. Glistening tree-trunks heaved straight up, ten, twenty
feet of slick wood, like immense spears hurled at the bow or sides.
Fair weather smoothed out the waterway, masked subsurface currents that threatened to drive the craft into a tributary whose normal flow was overmastered by the Mississippi in flood, drive it
miles into the mystery of the interior. Below a spot that the boatmen called Barrancas de Margot, an enormous whirlpool spun
dizzily and at its edge a derelict keelboat shot in an unending
mile circle, would race on and on in the grip of that maelstrom
until time and the river's clutch disintegrated it. Facing all hazards, imperturbable under rain, sun and wind, Maître Charcot
stood by the stern oar, his only concession to the elements being
the inversion of his pipe-bowl against a downpour.

  Long miles and days beyond the Barrancas de Margot, the Poitou
suddenly bucked into a roaring surflike flood close under the east
bank where heavy black clouds hung low. As Markham clung to
the starboard gunwale, Brady's hoarse voice rasped in his ear, "By
God, Charcot's got us into real trouble now." The Virginian's

teeth were bared and his eyes were deep in their sockets. "Look to midstream!"

Midstream was even worse. There was less debris, fewer floating trees, but the current ran swifter and the waves lunged high. Markham drew a sopping sleeve across his eyes. "Didn't see that. He'll have to beach here." But as he spoke a long, towering section of the wooded east bank began a slow slide into the flood.

Markham's mouth went dry and his heart pounded against his ribs. Brady yelled, "God almighty!" and some of the older hands, wild-eyed, wrenched at a broad cabin door, trying to pry it loose to launch as a raft in the face of certain shipwreck. Then Charcot's great voice roared, "*Aux rames!*" Boat discipline was stronger than terror and oarsmen pounded ahead to the seats in the open bow. Markham ran with them. Brady shoved him aside. "Leave this to men who know their trade!"

Markham panted, "Go to hell. I'm on this watch," and jumped in among the benches, snatched up an oar and jammed it between the thole-pins on the starboard side.

The keelboat stroke had been hard to master, but Markham shut his eyes and his mind, concentrating only on the bite and lift of his oar. Down deep, with his whole body following through on the thrust; up, back, with the blade barely skimming the surface, down deep again. Up, back, down and up, back down. Someone was beating out the rhythm of the stroke and he soon caught it, knew that Brady, just ahead of him, was in time, that a wispy *coureur de bois* was straining at the port oar that paired with his own. Up, back, deep. Up, back, deep.

The sound of the beat was swallowed in a great roaring and Markham bit his lip, shivering. The new din was the full strength of the current pounding against the port side of the *Poitou*. *Charcot was leaving the east bank for the deadlier peril of midstream.* Row! As long as the boat could move, there was hope, faint — but a glimmer. Waves broke over the gunwale and water splashed about his ankles, rose. Row! His lungs were bursting and each breath felt like a blast of furnace air drawn into his chest.

He raised his head a little, ducked it quickly. That one look downstream showed nothing but a welter of wind-blown spray and angry white water. He tugged harder at his oar. Supple wood hissed and rasped along the gunwale, branches slashed at his face and he knew that the boat was skirting a giant water-logged tree whose butt was anchored in Mississippi mud. Once the oar jarred in his hands and he shouted in stark fear as a glance to starboard showed him slick, black rock above the surface. But the next stroke bit sharp and deep and he strained on.

His legs were on fire. His ribs and shoulder-bones felt red-hot. His thoughts beat dully in his head. "Five more strokes and I call for a relief. Man two rows ahead quit a long time ago." Then he saw Brady's back and shoulders bending, straightening, seemingly tireless. "Ten more strokes." The wispy man at his left was relieved. "Now it'll be just five more!" Brady kept on, his stroke smooth and regular. "Ten, then. One — two —"

The *Poitou* lurched. Someone bawled, *"Levez les rames!"* Uncomprehending, Markham looked starboard. The west bank lay less than a rod away and the boat was heading north. The ugly square sail crept up the mast, shivered, bellied to the touch of a quartering wind. A rustle under the keel proclaimed that Charcot had brought up in a current which inexplicably flowed north. Somehow he had crossed the wide Mississippi through reefs, eddies, whirlpools and heavy debris as surely as though he had been following a well-blazed forest trail, and into favoring wind and flow.

Markham slumped over his oar, gasping, while his lungs labored and his overtaxed muscles jumped and twitched. Suddenly he jabbed a fist angrily at the sodden back in front of him. "God damn you, Brady, why the hell didn't you call for relief?"

Brady's sagging head shook dully. "Jesus Christ, I was waiting for *you* to, pig-headed bastard!" He rested his forehead on his oar. "Charcot. By God, he's a *riverman*, Mark!"

"Huh? Who? Oh, Charcot? Yes. Guess he is, Phil."

Men began to shout from the benches, from the walkway, in high-pitched relief. The fiddler scrambled to the roof of the deckhouse, tucked his fiddle under his chin, waved his bow in a wide, joyous circle and began sawing away. Voices from below caught up the thin fiddle-notes, shaped them in a wild chorus:

Ah, ah! Tenouich' tenaga,
Ouich'ka!

The *Poitou* lay moored to a tree in the lee of a wooded sandy island as Markham came out from the cabin, rifle slung at his back and haversack bulging at his hip. The rising June sun was strong on the low bank to the east where trees seemed to wade in a watery mist, miasmic and forbidding. A little to the north a great flood swept on to join the Mississippi and the surface was dizzy with eddies and countercurrents and calm patches and sudden tossings as the two rivers met.

"The Ohio," thought Markham. "Looks rather different from what it did on Pollock's map." He had mastered more than a thousand long miles of river travel and he felt a deep glow of pride as he thought of the paper, signed by Onesime Charcot, certifying him as an able river-hand, that lay sewn in an oiled silk cover along with his letters to Governor Patrick Henry and General Edward Hand.

Something stirred in the morasses of the east bank and Markham called over his shoulder, "Here come the hunters now, Phil. They're just launching their canoe."

Brady emerged with rifle and haversack. "Good. We'll get our route from them. Our canoe's all loaded and in the water off the port bow. Get in and be sure the stowage is done right. I'll talk to the hunters."

Markham nodded and crossed to the port side. Bearded men drifted casually up to him, shook his hand with a *"Bonne chance, le Bastonnais!"* or *"Au 'voir, Yanqui!"* with a shy friendliness that made answering difficult. On the port gunwale, he slipped off his moccasins, dropped into the shallow water and stepped gingerly into the canoe. Despite Brady's lessons he did not dare copy the Virginian's carelessly easy drop from the keelboat.

Provisions, a small powder-keg, another of taffia were stowed carefully in the swelling midships of the canoe. Markham took the bow paddle and tried a few strokes, swinging the canoe about at the end of its long painter. The graceful craft glided aft and Markham checked it, trying to imitate Brady's paddle technique.

"But I am sad," said a low voice just above his head.

He looked up. Rose-Claire, full cheeks dimpling and white teeth showing, was smiling at him, her head just above the gunwale. Markham announced that he was desolated to cause sorrow to a distractingly beautiful demoiselle.

She put her hands on the gunwale, leaned her cheek against them and looked sidewise at him. "You are much more *beau garçon* since you shave off that black beard of a buccaneer."

Markham flicked his paddle and drops pattered bright in the sun. "That is so Mademoiselle will not remember me as a *loup-garou* when I am gone."

She pouted. "I know that you go, else it would not be permitted that I speak to you. You go far?"

"To Boston."

The end of a pink tongue showed between her teeth and her head rose as though she were standing on tiptoes. "*Dites!* You take me? Afterwards I walk back to Cahokia. It cannot be far."

"Again am I desolated. You should travel in a coach with white horses and a fine young *seigneur*, not a riverman like me. And Boston is very far. Ascend the Mississippi three times and still you will not have measured the distance to Boston."

"*Ah, oui.* That is far," she sighed.

"*Très.*"

"So you will find a horse to bring me back to Cahokia! Now be silent! I get my little bundle and — *mais enfin!*"

The canoe shot toward the bow as Brady tugged at the long painter. "All right. We're off." He dropped lightly into the canoe and caught up his paddle. "The hunters met a party of Chickasaws and they say the left bank's pretty safe, so we'll hug that." He drove the canoe around the bow, sent it out into the stream. "I'll paddle alone till we get rightly into the Ohio. It's risky going here with these boils and crosscurrents where the two rivers meet. After that we'll both work."

"Anything you say, Phil, so long as I'm pointed home." As Brady worked the canoe skillfully on, Markham looked back at the *Poitou* which would soon be butting its way up the mysterious northern reaches of the Mississippi. Some of the crew were waving from the gunwale. Aft — Markham grinned. A little of Charcot's discipline seemed to have broken down. A young boatman was crawling along the cabin roof, carrying a twenty-foot pole from whose iron-shod end a folded white paper dangled. Rose-Claire, her back to the canoe, was reaching eagerly up for it.

III

Challenge of Wilderness Trace

CAPTAIN James O'Hara's little flotilla, about which Oliver Pollock and Phil Brady had talked so earnestly back in New Orleans, had nearly slipped west downstream unobserved past Markham and Brady's riverside camp on the morning of June 24, four days after the pair had left the *Poitou*. Markham had been first to note the flicker of oar-blades in the predawn gloom and Brady, slinging on rifle and haversack, had sprung into the canoe and paddled furiously out into the current, shouting.

Markham had seen him pull alongside the rearmost of the two bateaux and climb into it. Then the river haze had swallowed up canoe and bateaux. That had been a good two hours ago, Markham reckoned, and now he waited, alone, on the low bank where they had come ashore after sundown the night before.

He was not really worried. Brady had a long and complicated story to tell O'Hara, a note from Pollock to deliver. Then he would have to cast off and work his way back upstream to the camp. It might be noon, actually, before he returned, especially if O'Hara insisted on asking questions. But the delay was annoying, particularly as the Virginian had counted on reaching the Falls of the Ohio and the two-mile portage before midday.

The sky brightened and minutes dragged reluctantly past. Markham had his rifle, plenty of powder and all the stores that the two had unloaded from the canoe the night before. Just the same, he did not dare light a fire to cook breakfast and he did not want to venture far from the campsite. Had Brady been there it would have been different, for the Virginian could read the ground and the trees and the sounds of the riverbank as surely as Charcot had read the Mississippi. He did creep down to the water's edge with what he hoped was due caution to scoop up a cup of water and dart back to shelter. He sprinkled cornmeal into the cup to settle the river-mud and drank slowly. Older hands of the *Poitou* had jeered at those who used cornmeal. River-mud, they said, scoured out a man's tripes, kept him young and healthy, *quoi!* Perhaps there was something in their notion. They never seemed to tire or go sick.

He flicked away the last drop. Just how far downstream had Phil been carried? "Damn it, though," he thought. "Phil will be worrying about *me*, stranded here with no canoe." He sat motionless, watching the downstream drift where river-birds had begun to skim and dip, but no trace of human life showed.

As the sun climbed, he got out a slab of rank, greasy bear-bacon and gnawed at what he figured was his share. Breakfast over, he took up his sewing-kit and with waxed string mended a rent across the knee of his buckskins. Bushes began to wave on a spit of land that jutted far out from the north bank and his hand dropped to his rifle, then relaxed as a vast, shaggy head with short, curved horns thrust through the branches, withdrew in a swirl of green. A buffalo! So Phil's accounts of the huge beasts that herded off there in the Illinois country had not been overdrawn. Markham went on with his mending, then put his kit away, noting that the sun was about nine o'clock high.

The sun. What was wrong with it? The morning was fading out in a weird, unhealthy glow and a hard, sinister shadow crept across the sun. River and banks took on an eerie shimmer like tarnished silver and the endlessly dipping birds whirred away to the shelter of the trees. The black disc slid on over the face of the sun. Markham got uncertainly to his feet. Long months ago he had seen another eclipse off Bastia in Corsica and had been tolerantly amused at the terror of the xebec's crew. Now, alone by a dimming American river, he tasted something of their superstition-bred panic, knew a blind impulse to run — anywhere.

He saw movement out on the water, a stirring and a ruffling coming from the east. At first it was movement, nothing else. Then he made out two, three canoes whose flicking paddles gave out no glitter in the thickening gloom. Behind them was a mass of distorted shapes gliding silently west as though floating through the air of a devil-world. The masses swelled and he caught the steady lift and dip of oars, many oars. He backed away one step — another —

There had been no warning rustle in the bushes about him, no snap of twigs, but all at once two buckskinned men, their rifles ready, closed in on either side of him. One, a blocky, wide-shouldered man, planted a moccasined foot on Markham's rifle. The other, tall and lean, pushed the muzzle of his piece forward. "Start talkin'," he said. "Who? Where? Why? Stuff like that, and fast."

"Markham Cape. Out of New Orleans. Boston-bound."

A hard grin split the other's beard. "Starts like a real good story, only we ain't got time to listen. Try again."

Markham, hands high above his head, cried, "It's true. I'm from Oliver Pollock. Feel inside my shirt. I've got letters from him to Governor Patrick Henry, to General Edward Hand."

The shorter man picked up Markham's rifle. "Maybe you got one for Mr. Hair-buyer, too."

"Who's he?"

"You ain't never heard of him?"

"No!"

The other man gestured riverward with his rifle. "He's either a God damn liar or a God damn stranger. Whichever, he's got to get talked to. Quit hollerin' 'bout your letters, Bub. The Colonel gets paid for readin' things like that. Us, we just fetch 'em to him. Get busy with the rawhide, Shad."

Before Markham could move, the man Shad had pinned his arms deftly behind him, bound them at elbow and wrist with harsh rawhide while his fellow, huge in the macabre half-light, covered him with his rifle. "That'll do, Ep," called Shad, pushing Markham forward. A buckskin at each elbow, Markham stumbled on through the undergrowth, scrambling awkwardly over a fallen sycamore, wading a muddy brook. There was no sign of path or trail, but Shad and Ep pushed on unhesitatingly. On a steep downslope, Ep reached ahead, parted a mass of bushes to show a canoe riding in a narrow backwater. "Ease him in, Shad," grunted Ep, steadying the frail craft. Resignedly Markham stretched out on his back and the pair climbed in and pushed off, Shad paddling stern.

From the bottom of the canoe, Markham could see only the sullen livid sky above him. It seemed to be brightening a little and a thin crescent of pure light, like a fingernail paring, showed on its lower rim. Underneath him the river hissed gently against the canoe. Then, from somewhere out of his vision, he heard the flip of oars, the whine of thole-pins and occasional muffled voices. Once progress was checked and he looked up to see bearded faces peering down at him from another canoe. A man asked, "Where'd you fetch him from?"

"Just below Panther Riffle. How's doings to the north?"

"All quiet. Jake and Bill's gone ahead to the mouth of Horseshoe Crick."

Then the faces were gone and the canoe shot ahead.

Oars and voices were much louder now. Markham felt the canoe swerve sharply, grate against something and come to a halt. Shad prodded him. "Set up, now. Ep'll ease you by the collar." A strong hand heaved Markham to a sitting position. The sun was almost clear and he saw a long column of bateaux crammed with men gliding down the deepening blue of the Ohio. Shad and Ep were holding their canoe close to the stern of a boat and a buckskinned man, coppery hair bright in the sun, was staring at him from hard blue eyes. It was a strong, handsome face with good features and a thrusting chin. Markham could read neither patience nor friendliness in it. Holding himself as erect as he could, he returned the other's stare, noting the sweep of the powerful shoulders, the muscular neck and the play of tough tendons in the hand that lay on the tiller. There was a world of authority about the man, though he seemed no older than Markham.

The first question snapped out. "What were you doing on the south bank?"

Markham's head went back. "Who's asking me?"

The blue eyes darkened. "George Rogers Clark, Lieutenant Colonel, Virginia State Troops, and I'll ask the questions. Who are you? Where are you from?"

"You're a long way from Virginia to be demanding answers," began Markham. Clark's expression did not change, but Markham had quick sense of actual, physical danger. Changing his tone he gave a rapid account of himself from his quitting Genoa up to Brady's disappearance with the O'Hara party. The other's face remained impassive as Markham probed it, hoping for some flicker of belief.

"You say you were trying to get home. Where's that?"

"Boston."

"In Massachusetts? Then you wouldn't know many people or places here or in Virginia?"

"Never been twenty miles west of Boston till I raised New Orleans."

"Anything to back up your story?"

"Letters from Oliver Pollock about me to Governor Henry and General Hand. They're sewn into my shirt-front in oiled silk."

Clark gestured curtly to Shad who ripped out the packet and gave it to Clark. The latter broke the stitches and ran his eye over the script. "Hell, anyone could have written this." He raised his voice. "Pass the word to Captain Bowman and Captain Helm. Do they know Oliver Pollock's fist?" He faced Markham again, his hand out. "Let's see your letters to Colonel Henry Hamilton."

"That's all I've got. Don't know any Colonel Hamilton."

Clark's jaw muscles bulged. "You don't? How about de Rocheblave, then, or Arendt de Peyster? You say you never heard of them?" He stared hard at Markham, then gave a sweep of his arm. "Take him to Bateau 8. Sergeant Harrison's shorthanded there. Have him put this man to work and keep him at it. Bind him to someone reliable. No one's to gab with him or answer his questions." He shoved at the stern of the canoe, sent it out into the current.

His bonds removed, but linked by a four-foot thong to the man next him, Markham pulled doggedly at a heavy double oar. Eight oars and sixteen rowers. Red-haired Colonel Clark must be in a hurry to get somewhere. But where could he be going with these Virginia troops in their buckskin or linsey-woolsey, with this tiny wilderness army without uniforms or drums or flags or insignia? Markham had counted at least eight sharp-prowed bateaux and there might be more ahead on the far flanks. One hundred and fifty men or more, all armed with long rifles, bound for where and to do what? He remembered the Willing expedition down the Mississippi, Pollock's exasperation at its final futility and Brady's tenuous connection with it. But Clark had expressed no interest in Markham's mention of Brady or O'Hara. The flotilla's business lay elsewhere.

This was no concern of his. What did concern him was the repetition of a familiar pattern; once more he was forced to double on his tracks, to head far away from his goal. He began to laugh, silently. "And I *thanked* Pollock for getting me on the *Poitou.* Well, this is no fault of his."

Two hours of rowing. Two hours of rest while a relief manned the oars. At noon he was given a ration of smoked venison, rank and salty, with a mug of river water before resuming his post. The men about him talked little among themselves, addressed him only in brusque monosyllables. Even resting, they seemed to be straining toward some goal which Markham could not guess, gripped by the same tension that held their Colonel. By the stern oar, Sergeant Harrison sat alert, the westering sun full on his face where a bristly beard grew in patches about broad scars that looked like old burns. One eye-socket was empty, red, and rough with more scar tissue. The remaining eye seemed to take in the whole sweep of the bending river, the slow-passing green banks, while never leaving Markham.

During a rest a canoe glided alongside and a red-faced man shouted to Harrison: "Colonel says ain't no one here knows Pollock's writing. Keep a tight clamp on that bastard."

"Ain't aimin' to miss," grunted Harrison.

Markham called, "Does that mean I'm still under arrest?"

"Sure does."

"We're not in Virginia. He's got no authority to hold me."

"Sure ain't."

"Will you send a message to him for me?"

Harrison leaned forward and Markham saw the hilt of a heavy knife against the horribly scarred skin of his chest. "Save your breath. Could be you'll need it, danglin' by your neck out'n a sycamore-top. The Lord's lovin' forgiveness ain't apt to reach down and light on spies the Hair-buyer sends out."

"Oh, so I'm a spy, am I?" cried Markham.

Harrison nodded. "In this year, in this hunk of the world, you kinda got to be, till we're showed different. Keep rowin'."

For three full days and three full nights the flotilla plunged its way west down the Ohio River. The rowers labored, were relieved, ate, slept, took their places again with a clockwork precision that told not only of good training but of a fixed will on the part of each man to push on to the end of the journey. What that end might be, where it might be, and the purpose of the journey itself were still mysteries to Markham. The crew about him stayed noncommittal as ever, limiting their talk to the needs of each day, never speaking of the past or the future. There were probably many danger-spots on the route, but he, back to the bow, never saw them, knew only that the general course scrupulously avoided the north bank, hugged the south as much as possible. Canoes dropped down the column with messages for the commanders of each boat, shot west again, but the news that they bore never reached him. Twice he saw a light skiff moored by the bank with Colonel Clark, accompanied by two men nearly as big as himself, watching the progress in tight-lipped silence as they leaned on long rifles.

No doubt the steady flow of bateaux meant something to them, Markham thought. For himself, each riffle skirted, each point rounded was merely impressed on his mind as a landmark that he would have to pass all over again, once he was released. Anyway he could be sure of one thing. Phil Brady had not yet come back up the Ohio from O'Hara's craft. Canoe-borne scouts ahead, on the flanks, in the rear would have picked him up by day or nosed out any campsite by night. As a Virginian, he would have been among friends, would have quickly heard of Markham's capture and spoken up for him.

Toward noon of the last day, Markham became aware of a strong current butting against his bateau's port side, looked over his shoulder to see a broad river-mouth, a shaggy island. The mouth of the Tennessee River! He remembered Phil Brady pointing it out to him a day or so after leaving the *Poitou*. Then the Mississippi itself must be less than forty miles ahead. He felt his stomach contract as he saw himself rowing down that vast river in a new coup against those places of which Pollock and Phil Brady had spoken — Natchez and Baton Rouge and Manchac. All the weeks and months and toil and danger of working upstream under Charcot would be tossed into the discard like the worn-out moccasin (carefully weighted to insure sinking) that a man to his right was dropping overboard!

The south bank was very close, the rowing was harder. The column must be pushing into the mouth of the Tennessee. Sergeant Harrison threw the tiller over and the bateau headed into the lee of the shaggy island. The keel grated on firm sand. Harrison barked, "Ship oars! Git ready to beach!"

Markham swung his oar inboard and stood up as the stern rocked gently in the shallows. "Bill! You and Abel run him ashore! Lash him to that sap-tree yonder and stand by till the Colonel hollers. The rest of you, make fast to that stump."

Markham's oar-mate and another man hustled him into the water and up a muddy beach where other bateaux were unloading men and supplies. "Here's the sap-tree," said the man Abel. "What we lash him with? Hey, cast off that thong that's round your arm and we'll hitch him with that."

"You figger that's all right?" asked Bill dubiously.

"Long's we're here, it is. Ain't never liked tying human-folk up like cord-wood. It's humileratin'." He knotted the free end of Markham's thong about the sapling. "Now we'll stand just a-hint you, Mister, and please don't do nothin' to rile us. Gettin' riled makes my guts sour."

"I'll stand easy," said Markham shortly. Rubbing his cramped arms and legs he surveyed the crescent cove where the last bateaux were mooring. Ten, twelve of them he counted with a fringe of canoes riding gracefully at the right. Men were lugging sacks and bales and kegs ashore, overturning the boats, driving nails into bottoms and keels. He tapped a foot impatiently. Where was Clark? He was sure that he could clear himself in a five-minute talk. Then, since Clark would certainly be sending messengers back up the Ohio, he would be bound to see that Markham was set on his proper route again. He watched the come and go of men, all maddeningly alike in their buckskins or linsey-woolsey and broad-brimmed hats and slung rifles, dressed and armed as their Colonel was.

George Rogers Clark suddenly stood out as though a shaft of strong sunlight had touched him. It was not merely that he was tall and powerful. There were others taller and stronger. Nor was it his coppery hair as he stood there, bare-headed, for that same shade was repeated half a dozen times. There was something in the lift of head and chin, the set of the shoulders, the way he turned his head, gestured, stood relaxed with one foot on a rock and forearm resting across his knee. He was at the water's edge. He was back among the pines, he was alone in a canoe studying the campsite from the water, he was ashore again. George Rogers Clark simply could not be anonymous. He was his own living insignia of rank that men would recognize anywhere at any time.

Out on the river there was a great hallooing and into the mouth of the Tennessee shot a canoe with a lone paddler who shouted,

"George! Oh, George! Got something for you! Oh, by God I got something!" The canoe was beached and the paddler sprang out. Behind Markham, Bill cried, "It's Will Linn! What's he doin' here? Thought he was to the Falls of the Ohio."

Linn was running up the slope toward the pines and Clark darted out to meet him, snatching at what looked like a letter that the former held out to him. Clark ripped it open, stared at it. Then he whirled about, flinging his arms high in the air. "All captains!" his voice crashed out. "Bowman, Helm, Montgomery, Harrod! Here! On the double! We've got it! We've got our lever!"

The triumphant lift of Clark's tones set Markham's spine tingling. As the company commanders ran to Clark, another canoe swept around the corner of the island and a man sprang out yelling, "Mark Cape! Where the hell's Mark Cape? Hear you got him tied up!"

Markham started forward, but Abel's rifle-butt checked him gently. "Orders is you ain't to squawk and you ain't to ramble."

"Prob'ly be all right," said Bill. "I'm dinged if that ain't one of Ed Brady's boys. Ain't a soul in the Shennydore Valley don't know Ed's boys!"

Phil Brady paused by the beach, caught sight of Markham, gave a quick wave of recognition and pushed on to the pines where Clark sat on a rock among his officers. Markham saw the Colonel look up abruptly, make a gesture of annoyance as Brady stopped before him. Then Clark relaxed, seemed to be listening intently. At last he rose with a nod to the men about him and strode toward the sapling, Brady close at his heels.

As the pair came near, Markham found himself wondering how he could have associated brusque harshness with the tall Colonel. He was smiling now, a smile that began in the steady blue eyes and reached out with an infectious warmth. "Cut him loose, boys," said Clark. "Mr. Cape, my apologies. We're running on mighty thin ice these days and I couldn't take chances. Too many lives at stake, perhaps more than just lives."

"Don't have to explain much to Mark," put in Brady. "He doesn't miss a lot."

Clark's smile wrinkled the reddish stubble of his cheeks. "Mr. Cape, I'll try to make amends for snapping you up the way we did. I know from what you and Brady told me and from Mr. Pollock's letters that your intent is east."

"You had no choice, Colonel. I can see that. It just means time lost that Phil and I can make up easily. We could use a few supplies, though we've a fair store cached up there where your men caught me."

Clark's smile faded. "I wish that I could say Godspeed. I really do. But I need Brady. So I'm taking him. Alone, you *might* try walking to the Falls of the Ohio. I doubt if you'd get there. So you'll have to come with us, I'm afraid."

The glow went out of the bright day. "Where to?" asked Markham hoarsely.

"Where we're going to do what we've got to do," answered Clark.

"You'll tell me no more?"

"Not right now."

"When you've done your job, I'll be free to cast loose again?"

Clark gave him an odd look. "So far as I'm concerned — yes. Beyond that, I can't promise — not for you —" he paused "— nor for any of us. You'll excuse me now. I'll have your rifle and equipment returned to you. I'll assign you to a company before we re-embark so you can draw rations properly."

"When will that be?" asked Markham dully.

"As soon as we reload. Say about half an hour." Clark nodded, turned on his heel and swung off toward the pines.

Markham slowly lowered himself to a rock by the sapling. "Christ! Does it always have to happen like this? I get a few feet up the ladder and then someone starts sawing the rungs out from under me."

For an instant, Brady's hand touched Markham's shoulder. "Yuh, that's the way it goes, God damn it." Then his voice took up its old, bantering tone. "What are you pulling your chin down among your knees for? Boston'll still be there. It always has been,

God knows why. Anyhow, you'd have to stick to me. Soon's I'm out of sight you get into trouble."

Markham shook himself. "I'll make do." He punched Brady lightly in the ribs. "*I* get into trouble? You sneak out of camp when I'm asleep and what happens to *you?* Damn near get carried down to Arkansas Post with O'Hara."

Brady rubbed his lean jaw. "You're not as wrong as you might be. O'Hara swore I was under his orders and tried to nail me to an oar for the rest of his voyage. He didn't like the news about Willing for sour owl-feathers and sort of took it out on me. I had to tell him that you were stranded with dispatches from Pollock to General Washington and Robert Morris but even so we were damn near down to the Mississippi before he'd let me go. I ran onto one of Clark's scouts a mile below this island and learned about Clark. Likewise about you. Don't mind admitting you'd been sitting heavy on my mind coming back upriver."

"You sure cleared me quick enough and I tell you I won't forget it. A sergeant named Harrison was talking about hanging me."

Brady nodded calmly. "Could have happened. There've been some mighty queer people wandering around the river and a man's got to have a story, swift and convincing, these days."

"How'd Clark happen to believe you?"

"Believe *me?*" Brady stared. "We're Virginians. Everyone in Virginia knows everyone else. The Clarks are mighty important folk in our state. George Rogers he's got about eighteen brothers and all of them are generals or something with Washington, well-scholared men. But *he*, he kind of ducked out of school and took to the woods. Don't guess there's many that knows the woods and Indians better than he does. Knows folks, too." He rubbed his jaw again. "Just the same, I'd admire to know how he knew I'd been out before. That's why he wants me along."

"Out where?"

Brady went on unheeding. "It was before the war. I went west, trading, when George Morgan was trying to open things up for that Philadelphia company, Baynton, Wharton and Morgan. Funny he'd know that."

"Trading where?"

"Where we're going, like Clark said. Yes, *sir!* That's where we're going. One hundred seventy-seven of us. Add Clark and that makes it two hundred seventy-seven. Hey! They're loading up the bateaux again. And here comes Abel Twitchet with your rifle and kit. Best be stirring."

The flotilla was heading west down the Ohio again, and again Markham pulled at an oar. Except that he was no longer bound to his seat-mate there was little difference between this stage of the journey and the earlier ones. The other men in Bateau 8 were silent as ever and Sergeant Harrison's good eye still looked coldly out from a fire-ravaged face. Markham worked doggedly on, thinking grimly with each stroke, "There's another damn yard of water that I'll have to churn up again when I head back east!" If only he knew where he was going, how far he was being thrown off course. From what Phil Brady had told him, there was less than forty miles to cover before the Mississippi was reached. If Clark should enter that river and head south —

Suddenly Markham noticed that Harrison's tiller was edging farther and farther over. The bateaux left the shelter of the south bank, headed out into midstream, their prows boring on toward the northern shore. Scout-canoes swept in, glided on between the main flotilla and the nearing bank.

The sun dropped and summer dusk settled over the river. Markham, off duty, rubbed his aching arms and thighs as he watched the slow-slipping north bank and wondered what lay beyond it. He tried to recall the map that he had studied so long ago at Oliver Pollock's. In his mind he saw the great black rope of the Mississippi stretching north and north, saw the Ohio driving into it. The merchant's brass ruler had circled over the area east and north of the two rivers, but his memory held no details of the vast expanse of land that rolled away to the Great Lakes. It probably didn't matter. All the talk that he had heard in New Orleans and on the *Poitou* was concerned with those British posts down the Mississippi. Very likely Clark was on his way to join O'Hara's little party at Arkansas Post for a fresh move against Natchez. Down the Mississippi again! He shook his head wearily.

Harrison threw the tiller over hard and branches whipped across Markham's face as the prow butted into a narrow creek. Ahead a low voice called, "Beach your craft," and the thick undergrowth was loud with tearing, grating sounds. Someone prodded Markham and he sprang out into ankle-deep mud, heaved and dragged the boat with a half-dozen other men onto a soggy, shelving beach, strained on step by step until the stern was lost in a woody tangle. All about him in the dimness, other crews were wrestling their craft ashore, slashing down branches to mask sides and sterns. Harrison called, "Cap'n Helm's company! Up to the ridge and wait there."

Helm! Markham had almost forgotten the assignment given him so casually on embarking back at the island. Rifle slung and heavy haversack tugging at his shoulder, he pushed ahead, feeling for the ascent with his moccasined feet. Light was better toward the crest and men were ducking and weaving easily through the undergrowth, past the clutch of snagging branches, and he envied their lithe progress.

There was a red glow in the west as he reached the top. He halted by a tall pine and saw the last rays of the sun touch the sweeping curve of the river, light up a high, crumbling log palisade less than a half-mile away on the north bank. Then day faded as though a vast curtain had been drawn and night rushed in among the trees about him. A heavy-set man, broad hat crammed on the back of his head, loomed at his elbow. "Cape?" he asked in a rumbling voice.

"Here."

"Here!" said the other, holding out a flat wooden canteen. "Have a snuffle with me."

Markham took the canteen, tried a cautious sip, then tilted his head for a long, full swallow. The liquid was strong, spicy, with a fine, full body. A first hint of sweetness was replaced almost at once by a mellow dryness. His host's hand reached out, took the canteen firmly from him, tilted it himself and replaced the cork. "Hah! You take a real grown-up snuffle. Like it?"

"Don't recall gagging," said Markham.

"No, now that you mention it I don't recall seeing you. It's a brew of my own." A wistful note crept into his voice. "Must say it's better drunk out of silver or pewter and it really ought to get a red-hot toddy-iron swizzled into it. Folks back in Fauquier County call it Helm's Heartener."

"You're *Captain* Helm then?"

"Uh. Now let's sit on this rock and you do some listening while I tell you what George — that's the Colonel — wants you should know. You've got to be with us and he didn't figure it was all ways square for you to trail along blind." He dropped onto a flat stone and Markham seated himself beside him.

Helm took off his hat and rubbed his head. "Things are bad, powerful bad this side the Alleghenies. Western Pennsylvania and Virginia are bad. Kentucky's just pure hell with a lot of fixings added. Indians. They ambush the river-banks and the trails and the fords. They raid the settlements. They burn and murder and torture and scalp and drag folk off to Canada. Hardly a man on this ridge but's lost kin, one way or another."

"Sounds like New England in the old days. Indians used to come across from Champlain or down the Merrimack and the Androscoggin."

"Indians is always Indians. Used to be the French supplied and led them. Now it's the British, only they do more supplying than leading. We got to stop the Indians somehow. If not, folks won't stay in Kentucky or western Virginia or Pennsylvania. The frontier'll shrink and shrink till one day you'll see palisades around Philadelphia and Williamsburg and the west edges of those towns'll be the frontier and then what'll happen to our armies on the coast? What'll happen to *independence?*"

Again Markham could see Pollock's neat office, could hear the merchant's calm voice saying that the Allegheny Mountains could be no true frontier. Why hadn't he listened more carefully?

Helm went on. "So, if we can beat back the Indians, we're safe, kind of. And the best way to do that's to cut off the supplies and the presents and the bribes they get from Detroit where Henry Hamilton's in command."

"The one they call 'Hair-buyer'?" asked Markham. "A lot of people wanted to find out if I knew him when I was first picked up."

"Kind of have to want to. He scatters spies like a dog sheds fleas. Not that he really buys hair. Just pays the Indians for the prisoners they bring in. If they fetch in a mess of scalps, why that's evidence they've messed up some Americans, so he pays a bit for them too. Well, now, do we take Detroit, the Indians won't be getting supplies and presents and bribes and they'll go skittering off like dogs that've been dapped with turpentine. This here move is George's, mostly. He spread it out to Governor Henry and Tom Jefferson and a few others and *they* liked it enough so they got the House of Burgesses to vote men and money for the job." He cleared his throat apologetically. "Of course, there was a lot of skulduggery in that vote, because the legislators didn't know what they were voting for. Whole thing was secret as hell. Matter of fact, none of the boys knew where they were going until the day they left Corn Island, up by the Falls of the Ohio that day the sun got swallowed for a while. Kind of late to turn back then."

"Detroit? Where's that?"

"North, up on the Great Lakes. But we ain't going there. We're intending for Kaskaskia."

Kaskaskia! Markham's mind clung to the one familiar name that bobbed up in all this talk of the Northwest. That was where Louis Boudreau and Mathieu Granet and Georges Herriot of the *Poitou* came from.

Helm was talking on in his comfortable rumble. "We take Kaskaskia. Don't rightly know how. Don't know what we'll run up against there. We didn't even know the best route till we picked up some hunters back on that Tennessee island and persuaded one of them to guide us. But George says we'll take the town, so we'll take it."

"Kaskaskia. On the Mississippi," said Markham slowly. "More rowing!"

"Oh, no." Helm spoke soothingly. "We leave the bateaux hid right here, close by that old Fort Massac the Frenchies built near fifty years ago. Then we take a nice little walk, three, four days, up the Massac-Kaskaskia Trace. Kind of a holiday, if our rations hold out, because we're just taking what our haversacks'll hold. No fires to light because we don't crave to be seen. No cooking to trouble us. Just good, easy walking."

Markham's jaws set as he looked out into the mystery of the forest night that was softly astir with the sound of many men settling themselves. Somehow the long days of struggling through snake-infested marshes with the *Poitou*'s cordelle gnawing at his shoulder seemed suddenly carefree, almost gay. He said slowly, "Of course, I've no choice at all but to keep on with you."

"Not a mite," said Helm cheerily.

"But I was just wondering what will happen if we meet people who don't like the notion of our nice little walk."

The canteen-cork popped softly. "Just another snuffle. I'll take mine first because I want to feel real optimistic when I say this." Helm drank, handed the canteen to Markham. "We've seen plenty of Indian-sign both banks of the Ohio. But far as we can figure, there ain't a soul in the whole Illinois country got even a ghost-mouse of an idea that there's anyone stirring south of the Kaskaskia River. We — Hey! Here comes George. I want a word with him. Give me the canteen." He took it and slipped off among the trees.

Markham, his throat still tingling from the last drink, could just make out Helm's light tread in the dark, but that was all. He was startled to hear Clark's voice, low, musical yet carrying, quite close by. "That you, Leonard? Come along with me." His tone grew louder. "You've got your orders, boys. No fires. No straying. We start an hour before sunup. Get your sleep." The words died away as Clark moved on. Markham could still hear Leonard Helm's gentle pad-pad, but George Rogers Clark seemed to float along, leaving no footfall to underscore his words. "No fires. No straying. We start —"

The night was warm above the little creek that fed into the Ohio and a breeze off the big river played softly through oak and pine and sycamore branches. Markham lay down among thick pine-needles, rubbing his eyes while nagging thoughts raced through his brain. He was badly off course again, apparently heading on a bearing that would take him on and on to the northwest instead of the proper northeast. Except for the fact that he was no longer alone, he was no better off — in fact he was now worse off — than he had been while waiting for Brady's return at the little camp by the Ohio. Now he was caught up in what he could only think of as a hare-brained expedition to take a French village in British territory held by an unknown force that would surely be made up of local militia bound by oaths of allegiance to the English Crown and might quite possibly include tough, war-wise British regulars. And why? How could the capture of a Mississippi river-port have the least bearing on the flow of money, arms and supplies from Colonel Henry Hamilton's stores at Detroit to the Indians? How could the presence of less than two hundred Virginians and Kentuckians in Kaskaskia keep a single tawny savage from killing and scalping in the frontier settlements hundreds of miles to the east?

He rolled over, careful to keep an arm through his rifle-sling. He had no particular fears for his own survival, unless disaster overtook the whole column. The past years had toughened him physically and mentally enough to meet most situations. His powder-horn was full and so was his shot-pouch. His wooden canteen was brimming and his haversack held several pounds of corn-meal, some parched corn and hard slabs of what he had been told was dried buffalo meat that smelled like a wet dog. In the past he had kept alive on far scantier rations.

From what he had seen of his fellows they were as hard and resourceful as himself. More than that, they moved in a familiar setting, knew each other and their leaders, and, to judge from Helm's words, had an accumulation of highly personal memories of what Indians could do and had done. He turned again and his knee brought up against something solid, yet yielding.

A voice growled, "What you doin', ramblin' about all over the place? Ain't you heard what the Colonel said 'bout strayin'?"

"Sergeant Harrison? Sorry. I wasn't straying, just turning over."

"Same thing. Don't do to get fretsome. Just lie still and no one'll hatch an idea to poison you with lead. You foreigners got to be careful."

"I'll take care."

"I'll kind of help you take care. Say, how come you ain't armed proper?"

"Am," said Markham.

A hard hand fumbled about his waist, his chest. "Ain't," said Harrison. "Here, grab this."

Markham reached out and his fingers closed on the hilt of a long-bladed knife, felt a leather sheath, a dangling rawhide loop. Harrison went on. "Hitch it to your belt or sling it round your neck. Come you have to use it, keep the point level, the edge up and your thumb along the hilt. Strike up a mite and you'll go into meat like it was butter."

Markham stowed the knife away. "You're giving me this? Thanks and —"

"Ain't givin'. Loanin'. When I want it back, I'll pick it off'n your body. Now git some sleep. There's wearin' work ahead."

IV

A Bewilder on Prairie Trails

THE FOREST was interminable. Oak and walnut and butter-nut, white pine, ash and wild cherry swept up from the wil-derness floor, reaching higher and higher toward the hot blue of the sky and the touch of the sun. Sometimes their massed tops, thick with ever-climbing wild grape, shut out the day. Then the Illinois Regiment, as Markham had learned to call it, wound on in endless single file through a twilight hush to emerge into the gold and green and brown open glades.

By a brook that drained off into the Cash River, now far to the south, Markham stood on a rock and counted the steady flow of gray-brown men and bobbing rifle barrels. There was no one in sight down the old trace behind Captain John Montgomery's company and Markham hailed the last man. "Any more of you?"

The man shook his head. "Not unless someone's give birth since sunup and I ain't heard of such."

Markham studied the notched stick and the strip of bark on which he had been keeping tally for Clark, carefully verified his count once more and stowed stick and strip inside his shirt. A clear spring bubbled up close by the rock and he knelt by it, drank deeply, then emptied and refilled his canteen. As he rose and started on after the others sudden cold fear gripped him. He was alone and his straining ears could catch no sound of voices or the rustling swish of moccasins. He took a few steps forward, only to come to a halt, heart pounding. The trace petered out on the far side of the brook and the towering trunks seemed to be moving slowly toward him as though to swallow him up.

Lost! The thought beat at his brain. There would be little

chance of picking up the route of the column for the men were scrupulously obeying Clark's orders to leave not even the smallest litter behind them. Then his eyes caught an old scar on an oak tree and he made his way clumsily across the brook to it. There it was, the old, old blaze with some forgotten code-mark deep-carved and still showing smears of the red paint that the careful French had put there when they laid out the Fort Massac-Kaskaskia trace so long ago. And there, above and to his left, the last of Montgomery's men were climbing a steep slope that, with a sharp turn, had taken them out of his sight for a few short moments.

He shook his head angrily as he hurried to catch up. He had been an idiot to panic at the thought of being alone in the forest. Just the same —

The men of Helm's company, of other companies, had been talking more since they left the river. They had spoken of Indians. Phil Brady's bald statement in New Orleans that very few settler families had dared stay in Kentucky in the winter of '77-'78 suddenly became horribly vivid to Markham, took on reality and straining life — and death.

Solid blocks of talk still hung in his mind. "Comin' in from hayin' we found Ed Whittemore and Doug McNeak all bloody and skelpt, lyin' right across Doug's mother's door. Ain't never heard what betided her or the young ones." "We managed to git Arch Pendergast shook clear, but them devils snuck Pete Flynn and Tom Good and the Barnes gal back into the bush and outa reach. But we c'd smell the burnin' right enough and Pete, he ain't stopped screaming till next sunup." "Sure, I know they ain't got away. There was my cabin burnin' an' Abby and the twins an' Martha hollerin' an' me tied to a tree with Shawnees flickin' knives at me. It was that rescue party outa Riddle's Station that set me loose, but by the time they come, they wasn't no more sounds comin' outa my cabin. Just smoke an' — oh God! that smell." Sergeant Harrison had lived long hours over a slow fire while lighted pine splinters, inserted with fiendish skill about one eye, burned until the eyeball began to boil. The sergeant allowed that he had been real glad to see that rescue party from Logan's Fort.

Such men, with such knowledge and such memories, might know a moment of terror on finding themselves alone in a forest that could hold a score of hidden, hostile watchers. And they were at home in such a forest, whereas he — "Quit making excuses." he told himself. "If you don't want to get left behind, don't dally." He was abreast of Harrod's company where Shadrack Mason and Eppa Cox, the scouts who had picked him up back there on the Ohio, hailed him as he trotted past. Markham knew a sudden wave of affection for this drab column of sweaty, greasy men. It was something secure and solid to which he could cling, as he had clung to the *Poitou* coming up the Mississippi. There he had been safe, no matter what hazards, so long as he had planks under his feet and Charcot guiding those planks. Here, little short of a vast-scale calamity could touch him if he stayed close. If only he didn't feel so weak. There had been a pooling of rations before leaving the night camp near Fort Massac and his haversack no longer bulged. On this the third day of the northwest march he had breakfasted on a thin cornmeal cake and a sliver of dried elk-meat and that would have to do him until the night halt. He wondered if others in the column were feeling the pinch, but hasty glances at their set faces told him nothing.

The trace led on, dipping down a long slope where the trees were thinner, and Markham saw the head of Leonard Helm's company with Bill Moon and Abel Twitchet, his guards at the Tennessee island, a dozen yards in the lead. The captain, easily the oldest of all the officers, plodded doggedly on. He winked as Markham passed, grimaced and slapped the canteen that had been long since drained of Helm's Heartener. At the foot of the slope Markham saw George Rogers Clark swinging easily along, flanked by Phil Brady and Lieutenant John Gerault, a London-born Huguenot who had somehow made his way to New York and thence out to the Ohio Valley. Markham had at first disliked Gerault, distrusted his eternally dapper appearance. He always looked fresh-shaven, his equipment was spotless and his buckskins were almost white despite the fording of muddy brooks, the passage through long swampy stretches and the touch of pitchy pine-boughs. It had to be admitted, though, that Gerault kept up with the best marchers and seemed to do with very little sleep and the scantiest of rations.

Clark looked around as Markham came up. "What's your count?" he asked.

"One hundred seventy-eight all ranks, counting yourself," answered Markham stepping up beside Brady. "No stragglers. Captain Harrod reports he's having trouble keeping his men in line. They break every time they pass a blackberry or dewberry patch. Captain Bowman says the same. The men are hungry as hell."

"Can't have that," snapped Clark. "A good woodsman's got to be able to starve well." He touched Gerault's arm, jerked his thumb backward. Gerault nodded and started off down the column. "He'll tell 'em."

"Can't blame the boys," said Phil Brady. "They're getting empty. Walk past a company at a halt and you'd think a thunderstorm was coming up, the way their guts rumble."

Clark shook his head. "Rumbling doesn't carry. But let some damn fool who thinks more of his belly than his scalp loose a shot at a deer or a turkey and we could have trouble. Simon Kenton's been ranging both sides of the trail and so far hasn't picked up Indian-sign. One shot could fill these woods with Shawnees and Delawares and then where'd we be? The lucky ones *might* get off as light as Joe Harrison did, but I doubt it."

"John Saunders sighted anything?" asked Brady, pointing to four men some fifty yeards ahead.

"He's just supposed to find the route for us, that's all." Clark swept his knuckles across his forehead. "Wonder if I was wrong, picking him up at the Tennessee island. Christ, I still don't trust him, but he was the only man who'd been over the Massac Trace."

"He's been all right so far and you've got three men watching him all the time."

"So far. But we've got all the rest of today and all tomorrow before we hit Kaskaskia. Maybe friends of his have been dogging us. They could send word ahead and Rocheblave could drum up the militia in Kaskaskia and Cahokia and Prairie du Rocher. He could send word damn fast to Arendt de Peyster at Michilimackinac and we'd have Canadians and British regulars cutting in behind us. Also, a hellish cloud of Indians." He threw back his shoulders. "We're doing what we can with what we have. Time for a halt. Get on with your talk about Kaskaskia. So far you've seen nothing familiar?"

"Much too early," answered Brady. "When I was out here in George Morgan's time, I came over the Vincennes-Kaskaskia Trace. That's about at right angles to us and way to the north. How far, I couldn't say." He seated himself on a big jutting oak-root and tugged at the fringe of Markham's buckskins. "For God's sake, sit down. My knee joints have sagged down so far they're resting on my ankle-bones. Melts my marrow, seeing someone prancing around like you are." Markham joined him on the root while Brady pulled out a sheet of rough paper and flattened it. "Kaskaskia. Here's Garrison Hill. Used to have a fort on it. They built a new one closer to the river. Here's the town. One big, wide street, couple of little ones leading off it. Houses mostly wood, built of upended timbers. Two or three stone ones —"

Markham leaned back against the trunk as Brady talked on. To his surprise, Clark did not look over Brady's shoulder. He paced slowly up and down, hands behind his back, eyes on the trace or searching the tree tops, seemingly little interested, tossing out curt comments almost absently. "I see." "Like that, is it?" "Might be." "Can't always tell." "No knowing how many are in the fort now." "Sometimes happens."

Along the trail the men of the four companies sprawled, tilting up canteens or gourds or horns, rinsing mouths, stripping wild raspberries from branches that they had torn off in passing. Gerault came trotting up, nodded to Clark and squatted quietly beside Brady. Far up the trace, the guide Saunders lay with his hat over his eyes while his watchers knelt close by.

In the middle of one of Brady's sentences, Clark said abruptly,

"The rest'll keep. We've got to be stirring." He signaled down the column, then to the group ahead. As the four men got to their feet, Markham heard him mutter, "Just wish I was sure of that bastard Saunders."

The end of the forest came so abruptly that it was almost a shock to Markham. At one moment he had been plodding along the shadowy trace among the trees. Then light grew stronger, stronger and he stepped out into the full morning glare. Ahead of him were acres, miles of rolling grassy country dotted here and there with tidy copses of walnut and sycamore or green-streaked where young ash marked the course of a stream. Overhead the morning sun, climbing toward noon, poured its golden flood out of a deep blue sky where immense white puffballs of cloud sailed to the touch of a steady wind.

The hypnosis of the forest left him. He felt as though, weary with endless swimming, his feet had touched firm, sloping bottom where each step brought him closer to his own element. He swung his arms out, breathed deeply, snatched at tall grass-spears and chewed their pulpy ends. He could see two miles, perhaps five miles, in any direction but the rear. If he strayed from the column now, there would be no trouble about finding it again, winding over these grassy plains dappled with sunlight and cloud-shadow. Off to the north he caught sight of something moving, something slow and dark and massy. He felt almost like a veteran long-hunter as he identified the movement, laughed at his own fright back there on the Ohio at what had seemed to him a nightmare vision. "Phil!" he called. "Look yonder. Chuck away your berries. There's dinner! Forty, maybe fifty buffalo!"

Brady pushed him. "You gone light-headed or something? Maybe that's somebody's dinner but not ours. The sound of a shot'd carry miles in this air." He said over his shoulder, "George! Mark spotted a herd. See 'em off there to the northeast?"

Clark came abreast of them, flanked by Gerault's spruceness and Helm's lined, full face. "I saw them. That's good, Cape. Always holler about what you notice."

"At least that tells us there's nothing in that quarter," rumbled Helm. "The beasts are just movin', not fleein'."

Brady squinted toward the horizon. "Could be that someone's shifting them off there, just enough to keep 'em stirring."

"Yes," said Clark tersely. Almost to himself he muttered, "I don't like it. I don't *like* it."

"Seen better," observed Helm calmly. "Ain't a scrap of cover and the regiment'll stand out like a brick blab-school in a snowstorm."

Brady said softly in Markham's ear, "Just one man in that copse off yonder could see us and send word of us to quarters where we don't want it to go. And we'd never know it until too late."

The exhilaration of the vast spread of open country died abruptly for Markham. The wide prairie could be as deadly as the close-packed trunks and half-light of the trace. He hitched at his belt, touched the thong that held Harrison's big knife about his neck. "Always something new, Phil. God damn it, maybe if I live to be a hundred I'll learn enough to look after myself wherever I am." He managed a laugh. "Anyhow, I got to be pretty thefty with a swivel-gun. Once I wiped out a whole boarding-party with one blast when our felucca had a wicked list to port. Maybe I'll learn some of your land tricks before I'm done."

Clark's coppery head appeared between him and Brady. "What's that about swivel-guns?" he asked sharply.

Markham flushed. "Just telling Phil that I'd used them in the Mediterranean."

"H'm," grunted Clark and dropped back. Presently Markham heard his voice again. "Leonard, what the hell's Saunders doing up there?"

Brady nudged Markham and pointed ahead. Saunders and his guards were a scant fifty yards in advance of the column instead of the hundred or more that they had been keeping earlier. The guide was moving slowly, stopping every now and then to look around, walking on again, rather uncertainly, Markham thought.

"Saunders is all right," put in Helm. "Just ain't many landmarks hereabouts."

"I *think* he's all right," said Clark. "But Christ, that isn't enough. I've got to *know* he is. Too much is riding on this for just thinking. And I'd like to know what ever happened to the guides who were supposed to join us at the Tennessee island."

"Maybe he'll do better than they would have," said Helm soothingly. "Looky. Seems to have caught a better scent. Striking out right briskly, he is."

"He'd better," snapped Clark.

Markham moistened his lips. It was an eerie feeling, pushing ahead over the prairie, following a man who might be knowingly leading on to disaster. At least, he reflected, he was not alone. He turned to look down the long drab column of the Illinois Regiment, marching on one by one. They were all seasoned wilderness men, taken individually. Could they act as a unit when danger came? They had nothing that he knew of to hold them together, no backlog of military tradition and practice and law and discipline. He thought of various European troops that he had seen, like the Spanish Hibernia Regiment, so largely manned and officered by transplanted Irishmen. But these men, hastily gathered together, highly individualistic, seemed to him to be bound by two common ties — a deep-seated rage against the Indians and an equally deep wish to strike some blow that would end, or help end, the Indian menace.

Their strength and their effectiveness as a unit would rest almost entirely on their leadership, they would have to be held together and made to act together by ties of confidence in and trust and affection for Clark. So far, those ties had seemed very strong. The men all knew him, had seen him in wilderness fighting. But so far, the ties had had no great strain put on them. For himself, Markham was not sure. George Rogers Clark stood out as a leader. There was no doubt about that, at least so far. He was apt to snap out with biting harshness when his suspicions were aroused or when he saw work or precautions scanted, a trait which might or might not be good. When reports were brought him, he often seemed to listen abstractedly as though he had lost interest. Or he might cut short answers to his own questions, as he had with Phil Brady that morning, leaving Markham with the feeling that the information in Clark's estimation was not worth hearing.

Yet Markham had seen him plunge into bad going, like the alder-swamp the day before, as though getting through it were some-thing of a frolic, laughing and bantering with the men, link-ing arms with seeming laggards and rushing them along with him, drawing the whole long column onward by the very conta-gion of his own whooping progress. And a few moments later, Markham had been with him near the head of the column and knew that his face was set and his eyes hard as he juggled the problems of miles and rations and the future and possible treach-ery. "I wonder," Markham asked himself, "if I underrate him sim-ply because he's just about my own age and doing a job that I couldn't even start. But maybe I'm just beginning to *think* that he may be all right, but all the time feeling that I've got to know — like Clark about Saunders."

There were halts in the swaying grass, a detour to a spring to refill canteens and gourds, a wide, circling movement past a dense copse where Simon Kenton, tall and red-headed like the Colonel, thought he had detected suspicious stirrings, then on again. At one halt Captains Bowman, Harrod, Montgomery and Helm squatted in a ring, apparently reviving an earlier discussion con-cerning the reported attitude of the French people of Kaskaskia, the Creoles as they called them, although Creole could also mean Spanish, as Brady, shamelessly eavesdropping, murmured to Mark-ham. Once again, Clark paced absently about while his captains gestured at him, saying that the Creoles were against the English, would welcome a change of rulers; that, thanks to carefully planted stories, they were terrified of Virginians and Kentuckians, of the Big Knives, whom they looked upon as murderous barbarians, rather worse than Indians. Given all that, how should the Creoles be treated? The only answer was a curt, "We've been here too long. Get the boys moving."

"Wonder how much longer the boys *can* keep moving," said Markham as he struck out beside Brady.

"I'm done wondering, Mark. My head feels stuffed with cotton and my knees swivel every time my feet hit the ground. Wish we'd see more of those bushes with the little green leaves like you spotted this morning. How'd you know they were good to eat?"

"Didn't. They just looked like some I found once when I was — when I was hungry somewhere else. Look at Saunders up there. See his track in the grass? Looks as though he was tacking with a rocky coast to leeward of him. Back and forth, back and forth."

Clark swung up beside Markham. "Cape, you've never seen Saunders close to, have you? Or he you?"

"No, to the first. Doubt it, to the second."

"Come along with me, then. Something's wrong. I'm going to talk to him. Unsling your rifle. When we get there, stand a bit behind me and to one side. Don't talk. Don't do anything. Just lean on your rifle and look at him, keep looking at him, right in the face."

Markham had to set his jaw hard as he grounded his rifle and crossed his hands on the muzzle, eyes fixed on Saunders. Something — perhaps everything — *was* wrong. The guide's face was an unwholesome clay-color under the brownish bristle of his beard. His rather slack lips quivered and cords danced and flexed in his thin neck. His hands ran ceaselessly along his rifle-barrel and left shiny marks like snail-tracks.

"Well?" Clark's voice snapped like a whiplash and the little escort edged away as though to disassociate itself from the guide.

Saunders stammered, "I — I don't know — I jus' don' know. Honest! I'm jus' — well, like I said — honest —"

"I'll judge the honest part. Talk!"

Saunders's glanced flicked away from Clark, met Markham's, fell to the ground. "I — can't figger out where I am — Christ, Mister — Colonel — it was easy in them trees. Out here —"

Clark's tone was dangerously soft. "You told me that you could take me up or down the trace, daylight or dark."

"I meant that." Saunders hugged his rifle to him. "So help me Christ our dear Lord I did. But it was turn of spring when last I come this way. It's all different. Looks different. Feels different." He swept a sleeve across his face. "What you got that man with the rifle hexin' at me for?"

Half pitying, half hostile, Markham watched the guide while Clark's face remained rock-hard, unmoving. Saunders babbled on. "A little more time! Lemme cast a mite east, a mite west. Maybe I can pick up a tree or a slope that'll talk to me. Lemme go alone. I get frazzled with them fellers followin' me."

Without turning his head Clark spoke to the escort. His voice was still low and sent cold waves along Markham's spine. "We've got a spy here. You know who'd pay him. Take him into the copse off there. Lash him to a tree. Don't bother to cut him down afterwards. Then catch up with the column. Come along, Cape." He turned on his heel.

All at once Saunders's face was wet and bubbling noises came from his throat. Clark wheeled about. "You still think you could pick up a landmark?" The guide's reply was unintelligible. "You three!" snapped Clark. "He's got one hour to find it. Go with him. Don't let him get more than ten yards ahead of you. One of you always keep in sight of me. Until he finds the trace, he's still a spy."

The escort closed about Saunders, who scuttled off panting, "I'll find it, by God I'll find it."

Markham pushed his hat back, wiped his forehead. "Jesus!" he muttered.

"I'm handling this job," said Clark sharply.

Markham was silent, stood watching the four men moving off across the grass. Now they dipped into a swale, now entered a clump of trees, but there was always one of the escort in sight pausing to look back at the Colonel. Markham found himself breathing out a silent petition. "Find it! Find something, for God's sake!"

Time dragged on and the sun dipped lower. Suddenly an escort sprang on a rock, rifle held high in one hand, his round fur cap waving in the other. "Looks as if he'd hit it," said Clark carelessly. Then the tall red-haired man sat down, forehead on his knees. "Thank God," he said and his voice was no longer careless. "I was scared — scared I'd have to shoot him." He rose stiffly. "It was his weeping that swung me. Till then, I couldn't prove to myself he wasn't lying."

"What could his weeping tell you?"

"That he was in a bewilder. He couldn't find the signs he knew he ought to find and sort of lost grip on himself. I've seen it happen before to others."

Markham nodded slowly. "I've seen it, too. Just this morning a man thought he'd lost the column back in the forest. He was so scared a chipmunk could have chased him clear to the Mississippi. He never could have accounted for himself if he'd been accused of trying to desert. A man named Cape, it was. Here comes your party, all laughing."

"Come on. We'll go to meet them. I've put him through a bad time."

"Put yourself through one, too, Colonel."

"Part of my job." He called, "John Saunders! Get over here quick and give me your hand. You've stood up like a real woodsman. I'm going to send Dennett and Post and Jones back to their companies." He caught Saunders's grimy hand, thumped him on the back. "You just keep right on ahead and holler back at us if we get lagging."

Saunders shook his head. "I'd kinda like to have the boys stay with me. It's more sociable. And God damn me if I know what I seen or heard that set me right. Jus' looked back over my shoulder once and every grass-spear and tree suddenly begun wavin' me along and the whole prairie fell into place as homey as if I'd covered it a hundred times before." He motioned to the rear with his rifle. "You jus' go on back and look after your boys. Keep a-follerin' me and you'll sight the Kaskaskia River by sundown tomorrow."

Clark started to speak, but checked himself. Then he said, "Keep a-plodding, John. Send back word if you want anything. I'll be down by the tail of the column for a while. Come along, Cape."

Markham knelt by the dark brookside and splashed water lavishly about his face and neck, rubbing it vigorously into the beard that had sprung back since he had last shaved it before leaving the *Poitou*. Someone edged along toward him out of the grove where Clark's command had spent the night. "That you, Phil?" he called softly.

"Guess so. Going to be hot today once the sun's up, and we'll be marching on empty bellies again. Cram down all the water you can hold. There's no real meat to it, but it helps fill you up — for a while."

Markham pushed his hat toward Brady. "Feel inside the crown. Got some blackberries and dewberries under that wadded handkerchief. They'll be squishy, but they'll go down. I mean it! Dig in. I had all I dare eat. Fruits and berries get too damn active if you don't have bread and meat and things to go with them. Besides, we'll be certain to strike more berry-patches today."

Brady hesitated, then plunged his hand into the hat. "I'll remember this, Mark. God, these are good, especially the blackberries. You can really set your teeth into the seeds. This is a hell of a good way to celebrate the fourth of July."

"Or the fifth or the sixth or the seventh, if we last that long."

"Your wits diddling you? The fourth of July, July the fourth! Oh — I forgot. Talking to you is sometimes like handing a book to a man who's never even been to a blab-school. Listen — two years ago today, our Congress, off in Philadelphia, kind of rose up and cast the States loose from England."

Markham rubbed his beard dry on his shirt-sleeve. "I knew what they did, of course. Heard about it at Ponta Delgada in the Azores, but the date didn't stay with me. I've been getting history lessons crammed into me on this march, too. Hell, it's funny. Those two little villages north of Boston! Never were much in my mind when I was at home and now I run into a mess of Virginians who seem to know as much about Concord and Lexington as if they'd spent their lives in Middlesex County, Massachusetts. Have the scouts come in yet?"

"That's what woke me. Simon Kenton and Hi Bales took an extra wide cast and came whooping in to tell Clark there wasn't as much as a hopper-grass stirring."

"Hope they're right."

"Apt to be. Kenton, he's about the best scout on the continent."

"What do we hit? More prairie?"

"Same as yesterday, they say. It'll be easy marching."

"Hell and death! Easy for us — and for others. I tell you, Phil, I keep thinking of a country inn I saw once. The table had a nice white cloth and a big black ant was crawling across it. The man sitting next to me waited till he got within easy reach and then just sort of buttered him over the table-top. That's the way I've been feeling out in the open. Someone's lying back just out of sight, waiting for this command to get where one swipe'll spread us all out over the grass."

"That's one thing that George Rogers Clark never learned how to do — to get surprised. He makes surprises happen to other folk. On your feet now. The boys are forming up."

The column wound on with a fair-weather sunrise at its back and a soft summer wind sending swift ripples over the grasses that were diamond-tipped with dew. Marching as connecting file between Helm's company and Harrod's, Markham watched the new day come on. The terrain looked to him exactly like yesterday's and he had an uncomfortable feeling that time was running backward, that he was moving through July 3, 1778 all over again instead of entering into July 4. There was the same distant horizon, shutting down bowl-like on all sides. There were the same rare rock outcroppings and the same great canopy spreads of groves and copses. Cardinals swept up in vivid scarlet arcs toward the deepening blue of the sky. Meadowlarks poured out their morning songs by the edges of fringed pools. Once or twice in the far distance buffalo herds moved like slow, black clouds. Markham stood stock still an instant. "Yesterday's saying itself all over again."

Yet there were changes. One thing: the route from the Ohio had held pretty steadily north. Now it was pushing sharp west. Another thing: yesterday, John Saunders had been casting about like a lost dog with three men hanging, watchful, at his heels. Now Markham could see him far out in front, swinging along with his head back and laughing with his companions, a free man among his peers. There was something else, too, to set this day off. Markham and the rest were twenty-four hours hungrier than they had been yesterday. He could read that hunger in the sag of shoulders, in the occasional stumbles and the sunken eyes of his fellows just as surely as in his own flashes of dizziness, in his feet that were sometimes so aimlessly light and sometimes so heavy, in the running cramps that stabbed through his belly and in the thoughts that darted erratically through his head, as uncontrolled as dreams. If the column halted and the men scored the soil with their long knives, they could scatter seed-corn or wheat in the furrows and in time the grains would sprout into tall ripe stalks. Then ears could be gathered and finally made into bread, into thick, crusty loaves that the four companies could chew and chew and then go on refreshed. Markham was no farmer but he could see that the soil was rich and black. He was quite sure that no plow had even broken the surface since the beginning of time, that no axe had ever been laid to the oak and sycamore and ash clumps. How long would a halt have to last to bring bread out of the ground? Probably the Colonel could find some way to hurry things.

The Colonel. A lot of odd things about him. Plenty of men in the command were older, more seasoned than he, yet they followed him unquestioningly, accepted his sudden silences, his seeming withdrawals into himself, his habit of marching on alone and paying little attention to what was said to him, his quick decisions that often seemed to Markham like whims. And there was the way people spoke of him. He was "the Colonel." He was "George." But more often he was "George Rogers Clark" with never an abbreviation or nickname. Men spoke of "Lennie Helm" and "Joe Bowman" and "Will Linn" but never of "George Clark." And speaking of Will Linn, what was the great news that he had brought Clark back there at the Tennessee island, the news that had the Colonel shouting that he had a "lever"? Perhaps it had to do with a cache of supplies on the road to Kaskaskia. Markham began to inventory the cache, to count up sides of fresh beef, smoked buffalo-hump and tongue, rich, luscious bear-bacon and sheets and sheets of good thin hard-bread that would crackle and snap between a man's teeth.

There was a halt in a great tract of waist-high grass into which the men vanished, sprawling among the roots and the grass-tops waving above their heads. Markham, hat over his eyes, tried to re-capture his thoughts about the cache, but they danced away and he found himself wondering once more about Oliver Pollock and how that merchant had first come to New Orleans and what had enabled him to sail so smoothly and confidently through the diffi-cult mazes of Spanish officialdom. A brilliantly logical explanation formed in his mind, only to be shattered by a sudden start.

A man was prodding Markham's ribs and asking if he really craved to git lef' behind. Markham rolled to his feet, adjusted his equipment and fell in behind Helm's company. If he had actually slept, it had done him good. His lungs and legs and head felt better and he struck out through the whipping grasses. He knew from ex-perience that this renewed energy, this second wind, was nothing but a further symptom of overexertion and privation, but it would carry him on for a long time. There was no sense in worrying about what might happen when it gave out. Then men were shout-ing his name, saying that the Colonel wanted him up at the head of the column.

When Markham reached Clark, John Saunders was still well in advance and far out beyond him a few men moved westward over the prairie. He thought he recognized Simon Kenton and Will Linn among them. Scouts, out ahead and not on the flanks! Some-thing was going to happen. Markham nodded to Phil Brady and Gerault who walked with Clark and Harrod. The Colonel said abruptly, "Gerault tells me you speak pretty good French."

"It's spotty, I'm afraid."

"Can you understand it? Do French understand you?"

"I manage to make do," answered Markham.

Clark stared at him. "That doesn't tell me anything."

Beyond him Brady laughed. "He means he'll get along, Colonel. It took me about six weeks to translate it."

"All right," said Clark. "Don't stray." Then, seemingly dismissing Markham from his mind, he strode on, eyes on the scouts far, far ahead.

Slow miles went by underfoot. There was a halt, more miles, another halt and forward again. Topping an abrupt rise in the prairie, Clark stopped short, pointed west. Off on the utmost western rim of the rolling grasslands, Markham caught a glint of water touched by the dropping sun. Saunders galloped up, joyous as a wagging puppy. "Told you I'd raise it 'fore sundown."

"That it?" asked Clark, his face set and eyes narrow.

"Nothin' else but. The ol' Kaskasky River!"

Clark's breath went out in a slow exhalation. "You've done a man's job, Johnny. When you start for home, I'll give you a letter to Governor Henry about you." He threw back his head. "Phil Brady! Double back down the column. Tell all company commanders we'll wait out a bit more of the daylight in that oak grove yonder. Tell them to be sure no one straggles and have every man awake and alert. I'm going to talk some."

V

"Attack — Quick, Hard and Positive"

"The odds don't look good. So I reckon the best thing
for us to do is attack — quick, hard and positive."
— G.R.C.

A SOFT green light that was just beginning to take on sunset tints filtered down through the oak-leaves of the grove. Markham sat at the foot of a great tree, his knees drawn up to ease the hunger-cramps that kept lancing through him, and watched the men of the Illinois Regiment sprawl out in a wide semicircle. Brady squatted wearily beside him. "Want to be right here," he said. "George'll want a real look at my map before he starts in orating."

Markham stifled a persistent yawn. "Every time we halted I saw you two scrunched down over it. He must know it better than you do by now."

"Hell." said Brady, chewing at a spear of soft wood-grass, "I was scrunched but every time I started talking he'd get stray-foot and begin counting the squirrels up in the tree-tops. Here he comes now." He rose. "He'll be hollering for me any minute."

Clark strode into the grove, handed his rifle to John Saunders, who tagged devotedly at his heels, and faced the semicircle. Brady sat down again. "Well, later then." Clark looked coolly about him, began to speak in a low-pitched but carrying voice.

"All right, boys. We've got close to where we're going. That river you saw to the west's the Kaskaskia. The town and the fort are on the far bank. Here's what we know. The fort's strong enough to hold off a thousand men. It's got a dozen cannon at least. The militia's well organized and armed. There are about two hundred fifty families in Kaskaskia, so let's say they'll have a good three hundred militiamen. That clear?"

There was dead silence from the semicircle, but Markham saw that men were sitting forward, gripping rifles or knives. He hoped, as he thought of the fort and the hundreds of militia, that he looked as determined as his fellows.

Clark went on: "Here we are. Some of us a thousand, twelve hundred miles from home. No one can help us. We haven't got a hell of a lot of powder. We've marched hard and lived on berries for the last forty-eight hours. We don't know what sort of a reception we'd get if we tried to rush the town. The odds don't look good."

Markham listened incredulously, caught a stir as the blur of faces seemed to sway toward him. Was Clark, after all this effort and toil, going to —

"So I reckon the best thing for us to do is attack — quick, hard and positive." The faces stopped swaying and Markham felt prickles running along his spine. "Here's what we do. We get across the river. Captain Bowman's company will come with me to the fort, just south of the town. Captain Helm's and Captain Montgomery's companies will circle the town from the north. Montgomery's will drop out there. Helm's will swing to the west side. Captain Harrod's company will stay at the crossing-place." He paused, letting his glance sweep slowly from one end of the regiment to the other.

A man said uneasily, "Sure. But what we do then?"

Clark grinned, tossed an acorn at the questioner. "Sit right there and listen. There's a bit more to come. About the French, the Creoles. They'll be against us to the last soul. It won't be because they love living under British rule. They hate it. But the British have spread so many yarns about us people from Kentucky and Virginia that the Creoles are scared as hell of us. They think we're worse than the worst Indians that were ever spawned. We burn, loot, rape, scalp, torture enough to make a Shawnee or a Piankashaw blush. That's what they think, that's what the British have drilled into them. They'd rather see all the devils from hell swooping down on them than a dozen Big Knives, as they call us."

Sergeant Harrison's hoarse voice spoke. "I don't take that as neighborly of the Britishers."

Clark laughed. "But it was! It gives us a wolf-trap hold right at the start. Now we go back to the three companies. Bowman's men and I will hit the fort and seize the commandant, de Rocheblave. You others, wait till you hear a single rifle-shot from the fort." He smacked his palms together. "Then you hit right into town. Hit hard, hit noisy. Yell your damn heads off. Pound on anything that'll make a din. I want you to sound like a herd of panthers and buffalo, all mixed up, smashing in." He held up a hand as an approving rumble followed his words. "*But — that's all!* Chase any people who come out right back into their houses. Let them alone! No violence of any sort. Sergeants and officers are to shoot any man of ours who as much as crosses a threshold. You're not to take even a potato-paring or a scrap of bacon rind. Just stay outside, keep the people inside and keep on brewing up the damnedest racket that was ever heard this side the Mississippi. The Creoles have been taught to fear us. Make certain that they do. But —" his voice dropped lower — "they *must not hate us.* If that happens, we all might as well blow our brains out. It'd save us a lot of trouble. So keep the town tight and scared, wave your rifles and your knives and hatchets. You'll get word from me soon enough. Now about the town —"

Clark spoke on, describing the houses, streets, palisaded gardens clearly and concisely. Phil Brady tugged at his hat brim. "Reckon those squirrels must have told him a lot while I was rustling out my map. Got every God damn thing perfect — yep, hear him mention that well by the big stone house? That was just an 'x' on my sheet."

Markham nodded. "And all that stuff about how the Creoles feel. Don't know how many times Helm and Bowman tried to get him excited about that on the trace. And he'd just say 'Um' and walk away. Hey — he's about done."

"That's all," Clark was saying. "Captains, lieutenants and sergeants will go over all of this with their companies to make sure every man understands. Remember, no blow to be struck, no knife used, no shot fired unless it's life or death. Rest easy now. We start at full dark."

The dancing yellow point bothered Markham. It might be five miles away or five feet. Or it might not exist at all. He remembered night-watches at sea when a belly scantily stocked with bad food had set whole constellations winking at him from thickly clouded skies. Moistening his fingertips, he passed them over his eyes, blinked hard. The yellow point was gone. There it was again, no matter how hard he rubbed. He reached behind him, caught Phil Brady's shirt and pulled him forward. "A light!" he whispered. "Shining on water. No mistake."

Brady panted. "I'll be God damned! It's from Lernault's Ferry. It's got to be. How come Saunders didn't spot it? No one ahead of us but him."

"Maybe the ground hides it from him. Who's behind you? Tell him to pass the word to Clark."

Markham stood leaning on his rifle and staring at the yellow pinpoint incredulously. There it wavered across the empty prairie, the first ray not from sun, moon or star that he had seen since he had left the *Poitou*. It told him of a roof, doors, windows, a fireplace and the quiet peaceful stir of human existence and he had an odd, uncomfortable feeling that he was somehow spying on the creators of that light and on their life, that he should mumble an apology and slink off into the dark where he belonged. He started as a voice close behind him said, "A light? You're sure? Where?"

Clark glided up beside Markham, who pointed silently. The Colonel said "Hah!" softly. Then he gave Markham a gentle shove. "Keep on going, right to the house, you and Brady. Joe Bowman and some of his men are right behind me. We'll pick up Saunders. The rest of the men'll be following right along behind us. Take your tone from me when we get there. Come along."

Markham kept on behind Clark, heard Brady and the others just in the rear. Saunders was overtaken, carried on in Clark's wake. Suddenly a steep-roofed house with wide galleries showed dimly, one wall split by a steady golden glow. Clark broke into a trot,

making for the front door. Markham caught a whiff of roses, felt
thorns skid off his buckskins as he jammed through the narrow
gate. Then the boards of the gallery were under his feet and he
halted beside Clark, who held up a warning hand.

"No noise," whispered the Colonel, rapping on the solid door.
Inside someone stirred, an angry voice growled, *"Qui ça, à cette
heure?"* The door swung grudgingly open and a thickset middle-
aged man peered out, a candle held high. The candle and its brass
stick clattered to the floor, went out, and the man's voice cracked
in a scream. *"Miséricorde! Les Bastonnais! Les Grands Couteaux!"*
He tried to slam the door shut, but Clark's foot wedged it open
and light from another candle shone on rifle-barrels, bearded faces
and buckskins. The man dropped to his knees, babbling that his
cellars, his storehouses, his kitchen were at the disposal of the Big
Knives, that he was a very poor man, but what money he had —

Clark spoke almost gently. "Tell him he won't be harmed, Cape.
He and his family are to stay indoors and keep quiet, that's all. Tell
him I'll post a guard to make sure he isn't bothered."

Markham began. *"Soyez tranquille. Pas de mal, comprenez?"* He
gave the rest of Clark's message as best he could. The door swung
wider and he caught sight of a thin, pretty, dark-haired woman, a
heavy-faced girl crouched by a table covered with white dishes that
were gay with painted flowers. He nodded to the pair, saying, *"Pas
de mal,"* but they only stared at him from fear-haunted eyes.

At a sign from Clark, Markham closed the door. "No use slamming around unless we have to," said the Colonel. "The less noise
the better. Who's that coming toward us?"

Simon Kenton's soft voice called, "Found the boats, George."

"That's the beginning of our luck. Let's not lose it." Clark
looked past the high fence where the rest of the regiment was a
dim, moving mass. "Cape, can you swim?"

"Yes."

"Follow me to the bank, then strip down. We'll swim the boats
across. Oars are too loud. Come on." He started out at a swinging
lope.

Markham kept close behind him, found Harrod's company hauling some unsteady-looking boats close to the low bank. Other men were stripping to leggings and breechclouts while someone was saying in a hushed voice, "Stack your fixings right here. Last boat'll bring 'em over."

The summer air was gentle on Markham's skin as he wrapped his shirt about his rifle and pouches, tied his moccasins to the muzzle of his piece, but little chills kept running across him as he eyed the dark flood, tried to make out the west bank. It was invisible now, that far shore, but its dark reaches might mask alert Kaskaskia patrols, solid bodies of aroused militia waiting with poised muskets, or painted Indians lying in silent ambush. A sense of heavy menace crept toward him across the water, an unspoken warning that was only intensified by the muted voices, the cautious movements, the gentle splashings about him. He remembered a time when he had watched, frozen, while a long fuse spluttered its slow way toward a powder keg. He and a Cypriot smuggler had managed to spring forward and stamp out the spark with a few seconds to spare. Now —

Someone pushed him, with a whispered "In with you," and he slipped into the water beside the first boat, a stubby, high-prowed craft that sagged and rocked under its load of a scant dozen men. A voice breathed, "Shove!" The boat glided heavily out into the stream. Markham caught the gunwale with his left hand, began paddling with his right while his feet fluttered out behind him. Ahead he could make out two other swimmers and muffled splashes and swirls behind him told of at least one more. The going was hard, even for Markham's muscles toughened by cordelle and oar and pole. There was little current but the bottom rose and fell beneath him. Sometimes his feet kicked in deep water. Sometimes sudden shelvings or rises rasped his down-plunging hand or brought his feet against sunken roots and logs. Stroke by gasping stroke he kept on, trying to catch the rhythm of the man ahead of him. In the boat, the non-swimmers crouched low, rifles huddled close against flying drops of water.

A mud-bar shouldered near the surface and Markham found himself and his fellows pushing on through a waist-deep stretch.

He brushed water from his eyes and as his vision cleared he saw the far shore. There it lay, black and silent, a bare twenty feet away. Instinctively he crouched low. Then the mud-bar shelved and he was swimming again, keeping his head as much under water as he could.

The boat suddenly shivered, tilted, became light under his hand. They had reached shore and the passengers were leaping out, running silently inland, bent double and rifles ready. Two, three minutes crept by and no sound came from the bank. The man ahead of Markham spat out water. "Not a God damn thing stirring. Head her for the other bank. We ain't done yet."

After a third round-trip, quick hands hauled Markham out of the water and a voice whispered that he and his fellows were to rest through one relay. He stretched out, panting, on the soft grass and his hands and feet began to burn from scrapes and cuts. The night hung black and heavy and still as ever but he could make out a wide semicircle of men reaching well inland to cover the landings against any possible attack. Nearby, vague masses showed where the rest of the regiment was forming into companies. Now and then he caught sight of Clark's big-shouldered form against the sky, heard him give terse orders.

South over the dark lands rose a distant huddle that could only be the town of Kaskaskia. A pinpoint of light shone yellow at its north end and Markham was sure that he caught the high, thin tones of a fiddle, briskly played. He stared at the light, trying to associate it with the night's mission, but it seemed too homely, too comfortable with that unseen fiddler sawing away beside it.

A bare foot nudged his ribs and he started violently. A dim shape muttered, "Join Helm. He's got your rifle and powder."

Markham rolled to his feet. "No more swimming?"

"No. They found another boat and kind of speeded things up."

"Everything still quiet?"

"So far, but there's a sight of time and a sight of darkness left."

Markham ran along the bank and Helm lumbered toward him. "Here's your rifle and powder and shot, Mark. Will Harrod's boys'll stay behind to guard shirts and such fixings. We're going to start in a minute. Keep by me so's you can tell me what he means if someone shouts Creole-talk at me."

"I won't be straying," answered Markham as he felt the lock of his rifle. He looked toward the town again. The distant crumb of light had died and the fiddle was silent. The hush deepened over the west bank of the Kaskaskia River and he knew a mounting intensity of apprehension.

Half an hour later Leonard Helm's company lay motionless in the grass some fifty yards to the west of the town. The march in from the river had been nerve-wracking in its very uneventfulness as the men breasted their way through cornfields, wove cautiously among beanpoles, fearful that each next step might bring forth the dreaded challenge or a bright spatter of musketry. Markham, his pulses still pounding, lay just behind Helm, rifle in the grass ahead of him. The rest of the company was close behind him, but he could find no comfort in its presence. He knew most of the men by name or sight but fatigue and darkness had turned them into anonymous strangers, intent on their own business and heedless of him.

Out in front, Kaskaskia lay utterly silent. He could make out steep-roofed houses surrounded by shadowy hints of deep galleries. The back gardens were protected by high palings that ran stockade-like, broken here and there by darker patches that must be the lanes and the two cross-streets of Phil Brady's map. Clark, with Bowman's company, should be near their objective, the fort at the south end. When that rifle-shot came from the fort, Montgomery's men were to strike into the town from the north, Helm's from the west. But what would that shot mean? A Creole finger could pull a trigger as well as a Virginian and the echoes of that shot might set that dim fence stabbing out in a ripple of fire to scythe down the pitiful handfuls of attackers. The militiamen would know every fold in the ground, every blind alley into which the assault might be drawn.

Leonard Helm's wheezy breathing was audible, rising and falling above the scurryings of crickets. Off by the river a night-bird croaked hoarsely. All at once Markham was on his elbows, ears straining. The sound came from the direction of the fort, thin, high-pitched and unmistakable, a woman's voice taut with fury. Helm murmured over his shoulder, "Lordy-lordy-lordee! Now I do pray that none of the boys has gone and got impulsions." The sound went on, distant but cutting, died away. Then the night was split by the clean, sharp report of a rifle.

Helm bounded up, roaring, "My company! Forward! Yell like hell and remember your orders!"

Markham pried himself erect, was swept along partly by the thumping feet and the din that erupted around him and partly by the fear of being left alone on the night plain. Men were shrieking, yelling out a shrill "Yi-yi-yi-yi!" above which rose nerve-jangling whoops. The long, long fence seemed to move toward him and the words "Now it's coming! Now it's coming!" beat through his mind and he braced himself for the hail of musket-balls that must surely sting out at the running men. The fence was thirty yards away, twenty! Now! Now!

He was in a lane that cut through the palings and led on past the gabled ends of houses. Lights flickered in windows to the left, to the right, but they came from hastily lit candles and not from muzzles. Helm's men yelled louder, banged on loose boards, on discarded pots they picked up.

The lane ended and the company poured out into a wide street with a three-story stone house dead ahead, lesser wooden dwellings stretching right and left from it. Helm shoved Markham. "Take Cal Fisk and Joe Ames and go visiting. Scare the Creoles into giving up their arms but don't push as much as a toe over a threshold!"

Markham swerved left, Ames and Fisk behind him, swung open a low gate and ran up a path to a front gallery. A candle wavered behind a curtained window and he pounded on the door yelling "Ouvrez!" The door gave a little and Markham shoved it with his foot, revealing a wispy man in nightshirt and nightcap, candle trembling violently in his hand. Markham panted, "Pas de mal! Donnez-moi votre fusil! Ne sortez pas." The man gave a clucking cry, pushed an old musket, stock first, through the door. " 'N'y en a plus?" snapped Markham, taking it. "Alors, faut pas sortir, vous savez. C'est tout!" He slammed the door.

"What we do now?" asked Ames.

"Hit the next house, the little stone one." They came down into the lunatic din of the street where rifle-butts slammed against loose boards, milk-pails, butter-firkins. A score of men had formed a circle and danced in a half-crouch with bent-kneed steps, occasionally leaping high as though lifted by the piercing yells that shot up on all sides. Somewhere a Creole was shrieking that "les Bastonnais" had come and that every throat in Kaskaskia would be cut.

Markham vaulted a fence, leaped to the gallery of the little stone house. The door swept open and a half-seen man ducked out. Ames caught him by the collar, shoved him back, while Markham cried, "Doucement, doucement! Pas de mal! Rendez votre fusil." The man clung to the door, shouting that he was a corporal of the Kaskaskia militia and that it was his duty — His voice died as Fisk brandished a long knife with mock ferocity, and in a few seconds Markham had another musket.

Back in the street they found Helm seated on an upturned bucket, oblivious to the awesome bedlam as he whittled on a stick, humming softly to himself. He peeled off a long shaving and nodded. "Stack those muskets right here. We're picking them up fast. Now kind of drop in on those folks 'cross the way." He raised his voice. "Sergeant Harrison! Take your men and watch every house that's been visited. Just see that no one goes out, and club anyone of ours that gets out of order or frets a Creole."

"Is it all right do folks have lights to their homes?"

"They can light a light, tan leather, build a ship, write a sermon — in their houses. Stir, now."

At some unmarked time later, Markham and his companions, slung about with confiscated muskets, stumbled along a path that led between two broad-galleried houses. "Dawnin's nigh," mumbled Ames. "Can see a mite."

Markham nodded, noting that blacks were fading into grays all about him. Suddenly he yelled, "Look out! On the right!" and stood staring at the half-naked savage, blackened and shaggy, closing in on him. He raised his rifle jerkily, then broke into a quavery laugh. "My own reflection in that shed window! Damn near shot myself!" He pointed at his image in the blurred glass.

"Close call!" agreed Ames in awed tones.

The two patted Markham gravely on the back and somehow their praise of his presence of mind lightened a little his burden of hunger and fatigue.

At the end of the lane the three broke into a wobbly run. Seated in the street on the same overturned bucket, Captain Leonard Helm gnawed away at a roast fowl as though it had been an ear of corn. By his side lay a vast loaf from which slices had been hacked and between his feet sat a deep tin pot and a dented cup. Without breaking the rhythm of his gnawing Helm called, "Stack your lethal weapons over there. More chickens in the basket behind me. Strike any trouble?"

Markham snatched up a crackly cold fowl and bit into it. All up and down the street Clark's men leaned against palings, hunched on mounting-blocks or lay flat on the ground, chewing blissfully. "Where'd this come from?" asked Markham between bites. "Did we levy on the Creoles?"

Helm tilted the coffee pot. "No Creoles, no levy. Jim McMurray and Dick Winston, American trappers and traders, have been living here a spell. A lot of the boys knew them out of the old days. Jim and Dick felt kindly about us and hustled up what fixings they could. We'll get more later. Now about any trouble you might or might not have stricken."

Markham tossed away a leg bone and reached for the coffee-pot. "How could a lot of scared and sleepy townsfolk make trouble?"

"Never saw a body too scared or too sleepy to make trouble," observed Helm placidly. "But I reckon you mean no. That's good."

"How did things go for the Colonel at the fort? I remember a woman yelling."

Helm munched on a thick crust. "Things went the way they most always do for George. He got the Commandant, Rocheblave. That squawking was just Mrs. R. telling George she didn't just approve of his busting in like he did. He had to put both under guard. Town's sealed up tight's a drumhead. No one comes in, no one goes out. We found a list of militia officers and they're all in irons down to the fort yonder."

Markham tossed a whole drumstick back into the basket. "Funny how fast you fill up when you've been eating slim for a while. Well, so we've got Kaskaskia. The Colonel'll be sending word back east pretty soon, won't he?"

"Apt to. Patrick Henry and Tom Jefferson, they'll admire to hear all about this."

Markham drank more coffee, frowning. "That'd be a good chance for me to get headed back east again."

"Might be. But there's always a couple of other things to figure on." He sighed. "Damned if I know why, but there always is."

"Such as what?"

"Such as George wanting you right now. Don't you see Gerault down there waving to you?"

Markham got up resignedly, slung his rifle and trotted stiffly along the street, eying Gerault in surprise. The dapper Huguenot had probably not shaved but somehow gave the impression that a skilled barber had tended him. His sodden buckskin shirt and breeches had been replaced by neat homespun that glowed an almost pipe-clay white. He nodded to Markham. "The Colonel wishes you, Mr. Cape," he said and led the way past the last houses of Kaskaskia, over a grassy stretch and into a log stockade with bastions at the corners, a two-story blockhouse and a few smaller buildings in the center. The whole place looked neglected and the light cannon in the bastions tilted or ducked at crazy angles. "All this troubles me," said Gerault, indicating the sagging works.

"Why? It's ours, isn't it?"

"Yes. Ours — to *defend*, now that we have taken it. I fail to be amused by the thought of being penned here by Indians who have only to wait until regular soldiers and artillery come against us from Detroit."

"Damn!" said Markham. "That could be another of the 'couple of things' that Helm mentioned."

Gerault thumped on the broad door of the blockhouse and a voice growled, "Who's that?"

Without answering, the Huguenot pushed open the door, waved Markham in. The latter crossed the threshold, then stopped. The bulletproof shutters were closed and a couple of candles burned feebly, adding their glow to the slow flicker from the fireplace and vaguely lighting up unkempt heads, bearded faces, bristly faces, naked sweating arms and shoulders and chests, mud-smeared and streaked with dried blood from small cuts and scratches. Among the close-packed bodies standing along the walls, squatting on the floor, seated on benches and tables, rifle-barrels and bared knives reflected fire and candles.

The reek of sweat and dirt and damp buckskins and grease caught at Markham's throat. "Christ, this place stinks like a mink's den," he muttered. "Where's the Colonel?"

Clark's voice sounded from the gloom. "Good and strong, is it? Then close that door quick. Don't lose a whiff. Gerault, you're too God damn clean. Get out of sight toward the back. Markham, stay here near me. We're going to have visitors. You listen to them, talk to them. Here, take this venison-shank and keep gnawing at it."

"He's always called me 'Cape' before," thought Markham. "Something new must be stirring."

Then a dull rustle of voices sounded outside. The door opened slowly and a stocky man in a rusty black soutane entered. After him, outlined against the new glow of the sky, came a huddle of middle-aged men. They held laced cocked hats under their arms and their full-skirted coats brushed against silver knee-buckles. Markham made out a flowered waistcoat here, the sheen of silk stockings there. When the priest stopped, the rest halted. It seemed that a sudden cough would send the whole delegation scurrying out like mice — except for the priest, who looked calmly at the half-seen, silent faces before him. Suddenly he spoke, marshaling English words with obvious difficulty. "The man — who — command, please?"

From the murk Clark answered, "*I* command this force — and Kaskaskia. George Rogers Clark, Lieutenant Colonel, Illinois Detachment, Western American Army. I've no time for formality. Speak French if you like. What do you want?"

The tonsured head went back. "I am Père Gibault. We know, we others, how your settlements have suffered from Indian attacks sent out from the north. So we may guess the intent of your coming here."

Markham gave a quick summary to Clark who nodded, saying, "Tell him to go on."

Gibault kept his eyes on the dimly seen Clark and continued, Markham making a running translation. Though the Creoles of the Illinois country, the priest said, had had no part in any such attacks, nor in the war between the British Crown and the Colonies, indeed knew little of that war, its causes and its progress, they realized that Kaskaskia, being under British rule, could hardly hope to avoid retaliation for those attacks. Accordingly —

Clark cut in sharply, "This isn't a debate. What does he *want?*"

The answer came quickly. "He wants your permission," said Markham, "to get all his people in that church up the street. He wants to prepare them for — well, for what may lie ahead, to give them his blessing. He also wants you to understand that your capture of Kaskaskia has nothing to do with his duties as priest. He'll tolerate no interference from you or anyone with those duties."

"*He'll* tolerate —" began Clark, his voice rising. "Damn it, tell him his duties are — no concern of mine. Sure! He can cram every living soul into the church if he wants to. No one'll bother him or his congregation. I'll be obliged, though, if he'll pass the word that no one is to leave town without my say-so. And another thing — bear down hard on this — he and his people are *not* to discuss our taking the town, *not* to speculate on *why* we took it or what we'll do next. Get going."

Père Gibault looked a little dazed when Markham gave him

Clark's permission. Then he turned to the other Creoles, who seemed profoundly relieved, then more shaken than ever as they heard him. Markham caught a quavery whisper, "But our houses, unguarded while we enter the church? What of our possessions, our goods?" Gibault said sharply, "Why concern yourselves with what may be already lost? We must work to save lives, to keep families from being broken up and carried off prisoners to the New York, the Virginia, the Pennsylvania. Remember what has happened to the families of most of these men who came among us in the night." Then with a series of bows, quaking on the part of the townsmen, dignified on the part of Gibault, the delegation left.

Clark stretched himself. "For God's sake shove back those shutters and let some air in here! Douse that fire. Damnation, that priest's a man! Did you hear him say *he*'d have no interference from *us*? Joe Bowman, get out among the companies and tell the other captains it's all right for people to leave their houses to go to church. Put guards front and rear of every house. None of our men to enter. And be sure there's no sign of a guard at the church!

"Now everyone get cleaned up. Some of Harrod's boys are bringing down the extra truck we left up at the crossing. Get shirts on your backs and muck off your faces. No one's to quit the stockade without my leave. Shove that rum-jug over here, someone."

VI

Word from Louis XVI

THE SLOW, vibrant chant of a church bell broke through the veil of uneasy sleep into which Markham had fallen. He rubbed his sleeve across his eyes, swore mechanically and rolled to his feet, blinking in the swelling sunlight that flooded the enclosure about the fort. A few of Clark's men were stumbling sleepily toward the sag-fronted stockade where some of their fellows peered through untidy gaps that commanded a view up the broad street of Kaskaskia. Markham hurried to join them, then slowed his pace as he noted that no one had troubled to unsling a rifle or shout a warning. Smothering a yawn, he took a casual glance between two tottery uprights, started to turn away, forgot to complete his yawn and muttered, "I'll be damned!"

It was close to six o'clock and the rising sun was lighting up the steep roofs on the east side of the street, turning the windows on the west into sheets of gold, playing on the vertical timbers of façade and side. Above window and roof the little belfry of Kaskaskia Church was like a finger raised in command, supplementing the slow boom of the hidden bell. Bright movement flowed from every door and from every low gallery. Red and green and blue and orange of headkerchiefs, of bodices took the new sun, knee-length skirts were silvery gray above the crimson and purple and yellow of long petticoats as the women came into the street. They went hand in hand, they carried babies, they led small children who tramped on uncomprehending over the soft ruts. The men were there, broad-hatted with long, red-sashed blouses and baggy knee-breeches. A few were dressed like the merchants who had come with Père Gibault to the meeting with the dreaded leader of the

Big Knives. Some clutched awkward bundles whose wrappings the wind flipped back to show silver candlesticks, a gold-framed mirror, a brass-bound casket of glossy wood. On went the Kaskaskians heading for their church where Père Gibault stood motionless, waiting. They walked with their eyes on the ground as though not daring to look at each other and their pace was slow as though marked by an ominous drumbeat. In front of each house a bearded, buckskinned man leaned on a long rifle and watched the uneasy flow in silence. As the last kerchiefed head, the last broad hat vanished into the church, a shadow fell between Markham and the shaky uprights. Clark's voice called, "All through sleeping?"

Markham turned, saw the Colonel coming toward him, a splendid figure in clean buckskins, freshly washed and shaven, his coppery hair bright in the morning. "I didn't get started," answered Markham. "I never can sleep when I'm too tired. Always feel as though a hundred thousand mean bees were crawling under my shirt."

"Then I'm not breaking in on your rest. Gerault's busy with letters and fixings, so I want you to come for a walk with me. Stack your rifle, pouch and powder-horn over there. No one'll touch them. Keep your knife inside your shirt."

"Thought you looked sort of naked," said Markham, ducking out of his equipment. "Must have missed your rifle and truck. What am I supposed to be doing this time?"

"Just walking up a village street, walking and seeing and listening and talking French when you have to. Come along." He led the way out through the sally-port.

Some signal must have been passed, for all the house-guards had fallen back into side lanes and alleys and Markham and the Colonel moved out into a seemingly deserted town. Idly they sauntered on past gardens where blue and pink and white hollyhocks nodded to them over white palings. The sun struck through glazed windows and Markham saw in one room a vast, square bed with a dark crucifix over it, in another a polished table, a curved armoire whose china-stacked shelves ran from floor to ceiling. Here was a black-framed picture of the Madonna, reminding him of the sleepy dimness of Italian churches in a hot, country noon. There he caught the glitter of a long mirror cased in gilded wood. A spinning wheel with a betty-lamp nearby might have been in any farmhouse in the country back of Boston. He himself had shipped dozens of sleek marble slabs like the table-top in the next house.

But he shook his head over farming tools so primitive that they suggested relics of long-dead peoples such as eccentric scholars were always digging up in Italy and shipping to the British Museum in London. Another crude betty-lamp, a gold-hilted sword on a wall, thin porcelain whose fineness made him catch his breath, a wooden harrow that the rawest New England settler would have scorned, a mahogany stand holding a court wig. "Just as if Noah's flood had picked things up all over the world and dumped them here in the Illinois country," he thought.

Bees buzzed lazily among hollyhocks and roses in the gardens. Down from a low gallery came an inquiring silver-gray cat, head lifted and tail high. Markham spoke to it. It greeted him courteously, rubbed its nose against the fringes of his leggings and then fell into grave step beside Clark. A quick pang struck Markham. A warm Sunday at home, a walk up Summer Street in the noon hush heading for Boston Common and the shade of its elms — the illusion left him instantly as he caught movement up ahead. He plucked gently at a dangling thrum on the Colonel's sleeve.

Without looking up, Clark nodded. "I saw it, too. Someone's head and shoulders popped back into the church like a woodchuck into its hole. We're being watched from there and probably from some of the houses. Let's slow down a bit more and give 'em something to wonder about."

Progress became more haphazard than ever. Clark stopped before one house and kept up a lazy flow of talk that had nothing to do with what was before him or with the sudden quick gestures that he made. He turned suddenly, pointed back toward the ruinous fort, then spun about quickly, went a dozen paces farther on and stopped, scowling at the inoffensive west. Markham adapted his own pace and actions to the Colonel's, playing out an elabo-

rate pantomime whose only visible audience was the cat who sat at
Clark's feet during each pause, solemnly following every move with
its big eyes. When the pair moved, the cat marched on just ahead,
looking back to be sure that its charges were not lagging. Markham,
putting himself in the place of an unseen human observer, realized
that they were creating a very real enigma. Was the chief of the Big
Knives surveying the town as a looter? As an incendiary? As a ruthless conqueror?

They were abreast of the church that looked as silent and deserted as the rest of Kaskaskia. The double doors swung slowly
open and out into the sun stepped Père Gibault. A few men trailed
after him, looking even more gray-faced and fearful than they had
at the fort earlier. Clark glanced casually at them, nodded, then
kept on talking to Markham.

Gibault came forward. "*Monsieur le colonel!*" The men halted
under the little porch and behind them a swarm of women's heads
swayed, haunted eyes dark in white faces. Clark turned with an air
of absent politeness. "Yes, Father Gibault?" The cat seated itself
between Clark's feet and began to wash its face.

The priest spoke in a clear level tone. His people, he said, were
reconciled to the loss of their possessions, even of their homes. His
voice rose higher. "But I appeal to your humanity, Monsieur, in
the name of Him whose teachings my people and your people follow, that there be no bloodshed." Markham translated rapidly,
nodded to Gibault to continue. "And I appeal to you in that same
name that if exile there must be, families be not broken up, husbands parted from wives, children from parents, affianced from
their intendeds." There was a stir about the porch and a few
women came out, babies in their arms.

Markham, rendering the priest's plea into English, saw Clark
flush and his face set in tight lines. "Tell him to go on," said Clark.

Gibault held out his hands. "We do not know your plans, we
others, but I must beg that women and children be allowed to
take some of their clothes, that the men be permitted to prepare
stores of food against the long road into exile." More women, some
half-grown children, an old man edged out into the sunlight, eyes

fearful. Gibault went on, "We know that such mercies have rarely been granted to your people in this war which we do not understand." He pointed suddenly at Clark. "Because those mercies have been denied your people, the faith that we both follow, each in his own way, demands ever more strongly that you, as Christian, extend those mercies to my people, it being in your power."

Markham could detect no yielding in Clark's face as he translated Gibault's words.

This time Clark spoke directly to the growing semicircle about him and there was a sharp edge to his voice. "What do you think we are? Hell, we don't make war on women and children and old folk!" His tone was suddenly gentler, lower-pitched. "You're all safe from us. Forget about your houses and your goods. We won't go near them. You're afraid for your church? In the new nation my people have started back east, in the United States, all churches stand equal and respected. Why have we come among you? We're on our way to stop the shedding of innocent blood in our settlements — and in yours, if they're threatened."

Some of the lines left Gibault's worn face and his eyes softened as Markham, deeply relieved, translated. Behind the priest, bolder men edged closer and women with timid smiles stepped into the street, clucking to their children.

"You see," Clark went on as though sharing a confidence with trusted people, "we had to come here hard and fast. De Rocheblave would have fought us if he'd the least hint about our coming. Your militia would have had to obey him. But that's all over and without any fighting. Go about your affairs as though we weren't here. No one will bother you. I'll take the guards away from your houses unless you feel safer having them there."

Markham watched the faces before him as he turned Clark's words into French. It seemed to him that their relief was strongly tempered with incredulity. ("And why not," he thought, "after the way we pounded in last night!") Clark must have caught the same impression, for he reached down, picked up the cat and held it against his shoulder, stroking it under the chin. Somewhere in the crowd a girl laughed, an easy, happy laugh. A man cried, "*Mais enfin!"* as though that homely gesture had lifted a weight from his mind, had endowed this tall stranger with a home of his own, a family, possessions, had turned him from an enemy out of the dread unknown into a comprehensible human being whose roots might well run back to some other river town, perhaps to a town almost like Kaskaskia, *quoi!*

Slowly the people flowed forward, engulfing their priest and the two unarmed strangers. All at once they found their voices. Phrases in quick French, in rusty English welled out. "Ah, had we known of all this we would have welcomed . . ." "Goddam Angleesh! Tell us, 'You lose war! Take off hat when spik to officer Angleesh!' 'Stand here!' 'Do zat!' 'We gif order, you obey!' " "And always, Monsieur, they say that they protect us from the Big Knives who, they say, are all that there is of the most barbarous."

There was little need to translate. Minor British officials, many Frenchmen like de Rocheblave, obsessed with the idea of the sanctity of any kind of king, had dinned into Creole ears the tale that the colonists had risen in unholy revolt against the Crown, that they butchered, tortured like the worst Indians, that they meant to enslave all in the King's domain, to abolish the Catholic Church, the old French laws and customs and language which British rule had guaranteed and scrupulously maintained.

Clark nodded when Markham had finished a quick summary. "The same old story. That's why they scared so easily when we bust in last night. Now they're getting a shock of a different kind. Look. They're all clustering about Gibault near the porch, leaving us stranded. Keep your ears honed. There — what's he telling them?"

Markham edged closer to the church where men were suddenly shouting and gesticulating. Gibault held up his hand, shaking his head as though repeating something that he had said before. "It is not in my province to advise! I may not consent, neither may I forbid!"

A pudgy, swarthy man whose gold-braided coat was huddled over a brown smock broke from the crowd, marched boldly up to Clark who stood quietly, still holding the gray cat. "*Monsieur le colonel!*" he began confidently enough, though the puffy calves under heavy wool stockings were quivering.

Clark nodded to Markham who said, "*Continuez, Monsieur. On écoute.*" A flood of French burst out and Markham looked dubious as he said to Clark, "He keeps saying that he wants to place himself under your protection. I think he really means the whole town, not just himself."

Clark grinned. "Nothing much can happen to the town without happening to us first. See if he's thought of that."

The Creole had, it seemed, but it only made him more voluble. Others joined him, were equally clamorous and Markham found himself stuttering a little as he channeled the meaning to Clark. "They feel safe as long as you and the Detachment are here. But suppose you go on? They're sure that you have other 'vast conquests' in mind. They want — wait a minute — I'm going to make him say that again — it's —" Markham threw out his hands. "There it is, Colonel. How can they come under protection of the United States?"

Clark's face showed only polite interest. Then he picked the cat off his shoulder, handed it to a little button-eyed girl in cerise and gray who stood staring raptly up at him. "Well," he began almost casually. "They're under protection as long as we're here. After that — why, I don't know any way of doing it except by taking an oath of allegiance to the United States."

A storm of French assured Markham that that was what the Kaskaskians desired beyond anything else. Clark ran his hand through his hair, looking rather diffident as though being called upon to act beyond his proper sphere. "Well, I reckon I could administer the oath. But — oh, Lord, this'd be a rather serious matter. Ask them to sleep on it, to wait a few days or so, think it all over. Besides, they've got that news from France to consider."

"*What* news from France?" Gibault's voice was hoarse in a sudden hush.

Clark looked surprised. "You mean you don't know?" He glanced at Markham, muttered, "Be sure they get this." Then he raised his voice. "His Majesty Louis XVI of France has declared war on England. He has made an alliance with the United States; he will support us with his army, navy and treasury until England recognizes the independence of the United States."

The essence of Clark's words seemed to reach the people almost before the translation and they stood still staring. Markham suddenly remembered a green island at the mouth of the Tennessee, a canoe shooting ashore and Clark shouting that at last he had his "lever." He whispered, "So that was the news that Will Linn brought you, Colonel?"

"Yes. The alliance. I held it back until the people took the first step toward us." He glanced toward the fort. "Wonder if Len Helm has — yes, just in time!" Men were at the peak of the blockhouse where a flagpole stood high and slim. A darkish mass climbed slowly, shivered as the morning breeze caught it and tossed it wide. Through a sudden blur Markham saw bold red and white stripes, a blue canton spotted with white. Clark and Markham whipped off their hats. All about them Creoles stared at the fort. The men were bare-headed. Some of the women crossed themselves while others merely gazed. A mother held a baby high in air, a neighbor bent to point out the rippling colors to a sturdy-legged child.

Slowly Clark replaced his hat and the Creoles began shouting, "*Le serment!* The oath!"

"Wait a minute!" called Clark, laughing. "Markham, tell 'em to talk to Gibault first. I won't listen to anything that doesn't come to me from the Father!" He drew a deep breath, squared his shoulders. "Looks as if a few things are getting settled the way I'd hoped. Now I've got a thousand matters to attend to. You can save me a lot of time by walking around this town. Look at the people, their stock, their tools, their goods as if you were going to open a trading-post here. Then tell me about it. Go where you like, only don't cross a threshold or go under a roof unless you're invited."

"Another job for me?" grinned Markham. "Guess I can make do. Where can I find you when I'm done?"

"Come sundown would do, at the fort," said Clark and started off down the street, a clamoring escort of very junior Kaskaskians milling about him.

Markham waved and turned up the wide, grassy street. When he reached the crest he looked west. Some two miles away a broad blue band glistened as it stretched north and south. There was no way of gauging its width, since the far bank was masked in haze. Shaggy islets rose green in the middle distance and between them a keelboat worked north, flashing oars laboring. "The Mississippi again!" muttered Markham. Then he laughed at the great river. "Foam and rage all you like. You'll never get me in your current again!" He turned his back on his old foe and sauntered off toward the fields that lay to the south of the town. He found long, narrow strips where peas and beans and corn and wheat seemed to burst out of the ground, where pumpkin and squash vines trailed their green lines under a bright sun. He saw vast barns of stone or wood, an endless fenced stretch where scrawny cattle grazed beside little, chunky horses. He peered into sheds and frowned in disapproval over the tools and farm implements. He wondered why there was no one about in these fields and pastures that lay separate from the town, then remembered that it was July fifth, a Sunday.

Toward sunset Markham walked contentedly down toward the fort. In a few minutes he would be arranging with Clark for passage south to the Ohio, and then farewell to the Illinois country. In the meantime he had been amply fed, wined and, in general, been given the key to the town that lay on its tongue of land between the Kaskaskia and Mississippi Rivers. He had been made welcome in a dozen houses, had met scores of Kaskaskians of all degrees. Barns, storehouses, shops and warehouses had been flung open for him. He had even been led to the church to marvel at the great bell sent out in 1743 by King Louis XV himself and had fingered the inscription cast into the lip: TO THE PEOPLE OF THE ILLINOIS FOR THEIR WORSHIP.

His head buzzed with data, impressions, opinions, all of which would be well worth passing on to Clark. Still more valuable had been the breathless comments that he had heard from time to time as excited and delighted Creoles brought word to their friends of the results of Clark's conferences with Père Gibault and other town notables. It was evident that the Virginian was building up a solid store of genuine good-will.

As he neared the great stockade the double gates were flung back and out poured a mass of mounted men in an unbroken trampling of hoofs. Captain John Bowman was in the lead, riding beside a swarthy, keen-faced man who wore an officer's sash and straight sword over the white and blue uniform of the old French militia. On they came, Clark's riflemen and Kaskaskians all mixed together. Markham caught sight of Phil Brady on the far flank, darted in between the lurching horses and clutched at his stirrup. "Hold on! Where are you going?" he shouted.

"Watch out!" cried Brady. "You'll get rid down. We're heading upriver to capture Cahokia!" Markham watched him ride away and then ran up the steps of the building where Gibault had come with his terrified fellow-citizens at dawn.

Clark was seated at a long table by the south window calling something to Gerault, who was shepherding two well-dressed Creoles through the side door. He turned quickly, frowning, as Markham entered. "Well, what have you got to tell me?"

Markham drew up a chair and sat down. "A lot, I guess. For the most part I've been thinking over something that Oliver Pollock said to me in New Orleans."

"I didn't ask for —" Clark began impatiently. Then he went on more slowly. "Oh — Pollock. Yes. What did he say?"

"Something like this: 'Put a hundred stirring American families in the towns north of the Ohio and you'd change the face of the continent.'"

"What's that got to do with us?"

Markham swept up a stack of loose papers, riffled them mechanically into order, slapped them down. "Just this. I've seen Kaskaskia. Founded near the start of this century and hasn't changed since. They use the same kind of tools that peasants used in France two hundred years ago. Some of them plow with forked sticks. They never fertilize their fields. The crops look as if they'd been planted by a gang of drunken bears. It's low-lying country and they lose a lot from floods. Droughts kill their crops. And, by God, with all this they've never even troubled to think about a drainage system against floods or reservoirs to use in dry spells."

Clark's face was expressionless. "Never heard of anyone starving here."

"That's my point," cried Markham. "With all this hit-or-miss life, they raise enough to ship produce down to New Orleans along with their furs and still have plenty for themselves! A third to a half of what they grow is surplus. The soil's wonderful. See what Pollock meant? If the first settlers had been Americans, whether they came originally from the British Isles or France or the German States, if they'd been the sort of people you and I know back home, Kaskaskia'd be a big trade-center by now with twenty-five hundred families, not just two hundred and fifty. There'd be other big towns, north and east. People'd have pushed across the Mississippi so strong that every Spaniard there'd be whistling 'Yankee Doodle.' Our people'd make up the bulk of the militia on the west bank and Governor Galvez down in New Orleans couldn't put through a law they didn't like even if he sent the whole Louisiana Battalion to back it up."

Still frowning, Clark reached under the table, dragged up a bottle and two pewter mugs. He mixed rum and water in the mugs, pushed one across to Markham. "Keep on talking," he said.

"All right, let's look at the town today. About everything I know comes from listening to Creoles talking to me or each other. Unless I'm mighty wrong, you've done some damn smart things. You've won over Père Gibault and his word means a lot here. Just the same, I think the town would have been with you anyhow."

"You're wrong if you figure I wasted time on the priest. He's a good man. Besides, I like him."

"The Creoles can see that, too. But here's what they're remembering. You went out among them unarmed. They could have shot you down or kidnapped you. Without any pressure from them

you told them you wouldn't interfere with their church, that no
one would be harmed, that there'd be no looting, no driving off
people as prisoners. They believed you. When they asked to come
under our flag, you told them to take it easy, to think it over. All
that I heard with you. Since then, you've advised them to set up
an elective government of their own. You've moved most of our
troops out of town and camped them along the river. You've
given back all the arms we seized and released the militia officers
from arrest."

Clark ran his fingers through his coppery hair. "Hell, that was
only common sense. All I've done's to put them back where they
were when we bust in on them. They're no better off."

Markham grinned at him. "Do you really believe that?"

Clark grunted over his mug, "Why don't you?"

"For the same reasons you don't. But if you want me to tell you
what you know already, here you are. All their lives and their
fathers' and grandfathers' and great-grandfathers', the Creoles
have been told what to do. They've been told how much they can
plant, how much land they can use, how much forced labor they
have to do. And they've been told these things by someone appointed from Quebec by someone who was appointed by Paris or,
more lately, by London. The idea that they can run their own
affairs really staggered them, though they're hard-headed enough
to realize that town has got to mesh with county and state and nation. Mind you, they haven't fretted under British rule particularly. It's just that you've shown them something better. And you
don't treat them as conquered people but as possible fellow-
citizens."

Clark refilled his mug, pushed the bottle toward Markham.
"Maybe you were just getting polite answers to your questions."

Markham shook his head. "This stuff just kept bubbling up
through talk about the betrothal of the Boudreau girl or a dispute
about whether old Ferrié built his wharf in '51 or '52. But someone
was always coming into whatever house I by invitation happened
to be with something he'd heard from Père Gibault or what you'd
said to a particular delegation."

Clark drew a long, slow breath and some of the weary tenseness seemed to leave his body. "So that's what they're saying, is it?"

"Two more things," said Markham. "You couldn't have timed your announcement of the French alliance better. It won over a lot of them who felt that any revolt against any Crown was wrong, even the British Crown. And you didn't use it to clinch anything, just tossed it out as something they might like to know about. The other is that close to twenty Creoles rode out with Bowman and his men against Cahokia."

"Thirty-one," said Clark.

"Better yet. I heard them shouting that they'd volunteered to go, that you'd given them the *right* to bear arms. European laws are wicked about such things. In some places they hang a peasant for owning a fowling-piece. It's not so strict here, but the old memories last." Markham pushed aside his mug and rose. "I could give you a lot more detail about this town, but it wouldn't change my story, just lengthen it."

Clark rolled his mug between callused palms. "Yes. You used your head and your eyes and your ears and all your past experience, Markham. A good job. Now I've got another for you."

"Thanks," said Markham, shaking his head. "I think I've done my last job for you."

Clark's eyes hardened and his chin set. "I'm ordering you, not asking."

"You can't," said Markham calmly. "I don't belong to your Detachment, took no oath. I owe you nothing. You forced me to come with you. You said when the march was over I'd be free."

"What makes you think it's over?" asked Clark, rising.

Markham laughed. "Don't try to scare me the way you scared the Creoles when we first came here. Look, you're not going much farther with your weak force. If you're crazy enough to try to, nothing that I can do will help you. If you've got more men coming up from the Ohio, you won't need me."

"So you'd turn tail and run away." Clark's voice was almost a whisper.

"Oh, no! You'll be sending word back to Virginia and it'll cost you nothing if I join the party."

"I've given you an order."

"So you said. But I'm going out that door. Want to try to stop me?"

Clark laughed. "Not I. You'll do your own stopping. Quit glaring at me and pull up to the table and have a drink." Markham hesitated, then seated himself, taking his mug. Clark went on, "About those couriers to Virginia. They left hours ago, Simon Kenton and Shadrach Bond, the two best scouts in the country. You couldn't have kept up with them. Doubt if I could. So you can't stray far alone, and that puts you right here in Kaskaskia."

Markham eyed Clark warily, then shrugged like a gambler who has lost against very long odds. "So they've gone and I'm here in Kaskaskia. I can figure that last part for myself. What I can't figure is *why* I'm here, or you or the rest of the Detachment for that matter. Got any objections to telling me? And don't sing that old tune about 'defending Kentucky' by being up here so close to the Mississippi that we can almost hear the wake of a keelboat."

The Colonel studied Markham over the rim of his mug, then nodded slowly. "Yes, I reckoned you'd see through all that." He planked his mug on the table, rose and began to pace up and down. "Just the same, as a matter of fact we *are* defending Kentucky, but it's kind of by accident."

Markham tilted his mug, frowning. "Going to make me try and guess the answer to that?"

"No. I'm just telling you what I had to tell myself, a long while back." He paced on, swinging his arms loosely. "I came into Kentucky, back in '74, one of the first. It was everything the boys have been saying about it. Settlers came in all a-steaming. The big war against the Crown started, but it all seemed 'way off yonder somewhere to most of us. Then, in '76, the Indian raids came. Seemed as if all we did was defend fortified houses, get provisions, ambush Indians when we could, bury our dead and bandage our wounded. That was our life. Reckon we'd have seen every settler light out east for home, except that he was usually safer staying put than moving. Everyone had to pitch in and do what he did best. Some hunted, some scouted, some built forts, others tended cattle or crops. They made me military commander, rank of Major, militia of course."

"They did? You were pretty much of a greenhorn then, weren't you?"

"I sure thought so. There was Dan Boone, Simon Kenton, Ben Logan, all better frontiersmen than I, older, cannier. But, hell, they said a job like that takes more writing than fighting and I was handiest with a pen."

"They may have said just that," Markham observed, "but they thought a whole lot more, giving you that load to carry."

"They'd know more about that than I. Anyway, I got to thinking about Kentucky a bit more and I saw that it was only a part of the rest of our country, and by 'rest' I don't mean just Virginia. I began to see that what happened in Kentucky could get felt a long way east and northeast. Else we'd have done a lot better to have given up and gone somewhere where we wouldn't get killed quite so quick and so frequent. All of a sudden I saw Kentucky the way an eagle might have seen it from way, way high. It was like an island lying off there west of the Alleghenies. No Indians lived there, but a lot hunted it. I looked east and Kentucky seemed to me like a mighty strong door barring unneighborly folks from the west. If the Indians were able to bust through it they could smash across the mountains into what people back home call the 'frontiers,' into the far edges of Virginia."

Markham snorted. "How could they do that? Just look at the past. They'd bounce back off the frontiers the way they always have."

"By God, no!" cried Clark. "This is damn different. They hit into what I call our 'interior frontiers' and what happens? They hit deeper and deeper. They fan out north and south, they sweep the regions that send grain and corn and beef and cloth to our armies and the armies begin to starve. No more recruits from the back-country join the army. The frontiers move east and west until all we've got left is a ribbon of beach with the British Army and the Indians hemming us on one side and the Royal Navy on the other."

Markham tilted back in his chair, watching Clark. "That's a mighty long view you're taking from your eagle-back ride."

"It's all damn plain, but I was blind to it until I got thinking high. Then I saw right away what I had to do, that I had to lay aside every private view and engage seriously in the war. Now understand this: we could hold Kentucky against just Indians with what we had right there to hand. Indians can't stick to a job by themselves. A little killing discourages them, or they run out of food or they suddenly think of something else they'd rather do and they quit. But the British up on the Great Lakes, along the Wabash and here in Illinois are keeping them at their work. If one tribe gets the idea it'd be more fun to go back north up to the Muskingum and build fish-weirs, off they go, but another tribe strikes south into Kentucky and a third follows it. They're all supplied and equipped and paid by the Crown, mostly through a Colonel Hamilton at Detroit. That combination will finish us off and open the Kentucky gate to a flood of Indians."

He paused. Markham waited a moment, then said, "You were going to say 'finish us' and all that — *unless?*"

Clark started as though Markham had broken into his thoughts, "Yes. 'Unless.' That was it." He talked on more rapidly, his voice sinking until Markham had to sit forward to hear. Clark had sent scouts north across the Ohio and had pondered deeply over the full reports they had brought him. Last fall he had beaten his way back to Virginia and sought out Governor Patrick Henry and Thomas Jefferson, both old family friends, and had dinned his message into their ears: five hundred men to go down the Ohio, then hit north against the towns where British commandants kept the tribes on the warpath. Henry and Jefferson had been won over quickly, had brought the powerful George Mason into their camp. But everything had to be done very secretly. The least hint would have gone north with lightning speed, warning the enemy. At last, when the plan was finally approved by the legislature, that body had not the vaguest idea of what was really being voted when they authorized "a force for the defense of Kentucky." The command of that force had fallen to Clark, unsolicited by him.

"Of course, I didn't get the men or money I needed," Clark went on. "Just one hundred and fifty finally joined us at Corn Island in the Ohio. I had twelve hundred pounds, Virginia paper money, for the whole job. If I'd had the full five hundred men, I'd have struck up the Wabash and gone right on to Detroit. That's the big prize. Smash Detroit and you won't need as much as a fowling-piece in Kentucky. We could have brought it off, too." He grinned suddenly. "Never did dare mention Detroit to any of the Virginia people. They'd have thought I was stark mad to try it even with a thousand men. So I had to do what I could with what I had. My biggest trump card was that, until the day we left Corn Island, no one but I knew where we were going or what we were going to do, not even Will Helm or Joe Bowman. Never knew a secret kept like this one before."

Markham passed a hand over his forehead. "You're telling me that this mighty Western American Army, from which our Illinois Detachment is drawn, amounts to —"

"That's it," said Clark happily. "Amounts to that same Detachment. There's nothing at Corn Island but a few settlers."

"I've seen gamblers and gamblers," said Markham, shaking his head in wonder. "But this —"

"This is our first step, not the big one to Detroit that I wanted to take, but the one that was possible. We've found out we'll have no trouble from the Creoles. By being here we'll keep the Indians wondering if the British really are so powerful, if it's really safe to tie to them. Another thing is that we'll prevent a whole lot of supplies going from this area to the British posts on the Lakes. Also Rocheblave's not going to be sending any more bribes or inflammatory letters to the tribes." He broke off, swept his hands through his hair. "I'm tired of talking. Pour me a drink, will you? Won't take long to tell you all about this next job I want you to do for us."

"You still think I'm going to do it?"

"Sure."

"And just why, for God's sake?"

"From the way you've been listening. And where would you go from here except on that job?"

Markham reached for the bottle. "Guess I've got to chuck my cards away. You've won. If I didn't go on this job, what else could I do except burrow in here and drink with my Creole friends? So — what is it you want this time?"

The heavy door shivered on its hinges, burst inward and Leonard Helm entered, walking just the least bit on his heels. His broad face glowed like a summer sunset and his weatherbeaten cheeks creased in smiles that embraced the whole world in beaming goodfellowship. In one hand he held a bottle, in the other a bulbous gourd. "George!" Helm's voice boomed as though he had run onto a cherished friend in some unlikely spot. He marched across the room, thumped the bottle down by Clark. "Heartener! Best ever made!" He swung toward Markham, thrusting out the gourd. "Mark! Heartener! Helm's!" Then he paced up and down, rubbing his hands and chuckling. "A real nice town. Oozin' with real nice people!" He took the gourd from Markham, swigged at it, handed it back. "Reckon Cahokia's nice as this?"

"They keep Cahokia settled by shipping the best Kaskaskians up there. Like a reward. Every five years," Clark assured him gravely.

"Fact?" asked Helm, beaming happily.

"Fact. Now, Len, we're due for a good moon tonight. Take your company and patrol this bank of the Kaskaskia River right to where it curves into the Mississippi. It's only a few miles."

Jovial irresponsibility left Helm. He nodded briskly. "Can start in half an hour, George. We'll cover right to the mouth."

"That's it. And keep an eye out for —" Clark rose as a fearful bawling sounded outside. In through the door stumbled a man of the regiment, an arm about the shoulders of a Creole in a brown coat and baggy blue breeches.

Helm turned quickly. "Going to be trouble, George. He's hurt bad. What happened, Zeke?"

Zeke's leathery face was working and he could only point to the Creole who entered, step by slow step, hands before him and eyes streaming behind square spectacles. Zeke clattered, "Ain't they a goddam physic-man in the town? It's brother Beaulac! Him and me was liquoring friendly and all to once he was strick blind! Someone gotta fix brother Beaulac!"

Markham crossed to the pair, gently tilted Beaulac's head to the light, saying *"Doucement!"* while Zeke, panting heavily, watched slack-jawed.

"Someone gouge him, Mark?" asked Clark quietly.

Markham gave a sudden snort. *"Fermez les yeux!"* he said and the Creole obediently squeezed his lids into tight creases. Markham reached out, slipped off the spectacles, drew out a cloth and carefully removed the thick layer of butter that someone had smeared over brother Beaulac's lenses. He replaced the spectacles, saying *"Ouvrez, alors!"*

Timidly the eyelids shivered, opened. Incredulity, then a sort of mad joy spread over the Creole's face. He screeched, *"Mais je vois!"* His arms fell about Markham's shoulders and before the latter could dodge, a moist bristly smack fell on each cheek. Then brother Beaulac turned, plunged toward Clark and Helm, *"Et vous, Monsieur le colonel —"*

Zeke's hands clamped down on Markham's shoulders. "Bes' God damn doctor west of the mountains! You done cured brother Beaulac as was strick blind! You c'n have my knife, my cabin back home, my spotty ox! Know why?" He swung up a heavy arm, swept it down, missing Markham's shoulder completely. " 'Cause you done heal a frien' of Zeke Slemp, that's why! Anything a Slemp's got b'longs to you. Any Slemp, anywhere!"

Beaulac swayed back to the center of the room, arms high and feet drumming in a clumsy dance. *"Je vois! Je vois!"* he trumpeted. His voice soared higher. *"A boire! A boire! A la bouteille!"* and he lurched toward the door.

Zeke loosed his grip on Markham, started after the Creole. "Boo-tay! Means he's aimin' to open another bottle. Maybe I better help brother Beaulac!" The pair erupted through the door in

a tangle of arms and legs, began a weaving course up the wide
street of Kaskaskia.

Helm beamed approvingly on Markham. "That was a right
neighborly thing to do. Brother Beaulac's family's going to be
mighty happy, seeing him cured and all."

"You're appointed surgeon to the Detachment right now!"
laughed Clark. "Be sure and call him Doctor Cape, Len. Now
about this job, Cape. Get a good sleep tonight. Tomorrow morning you hit west across the fields for about two miles from the head
of the street. There you'll see Paquin's wharf and a pair of Creole
canoemen waiting for you. They'll take you across the Mississippi
to that Spanish town, Ste. Geneviève. Go ashore and hunt up the
commandant. Find out what he thinks about our being here. Find
out what he thinks the Lieutenant-governor up at St. Louis will
think. Find out anything else that interests you and may likely interest me. Then get back here and start talking again. Clear, is
it?"

"How about Cahokia?"

"We won't know for some hours just what's happened up there.
Use your own judgment about mentioning it."

"H'm," said Markham. "Sounds clear enough. Did you ever
figure, though, that I might find something better to do there than
come back here? I hold myself a free agent, whatever you may
think."

Clark nodded calmly. "If you don't come back, I won't be singing hymns very loud. But I'd rather have your reports than your
person. You'll send me, by word or by writing, what it is I want
to know, and that's the important thing."

Helm dropped a heavy arm over Markham's shoulder. "That's
fair enough spoke. Now come along with me, Doctor, and tell
me if the medicine I'm brewing will cure swamp-fever and croup
as well as the dumb-aggers."

VII

In a Spanish Garden Diplomacy Thrives

THE SUN was climbing the morning sky and the wind was cool on Markham's face as he swung along toward the great river, a wind that whispered of the mysteries that it had known in its journey over thousands of miles of untouched country. He whistled *"Tenouich' tenaga"* as he topped the last slope. Then the Mississippi lay below him, glowing like a cobalt lake close to shore, softening to a greenish plain toward the tufted islands of midstream, the channels between them smooth avenues or swiftly silver flumes. He called *"Ohé!"* and ran down the path to a flimsy wharf where his Creole paddlers, Saindon and Archambault, waited by a twenty-foot canoe.

They took charge of him at once. The crossing? Always a troublesome one at low water, but one took precautions. If Monsieur Cape would seat himself — The canoe glided out past thick bushes where birds were going mad with the glory of the new day. Aft, Archambault began to sing:

La fille du roi d'Espagne (Mon joli coeur de rose),
Veut apprendre un métier (Joli coeur du rosier).

The bow worked on, now knifing through pond-like reaches, now rocking in a maze of white water that made Markham grip the sides of the canoe. Smooth water again, more swift waves. Suddenly the Creoles sang again. *"Nous étions trois soldats, Du régiment St. Onge!"* and as though the song had been a signal, the western mists lifted to show a disorderly straggle of steep roofs stretching north a good mile. There was no trim village street, no

linking of well-tended fenced gardens. It was as though people fleeing some unknown danger had made a hasty night-camp whose
disarray the sun was just revealing. A few figures moved along the
waterfront and there were more out in the narrow ribbons of
fields that reached away to low hills in the west. Markham gathered his rifle and other possessions as the canoe headed toward a
low wharf beyond which stood a sentry-box banded with diagonal
red and yellow stripes. The beaming Creoles landed him and
then paddled off on some happy, secret quest of their own with
a cheery, "A *quatre heures alors!*"

Markham walked up toward the sentry-box, noting that the
gallery-posts of the nearest house were painted red and yellow,
while the Spanish flag hung limp from a pole in a yard some fifty
paces away. Out of the sentry-box slouched a bored man in a
rumpled gray-white uniform, trailing his musket-butt wearily over
the ground. Markham called, "I am from the Illinois Detachment,
Western American Army," while thinking how impressive Clark's
invented designation sounded in Spanish. "Where is the commandant of Santa Genoveva?" he added. The sentry only stared
stupidly, whereat Markham produced Galarmendi's impressive
passport. The effect was startling. The guard, eyes bulging, tried
to salute, bow, present arms and cross himself all at the same time.
Then, in understandable confusion, he called for his corporal.

A lemony-looking man, corporal's knot on his shoulder,
bounded from the nearest house, indignant at this intrusion on
his leisure. He ordered the guard to arrest himself. Then he looked
at the passport, gulped, ordered the guard to release himself.
Townsfolk drifted up and the corporal roared that someone should
run for the priest, have him ring the bell of San Joachim's church
in honor of Markham. A volley of French informed him that the
priest was away for a fortnight and that the church had never had
a bell.

The corporal rallied himself, shouted, "Present arms!" as though
to a full battalion. The guard's musket snapped up smartly, but it
was plain that the corporal had sinned militarily by answering a
duty-call unarmed. Nothing daunted, he snatched the rifle that

Markham held loosely and fell, statue-like, into position beside the guard. Markham, fighting back laughter, repeated that he only wanted to see the commandant, but his words threw them deeper into the paralysis brought on by Galarmendi's seals and signature.

Then he saw two more uniformed men coming toward him, a swarthy hawk-faced but almost smiling lieutenant and a bull-necked sergeant with needle-pointed mustaches. Markham swept off his hat to the officer as he identified himself, adding that his soul was lacerated at being the cause of taking so valued and valiant a warrior from the weighty tasks that His Catholic Majesty had surely placed on such shoulders.

Tcniente Ramón Nieto, hand over heart, protested that his highest privilege, no matter what the risk, would ever lie in being of service to so welcome and honored a guest. In the meantime, if he might trespass on his guest's boundless tolerance and cast a glance at this bit of paper — as men of the world Señor Cape and he knew what such things were, eh?

It appeared that they did not. Nieto, reading, stiffened, gave a curt order to the sergeant who raced off to the stripe-pillared house. Then he turned a glacial eye on Markham. "One does not tamper lightly with official signatures and royal seals, Señor. You are under arrest."

Markham answered evenly, "There has been no tampering."

"That I should be happy to believe."

The sergeant returned with four Spanish soldiers and three sulky Creole militiamen, red pompons garish on their wide hats. Nieto gave a sharp order and the escort led Markham from the wharf. For the moment he was not too worried. Nieto's turnabout was inexplicable, but the best way to meet it was to keep his mind clear. Anyway his paddlers would come for him at four o'clock, find nothing and make inquiries among the local Creoles. Then they would report to Clark and a mere handful of Big Knives could make a demonstration heavy enough to force Nieto to think deeply.

The procession wound on, reached the rear of the house where the Spanish flag floated. A fieldstone foundation, broken by tiny barred windows and a heavy door, lifted the first floor a good six feet above the ground. Nieto unlocked the door and Markham, with a shrug, stepped into the half-light of the interior. The key grated in the lock. Out in the sunshine he heard a few words in Spanish and knew that guards had been posted. Time dragged on.

Then footsteps thumped on the floor above. Something rattled and creaked and a thin blade of light cut into the cellar and a trap door was flung back. Markham started to his feet, staring as he found Nieto looking down at him. The Spaniard said in careful, heavily accented English, "My very dear fellow! This truly had to be done. Now ascend yourself that I make apologies."

Markham stood on a packing case and heaved himself up into the room, glancing quickly about him. There was a rather good rug from the Near East, a pair of armchairs, inlaid Moorish coffee tables, decanters, glasses, oily cigars in a cedar box. Nieto waved him to a chair, filled two glasses and placed the cigar-box at Markham's elbow. Then he caught up a glass, seated himself. "Your very good health. Now I explain how your arrestation was so deeply necessary."

Markham raised his glass. "Your health. I'm sure of that necessity."

"Yes, yes. Tomorrow, perhaps ten Creole traders leave this place, bound for Arkansas Post. Instead, they will visit British Natchez to trade. They get better terms if they report to the British commandant news of value to him."

"Such as?"

"Ah, such as seeing a man, calling himself American, who comes from far in the east bearing a Spanish document of the most official. All this I saw — you, document, traders — while I confronted myself to you. I recall in a flashing that an American Captain Gibson came once to New Orleans to buy powder for his armies. Our governor there flew into a very public rage, imprisoning that Gibson." He smiled, blew smoke at the ceiling. "Soon after, that so-wicked Gibson escaped, fleeing north. Also, several hundredweight of powder flew north. The British at Natchez knew only of the arrestation, not of the powder. They thanked our Governor."

Markham ran his thumb along his chin. "So I might have gone free today if a very astute Spanish officer had not seen my documents as arrant forgeries and arrested the bearer? You are a man of very quick decision, Señor."

"But no! It was my only course. Consider what could have happened had I welcomed you!"

"I think I can see. Your traders would have told Natchez that an American rebel had come from the east bearing Spanish documents which assured him a warm welcome. Natchez would think that a secret understanding existed between Spain and the United States with whom Spain's friend England is at war. Britannia, ruling the waves, would have stopped all traffic under Spanish colors on this river. As it is, the British will applaud your zeal as a neutral. Your Governor will hear of it, too. He, too, will applaud you."

Nieto grinned. "Exactly. To the British, I am true patriot, opposing rebels against *any* Crown. Your arrestation is now forgiven? Good. Then tell me how I may serve you."

"By answering two brief questions. The first, how do you, as a Spanish officer in command here, view a piece of news? Next, how do you feel that your Lieutenant-governor up at St. Louis will view it? The news: between midnight of July fourth and sunrise of July fifth, a Virginia regiment, under Colonel George Rogers Clark, captured the British-Creole town of Kaskaskia. No one was hurt. Clark raised the American flag over the town. He will administer the oath of allegiance to the United States to any who wish to take it. Nearly all will so wish."

"Ah, now!" began Nieto judicially. "You ask —" Then he started. "What do you tell me? Captured Kaskaskia?" He jumped up with a happy shout, tossed his cigar in the air, caught it, drained his glass, then Markham's, refilled them both, shouted again. "But it delights me! Ha! I slap my shoulder, I make giantly merry! As a Spaniard I wish only successes to the friends of my new friend. As Spanish officer —" he raised a cautioning finger,

"I remain neutral, but so benevolently that I am benevolence myself."

Markham rose, bowed, reverted to Spanish to express his thanks as floridly as possible. The word "benevolent," particularly as applied to Clark's little band, teased at him. That benevolence could hardly be turned to any practical benefit to Clark. Then there flashed into his mind a half-forgotten reference of Galarmendi to military supplies shipped north from New Orleans in Governor Galvez's name, but secretly charged to Oliver Pollock, Agent for the Congress of the United States. Military supplies. But such a tangled transaction, involving as it did Spain's very neutrality, could be known to few people, certainly not to a mere *teniente* at a post like Santa Genoveva. He stowed the memory away in his mind for possible future use.

Nieto was speaking again. "As to the Governor of Upper Louisiana, and his views on transpirations, we may only wait with knitted brow. Don Pedro Piernas has only but now been relieved at his capital of San Luís by Don Fernando de Leyba, who has re-emplaced him. The opinion of Don Pedro I may guess. That of Don Fernando, no, we being barely known one to the other."

Markham nodded slowly. "H'm. I see. A new official, fresh from New Orleans." Such a man would have been there at the time of those mysterious shipments, ordered by Galvez and charged, in greatest secrecy, to Oliver Pollock. He rubbed his chin thoughtfully, then began to speak. "Don Ramón, you are a most devoted servant of the Crown. You have just captured a dangerous, desperate character named Cape. Might it not be well for you to set out as soon as possible with an armed, mounted escort and deliver so infamous a prisoner into the hands of Don Fernando de Leyba, your superior officer? I think that it would produce an excellent effect in San Luis — not to mention Natchez."

Nieto stared. "But I do not —" He clapped his hands. "Ha! But of course! My sole duty and only! Yes, to San Luís! We shall follow an old Indian trail which is not genteel, but I have ridden it before. Late in the day we make our departure, for which I shall prepare great fomentations and dazzlements. Every eye in Santa Genoveva will witness and every English ear at Natchez will hear of it. Here are pen, ink, good paper, sand. Write what you please to your so-valiant Colonel and your canoemen shall bear the whole tale back to him, together with my most devoted and benevolently neutral considerations!"

The departure from Santa Genoveva was a huge, noisy success. Markham, bayonets hedging him, shuffled out from the cellar, irons at wrists and ankles, while swarms of Creoles cried, "Ah, *le pauvre!*" and cursed the guards who drove them back. By a knot of horses, Aspromonte removed the irons, heaved Markham onto a scaly saddle and bound his feet together under the horse's barrel. The Creoles howled, "*Au secours!*" Markham began seriously to worry about an attempt at rescue. Then he bit his lip as Nieto, waving a red-pomponed cocked hat, yelled for "the pack-horse with the evidence and the confession of the prisoner!" A weary nag was hauled up, saddle loaded with Markham's rifle, long knife and ammunition, together with ominous ledgers agleam with blobs of sealing wax. As one man, Nieto, Aspromonte and the mounted privates glared at Markham. Then an order was barked, the horses broke into a trot that scattered the Creoles like a bow-wave and clip-clopped out of Ste. Geneviève pursued by a few clods and stones.

After ten minutes steady going, the horses topped a long rise, wound down the far side. Nieto reached down and pulled away the cord that bound Markham's ankles. "Now we make you free man. If we meet walkers, press your feet against the horse's barrel as though still bound."

Markham nodded, then set himself to the task of riding. Nieto had been right in saying the road to San Luís was no "Camino Real." Rocky, twisting, dipping, it snaked through country as unmarked, untrodden as the wilderness miles between the Ohio and Kaskaskia. To the right the Mississippi rolled on, its waters darkening as the day ebbed. Ahead lay limestone outcroppings, stretches of forest somber in the fading light. Off to the left, low hills bulked.

Day ended and the ride drilled on into the night. A full moon turned the great river into an endless bar of bright gold. Black clouds massed, veiling moon and stars and the old trail. The moon came out again and at times Markham shivered as he looked down and saw how close that trail clung to a cliff-edge two, three hundred feet above the river. During a rain-squall the little party sheltered in the lee of a vast boulder and shared cold fowl, bread and cheese and Alicante wine. "We have passed the Plattin River," announced Nieto as the wine splashed into leather cups. "Next comes the Meramec, flowing east. Beyond it we shall seize an hour or so of sleep. Thus we appear alert and smart as we hand our desperado over to Don Fernando de Leyba. Now we equitate once more. No need to bind you, since we shall meet in San Luís with no inimicable eyes."

Early morning sun spread a silvery dazzle over green-brown prairies and brought mirror-flashes from dew-drenched stands of oak and pine far off to the west. Markham wondered if the river capital would ever materialize from the infinity through which the party rode, and then all at once St. Louis seemed to flow toward him over the rolling lands that edged the river-bluffs.

At first it seemed like Kaskaskia and Ste. Geneviève all over, with the same vast fenced common-lands, the same ribbon-farms running back to hill and forest in the west. Then the town showed its three wide streets running north and south, each clinging to its own sandstone ledge rising tier on tier. There were wooden houses, many stone houses, all with neatly fenced grounds, steep-pitched roofs and deep galleries that spread out like flaring skirts. A wide Place d'Armes was bitten out of the lowest street. There lay St. Louis, seemingly immeasurably older than the other up-river towns, though established less than fifteen years before. Below the town's eastern edge was a broad beach and then the roll and heave and glide of the vast Mississippi.

Into the lower street they clattered, past flowering gardens and tight fences, to halt at the edge of the Place d'Armes. Nieto dismounted and ran into a high stone house where a well-turned-out sentry stood below a plaque bearing the arms of Spain, and darted inside while the others sat patiently in their saddles. At the end of a good half hour he ran out, beckoned eagerly to Markham who dropped to the ground and followed him into a wide dim corridor. Nieto flung open a heavy door and waved Markham into the room crying, "Excellency, this is Don Markham Cape, friend to his Excellency Don Julio Galarmendi and to Don Oliveros Pollock!"

The man who rose behind the desk was short and fat and he wheezed as though his uniform of the Louisiana Regiment stifled him, as though his broad scarf of office were too tight. The room was quite cool but his round, sallow face and the backs of his hands shone with perspiration. "He's a sick man. Why the devil do they send him up here?" thought Markham, bowing deeply, hat under his left arm as though it were feathered and gold-laced. Without seeming to, he watched Don Fernando de Leyba carefully to see if Pollock's name brought forth any comment, any change of expression, but he could detect none.

There was no doubting the cordiality of the greeting, though. Flowery compliments were tossed back and forth, waved aside, elaborated still further, capped once again. At last de Leyba settled himself in his high-backed chair, waved his callers into other seats. "It was courteous of you, Señor Cape, to undertake such a journey to share your news with me. I listen eagerly."

Markham told of the taking of Kaskaskia and, at a venture, added Cahokia. De Leyba sat silent for an instant. Then he exploded in a burst of words, laughter and wheezes. He proclaimed his official but benevolent neutrality, his profound personal delight, rained questions, interrupted answers, embraced Nieto for arresting Markham. "So now your Colonel moves to further conquests, eh?" he asked between gasps.

"His plans I do not know. I met his expedition by chance far down the Ohio on its way to Kaskaskia. My knowledge of it begins at that moment and ends when I came to Santa Genoveva and San Luís." Markham was careful to use the Spanish forms of those place-names.

"You may inform your Colonel that I wish him well." Then an official shadow fell over de Leyba. "Of course there can be no question of diverting royal stores to help him against a nation with whom we are at peace."

"Oh, but Excellency!" Shock and respectful protest were carefully blended in Markham's voice. "Permit me to assure you that Colonel Clark would never contemplate so improper a step!" De Leyba looked relieved, in a quiet way, and Markham went on. "I do not know if he is, or is apt to be in want. It is to be doubted, since he is a far-sighted man."

"His every move shows that." Don Fernando sighed. "Ah, to be his age and a whole continent beckoning to one!" He pushed back from the table. Markham and Nieto rose. "Don Ramón, I have only highest commendation for your wisdom in bringing Señor Cape to San Luís. I shall inform Governor Galvez of this action of yours. He will be sure to mention it to Don Oliveros Pollock, whom I am proud to call friend. Señor Cape, please favor me by looking upon San Luís and all it contains as at your command. May clock and calendar fall mute as you look."

Markham bowed. "Your Excellency's courtesy is boundless." Inwardly he cautiously congratulated himself on not following a wild and earlier impulse to hint to de Leyba about the mysterious Pollock shipments. He was more than ever sure that any cue must come from the Lieutenant-governor.

De Leyba was saying, with a superb flourish, ". . . and now Don Ramón will escort you to my quarters and present you to Señora de Leyba, my wife, and to Señorita Teresa de Leyba, my sister."

Nieto led the way deeper into the building while Markham tried hurriedly to weigh events. It was more than unusual for a Spanish official to bring his family to a colonial post, far more so to introduce a stranger, let alone an alien Protestant, to it. De

Leyba must have been deeply impressed with the account of Clark and have judged Markham worthy of such a chief as well as acceptable in his own right.

Nieto was rapping at a thick door. Then he pushed it gently open and Markham followed him out onto smooth grass that was shut in by high walls. There were flowering shrubs, a little pool fed by a discouraged fountain, all presided over by a cynical-eyed cockatoo with a sulphur-yellow crest. Beyond the pool two women in low chairs looked up and two pairs of very black eyes showed polite welcome to Nieto, then black eyebrows arched high at Markham's stature and long-fringed shirt.

Nieto made a florid introduction, branching out into a wild description of the fall of Kaskaskia and the spectacular role that Markham must have played in it. Señora de Leyba, all in black and thin as her husband was fat, nodded occasionally. Markham was sure that "Americano," "Virginia," "Estados Unidos" held no meaning for her, though a line of anxiety deepened between her eyes. The sister, black mantilla draped over a tortoise-shell comb that Markham's trader's eye knew as Florentine work, sat demurely as befitted a girl in her early twenties, eyes downcast and hands folded. The older woman turned to Markham in the midst of one of Nieto's sentences. "Señor — this great army of yours — it will not spread its war into our Upper Louisiana?"

"Spread war *here?* Among our friends? Unthinkable, Señora."

Her fan trembled a little. "Many men are moving about. That always means war, sooner or later. Don Fernando — he is soldier as well as governor — he is not well — you understand — a hard campaign —"

"War will not come here," said Markham gently and was relieved to see tension ebb from her eyes.

A gate in the far wall creaked and a tall, brown-haired girl in a sweeping brown dress glided in. The sun touched gold braid at waist and throat, drew deep glints from wide gold bracelets. Markham thought, "Hello, you're no Creole or Spaniard! What the devil are you doing here?"

Madame de Leyba called in French, "Ah, c'est vous, Madame de Liliac! Quel plaisir! Don Ramón Nieto you will recall. I present to you, Señor Markham Cape, his friend."

Madame de Liliac bowed to Nieto, then her clear gray eyes widened as she saw Markham and she exclaimed in English, "You — you're from the Colonies!" Then, in French quickly, "Your pardon, Madame de Leyba."

Markham said, also in French, "I am from many places, Madame de Liliac."

"I spoke too quickly, Monsieur. Your clothes —"

"Such may be found anywhere, Madame. One wears what one may."

"And why not?" She smiled politely enough, returned Nieto's burst of compliments with calm courtesy, then fell silent. Markham glanced at Madame de Leyba, hoping that she would make conversation general, but it was obvious that the call was ended and the two men bowed themselves out.

Back in the Place d'Armes, Nieto sighed, "Ah, that Señorita! Were I not of the cadet branch of my family — but one may dream, even if one may not aspire."

"And Madame de Liliac, she is of the household?"

"Ah, no. Her tale would be of the most romantic were she not married. Picture to yourself that when little more than a baby, she was taken by Indians somewhere in your eastern States and carried off to Quebec. There she was ransomed — usual enough, I am told — by a wealthy French widower and placed in the Ursuline Convent. Later, still more wealthy and more elderly, he married her. Now he is at Havana where he seeks to unravel property matters still entangled as a result of the late war and its lamentable Peace of 1763. Now she waits word whether he will join her here in San Luís or she him in New Orleans or even Havana."

"I used to hear of captures like that when I was a boy," said Markham gravely. "They were bad. So now she has grown up as much of a Creole as though she had been born in New Orleans and her grandparents had come from Poitou." He shook his head.

"She looks so like my own people, but there is no link between us. No reason why there should be, of course, but not finding that link is a shock at first."

"Oh, but that is true!" cried Nieto. "A great-uncle of mine, shipwrecked among the Caribs, was lost to us for fifty years and when found was no longer of us. But I speak too much of myself. How may I serve you further? Surely, your army does not call you back at once?"

"As I told you riding up from Santa Genoveva, duty calls me just as loudly or just as faintly as I choose, a fact which Colonel Clark realizes. But I do hold myself bound to send him such information as I may have for him. Beyond that, I am no further use to him that I can see."

"Good, Then I take you under my charge, as Don Fernando directed. You will wish wine, food, sleep, ink, paper, pens, in whatever order suits you. There are quarters for you in the building next to headquarters where you may reign unchallenged as a high noble in his mountain castle."

Afternoon ebbed as Markham, seated at a paper-strewn table in the deep window of his quarters, looked out across the Place d'Armes to the river. The stone buildings, the uniformed sentry at the head of the steps leading to the beach suggested so strongly a corner of Europe that he found it hard to relate his thoughts to the unfinished letter before him. Then a keelboat, oars bright in the late sun, crept slowly up from the south. Two heavy canoes glided downstream, six paddlers bending and dipping in effortless rhythm. The illusion of Europe vanished and he picked up the paper.

His eyes skimmed along the firm, black lines beginning with the date, "July 12, 1778," and the salutation, "Dear Colonel Clark" . . . "and as stated in mine of the 9th inst. I see no reason to return to Kask'ia, not yet at least . . . am newly back from a trip well up the Missouri . . . told I might meet voyageurs planning a journey east up the Ohio . . . seems to be little such traffic, though opportunities do occur . . . attitude of de Leyba and Creolcs continues benevolent . . . news of French alliance, coming across river from Cahokia, produced an excellent effect . . . learn that all Captain Bowman's measures for Creole elections to town offices there proceed smoothly . . . St. Louis has nothing beyond it but frontier, yet it is far less of the frontier than Kask'ia, more urban . . . may be due to its origins, as it did not grow slowly from a cabin or two near a mission or fort. Instead, Pierre Laclède (Maxent-Laclède Co., New Orleans) moved here with all his workmen, materials, supplies and credit over a decade ago and the town sprang into life full-fledged."

He sat back in his chair and wondered if there were anything that had come to his notice since his arrival on the seventh, items that Clark ought to know ex officio or which might appeal to his ever-active mind. Earlier letters had touched on military aspects, such as there being no fortifications at either Ste. Geneviève or St. Louis and barely forty Spanish troops in the two places. He had stressed the importance of referring to those towns as Santa Genoveva and San Luís in all dealings with Spanish officials. The lead and iron mines in the interior had been covered. Satisfied, he wrote below the final line, "I beg to remain most respectfully, my dear Colonel, your obedient, if involuntary, servant" and added his name. He sanded the sheet, folded it, sealed and addressed it to "Lt. Col. George Rogers Clark, the Western American Army, Illinois Detachment, at Kaskaskia, Illinois Territory."

Later, he sauntered out of the house and across the Place d'Armes, the letter tucked into his shirt. Somewhere he was sure to find a reliable boatman, possibly an ex-colleague from the *Poitou*, to take the letter across to Cahokia, lying there barely visible in the late haze of the east shore. Then he was due to take wine with Nieto prior to a call on the de Leyba ladies. He rather hoped that Madame de Liliac might appear. He had not seen her since that first meeting, and though he had thought little about her, her calm good looks and the shadow of her childhood tragedy lingered in the back of his mind.

A sunburned Creole, red stocking-cap crammed onto a mass of curly black hair, was heading for the beach, a pair of paddles over his shoulder and a vast tangle of evil-smelling fishnet draped about him. Markham hailed him, spoke of the letter. The Creole exploded. Ah, but it would give him impassioned joy. One knew well where le Capitaine Bowman lodged himself there in the great stone house that men called the Fort of Cahokia. Markham thanked him, turned away, then checked his pace as the doors of a low warehouse swung open and out stepped Don Fernando de Leyba followed by a limping sergeant and a cadavarous clerkly man who hugged a heavy ledger to him.

De Leyba greeted Markham volubly, asked if he had news of further conquests by the ever-victorious armies of el Coronel Clark. Markham replied in florid kind and was about to pass on. De Leyba raised a pudgy hand, dismissed both sergeant and clerk and announced to Markham that he was baffled. In his predicament, he went on, he saw no relief until, in a flash, he bethought himself of that renowned man of affairs and trusted adviser to el Coronel Clark, Señor Markham Cape.

Markham, politely interested, stated that merely being thought of by His Excellency was a dazzling honor. He adjusted his stride to match the pigeon-pace of the fat little Spaniard in his white and blue, and the pair entered a street where flowers burst in explosions of pink and lemon and scarlet, white and blue and gold, where bees buzzed with fussy irritability among heavy blossoms.

De Leyba went on. "The circumstances are strange, Señor Cape. Sometime before my predecessor, Don Pedro Piernas, took his leave of San Luís, a number of cases arrived here from New Orleans. They were consigned to 'The Commandant at San Luís' and hence were most properly entered as royal stores." He paused, clasping and unclasping his hands behind his back.

Markham waited, then ventured a weighty, "Ah, I see," as though de Leyba had uttered some incomparably wise statement.

"I knew all would be clear to you!" beamed de Leyba. "Yes, royal stores, as attested by papers attached to the cases. But — and here we tread into the dread maw of an enigma — other papers touching on those cases arrived later. Discrepancies caught the eye of Garcia, my clerk. We examine, we make comparisons and behold,

Señor, these cases stand forth as *not* belonging to the Crown!"

"Not to the Crown?" asked Markham, still politely.

"No. Instead, through an error of the grossest, committed by some clerk in the Cabildo, they should have been consigned to an American merchant. What am I to do with them?"

"Why not merely transfer them to royal stores? From what I know of your methods, a simple stroke of the pen would suffice."

"Ah, but no! For then our New Orleans books would show no such shipment to balance our receipt. I cannot, under law, house them longer under royal roofs. No Creole merchant will accept custody of them. So there they lie, military goods, civilian goods, Indian trade goods. Ah, could I but wave a magic wand and melt them all into our river mists!"

"I see," said Markham again, but with a different inflection now. "Yes. Such stores. Quite." In the back of his mind there passed a quick picture of a cool, darkened room in the New Orleans Cabildo, of the deputy Galarmendi and the American merchant Oliver Pollock who spoke elliptically of supplies sent north in the name of Governor Galvez but secretly charged to Pollock. "A quandary," Markham went on. "The stores may not be moved and yet they may not stay where they are. I am correct?" Inwardly he asked himself, "Shall I risk direct inquiry about that mysterious American merchant to whom they are consigned? No. Not yet. Not yet. De Leyba is aware that the names of any stray American merchants in these parts would not be known to me. If these goods *are* mixed in with the Galvez-Pollock business, I can show no authority to ask questions."

De Leyba broke in. "It is as though he did not exist, this merchant, had never existed."

Markham nodded. That was natural enough. The man whom Pollock and Galvez expected to claim that shipment would have been amply documented. Apparently his mission, whatever it might have been, had never materialized or he himself had been waylaid or killed by Indians or had not been notified in time that such a cache was waiting for him. Who could it have been? James Willing, whose depredations about New Orleans had so distressed

Pollock? Captain James O'Hara, bound for Arkansas Post, who had so nearly dragged Phil Brady along with him? In any event, the proper "American merchant" had not appeared. He went on. "A vendue, of course, would be impossible under your laws. If a responsible American merchant could be found in the Illinois country, might he not be your solution?"

De Leyba flung up his arms. "Petty traders, vagrant trappers. No, never! Ah, my friend, what are we to do?"

"Some representative of the government of the United States —"

"Now, now, light begins to dawn! Find me one such and, if properly accredited, he might take delivery, to hold in trust. But how to find that man?"

Markham shook his head. "We should have to go far, far to the east, Excellency. Unless — unless we know of a man who represents *one* of the United States, a state which forms a part of that Union, eh? But we build cloud-castles, high-piled, beautiful but none the less clouds." He glanced sidewise at de Leyba.

The yellowish face that always glistened with perspiration showed a sudden, quiet satisfaction that belied his tones, gently sad. "True, Señor Cape. Turrets and bastions of golden mist. And in any event, such a man would have to exhibit proper authority from that member-State, he would — but we romance. Nonetheless, it has helped me greatly, your sharing your thought with me on this matter." He laid a hand on Markham's arm. "We are not yet vanquished, you and I."

Markham bowed. "My best thought will be bent to this, day and night." He talked on, but in his mind he was packing up his few belongings, composing hasty notes of leave-taking, hunting up the gaunt clerk Garcia, plunging into the string of boatmen's huts that clung to the river-bank by the beach in search of a craft for hire. A swift run to Cahokia where Joe Bowman would give him a mount — then Kaskaskia and his story for Clark — but such details could wait. He was now convinced that he knew in whose name those goods were held. There would be more waiting before de Leyba felt justified in abandoning protocol and speaking directly but that waiting time could be best spent in Kaskaskia.

VIII

Subtle Understandings and a Lady's Story

MAKING a decent exit from St. Louis had taken rather longer than Markham had expected and Cahokia, just across the Mississippi, had exacted its toll of time. So it was a good five days after his talk with de Leyba that he, with two Creole escorts, rode down the final prairie miles of trail on the east bank. Behind the party lay field and forest, pond and stream, the hamlet of St. Philippe, the amazing rock ruins of vast Fort de Chartres, half engulfed by the Mississippi, the house-cluster of Prairie du Rocher. Now, as the sun climbed, Markham saw the endless fenced common-lands and the sharp-creased roofs of Kaskaskia.

The sight of things half-remembered brought an unexpected sense of pleasure. There were the bean-patches where he had lain in wait with the rest of Helm's company for the signal to rush the town. There was the first door at which he had pounded. Turpin's three-story stone house lifted its ridgepole high to the clear sky. There were other homes that had opened to him in his first survey of the place after the capture. Louis XV's bell was pealing from the little church and the flick of a soutane told of Father Gibault's passage through an open door. "Must be more tired than I knew," muttered Markham. "This damn place is beginning to look like home to me."

The two Creoles, with friendly waves, left him at the head of the street and rode off in quest of innumerable relatives. Men and women leaning over gates or standing on galleries or in gardens called to him as though to a long-absent son of Kaskaskia. He rode on, answering. Then it struck him that most faces, despite beams of welcome, seemed full of some suppressed anxiety. He thought, "Hold on! This isn't Sunday. Why aren't they in the fields?" He could find no answer. There could have been no sudden upheaval, for the United States flag still flew over sagging old Fort Gage down by the Kaskaskia River. None of the Detachment were in sight, which was natural enough, but across the river, on old Garrison Hill, a group of familiar shirted men were throwing long knives at some invisible mark. Down the flats to the north, a mixed group of Clark's men and Creoles rode in from an all-night patrol of the silent prairies to the east. Markham shook his head. "Something's upsetting the town, but damned if I can make out what it is. Well, if it's anything really bad, Clark'll know all about it."

He rode into the sally-port of the fort where Sergeant Harrison's one eye glared up at him from a ravaged face. "Took your time, ain't you? When George tells a man to go somewhere and get back, he means there and back, not diddle-daddlin' over seven counties. Hope you got a story good enough to soothe him."

Markham dismounted and tethered his horse. "Thanks for your opinion, Sergeant Harrison. Colonel inside? Fine!" He ran up across the gallery and into the main room of the fort.

Clark was seated at the table with the Huguenot, Gerault, his back toward the door and a sheaf of papers in his big hand. He turned, then glared at Markham. "What the hell have you been up to?"

"Out on a job for you. Had you forgotten?"

"Oh, I got your letters all right, and I might ask if you got mine! I wrote you to obey orders and get the hell back here."

Markham dropped into a chair, fanning himself with his hat. "At Ste. Geneviève, I saw a chance to go up to St. Louis and meet the new Lieutenant-governor. Seemed to me if I were in command here, I'd want a first-hand account of what Señor de Leyba thought about our being in Illinois, not just some Ste. Geneviève subordinate's guess about it. So I went. You had all that in my letters, but you seem to have forgotten."

Clark glanced at Gerault. "God damn it, one of the hardest things to find is a man who'll obey orders and not go morrising off on some fancy whim of his own. And it's even harder —" he began to grin — "to find someone who knows enough to *dis*obey at the right time. You keep right on with that kind of insubordination. Your letters and reports —" he touched a packet by his elbow — "put the whole west bank right inside my head. And, between the lines, you told me a mighty lot about what's going on way beyond my range here on our bank. Now where are you going to be for the next hour?"

Markham hitched his chair closer. "Right here. I may have stumbled onto something for you —"

"It'll keep," said Clark. "I've got a real hell's brew going on about enlistments that I've got to clear up with Gerault before I touch anything else."

Markham said impatiently, "But this —"

"No! Back in an hour and that's flat."

Gerault, who had been looking out the window, said quietly, "I think you may wish Mr. Cape's presence now."

Clark leaned cautiously toward the window, then called, "Right. Stay where you are, Markham!"

Markham turned with the others as the heavy door swung open. For an instant he thought there might be a runner from Cahokia or even the Ohio. But it was Father Gibault who stepped across the sill, his rusty robes brushing the door frame. "I do not intrude, Colonel?"

It struck Markham that either Gibault's English had improved amazingly since that first day or his command was greater than he had admitted. Markham considered the latter possibility, then decided that constant practice during the past few days had polished up an earlier solid grounding. But carefully chosen as the words were, they seemed to hold a good deal of the anxiety that Markham had noted along the street on his arrival.

Clark rose with a cordial sweep of his hand. "This door is always open to you, Father. What can I do for you?" He pushed forward a chair.

Gibault seated himself with a smile for Gerault and an easily turned phrase of welcome for Markham. Then he sighed. "You have taken no steps here, Colonel, without consulting the Kaskaskians. Now I learn, though unofficially, that you bring perhaps four hundred men up from your base on the Ohio River."

Markham started. So that was why the Creoles had been leaning on their gates and fences, muttering uneasily.

Clark, hands clasped behind his back, looked keenly at the stocky priest. "It is not like you to be upset by mere tales."

Gibault nodded calmly. "That is true, Colonel." Markham watched the two, but could glean nothing from their expressions. The Father went on, "We are a solid little town, but not elastic. How can we accommodate the hundreds whom you plan to bring here? The walls of Kaskaskia will split with so many."

Clark said tersely, "Even if they do come, they won't just sit about here, Father."

Gibault drew a pipe with a reed stem and a carved reddish stone bowl from his robes, filled and lit it, then blew a wavery cloud upward. "So I surmised. You plan further expeditions. May a man of peace ask where?"

"A man of peace can at least surmise again," said Clark.

"Then I ask, where else is there to go save to Vincennes on the Wabash?"

Clark nodded. "That's one place if we're going anywhere."

Gibault inhaled again. "Yes. And to reach Vincennes — or some such spot — your force must be supplied, since I am sure that it could not bring much with it from the Ohio." He paused. "Supplied from Kaskaskia. That will be a heavy burden."

"We pay for what we need."

Markham thought that the pipe-stem trembled a little in the stubby brown hand, but the priest went steadily on. "You expect us to fit out — let me see — four hundred new arrivals, let us say six hundred men in all, for a long campaign. It can only be a long one. Our reserves will be exhausted. We shall have no surplus to ship to New Orleans to sell. Oh, you pay, yes, but can our women and children, our old ones, eat that money? Wear it? Winter will be upon us one day and what then, Colonel?"

Clark turned away abruptly. "We've *got* to make this move."

"But my people?" Gibault's voice was almost a whisper.

Clark, his back to the room, leaned his hands on the mantel and kicked his moccasined foot against an andiron. "I've people to think about, too. My regiment — and the settlers back in Kentucky."

"I know." Gibault sighed, laid his pipe on the table and sat studying the scarred floor.

Markham touched his arm. "It won't be so bad, Father. Clark's men starve well. They won't need as much as you fear."

The priest's lined face softened. "I know that the Colonel will be merciful as possible."

Markham glanced at Clark who stood, still braced against the mantel and his foot swinging against the andiron. What was he thinking about? If he stripped Kaskaskia and Cahokia, his men would march onto the prairies with swarms of angry Creoles in their rear. The American flag would be ripped down from old Fort Gage and the oaths of allegiance would shrivel like grasses in a drought. What news could have come in to make the coppery-haired Colonel toss away his undoubted gains? Also, Markham was quite sure that the move would not be well regarded in San Luís.

Gibault spoke softly. "Six hundred men to take Vincennes. More than you need, far more."

"I'm the best judge of that," answered Clark.

The priest rose, shaking out his robes. "I differ. You will send no troops."

"Who forbids it?"

To Markham's amazement Gibault was rubbing his hands and chuckling. "You yourself. I shall take Vincennes for you."

Clark spun about. "You'll lead a Creole force against it?"

Looking more delighted than ever, Gibault walked about the room, swinging the long cord about his waist pendulum-like. "Yes. A force of two. Please do not interrupt. Last night Dr. Laffond came into Kaskaskia. Once a year he visits our people along the Wabash, draws their teeth, cures their bellies, cools their fevers. I shall go with him, and take my rods, for there are many fine fish-pools on the way. And when we reach Vincennes, I shall have long hours of billiards with François Bosseron on the table he had shipped from New Orleans. Yes, a real holiday for me."

Clark spoke sharply. "Bosseron? I know the name. He commands the militia there for the British."

Gibault tramped happily about, his cord swinging in great arcs. "He is a man of importance along the Wabash. Lafond will tend the sick and also tell them how happy are the good Kaskaskians under your rule. He will drop a word about the alliance between France and the United States. As for myself, you know that I may have nothing to do with temporal matters. *But* I am quite free to give such spiritual hints as may be conducive to our business."

Markham, Clark and Gerault stared at the robed man pacing about so lightheartedly. "It's many miles," said Clark.

"Yes. Over two hundred and forty. I have been there often."

Gerault said quietly, "You realize that our march here may have set the Indians stirring off to the east where you'll be going?"

"They always stir. But I go armed, by special dispensation from my bishop in Quebec," replied Gibault calmly.

"I can't allow it, Father," said Clark suddenly. "There is a British official at Vincennes, perhaps some troops. You and Laffond would be hustled off to Quebec in irons."

Gibault joined Clark on the hearth, linked arms with him. "May a man of peace bring comfort to a man of blood? Not long ago I had sure word that that official, Edward Abbott, has given up his post and gone to Detroit, largely because he could not face the policy of using Indians against your Kentucky settlements. And there are no British troops there. I know that because now my friend Bosseron commands at Vincennes."

"All right. I accept. And I'll draw up some kind of proclamation for Vincennes for you."

"*Doucement!*" said Gibault warningly. "That would be a temporal matter." He smiled gently, gathering his robes. "But Dr. Laffond is quite free to deal with such things. I'll go fetch him now."

"I'll be delighted to meet him," said Clark. "And John Gerault!

Draw up an order right away canceling that move from Corn Island!"

When Gibault had gone, Markham sat staring at Clark. "What's been happening? Has Virginia finally sent you more men and supplies?"

Clark and Gerault exchanged glances. "H'm — ah — well," began Clark, "I had to do *something*. We're not ready to move anywhere yet. The Creoles are beginning to wonder if after all we haven't really come here to grab their lands. So I just let slip a few words and sat back to wait. I couldn't lose. The *rumor* of more men would stop the Creoles' fretting and then the longer heads would begin to wonder about supplying our expedition. They'd protest. I'd relent, revoke the order and we'd all be friendly again." He shook his head. "By God, I never expected anything like this offer of the Father's. If he can bring it off, it'll save us — well, I'd hate to say how much."

"But Virginia," persisted Markham.

Clark laughed. "I've heard no more from that quarter than you've heard from Genoa. Now I want to get back to this mishmash about enlistments. Come in after sundown tonight and we'll talk some more about your journey. Now, John, let's take Harrod's company —"

Markham hitched his chair still closer with a defiant rattle. "Let me use my own judgment for just a few minutes more, Colonel. What I've got may solve a lot of your problems, including the enlistments."

Clark looked impatiently at him, then scowled. "All right. Five minutes. Time him, John."

Markham reached out a long arm, seized the bulbous silver watch that lay between the two men. "I might as well hold this, John, or the Colonel will be telling you to throw it out the window before I've said fifty words." He faced Clark. "Now listen to this," he began, and told quickly what he had heard in New Orleans about the Galvez-Pollock upriver shipments. When he had concluded that part of the story, Clark started to interrupt, but Markham managed to drown him out by raising his voice and slapping the scarred table. "The whole story came back to me when I was at Ste. Geneviève, but I figured right away that Nieto, whom you know from my letters, was probably too subordinate to have known anything about such stuff and surely too subordinate to have dropped a hint to me if he had known. But at St. Louis I figured that there could be a chance — though I've got to admit it was all pretty much in the back of my mind, nothing that I was chewing over actively. I knew, too, that I couldn't come right out and ask him."

"Why not?" asked Clark abruptly, all impatience gone from his manner now.

"You can't deal with Spaniards like that. And you can't hurry them. If you try, you're done. But de Leyba apparently thought over what he'd heard about you and your expedition and decided to tell me in a very roundabout, noncommittal way that at least some of the goods were held at St. Louis, that he'd be glad to get them off his hands, that he'd turn them over to a proper person, if said person could show authority to receive them. You follow me?"

The room was suddenly very still. Markham was aware of Clark's quickened breathing, of the loud ticking of the watch and of Gerault's fingers rustling unconsciously among some papers. Then Clark said, "My God! Stores! Supplies! Just across the river from Cahokia!" He ran the tip of his tongue along his lips. "Got any idea of what's there?"

"The amount? No. I suspect that someone, perhaps James Willing or maybe O'Hara, drew against them on their way south. I did get Garcia, the clerk, to let me take a hasty look at the invoices. There are some powder, gun-locks, gun-worms, ramrods, pistols, but mostly trade goods. You know — horn and ivory combs, horn tumblers, scissors, razors, hinges, and, let me see, nails, mosquito-gauze, hats, shoes, stockings, and underclothes, male and female, silver gorgets, liquors, seegars. There's more, of course, but that'll give you a notion."

"My God!" said Clark again, eyes dulled by the shock. "Shipped in Pollock's name! How do we take title?"

Gerault suddenly began to stutter, his hands shaking as he fumbled with a flat leather case, "I have it! George, I must have it! Here?" He managed to pull out a few sheets, dropped some of them. "This one? No. This?" His voice cracked. "It is here! Attend me, George! 'And may draw drafts in the name of the Commonwealth of Virginia on Oliver Pollock Esq. of New Orleans in Louisiana in accordance with the letter received by me from said Oliver Pollock.'" He pushed the sheet at Clark. "It — it's signed by Patrick Henry as Governor!"

Clark let out a long, wavering breath. Then he said softly, "Yes. That's good enough. You agree, Markham?"

"No telling. It's certainly good enough to show to de Leyba."

Clark thumped the table. "It's got to do! Markham, did you tell him we needed this stuff mighty bad?"

"We hadn't gone that far, Colonel. And if we had, I'd never have told him."

"Why not? It might have speeded matters."

"God above, no! People are apt to feel a lot more benevolent toward a going concern than a shaky one. Hell's delight! I'd have sacked any clerk of mine who blundered like that!"

Clark started to expostulate, then said wearily, "Yes, you're right. That's smart figuring." He stirred restlessly in his chair. "Well, let's get onto the trail! Up to Cahokia and across to St. Louis and claim the stuff!"

"Sit still for at least a minute!" cried Markham. "I've told and told you that you can't deal with the Dons that way. Call it damn silly if you like, but they're dead earnest about punctilio. I'm on pretty good terms with Nieto, but if I tried to rush him into this or that he'd freeze up like a superbly polite iceberg and that would be the end of that bit of my cleverness."

Clark shoved back his chair. "All right. But, good God, we can do *something*, can't we?"

"Yes," said Markham patiently. "I've been telling you. We wait. Then one day you'll get a very florid and formal letter from Don Fernando. Then we can reason out what to do."

"Guess I've got to leave this in your hands," said Clark resignedly.

Markham laughed. "See, we're leaving you with nothing to do. I'm responsible for de Leyba, and Father Gibault's going to capture Vincennes for you with a batch of fishing-rods and a wilderness doctor."

"Guess I'm pretty damn lucky to have someone to tell me I'm lucky," said Clark with a sudden grin. "And speaking of the Father, if he's really going to Vincennes for us, we'd better outfit him and supply him. Take a run up to his rectory, Markham, and get an idea of what he'll need. And don't stop watching the trail for a messenger from de Leyba."

July days drifted uneventfully by. Markham prowled about Kaskaskia, listened to the Creoles talking excitedly about the coming elections for town offices, the first such balloting in their lives. Sometimes he rode out onto the infinity of the prairies with Clark's mounted patrols or stood with groups of fringe-shirted men and tried to learn their skills at throwing their stubby-headed hatchets at tantalizing small marks, learned a good deal about knife-throwing and, to his surprise, was able to teach them several refinements in that art. But most of his thought rested on the trail leading south from Cahokia, some fifty miles away.

Morning wind whipped a mist-like rain about as Markham watched a little cavalcade ride out of Kaskaskia. First came three Creoles, muskets balanced on their pommels. Next was Dr. Jean Laffond, immensely tall and thin with a great beak of a nose that jutted from his deceptively sad, lined face. He was all in black and his knees and elbows made grasshopper angles as he hunched on his stubby horse. But courtesy was also a permanent feature and his bony reddish nose suddenly swung toward Markham and dipped in mournful farewell. Close behind rode Father Gibault, his stocky body seeming to overflow from the saddle, bulbous with a dozen last-minute items crammed down the front of his robe. He waved genially to Markham. "Behold Sancho Panza who follows his Dr. Don Quixote to the windmills of the Wabash." He clapped a hand to his forehead. "*Sapristi*, but I grow forgetful! A packet on the table by my bed. It contains dried catnip for the good Bosseron's pet!"

Markham laughed. "Two men of the regiment will overtake you and your Don Quixote at Lernault's Ferry. I'll give them the packet."

"A thousand thanks. I am fond of Bosseron's *matou*, who rather expects a gift from me each time I arrive." He trotted off into the mists.

The riders changed from sharply defined figures to shapeless blobs, then vanished. "Off to take Vincennes, are they?" thought Markham. "I'd like to be with them. Two damn good men. Hey! What's this? Are they turning back?" He stared at the mist where new movement showed, then ran ahead shouting, "Señor Teniente! Don Ramón!" Hoofs squelched louder and in a moment Nieto, white uniform masked in an oiled-silk cloak, sprang from the saddle, shook Markham's hand vigorously. "Ah, so my old and good friend awaits me!" he laughed uproariously. "Now you make arrestation of me and march me off to a dungeon, as at Santa Genoveva? But first I am charged by Don Fernando de Leyba to deliver with all possible hastes a communicate of the most formal to your Colonel Clark."

"Our dungeon isn't quite finished yet," said Markham. "I abase myself before you while hoping that a slight delay in your confinement may not prove too irksome. Let me take your horse and we'll find the Colonel. It's more than good to see you again, Don Ramón. All goes well in San Luís?"

"To perfection. Don Fernando, Señora de Leyba and Señorita Teresa send their greetings to you, in especial fashion. Ah, and the letter I bring will not, I think, displeasure you, Don Markham. You and your Colonel, and such officers as he may name, are bidden most formally to come to San Luís where a banquet of honors will hold itself. A ceremonious barge will meet you at Cahokia."

Markham let out a breath of slow relief. Even a noncommittal letter from de Leyba would have shown an unwelcome lessening of benevolence. Also Clark could say, "See what happened from following *your* advice!" Now his insistence on waiting was fully vindicated.

Nieto went on, "Ah, a veritable fortress and stockade. Is that where we find your Colonel? No — there he is, at the right!"

Markham stopped, astonished. Clark was swinging out of a side lane, towering in his buckskins, carrying a paddle in one hand and his broad hat in the other. "Now how the devil did you know it was he, Don Ramón?"

"I — I do not know. I see him, I say at once to myself, 'But it *can* be no one else.' I cannot explain, but I knew that he commands many and that none command him."

"That's how I saw him for the first time," said Markham, then called, "Colonel! this is Lieutenant Nieto of the Louisiana Regiment with dispatches for you from San Luís!"

Clark turned, halted. There was genuine warmth in his smile, in his deep blue eyes, as he received Nieto. Most men, Markham felt, would have held out a hand for the dispatches, but the Colonel only said, "It is an honor to have word from Don Fernando de Leyba. Let's all go into my quarters." He led the way in, seated himself in the heavy chair and indicated places for Nieto and Markham.

Nieto moved a hand toward the leather case at his side but Clark disregarded the gesture. "You've had a long trip, Lieutenant. Kaskaskia is yours to command if you need food or rest. No? Let's have some brandy, then. Want to do the honors, Markham?"

The brandy was served and Clark talked on easily about affairs along the Mississippi, always careful to refer to "the Spanish shore," to say "Santa Genoveva" and "San Luís." Nieto, unmistakably awed and admiring, replied as befitted a mere "Teniente" in the presence of exalted rank. At last the letter was ceremoniously handed to Clark who gravely broke the impressive seals and studied the sheets of stiff paper. Then he handed them to Markham. "My command of the language of a neighboring and friendly power cannot match that of Lieutenant Nieto. Mind working this out for me, Markham? I want to be sure that I understand fully what Don Fernando de Leyba has had the courtesy to write me."

Markham began to rough out a translation while Clark kept up a pleasant conversation with the ever-impressed Nieto. "Look at that!" thought Markham. "In frowzy buckskins, not a tag on him to set him off from any other man in the regiment. But Nieto's staring at him as though he represented the Holy Roman Empire. So Clark needs me to 'handle the Dons' for him, does he?" He wrote on. From time to time men of the regiment tramped in to report on patrols completed, to suggest new areas to cover. Nieto seemed to accept their calling their Colonel "George" as just another mark of Clark's stature. Did not Julius Caesar himself allow many liberties to his tough legionaries?

Markham finished his work, handed the sheet to Clark, who read over the invitation, nodding. Then he rose and bowed to Nieto. "In the absence of the principal, I thank the deputy and through him do myself the honor of accepting. Markham, I want you really to sweat over a proper reply in Spanish for me to sign. We'll rush it up for Joe Bowman to send across to San Luís. We'll leave tomorrow morning for Cahokia and wait there. I'll just take you and Joe with me. Will Harrod can go up and take Joe's place while Len Helm sits on the lid here."

It was a bright day with a high, blue sky and a brisk wind whipped through the tall grasses edging the road that ended at Cahokia landing. The long thrums of Markham's shirt danced in the breeze as he shaded his eyes to look west. Plain on the far bank he could see San Luís crouched on its limestone terraces. Then he caught a glitter off the end of a deep green island half a mile from shore and called, "Here comes the barge, Colonel."

Clark, magnificent in pearly buckskins that threw his heavily tanned throat and features into sharp relief, joined him. Others followed. Joe Bowman, dark-eyed and serious-faced; Will Harrod, carrying a little fearfully the burden of the Cahokia command on his shoulders; Phil Brady, flaunting a piratical square-cut beard and bubbling with sinister predictions that the whole party would be handed over to the Inquisition on the far shore; a score of men from the regiment and countless awed Creoles, their eyes on Clark and on the great barge that drove steadily closer.

It was a full thirty feet long with an ample cabin where gilded carving and glass panes caught the light. Astern a vast Spanish flag seemed to preen itself over its reflection in the wake. Forward, a dozen rowers, red kerchiefs at head and throat and wearing gold-laced yellow and red jackets, bent to their oars. Flame and smoke gushed from the starboard side as a swivel-gun sent its echoes clattering downstream. Onto the roof of the cabin sprang three men in Spanish uniform. A drum snapped out a long roll, brass flashed and clear-toned trumpets blared.

The drum beat on. Oars were shipped and the barge glided smartly alongside. A gaudy boatswain sprang ashore, bowed and waved the guests into the midships cabin. Clark was about to step aboard when Bowman called, "Wait a minute, George! Where's Rame Neeto?"

As he spoke, a tumult swept through the crowd that parted to let Don Ramón Nieto beat his way forward. He still wore his little cocked hat but his body was swathed in an outsize hunting-shirt whose sleeves flapped over his hands, the skirt falling below his knees. His breeches were regulation, but huge moccasins flapped on his feet like misshapen bears' paws. "I made many hastes," he panted. "It is just that my so-good friends of the Company Bowman elect me an honorary member of themselves. See! I am now true Big Knife!" He brandished a long carving-knife that dangled from a cord about his neck.

Laughing, the others hauled him aboard and into the cabin. Overhead the drum beat again, the trumpet sang out, the swivel-gun slammed and the barge pushed off amid delighted cheers and shouts from the mixed crowd at the head of the wharf. Clark settled himself. "A carpet! Cushions on the seats. Real glass windows and sliding shutters. The Dons sure do things in style." He leaned back luxuriously. "I always did like traveling, Joe."

Bowman nodded. "Just the same, there's places I'd just as soon not get caught in, like, say, this cabin."

Clark's mouth tightened. "Yes. Penned like a coon in a hollow tree, the way Ed Bagley was this side of Redstone on the Ohio. Sealed himself up so the Shawnees couldn't get him, but he didn't figure on their having fire-arrows. Still alive, I heard, when the Indians broke in to him."

Markham shivered. It was so easy to forget, here in this ornate barge, the very real reason for the invasion of the Illinois country.

The journey was over and more drums and bugles echoed along the waterfront. Through the open cabin door Markham saw gleaming bayonets, white and blue infantrymen and in the foreground the short, fat figure of Don Fernando de Leyba in fullest uniform, ablaze with sashes and gold braid. Just behind him came two young aides and a half-dozen Creoles in outmoded finery, bearing long, silver-headed staffs.

Superb in his buckskins, polished rifle across his shoulders and with pouch, horn and haversack neatly slung, Clark emerged. Glancing upward at the Spanish flag floating from a high pole, he stood motionless for an instant, uncovered. Then he replaced his hat and came on toward the waiting Don Fernando.

Markham, hurrying along with Bowman and Nieto, edged up closer, ready to interpret. De Leyba produced a parchment roll, glanced at it, drew a deep breath that strained every button of his bulging waistcoat. Then, with a quick gesture, he thrust the roll into the grasp of an aide, took a few swift steps toward Clark, arms outstretched. He caught the Colonel's hands in his, stood looking up at him while the sun poured down on the fat, stocky Spaniard and the tall, forest-lean Virginian. De Leyba said in his halting English, "What use are words between us? A friend welcomes a friend."

"You give me a proud title, Don Fernando. May I ever merit it," answered Clark in a low voice.

Markham stepped back. That pair would need no interpreter.

There was another muted exchange. Bowman was presented and warmly greeted, Markham was hailed as an old friend. Then de Leyba's aides and the Creole officials came forward while Markham improvised equivalent titles for *corregidor, alcalde* and *justiciero.* Then Clark and de Leyba, side by side, moved off across the Place d'Armes, their suites following. Trumpets blared and drums pounded and the infantry escort fell in behind them. Creoles jammed the Place. Old men with lined faces stared in wistful envy at Clark's straight back and easy stride. Younger ones pressed forward. Mothers held their children high and knots of girls, arms linked, stopped giggling and pushing and a soft ripple of admiring wonder rose from them as the Colonel strode by. Then hosts and guests passed into the stone house where the Spanish flag flew and where the Spanish arms glowed by the deep doorway, leaving an unending murmur hanging over the crowds outside.

In his former quarters that looked east to the riverfront, Markham stripped to the waist, shaved himself for the second time that day and then sloshed hot water about in a vast basin whose steam bore a tang of almond-scented soap. Drying himself with a big soft towel, he shook his head at his reflection in a round mirror. "This is too good. A little more life like this and I'll be so soft I'll never dare start out on a trip east when the time comes."

There was a knock at the door and Clark's voice called, "At home, Markham?"

"As much as I ever am. Come in."

Clark entered with his noiseless tread. "Just wanted to tell you that you've made a real friend for us out of de Leyba."

Markham shook out his shirt, struggled into it. "You'd have made do without me."

"Damn it, aren't you ever going to learn to take credit, even where you don't deserve it?" He dropped into a chair. "I thought that reception would never end. There was no chance for any real talk."

"Official receptions never do end and there's never a chance for talk at them. That's why I told you not to try to bring the talk around to Pollock's goods and your paper from Patrick Henry. Everything could have fizzled out if we'd rushed things."

Clark sighed. "So we just sit and wait. Well, you were right about the invitation to come here, so I guess there's a chance you are right again. When is anything likely to happen?"

Markham frowned. "There are so damn many ways of guessing wrong that I'm not going to go blundering ahead. In — let's see — about an hour we're to dine with de Leyba, his personal family and his official one. After that, if custom still holds, we'll be asked to stay with him and one or two others and nibble at brandy. So — well, I said I wasn't going to guess, but I'd be surprised if we had a chance at anything except being cordial and friendly as hell until tomorrow. Maybe not then."

Clark rose, began to pace impatiently. "I can't stay here forever. Things are happening all the time across the river. Damned if I'll — oh, hell. Let's wait through dinner anyhow. But something's got to start."

The table nearly filled the length of the grassy court where Markham had first met the de Leyba ladies. A great awning, striped red and yellow, was hung from wall to high wall to keep the late sun from the spread of white linen, copper flower-bowls, bright crystal and silver that weighted it. Liveried Negro servants glided about with platters, trays and decanters. From the host's seat, de Leyba kept bobbing to his feet, one hand over the great expanse of white waistcoat, the other lifting a glass. He proposed toasts to Clark on his right, to Markham on his left, to Bowman at the far end by Señora de Leyba's right.

Markham wondered where else on earth the group might be duplicated. De Leyba, with Nieto and two very junior ensigns in full uniform; Creole dignitaries in outmoded but immaculate formal dress; the Americans in their hunting-shirts; Señora de Leyba, dark and dryly rigid in dull gray; Teresa de Leyba, lovely and sparkling in black velvet startlingly slashed with scarlet, between Clark and Nieto; Creole wives with spare pinched faces, broad

Breton faces, delicate faces above the willow-green or deep red or soft blue of long-cherished gowns; Madame de Liliac at his own right, light brown hair finely set off by plum-colored silk. A decade ago he could not possibly have been at ease in such a mélange, but the schooling of the years between allowed him to fit in now without effort. If only his partner had not been so hard to talk to —

She ate little, drank sparingly of French and Spanish wines. Markham's observations were answered pleasantly enough, then dropped, leaving continuity entirely in his hands. "And why not?" he reflected. "Young, very pretty, an elderly husband. Every macaroni in Quebec must have been simpering and grimacing in front of her." At least it was pleasant to watch her clear profile with its surprisingly impudent nose, its full lips and rounded chin, the calm glance of her gray eyes, the rounded whiteness of her arm as she reached for her wine-glass. She turned unexpectedly to him. "Señora de Leyba is worried since your army comes into the Illinois country." She used English carefully, like someone trying to recall the text of a page read long ago.

"I did my best to reassure her. Perhaps you'll remind her of that."

"And who will convince me so that I may convince her?"

Markham thought, "Your eyebrows have a beautiful arch and you've dimples like inverted commas on each side of your mouth," as he replied, "Haven't I convinced you?"

"Men talk, but war comes just the same." She sighed, folded her white hands and went on more rapidly. "I have lived with wars. I was in Quebec when Montcalm was killed, and the next year when de Lévis nearly took the city back from the English. People died under bombardments. Our Ursuline Convent was destroyed. There was peace for a while, but your Montgomery and your Arnold attacked the city in the snow nearly three years ago. Is it odd that I worry for my friends here in St. Louis?"

"There's no reason for alarm. I'm sure of that, even if I don't know much about our plans."

Her gray eyes widened. "But you must know! You, so close to

your Colonel. What were the orders when you first started for the Illinois?"

"That's something I'll probably never know. I am with, not of, the Detachment. I met the Colonel's flotilla as I came east up the Ohio. Its mission was most secret, so I was forced to come along. I've been useful to the Colonel in a few small ways, but as soon as the chance comes, I start east up the Ohio again."

She looked incredulously at him. "Why were you, no *coureur de bois*, alone on the Ohio?"

"I wasn't. Another man was with me."

"That's the same as being alone for one like yourself."

Markham smiled. "Now I did hope that at least I *looked* adequate!"

"Not for that life. I, who know wilderness travel, say that." She shook her head. "You are new to this element, even though you may swim in it. I — am I too inquisitive if I ask what you were doing on the Ohio with just one companion?"

"Not at all. But my story's longer than it is interesting." As briefly as possible he sketched out the events that had brought him over the years and the miles from Boston to St. Louis. Then, aware that she had been sitting, very quietly, with her hands in her lap and eyes on the table, he said, "I'm sorry. Even shortened, it is not interesting."

She raised her eyes, almost timidly he thought. "Oh, it is not that. Only — when you reach home will you undertake something for me?"

He tried to mask his surprise. "But — I'd be delighted."

She colored and her eyes dropped again. "Don Ramón Nieto has told you how I came to be in Canada, I know. It — it is all so vague. We lived on a river called the Royal that must have been in the Province of Maine, and we can't have been far inland because I remember the smell of the sea in the pines."

"Was this place in a town?"

"Yarmouth and Falmouth are in my mind, but they may just be names I've heard." He saw her eyelids close, perhaps to blot out old memories. "My family name was Gore. Merrill and Nason and Baxter must belong to that time because after them in my memory come only French names." Her voice was lower, more rapid. "They told me my mother and father, both my brothers were killed. Some other people were taken captive with me, but I've no idea what happened to them. You see, I was only four."

Echoes of Indian-talk on the march to Kaskaskia flooded Markham's mind. He could also hear Father Gibault pleading with Clark that families be not broken up. "Only four," he thought. "You poor little scrap."

She went on, "There *must* be more that I can remember. I'll try. I know it sounds hopeless, after all these years, but could you make inquiries for me in Boston? Is there a place called Salem in Massachusetts Bay Colony? That may be where the Gores came from."

"Of course I'll help. Did you ever set any of this on paper?"

"Not when I should have. I was so young and you really do begin a new life in the Ursulines. I was happy with the Sisters and soon felt that I'd been born on The Rock. Much later I began to wonder. Monsieur de Liliac made many inquiries, but they came to nothing. A lot of Convent records burned during de Lévis's attack in '60. Then this dreadful war came and there was no chance of finding out from Massachusetts." She sighed again. "There must be so very, very many like me."

"That may make it all the easier to start inquiries. I have one of my own to make, for example."

She started. "You did not tell me of that! No! No! I cannot add my questions to yours."

"But mine are so much simpler than yours. As of early '75, my father, mother and two brothers were alive. Once I'm within hailing distance of Faneuil Hall or King's Chapel, I can find out about them. Your case will take more time, I'm afraid."

"Time cannot affect what I want to know," she said sadly. "Was my whole family killed? Where are they buried? Have I close kin in your Colonies? I must know, not for myself but for my little daughter Annette. I will start trying to set my memories in order and write down everything. Could you call on me at my house to-morrow about five? Señora and Señorita de Leyba are coming to drink tea with me. You'll find my house in the Rue de l'Eglise just above this one, the Rue Royale. I'll give you what I've set down and then —" She gave a little cry of dismay.

All along the table people were rising. Señora de Leyba was looking almost reproachfully at Madame de Liliac. Don Fernando, grinning and wheezing, slapped Markham's shoulder, chuckling about "You young people — forget the whole world while staring into each other's eyes." Markham followed the others out, flushing a little.

Later the senior guests sat in the Lieutenant-governor's official salon that was heavy with Spanish leather screens, thick, somber hangings, massive carved chairs, and yet unexpectedly alive with bursts of color and light from Moorish brasses, inlaid coffee tables and vivid tiles whose deep blues and greens seemed to flow out into the room. While sound French and Spanish brandies circulated, Markham's mind was kept endlessly alert as he translated for Spanish, Creole and American.

The talk ranged from the price of prime beaver-pelts on the New Orleans market to the endless, towering grassy mounds left on both sides of the river by some vanished race. Clark very deftly parried questions about the expedition, limiting himself to speaking of the vast buffalo herds sighted by his scouts who did not dare shoot a few for the starving column for fear of drawing unwelcome attention to it. Markham told of his own awe at coming on the breathtaking ruins of Fort de Chartres between Cahokia and Kaskaskia, a staggering stone monument to military engineering slowly drowning there in the wilderness. "The river claimed it," he went on. "You'll recall, Don Ramón, how a whole casemate slid into the ooze as we rode past on our way up from Kaskaskia? A pity, all that work. Nothing to do about it, of course. Kaskaskia'll go the same way, some spring flood. So, I think, will Santa Genoveva." He caught Clark's eye on him, saw that the Colonel was frowning almost imperceptibly. Markham gave a slight shake to his head. This was *not* the time to speak of Pollock's goods.

Don Fernando broke in, "All swallowed up by the river, Don Markham? Our good Spanish town of Santa Genoveva?"

Clark said easily, "But such a thing cannot happen to your San Luís, built on its limestone ledges."

"And yet, Señor Colonel," began de Leyba with a rueful smile, "in one little corner of San Luís I might welcome such a flood to relieve me from embarrassment. Our good friend, Don Markham Cape, knows of goods belonging to an American merchant, consigned here by mistake, which I may neither hold properly nor properly rid myself of."

Markham repressed a start as he turned de Leyba's words into English with no warning phrases added. Clark remained utterly relaxed, showing only polite interest. "An American merchant, eh? Poor devil. A whole bag of *reales* or dollars or pounds that he'll never recover."

De Leyba laid his hand on Clark's shoulder. "You see it so? He may stand on the brink of ruin. We hold salvation for him here and may do nothing about it. His name? Ah, as I told Don Markham, foreign names elude me. But tomorrow or the next day or at some convenient time during your visit, we could step inside the warehouse and view the goods."

Markham saw the slightest flicker as Clark's jaw muscles tightened, but the Colonel only said, still politely, "Command me, Don Fernando, if I may be of the least service to you. But I fear — you will understand that my orders do not touch any fellow citizen west of Virginia." He shook his head apologetically. "Any fellow citizen, except, of course, a Mr. Oliver Pollock in New Orleans, on whom I am empowered to draw. But he is three months and more away from us here."

De Leyba nodded understandingly. "Ah yes. I see. None the less if you and I might talk over the plight of this American — not to speak of my own embarrassment, eh? You understand? In some idle time of your own, your own wide experience might ease my mind. H'm. Pollock. Could that be he whom we call Don Oliveros, friend to our Governor Galvez? But no matter. As you say, he is months from us here in San Luís. Don Ramón! Brandy for Don José Bowman and el Alcalde des Rosiers! Where is young Estavez and his lute? Our guests must have music. Señor Colonel Clark, a glass of brandy with you!"

Voices rose higher as the decanters made their steady rounds of the table. Clark's eyes from time to time sent impatient queries to Markham, "When — when — when?" only to meet stubborn replies of "Wait — wait!" And Markham was still saying "Wait!" when the gathering finally broke up and the guests trailed off to their various quarters.

Markham's room was pitch-dark and he groaned in angry protest as a hand tugged at his shoulder. Rising slowly from a deep well of oblivion he mumbled, "What you want? What's wrong?"

A dark shape bent over him and Captan Bowman was urging, "Get up! Get dressed! Meet George and me at the boat-landing right away. We're leaving!"

"Can't leave yet, damn it! Got to see Madame de Liliac and —"

"Folks don't say 'can't' to George. Hurry!" And Joe Bowman glided noiselessly out of the room.

IX

Winning Ways of *Gitchi Mokoman*

THE SUN was just clearing the low hills in the east as the canoe drove on toward Cahokia landing. Markham, crouched behind the bow paddler, bristled with resentment at the still unexplained move from St. Louis. The canoe swooped alongside the wharf and Clark was ashore in a single leap, Bowman and Markham following. Mists clung to the steep Cahokia roofs and in the fields to the north where Markham thought he made out rows of corn shocks. Then he saw that they were conical tents with people moving about, heard dogs barking, horses whinnying, caught the sharp tang of woodsmoke. Down the path to the wharf came muffled shapes wrapped in blankets with long feathers jutting from their heads. A cold chill crept up his back and he closed with his companions, staring at these Indians who personified for him all the ghastly tales he had heard on the trail.

They came on slowly, eyes fixed on Clark. One of them gobbled out what sounded like *"Gitchi Mokoman!"* Clark raised his right hand, palm out, spoke equally weird words. The Indians wavered, then faded away in the mists. To Markham's discomfort, Clark and Bowman slowed to a nonchalant saunter. A grove upstream disgorged more Indians and pack-horses. Dogs raced yipping about and children trotted soberly with the women. Half-grown youths chased each other, scuffled, whooped. Clark only glanced casually at the newcomers. "They're Stinkers — Winnebagos. Must aim to camp yonder."

The Indians halted. Men dropped onto the grass to watch the women labor over pitching camp. The dogs settled on their haunches and helped the men watch. Tent-poles bristled, were covered with great brownish sheets. Markham felt a little easier as the three crossed the log bridge that spanned the little Rigolet. Mists thinned more and Cahokia lay before him as he had seen it on his first return from St. Louis. There were the common-lands stretching away to the eastern hills, and in the distance loomed the eerie vastness of the ancient Indian tumulus known as Monk's Mound. The neat-fenced houses running north and south caught the sun as they seemed to close ranks toward the heavy stone building dimly marked with a great black crowned G.R. where he had talked to Joe Bowman before setting out for Kaskaskia. The whole village was coming to life. Virginians led horses down to water. Creoles and Virginians, riding two and two, showed on the Fort Chartres road as they came in from night patrol. Virginians and Creoles alike hailed the new arrivals and familiar faces and voices further scattered the cloud of uneasiness that had settled over Markham at the sight of the Indians.

He no longer pressed against the invisible barrier of his companions' slow gait, but strolled on with something like unconcern. As they came to the open space before the stone building, his breath went in sharply and his whole skin seemed to tighten. By twos and sixes and tens Indians were moving on silently. Their eyes were on the ground but he was sure that they saw more than he did. They were unarmed, but just the same — those incurious stony eyes, those sinewy coppery arms that showed through stroudings worn as a Highlander wears his plaid, those lean, flat-muscled legs —

Clark and Bowman favored them only with random comments. "Chippewas. Wonder if Blue Heron's with 'em" . . . "More Stinkers" . . . "Ojibways and a Peoria. Hi! There's Will Harrod."

Captain Harrod was leaning against a pillar of the stone house gallery. It must have been urgent word from him that had brought Clark racing across from St. Louis, but Harrod gave no sign of bad news. He blinked his rather sleepy eyes and said, "Howdy, George."

"Howdy, Will. Got anything to eat?"

"Reckon we ain't missing. Come in and sit by."

They all trooped into the big room where Clark spun a chair

about, dropped into it facing Harrod. Markham thought, "Now we'll find out!" Clark spoke quickly. "How about it, Will? The boys been quiet?"

"Tolerable."

Clark relaxed with a sigh. "I'd been fretting, Will. Thanks."

Markham rocked back in his chair. "God Almighty. You dragged me out of bed, got me half drowned crossing the river and hauled me ashore just to ask Will how the boys had been! Have you even begun to think about what you're going to do with those people out there?" With an effort he kept from pointing, but his eyes were on the open window behind Clark. In the grassy side street a crowd of Indians had gathered, staring silently up at Clark's wide shoulders and coppery head.

Clark only grinned. "Do? Why, first of all we're going to eat!" The gallery door opened and a gray-haired Creole woman brought bowls of onion soup thick with cheese and floating crusts, venison-steaks, vast pots of coffee, jugs of heavy yellow cream, loaves of thick-crusted bread, mounds of amber jellies and richly dark jams. Still deeply uneasy, Markham pulled up to the table and prodded grumpily at the bubbling crust that topped his soup. Slowly his ill temper ebbed and he accepted a cup of coffee from Bowman, passed a cream pitcher to Harrod.

Soon Clark pushed away his bowl, whose scalding contents had vanished with startling rapidity. "Shove the venison this way, Will. Now, Markham, I didn't want to say anything to you till we hit the east bank. I couldn't. I didn't know what we'd find. When we landed I figured it was best not to jabber about what we did find."

"It was done judgmatical," observed Bowman gravely.

"Anyhow, these people are here because I sent for them. Reckon I don't need to tell you anything more than that, do I?"

"You dodged Indians all the way to Kaskaskia," said Markham wearily. "Then you had patrols out guarding against them. And now you've sent for them. Quite logical, in a fashion."

"There's a time for dodging things and a time for meeting them head on. As soon as we were in Kasky, I drew up proclamations for all the tribes. Creoles and some of our boys ranged wide with them."

"*You* — sent proclamations to the *Indians?*"

"Why not? They had to be told why we were fighting the British. It was hard to put into Indian thought, but I said the Crown was trying to turn us into second-class tribes, something like that, and that they'd been stuffed with lies about us, just as the Creoles had. Sounds kind of good in Indian-talk — they'd 'been listening to the songs of the Bad Birds in the forest.' I went on that I didn't give a damn what the tribes did. If they didn't bother us we'd never harm them. If they joined the British, then we'd kill them all and throw them out for the dogs to eat along with their paymaster, Colonel Hamilton, at Detroit. It was up to them."

"You're trying to tell me that *that* was 'sending for them'?"

"My God, don't you see? I wasn't going to them, hat in hand. But one Indian's got more curiosity than a hundred geese. They'd want to *see* the man who sent out that proclamation. And I sent Creoles out among them saying how fine things had been since we came in. The Indians'd want to know all about that. So here they are, just as I said. Now let's hear Will Harrod's story."

Harrod spoke in venison-muffled tones. "Soon's the scouts told me Indians were on the move, I waited to see where they were heading and how many. It was full dark before I could tell. When I saw they were powerful ample, I passed word across to you in St. Louis."

"Any chiefs call here?"

"An Ottawa and a Peoria, asking leave to camp a spell. I said this was a Creole town and they'd have to see the head Creole, not me. What they really wanted was where you were and when they could see you. I said 'Don't know' twice and that, far's I knew, you didn't have anything to say to them."

Clark shook Harrod's shoulder gently. "Fine, Will, fine. You've kept our trail clear as a deer run. You follow all this, Markham?"

Markham shoved his plate away. "Damned if I do. You're figuring on the Indians doing exactly what you want them to do and that's a bad course in war or trading or navigation. Suppose they get ideas of their own. There must be several hundred of them around Cahokia and you can't have more than twenty-five or thirty of the Detachment here."

Clark and Harrod both shook their heads. "No, no," said Clark. "They won't start trouble. They've brought their women and children and that's a sign they're not on the warpath — yet. We're watching, and if they send even one squaw away, we'll know it. Hi! Who's outside?"

The gallery door swung open and Bowman, who sat facing it, cried, "Well, Rame! You sure got across the river like a bull-buffalo was after you!" Clark hailed, "Don Ramón! Didn't expect you till tonight!" Markham swung about in his chair, staring in surprise at Nieto who stood gravely saluting Clark, leather dispatch-case at his side and his cherished knife dangling from a long cord about his neck.

"With your permission, Señor Colonel, the papers which our Governor promised you." He handed a packet to Clark. "Also, I am to hold myself at your disposals for as long a time as you may have requirement."

Clark rose. "Thank you, Teniente. Let me see, you know everyone here except our Captain Harrod."

Nieto expressed joy at meeting el Capitán Harrod, saluted Bowman as leader of the company to which he himself had been duly elected Honorary Private. Then he seated himself. "Ah, it is good to see you all again. By ordinary I am not amused at being waked in the very tiny hours but when I learned of my mission, wings grew on my heels. Thank you, I need no foods. Now how may I serve you?"

Clark looked thoughtfully at him, then began to smile. "Tired?"

"In such companies as this? But never."

"You've never had a good look at Cahokia before, have you? Let's go out onto the gallery and see it from there. Come on, all of you."

They strolled leisurely out onto the gallery, were joined there by a spare, keen-faced man in a white uniform faced with blue. Clark introduced him as Major François Trottier of the Creole militia, then lounged to the railing, flanked by Nieto and Trottier. Markham edged up between Harrod and Bowman, fighting against apprehension as he looked down at the Indians who began drifting in through the stockade gate. They milled slowly about, seemingly aimless and incurious. Some squatted in sunny corners. Others filtered out through side-gates like desultory idlers, only to reappear at the main entrance. Markham sniffed the still, hot air. "I heard you call one tribe 'Stinkers,' Colonel. Why single out just one that way?"

Harrod looked surprised. "It's what they're called. The Creoles call them 'Puants,' not knowing better. Tribe name's Winnebago, but the other's shorter. Looky — Miamis yonder and Missisaugas and Michigamis and Osages. Looks like every tribesman and his brother's come to Cahoky to stare."

Slowly Markham lost a little of his instinctive dread and began to see them as individuals. There were heads topped with single feathers, clusters of feathers, with tall crowns of plumes. He saw roached heads, heads trailing tattery braids, heads from which plaits of coal-hard black fell neatly across each shoulder. There were flattish faces, small-featured faces, faces with proud, high-bridged noses and thin lips, lean wolfish faces and slack-jawed faces. The only common denominator was unchanging expressions and eyes like polished black flints that held no interest, no warmth, no reaching out. Many bodies were swathed in drab blankets but buckskin or linsey-woolsey hunting shirts were common enough. A few wore soiled and ragged French or British officers' coats with gorgets like brassy half-moons hanging by chains from sinewy necks. It seemed to him that the Indians were slowing their pace, tending to gather in groups facing the stone house gallery without actually looking up at it. Sounds drifted to him and he thought that he caught the two words that he had heard earlier. "Does that mean anything, Will?" he asked Harrod.

"Sounds like '*Gitchi Moko*—' something."

"Means ample. *Gitchi's* big. *Mokoman's* something like

'medicine knife' or 'magic knife' or just plain 'Big Knife.' It's what the Indians call us but the way they say it now points right at George."

Markham glanced along the railing. Clark, Nieto and Trottier chatted amiably on, three carefree men obviously enjoying each other's company. Suddenly Markham saw the group through Indian eyes. Clark, with seeming aimlessness, was letting all those tribesmen see him idling in patent amity with two uniformed officers, Spanish and Creole. The implications of this scene could hardly be missed by any coppery onlooker.

At last Clark hooked an arm through Nieto's, and turned away. "Don Ramón brought the Pollock invoices over with him, Markham, and you can start going over them right now. I'll send Phil Brady to help you. He used to know a lot about the Illinois trade. Shouldn't take the two of you more than six or eight hours, I'd say." He motioned to Nieto to precede him.

For an instant, Markham forgot the Indians swarming below. "Don Ramón brought you *what?*" he almost shouted, as Nieto entered the house.

Clark looked very innocent. "Didn't you know? Why, just as we were leaving last night, de Leyba said that it was a pity about those goods. I said I wished that I could help but all I had was written authority from Patrick Henry to draw on Oliver Pollock and that wouldn't serve in this case. Then de Leyba began wheezing and chuckling and said that the invoices for those goods *were* in Pollock's name. So we separated on that, I remembering what you said about not hurrying the Spaniards. When Will Harrod sent word we were needed in Cahokia, I routed de Leyba out. We had to talk through his bedroom window and he in a nightcap. I showed him the Henry letter and he whooped for a while and then said he'd send Don Ramón over here with the papers." He grinned again. "You sure were right about not hurrying them, Markham." He turned his back on the mob of Indians below and entered the house without a glance at them.

Markham followed him slowly. The invoices! There was no doubt that Clark had managed to place himself on very firm footing with the Spaniards, firm enough so that he had brought off his more than unceremonious exit from St. Louis without giving offense. Then he remembered again that he himself had promised to call on Madame de Liliac that afternoon to see how he could help her in her quest for her lost kin in Massachusetts and Maine. He would send a note of apology to her by the canoe that had brought Don Ramón. Another canoe would be coming over at midnight in case she wanted to acknowledge it.

An answer! "Why in God's name don't I tell Clark that the invoices can wait? That copper-topped slave-driver's got no hold on me!" Then he began to laugh. He called "Oh, Colonel! About those invoices! Scare up Phil Brady and we ought to be through with them by ten or eleven tonight!"

It was well past midnight as Markham and Phil Brady made their way up from the wharf along the sunken path on the east bank of the Rigolet. There was no moon and a haze dimmed the high powdering of stars. A steady wind from the north bent the tall grasses and brought with it a sour tang of smoke from the Indian camps above. Brady, gliding on behind Markham, spoke softly. "You got so you move real catty. You didn't make as much noise as a chip-mouse in those brambles."

"Self-defense. Every time Clark hears me stir, he gets ideas about another job for me. If it hadn't been for you, I'd be reefed on that Pollock stuff until tomorrow noon. And thanks for coming to the wharf with me, even if that canoe didn't bring anything back from St. Louis." The path was now shoulder-deep and Markham glanced casually west, looked again, stopped. "Phil! More Indians! Those tents weren't on the far bank when we came down tonight."

Brady halted. "Sure God new! That's good watching, Mark."

"Who are they?"

"I'd guess Meadow Indians. That's what we call them when a mess of young bucks from different tribes ooze off by themselves all mixed up. They grab young girls from other camps, get drunk, fight among themselves and have a nice, quiet sociable time.

They're safe enough so far's we're concerned, but it's best to keep quiet."

Markham started on, checked himself, his head cocked toward the shallow Rigolet. At least one man was wading cautiously to the east bank. Markham ducked low and the faintest of rustles told him that Brady was also crouching. The noises continued, became a muffled scrabbling on the bank. Then an Indian emerged, dripping, musket and powder-horn held high, stood poised then sprang across the path ten yards ahead. Phil Brady touched Markham's elbow and he looked west across the stream. Dim against the skyline he made out the heads of at least a dozen more Indians. He looked inland again.

The lone Indian was standing there as though staring at the high fences of Cahokia some thirty yards away. Then he faced about, slowly raised both arms shoulder-high, then swept his right arm upstream. The far bank bristled and Indians trotted north in single file. Seconds passed silently. Then without warning the far bank spouted fire and a ragged burst of musketry ripped out. Before the echoes died, the Indians plunged into the stream, floundered across it, reached the east bank and raced toward the stone house where Clark had his headquarters. The man who had crossed first pointed his musket toward the sky for what might have been a signal-shot.

Markham made no sound, yet his inner shout *"No you don't!"* seemed to him to blare into the night. His legs contracted, shot him forward like springs, driving his shoulders against the Indian's spine as his arms whipped about the coppery chest. The musket whacked to the ground and Markham and his opponent crashed among bushes and tall grasses.

Rank, greasy flesh jammed against Markham's face as he fought to wedge his forearms against the other's windpipe, but the Indian writhed, his arms and legs weaving like slippery snakes. A hard knee jarred into Markham's belly, a hand like an axe-butt sledged the back of his neck. His breath was gone and green and red and yellow lights spun behind his eyes. The Indian wriggled, slammed the heel of his hand against Markham's chin, forcing it back and sidewise. Markham gave with the pressure, twisted his body, using the strength of his enemy to help him break clear. He freed his right arm, clawed at the front of his own shirt and One-eyed Harrison's knife was in his grip. He whipped it out, struck once and felt the blade rip into solid muscle, then glide into something softer.

He heard a tight gasp, a horrible, grinding gurgle, retching. Blood was on his hands, on his bare throat and the Indian was limp beneath him. Panting, he rose to his knees, tugged his knife clear of the dead flesh, mechanically plunged it into the ground to cleanse it. He tensed again, relaxed as Brady dropped beside him. "Oh, it's you, Phil?"

Brady panted, "You all right? You get him?" There was a pause. "Uh-huh. Got him good. Christ, you took off so fast I couldn't bear a hand with you. Sure you're all right?"

"Right's I ever will be." Markham rose, sheathing the knife. "Hi! Look at the stone house!"

Across the field lights were gleaming. Indians were pounding at the main gates of the stone house stockade, yelling. The gates swung open, the Indians poured through and the gates closed on them. Brady cried hoarsely, "Come on. This can be God damn poison!"

The pair sprinted ahead, shouting, "Guard! Guard! Open the gates! Brady and Cape coming in!" The gates swung again. A few shadowy shapes that could only have been Indians scurried crouching from the flare of torch and gleam of lantern and tore blindly off into the night. Markham and Phil Brady pulled up at the entrance, stood staring in.

On the gallery Clark leaned negligently against a pillar, a red-bowled pipe in his hand. Joe Bowman and Nieto were with him, looking down into the yard where Trottier, lantern held high, turned its light on a knot of Indians who knelt under the bayonets of militiamen. Close by the gallery a line of Clark's men leaned on their rifles, glowering at the Indians. From the gallery, Clark spoke evenly. "Thank you, Major. Sure. Let 'em talk if they want to, for all of me."

Trottier jerked a thumb at the foremost Indian. *"Allez!"*

Still kneeling, the latter spoke at length in a high, singsong voice that broke into odd little quavers. Brady listened intently, then gave an incredulous whistle. "Christ, what a yarn! He says these poor innocent little chickie-birds were tending their own business on the *east* bank when Bad Birds fired on them from the west, so naturally they just flew off to their good friend *Gitchi Mokoman* for protection, and — hey! — here's something new. Bad Birds were fixing to rush in and capture *Gitchi Mokoman* and these good little fellers, they aimed to fight right alongside with him against those Bad Birds." He shook his head. "Maybe George'll have to accept the story, though. No one but us saw what really happened and how can we say these are the same Indians?"

Markham looked at Clark who was leaning on the gallery rail, talking coolly with Trottier. The yard was very still and he caught ". . . don't see how we can prove anything different, Major, so maybe —"

Brady gave a sudden grunt. "Where the hell have my brains gone?"

Markham growled, "Packed in a brine-keg along with mine. Come on." The two ran across the yard, Brady calling, "George! George! Make those bastards stand up!"

Clark raised his head quickly. "What good'll that do?"

Markham snatched a lantern from a guard. "You'll see. Get 'em up."

Prodded by bayonets, the Indians rose, their harsh voices gabbling a protest. Markham turned the lantern on them and its rays glinted on the slick sheen of soaked leather, on oozing moccasins. A hush fell, broken only by a sullen drip-drip.

Brady said sourly, "Must be a sight of water on the east bank."

Clark shook his head in mild wonder. "How'd we ever come to miss it?"

Trottier ran up to the gallery, Markham and Brady following. "What is it that you wish done with them, Colonel?"

Clark looked negligently down at the prisoners. "Done? Why,

they kicked up a row in your town, not mine." He dropped his voice. "But if I did have the say, seems to me I'd put irons on them and shove them into your jail for a spell. And Major — when we've beaten off an Indian attack back home, we most always roll out a barrel, get the fiddlers busy and the boys and girls dance till sunup and past! Now your town's sure beaten one off and if you've got something like that in mind, I'd be proud to toss in a mite of our rum, just to show our hearts are with you."

Trottier stared, then broke into a broad smile, nodded and ran on down the steps. Clark knocked a quick cascade of sparks from his pipe. "Let's go inside. I've got some listening to do." He led the way into the big room and took a chair. "How'd you two run into all this?"

"You tell it, Mark. You were closest," said Phil.

When Markham had finished, Clark sat for a moment with his eyes closed. Then he said, "You just never know with Indians. They might have been telling the truth tonight, but those wet leggin's gave them the lie."

"Mark forgot to say he jumped an Indian this side the Rigolet. Got him with one jab. Never hope to see slicker."

Clark turned sharply. "What the hell did you do that for?"

"I'm not too proud of it. His back was toward me. But he'd given the first signal and was raising his musket to fire in the air. I figured that could be only another signal and it seemed best to keep him from making it. I took the only way I knew."

Clark drummed softly on the table. "Yes. Reckon you had to. Wonder what that second signal was going to mean. At least, they didn't get what they came for — meaning me."

"You'd have been knifed?" asked Markham.

"No. They'd have knocked me on the head and bundled me off to Hamilton at Detroit. He'd pay plenty. Or maybe they'd have holed up around Green Bay and dickered to get a bigger reward."

Markham looked at him appraisingly. "Did you have an idea something like this might happen? You had at least quadruple guards inside the fence and no lights showing till the last instant."

Clark shook his head. "No. It was just —" he moved one hand

vaguely — "just something in the wind, in the feel of the night."

"Is there anything I ought to know about the wind or the night to keep on staying healthy? The Indians aren't going to like my killing one of them."

Phil broke in: "How'll they ever know it was you? Even then, they wouldn't hold it against you. You see —" he went on patiently, "you knifed him after the firing and on our side of the stream. They'd honor you for it as a good warrior. Lives, even their own, don't mean a thing to them. If you'd killed him in their camps, though, they'd come a-swarming and we'd fort up right here and get some praying done along with our shooting."

"Phil's right," observed Clark.

"Then that's settled, as long as the Indians agree with him. What happens next?"

"We're dead sure to have visitors tomorrow. Just a chief or two. Be kind of restful after tonight. You better stay and see what happens."

Markham turned to Brady. "I really believe we're going to get a nice long sleep tonight. I honestly do."

Clark sprang up with a shout of laughter. "I honestly don't. Didn't you hear what I said to Trottier before I had him iron those braves?" He looked toward the open door and called, "Bring 'em right in, boys!"

Two men of the Detachment trundled in a pair of rum-kegs. Creoles butted a fat wine-cask into the room. Clark shouted, "Set 'em up on those trestles! Shove the tables and chairs out of the way." He banged his hands together. "Ho! Here come the others!"

Markham cried, "My God, were you serious about Trottier and the fiddlers at this time of night?"

Clark slapped his shoulder. "Hell, Markham, a commanding officer's *always* serious. Haven't you learned that yet?" He made a sweeping gesture with his arm. "Keep 'em rolling, boys!"

There was a vague stirring out in the night. Nieto, who had changed his boots for silk stockings and light shoes, entered with a flash of silver buckles. After him came two Creoles brandishing fiddles and bows. Most of the reasonably adult population of Cahokia poured in after them, mingled with men of the Detachment. The Creoles had obviously dressed in haste. Wigs were awry, waistcoat buttons tugged at mismatched holes, bodice-laces zigzagged alarmingly, hands hitched at twisted breeches, tugged at ill-hung skirts, but every face was alight with gay anticipation.

The fiddlers scrambled onto the big table, the kegs were broached. Elders scurried for chairs and benches. Bulbous matrons and slim, nervous-footed girls ranged themselves along one wall, men of all ages facing them across the room. Clark, white teeth showing and eyes dancing, signaled to the musicians. The first notes sailed out, were picked up by voices in a great sweep, "*O-o-o-h, Al-ouette, jolie Alouette —*" The two lines flowed into life, advanced across the floor, arms linked, retreated, came on again, spun, stamped, broke up, re-formed. Virginians joined in, whirled about, bowed, advanced, fell back. Nieto, vivid in his white and blue, flew about like a bright shuttle while fiddle-bows slid and darted. Clark, standing by the musicians, shouted with the dancers and beat time with a great mug. Joe Bowman was out on the floor and Will Harrod, trying to catch the words that flitted up to the rafters, "*— je t' plumerai la tête, à la tête, Alouette! O-o-oh, Al — ouette —*"

The triumphant lift of the fiddles and the drum-drum of feet beat pitilessly through Markham's sleep-starved mind. Shaking his head he made for the door and the cool quiet of the night. People kept jostling him as they laughed and shouted. The door seemed an immeasurable distance away, the voices louder and more insistent. A hand caught his, swung him about and bright eyes in a sunburned face smiled at him, a head gay in a cherry-red kerchief swayed to the music. The bright eyes were gone and a wisp of a girl in vivid green, whose provocative full-lipped mouth denied the decorously lowered lashes above it, retreated before him, hands on hips and feet a-flutter, advanced as he fell back in the simple pattern of the dance.

Later he was in a long line, one arm linked with Nieto, the other with a stocky Creole in orange velvet. The fiddlers swung into a wilder, more joyous strain and voices picked up the air, *"En avant | La bande joyeuse | Dieu protège | Les bons vivants | En avant | La bande joyeuse | EN AVANT!"* The dancers followed the music into a quicker tempo, booted, moccasined and slippered feet stamping heavily at each *"En avant."* Faster and faster they went, pouring out of the wide door, spilling out on the parade-ground below. Markham's throat was raw from shouting, but he kicked out as lively as ever trying to match Nieto's spring-like agility. The gallery stairs were under his feet again and he seemed to float upward with the others, reaching the main room without effort. A tireless matron skipped and glided beside him, in place of the orange velvet, and her resilient, ample curves pressed against him at each step. The line had broken up into ranks and across the room Markham saw Clark, leaping high and joyously between Trottier and a slim, dark-eyed girl all in red. Feet pounded on, the fiddles soared and voices roared *"En avant!"* while every door and window showed masses of Indians outside, watching from a little distance in mute immobility.

Uncomfortably aware of a throbbing head and dry mouth, Markham went through the morning glare to the stone house. "Three hours' sleep!" he growled to Phil Brady who stumped along with him. "What's the Colonel want now?"

"This is George's way," mumbled Brady. " 'Go in and wait,' he says, so we go in and wait. God, what a head! I'm afraid I'm going to live after all."

Markham went up the stairs and when he reached the scarred threshold of the big room he stopped as though he'd run into a solid wall. The big room was jammed with forty or fifty Indians who squatted on the floor or stood awkwardly against the wall. Their smell was overwhelming. More so was their utter quiescence, the unbroken silence. No head turned as Markham stood in the doorway. No muffled word was spoken. But unwavering eyes, blackish or dark brown, fastened on him, cold, to him inhuman, incapable of any softening or lightening. The eyes of men bred to kill through uncounted centuries, to kill senselessly, unreasoningly, simply because the act of killing was the measure of a man, killing swiftly and silently at need, killing lingeringly with slow, inventive relish when occasion allowed. Heat and smell and silence were almost tangible and that piercing mass gaze seemed to drill through him like swift-flying needles.

He stood there for a long second, then a hand prodded his back and he knew that Phil Brady was close behind him. He rallied himself but his voice sounded dry and rustling as he called with forced bravado over his shoulder, "Hell, no one here but a bunch of Indians." He hoped that one or two of them would have enough English to catch his meaning.

Brady shoved again. "Go on in. We won't bother 'em if they keep out from under foot."

Markham crossed the threshold, thumbs hooked in his belt, and tried to look coolly about him. There were the same towering headdresses, some neat bunches of feathers set jauntily over one ear or draggled plumes with broken quills. Some wore scarlet or blue coats with tarnished gorgets dangling at the neck but most were wrapped in blankets, bright with green or red or yellow stripes or sodden brown as swamp-water. Here and there leg-irons under frayed blanket-edges showed that Trottier must have turned his prisoners loose to join the other tribesmen.

Trying to act as though he and Brady were alone, Markham lounged to a square table that took up most of the free space, looked idly down at it. "What's all this stuff, Phil?" he said pointing. On the scarred surface lay a long wide band or sash made up of thousands of shiny shell chips, gleaming, iridescent, superbly strung and woven together and edged with dyed porcupine quills. Beside it was an unmistakable pipe with a high, narrow bowl of some polished red stone. The broad flat stem, well over two feet long, was tightly bound with alternating red and white bands of beadwork and a great burst of red and black and white feathers sprouted from the lower side just below the bowl.

Phil Brady yawned. "That? Tacky trade-goods. Couldn't sell 'em to a blind possum-pup." He turned from the table and perched on the windowsill. Markham joined him, forced himself to face the squatting, silent men. The hush kept on unbroken until steps rang on the gallery. Markham saw Nieto in full uniform and wearing a sash and dress sword heading for the door. He called, "Come on in, Don Ramón. We're all alone here."

The Spaniard entered, looked coolly about as though the floor were empty and joined the pair by the window. Minutes went by, noiseless as moccasined feet on a forest-trail. Major Trottier, soldierly in white and blue, came through the door, touched a finger to his hat brim as he saw Nieto and ranged himself next to Brady. Markham felt tension pressing down on him like some tangible force, struggled inwardly to match the outward unconcern of his companions.

All at once Clark was in the middle of the room, tall, erect, his coppery head bare. A silvery gray linen shirt hung from his heavy shoulders and beads and quills and bits of bright shell glittered in its folds. In his right hand he carried a long knife sheathed in embossed leather from whose tip dangled a marten's silky tail. He glanced at the group by the window, smiled, started to speak. Then as though he had just noticed it, he stepped to the table, looked coldly down at it. The hush deepened. His sheathed knife moved slowly forward, touched the great shell sash and the pipe. Every Indian eye was following his least motion. Then his wrist flicked and the silence was broken by a soft hissing and a clatter as the sash slid with a rattling crash to the floor, the pipe whacking down beside it.

Phil Brady's fingers bit into Markham's arm. "Jesus Christ, Mark! He's chucked the peace-wampum and the peace-pipe back at them!"

The words, jarred from the usually unexcitable Brady, meant little to Mark, but the Indians were telling him a great deal. The cold, hard eyes became human. He read a savage anger in them, then bewilderment that slowly gave way to a deep, unmistakable fear tinged with awed respect. Clark perched casually on the edge of the table, swinging his knife back and forth at the end of its long cord. He jerked an elbow at the bright heap on the floor, spat out harsh-sounding words, his mouth twisted in contempt.

Markham glanced anxiously at Brady who answered as though his lips were stiff. "God knows what George is trying to do. He said something like *What's all this peace-pipe and fixings? What made you think I was at war with you?* Sounds a lot meaner in Indian."

Clark turned to Trottier. "All right, Major." Trottier gave an order in French and a militia-sergeant clumped into the room, butted his way among the Indians as though they were tethered horses. A key grated again and again and the sergeant shoved clear holding up a tangle of leg-irons. "Thank you," said Clark. Then without raising his hand he swung a long forefinger at the Indians and spoke again.

Markham edged closer to Brady. "Can you get this?"

Brady muttered, "Goes something like this: *You got my proclamation. I've heard you talking about it. By law I can have every one of you knocked on the head.* Hell, they know that! *Tribal custom. But you Stinkers just aren't worth it. You came here to catch a sleeping bear.* That means George, of course. *And you fumbled around like a passel of drunken badgers. I ought to drive you out into the woods but, hell, you've shown you're no hunters. You'd starve to death and I don't crave any kind of killing.* Oh, oh, oh! Is George crazy? You don't talk to Indians like that! You give 'em presents, flatter the guts out of them. Easy, George, easy! *You must be running scant of food in your camps and you sure aren't men enough to get any for yourselves. We got to treat you bear-hunters like squaws. We'll feed you and stock you with enough to get back to your home-lands. Now, you squaws, get the hell out of this house!* Oh, my God, George must have spent the rest of last night with a rum-keg!"

The Indians were as immobile as ever, but Markham was sure that along with the fear and respect that he had seen in their eyes something very like admiration had appeared. He muttered, "He's got 'em, Phil."

Brady shook his head. "It's all wrong! An Indian never shows what he feels. Hey, here it comes. That Peoria chief back there. Two Iowas are holding up their hands to show they're with him,

and an Ojibway and a Sauk-and-Fox. The Peoria'll spill out a lot
of slick molasses, swear we're all friends. Then they'll go home,
cook up some new hell and we'll be right back where we started."

The Peoria, a tall man with a broken nose askew in a lined face,
croaked out, "O Gitchi Mokoman —"

Brady sighed. "Won't matter much what he says. Same old talk!
He says his young men 'have been listening to the songs of the
Bad Birds in the forest' and got tricked into war by British lies
about us. Now they can see that the Big Knives are true warriors.
They want to shake hands with all of us. They ask mercy for their
squaws and children and for the crowd that raised hell last night."
Brady's mouth tightened. "This is the end of it. George can't say
yes and if he says no we'd better scoot back to Kasky and fort up
with the rest of the regiment."

Clark seemed to be paying only perfunctory attention. Then he
spoke briefly and Brady's eyes dulled as he translated. "He says
perhaps they better go back to their British friends. Maybe, he
says, the British are really as strong as they claim to be. Maybe.
But if they're not, the tribes'll get all slashed up when the Big
Knives finish off Hamilton. God! He ain't said yes and he ain't
said no, but he can't teeter forever. He's got to plant his feet. Hey
— what's happening now?"

There was a rustling in the crowd and a Winnebago chief faced
Clark, then turned and motioned to his fellows. Two young men
rose, drew themselves up, wrapped their blankets about them and
moved to the front. Heads high and with a fierce pride in their
eyes they met Clark's glance, sank to their knees and drew their
blankets over their heads. The chief spoke a few quick words, held
out a tomahawk to Clark who gripped it. The chief stepped back.

"What the devil's this?" asked Markham back of his hand.

Brady spoke dazedly. "I'll be God damned. The chief asked if
the lives of those two would soften the heart of Gitchi Mokoman
so that his mercy will extend to all the tribes here who listened to
the songs of the Bad Birds in the forest. Something like that."

"Hostages?"

"Hell, no. George'll have to split the skulls of those two to show the rest that he means all right. Easy job. Just a crack on the back of the head that won't take but a second apiece. And — hey — don't flinch! Those devils are watching the rest of us, as well as George. If they think we're queasy, they may swing back against us, figure we're not real fighting men."

Markham set his teeth, forced himself to watch Clark and the kneeling braves. The little hand-axe swung in a bright arc, then bit into the wood of the table. Clark took a great stride forward, flipped back the blankets from the pair, then levered them onto their feet with a great heave, turned them about so they faced the rest of the Indians. He spoke rapidly and there was an unmistakably gay lift to his voice. His arms went out, fell about the shoulders of the two braves. Brady, staring incredulously, kept up his translation but somehow Markham felt that he knew the sense of the Indian words as Clark spoke them. *These are my friends and the friends of my friends. You call them young warriors. To me they are chiefs. Let them come to me when they will. Through them you will hear my pledge that on our part there will ever be peace between the Big Knives and the tribes gathered here today at Cahokia. They will arrange meetings between me and all your principal men. What you have to say to me, I shall hear from their lips.*

It was too much for Markham to take in. Clark had brushed aside the peace-tokens. He had clearly said that what the tribes did was of no concern to him. He had spoken scornfully of the attempted capture of himself, had called them a pack of squaws, had told them roughly to get out of Cahokia. Now he was not only hailing as friends the two young braves who had offered up their lives, but had elevated them to chiefs' rank, calmly assuming recognition of his right to do so.

Phil's voice sounded as though he were being choked. "He's pushing his luck too damn far!" As though in rebuttal, an approving murmur rose from the packed Indians and feathered heads nodded in slow gravity. Across the room the broken-nosed Peoria rose, calling, "O *Gitchi Mokoman* —" Clark merely smiled pleasantly, indicated the two young braves. The Peoria hesitated, then went on, his tones wailing out, reaching unexpectedly high notes, breaking into weird quavers, rumbling deep in his chest. When he had done, the pair faced Clark and chanted out the Peoria's words.

"George has done it," mumbled Phil weakly. "The Peoria's speaking for all the tribes here and a lot that ain't. Says they'll keep out of this war if that's what George wants, but their hearts are with us." He passed his hands over his face. "I'm plain dizzified and that's a fact. I can believe anything now."

Markham started to speak, fell silent as, lit up by wisdom after the event, all of Clark's moves assumed a clear pattern in his mind. The Colonel had conducted himself throughout like a shrewd, wary merchant using his wits to make up for an almost total lack of capital. The Indians had had one commodity that he desperately needed — their neutrality. By careful steps he had forced them to come to him and then had shown a complete lack of interest in what they had to offer. And he had brazenly flouted the most cherished of Anglo-American tenets in dealing with Indians by refusing to send them even the tawdriest of presents.

He had consistently acted as though he had thousands of men, tens of thousands of dollars to call upon if he saw fit. Sure in the knowledge that the Indians knew of de Leyba's lavish entertainment of him in San Luís, he had further bolstered the notion that powerful allies stood with him by showing himself on the friendliest terms with uniformed Creole and Spanish officers who obviously deferred to him. And who could say what the Indian mind would build out of the news that the faraway monarch whom they had for generations personified as "their great French father" had joined the war on the side of the Big Knives?

Another point came to Markham's mind. Immediately after the bungled attempt at kidnapping, Clark had given a ball, where Creole, Spaniard and Virginian had gaily danced the sun in, without adding a single extra guard. All this, seen from the vantage point of time, had led most logically into the events just witnessed where the tribes, having been rebuffed and insulted, had ended by almost prayerfully tendering Clark their neutrality which he grudgingly deigned to accept.

It all sounded so easy, so logical in retrospect — Markham looked up hopefully as a slow hush settled over the packed room. Could this be the end? But blankets rustled, moccasins scraped on the floor as a Potawatomi, two Ottawas and a Sauk-and-Fox began clamoring for attention. Resignedly, Markham made himself as comfortable as possible against the wall, ready to weather another hour or two of orotund fetidity.

X

Victory for Father Gibault

THERE were more days of speeches, of meetings in packed, stifling rooms, of conferences in quiet spots along the banks of the great river, or in the crude shelters of the maple-sugar camps that lay not far to the north of the town. Sometimes all of Clark's men and the Creole officials were present, along with Nieto until duty called him back to St. Louis. At other times, Clark might meet alone with a few Indians. Once a single chief came in, unescorted, and was closeted with Clark for long hours that ended in a magnificent, oratory-filled banquet in the chief's honor. When it broke up, he was presented with a fine new officer's coat of British scarlet faced with deep blue and stiff with gold braid, the only gift, to Markham's knowledge, that Clark had bestowed on any of the tribesmen. Later he asked the Colonel about this odd guest and was told that he was a chief with far-reaching power, that he had come all the way from Detroit to see Clark and his command. He had liked them and, as a result, had given Clark the fullest details on Colonel Hamilton, the Detroit defenses, garrison, militia and available Indians. Perhaps even more valuable, he had assured Clark that Hamilton had had no word of the American invasion, knowledge that the chief himself had only reached by an involved process of deduction and reasoning. There was no danger, said Clark, of the chief's sharing his knowledge with Hamilton.

A few hours later, to Markham's astonished relief, the Indian villages vanished as utterly and swiftly and silently as the dawn mists of the Mississippi. Without a sound the tribesmen left, without a trace save for their ringed tent-sites and the circles of their dead fires. The empty fields had barely brought Markham their message before Clark was shouting and whooping in the *Place* by the stone house, whistling up a party for the trip back to Kaskaskia. Markham ran through the rising glow of the day, shouting for his horse, but Clark reached laughing from the saddle and caught the slack of his shirt. "Thought you were going back to the flesh-pots of Kasky, did you? Not with Pollock's goods coming across from St. Louis today!"

Markham ducked under Clark's forearm, neatly broke his hold. "You're getting soft, Colonel. Out of practice. What's that about Pollock?"

"Today. Phil Brady's staying behind with you. Rip everything open. Estimate the value. See what we can sell right now and what we should hold for a better market. Hell, I don't need to explain to a trader like you. Use the old Baynton, Wharton and Morgan warehouse at the southeast end of town. Keep me posted." With a final slap Clark wheeled and rode off.

Slow barges butted their way from St. Louis to the Cahokia wharf, were unloaded by Bowman's men and Creoles. Low-slung carts with small front and huge rear wheels trundled over the summer-crisped grass to the old stone warehouse to unload barrels and bales and kegs and sacks. In the main room where the sun slanted through deep-cut windows Markham and Brady directed the unpacking and recording, saw the long trestle-tops slowly vanish under cases of razors, of scissors, piles of bright blankets. Fat reels of glossy red and yellow and purple ribbons, of wildly striped and banded ribbons crowded against clusters of nail-kegs that gave way to stacks of men's wide-brimmed hats.

Creoles scratched away with busy quills as Markham or Brady called out the contents of each unit. "Ivory combs, Phil, right out of the Congo swamps or I'm a bumboat-man. What are these little pots of paint? Face-paint for Indians? Right. Vermilion, ochre, black, green, ten of each. Forty-eight boxes of Havana-carved rosaries. Here's three cases of muskets. *Allons-y, Pierre, ouvrez-donc!*"

Another sunrise and more ripping of boards and screeching of nails. "There you go, Mark! Gorgets, silver-gilt and brass, a gross of each for the Indian trade. Hi-yi, who's going to get these silk underpants? No squaw could keep 'em a second before her brave'd grab 'em for himself. Four bales ruffled shirts and twenty cards of gilt and brass and says-it's-silver buttons. Shoes, men's and gals'. I'll bid in a pair of men's. Moccasins are all right on the trail but after all they're nothing but a decent way of going barefoot. Pots, pans and kettles, all mixed up with beaver-traps."

Markham hoped for a break in the flow of barges so that he could cross to St. Louis and call on Mme. de Liliac, but the slow stream continued with just enough regularity to tie him to the east shore. Then on a melting summer evening, the head boatman shouted that only four loads were left, two of them small. "Good," said Markham. "Will you take a note over on the last return trip, Georges?" "*Entendu,*" shouted Georges as he poled away from the wharf.

Markham walked slowly up to the town, where he found Captain Bowman waiting for him by the big stone house. "Rider just in with a letter for you from Kasky, Mark. Here — catch!"

Markham caught the sheet and opened it, frowning as he scanned the black lines. Clark's script was legible but his treatment of foreign names was something more than carefree. Prairie du Rocher, a hamlet near Kaskaskia, appeared as "Parradaroosh" and "de Lebrau" could only be de Leyba. He nodded to Bowman. "All serene, Joe. He'd written 'Jerboath' for 'Gibault.' No word from him since he left to capture Vincennes all by himself for us. The Colonel's a bit worried. But the main thing is he wants quick action on that Pollock stuff." He stowed the letter away. "How does it happen he's worried? He sounds pinched."

"Oh, George'll be all right, Mark. It'll take time for everybody to get used to Virginia paper, that's all. Those close to us are all right but when they try to pass it to folks that don't know us, they get it shoved back on 'em. It'll all come out the way George wants it."

"Maybe, Joe. You know what I've been doing here and there for Clark, but I haven't been in on day-to-day doings like buying a bait of hay or a load of bear-bacon, so I can't judge. But I did hit this: a trader came through last week with a carved Indian pipe I wanted. He asked twenty-five shillings but backed off from ten dollars Virginia even at three shillings to the dollar. Then he saw this that I had and offered me the pipe and sixteen shillings, French and Spanish coin for it."

He held out a creased square of tough paper covered with writing. "Know all men by these Presents that Micajah Gremp hath deposited Four IV Beaverskins in My keep in good order and of the Worth of Six VI schillings each Skin and i have took from them Six VI Schillings for the Keep of Them and when they Be sold i will pay the Balance of XVIII Schillings for the whole Lot to any person who Presents this Sertification and Delivers it up to me at My keep by the great Rock close by the Shawnese town of Chillicothe on the River Scioto and done by my Hand this December 20 1778 (Signed) Jodab Buckpitt."

"Get that honored most anywhere," observed Bowman.

"Yes, I figured it would be worth a lot more than he offered me so I kept it. Wish I'd talked to him a bit more and found out why he was so set against our Virginia paper."

"Don't fret about bush-folk, Mark. Our paper'll always be solid with solid people. Come on in and let's open some brandy with Trottier before we eat a cold supper."

Through several rounds of brandy, through a protracted supper and, later, walking through hazy moonlight by the great river, Markham considered the question of Virginia paper money, reviewed in his mind the running account of the estimated value of the Pollock goods so far received that he and Brady checked and rechecked each day. He tried to recall all that he had heard of the origins of the expedition to the Illinois country and the various measures taken in its behalf. But here he had almost nothing to go on, since Clark had used him in a quasi-ambassadorial role rather than discussing financial matters with him.

Still brooding, he wandered away from the river, went up to the stone house and collected his equipment, left a hurried note for Bowman and Brady, the latter being off with some Creole friends on a rum-testing evening. Then he ran quickly to the stables, calling for Jacques Fournier, who saw to the Detachment's horses.

Markham broke his journey at the hamlet of St. Philippe just as dawn was flooding gold over the eastern prairies, then he was off again after a few hours' sleep and a meal at a Creole house. By midmorning he was skirting the ruined bastions and sagging walls of Fort Chartres. The great flood-ravaged stone wreck managed to look eerie and lowering even in the bright sun which struck through gaps in the masonry only to light up livid pools and dank caverns where unseen life rustled and slithered and plopped.

Beyond the fort, beyond the hamlet of Prairie du Rocher, the trail began a gentle ascent and Markham eased his mount to a walk. The dry, parching smell of summer-scorched grass rose from the ground along with whiffs of crushed aromatic herbs, pestled by the horse's hoofs, that were cool in throat and nostril. Locusts shot up in great arcs with a yeeeeing noise, spatted to earth like bombs from unseen mortars. Off to the right the Mississippi lay intensely blue, motionless in the still air as an endless band of cobalt glass.

Now the Kaskaskia River showed on the left, running with a dazzle of silver on the course that would finally swing it west to join the greater stream far below Kaskaskia town. There was a growing familiarity to all the land that lay before Markham under the brassy sun swimming in its high blue bowl and he touched his horse with his switch and resumed the thought that had been with him since leaving Cahokia. He felt an odd mixture of elation and apprehension as he considered his coming meeting with Clark, sure one instant that he was close to a solution of many major problems of the "Western American Army, Illinois Detachment," then shying away as he sensed unguessed factors that might upset his reasoning. The Pollock goods would mean a flood of cash that ought to cover immediate contingencies, but when that was spent or pledged —

He straightened in the saddle, staring off to the east where the ground shouldered up like rollers of the high seas. With a gesture that was automatic in its smoothness he unslung his rifle and caught the barrel in his bridle hand, then cleared the hilt of the knife that dangled under his shirt. The idiom of the trail sprang to his lips. "I'm a sad bastard if that wasn't musket-fire!"

Barely breathing, all senses straining, he brought his horse to an abrupt halt. Faint but unmistakable the sound came to him, the fuzzy *slap* of a musket. The lines on his face deepened as he caught the thin, hard crack of a distant rifle, then the musket's note twice. Muskets could mean only Indians, since the Creoles who had volunteered to ride with men of the Detachment in endless patrol far out on the prairies had been furnished rifles. The musket again, closer! A chill picture formed in his mind of a lone American or Creole, rifle empty, pursued by musket-armed Indians who reloaded as they rode.

A calm inner voice kept insisting that one rifle could do nothing to help that one fugitive. The sane, wise thing was to double back to Prairie du Rocher, collect a few Creoles and ride out again to possible rescue. Or it might be better to swing away from the sound of shots and veer into Kaskaskia on a wide tack. He gripped his rifle tighter, said, "Make up your damn mind" between his teeth, and gathering his mount, rode for the highest ground ahead.

The countryside opened up as though a curtain had been lifted. There was Kaskaskia off to the right, then a long sloping tableland running from the town to the center of focus and, off to the left, the Kaskaskia River with a little cluster of houses on the far bank. Lernault's Ferry, where Clark's whole command had forded the river on the night of the taking of Kaskaskia! A few faint eddies of smoke, visible in the still glass-clear air, seemed to hang above the stream. But where were the muzzles that had shot forth that smoke?

A wide sheet of silver suddenly sprayed out of the summer-shrunken river. Mounted men were whirling and weaving back of a sycamore grove on the far bank but still coming on — Indian, Creole, American? Due to the distance, the glare, and the gait of his own horse, Markham could not make out. He did not check his pace but gathered his reins ready for whatever the next move might be.

More rifle-shots stabbing quite close to the right front. Hoofs drumming behind a fold in the ground. Then a rider, four riders, a dozen burst into sight from behind the fold. They wore buckskin or linsey-woolsey and whooped as they rode, straining to keep up with the coppery-haired man who led them. A full length in advance he stood in his stirrups, reins loose, waved his hat with one hand, held up his rifle like a pistol with the other and fired high into the air.

Thick willows on the near bank stirred, shook, and an appallingly shaggy horse lurched out, bearing on its broad back a stocky, dark-haired man whose face, even from this distance, showed a thick black beard. He held a tattered green umbrella over his head like a parasol and his rusty robes fell back from sturdy bare legs and feet glistening from the passage of the ford.

Markham let out a wild shout of "Father Gibault!" and spurred his mount toward the priest, but Clark's bobbing head shot in from an angle long before Markham could come up. Clark's battered felt hat went one way, his rifle the other and his long-fringed arms nearly swept Gibault from the saddle. By the time Markham pulled up, Clark was alternately thumping Gibault's back and holding him off at arm's length, pounding his back again. The bed of the river spilled out half a dozen more men, scouts from the outer circle that always girdled Kaskaskia, who sat panting and grinning, shaking horrible rust-eaten muskets while their cherished rifles hung, muzzle down, between their shoulders.

Clark was shouting, "By God, Father, we've been fretted about you! Let me look at you. Thin! We'll feed you up. You're all right? Sure you're all right?"

Father Gibault finally managed to disentangle himself. "But

assuredly, *mon Colonel,* how may I be anything but all right when for long days I do nothing but tend to my prairie parish? A mere ride of a few miles each day in the finest of weather until I reach my Vincennes, then a few more miles for a few more days and behold, I return to my Kaskaskia. So have I spent many years of my life." He began to grin, almost apologetically. "But one day I do dally — the day just past, I play the schoolboy errant." He held down the shaft of his deplorable green umbrella with his chin, reached into his saddlebags and pulled out a dripping package, peeled off a thick wad of very wet leaves to show a mass of wetter moss, flipped that off to show more leaves and finally a pair of fine bass, each a good ten inches long. Looking more than ever like a truant schoolboy, Gibault went on, "I perhaps should not have taken the time, but I saw this stream of streams, this Eden of bass and I thought that I could not in decency return to Kaskaskia and face empty-handed my friend, *le Colonel.* So here is this pair. You and I shall sup on them at my rectory."

"You — you dragged yourself out of your way just to have something to bring to me?" shouted Clark. "Wonderful! But having you back, sound, is the best of all. I've been blasting and blasting at myself for letting you go out there alone. Now you're back and that's the big thing."

Markham, hanging on the fringes of the group that kept shifting as scouts and people from the town crowded about the pair, tried to get a good look at Gibault's face, but the shimmering green of the umbrella intervened. "Damn it, what did Gibault mean — 'empty-handed'? Trying to break it gently to Clark that he had had no luck at Vincennes?" He worked in among the wheeling horses and came almost abreast of the pair. Clark, one hand on Gibault's shoulder, was saying, "And what about Vincennes, Father?"

Gibault spread wide his fingers. "Peaceful enough to split itself. I made twenty-eight baptisms, nine marriages and was ready with extreme unction twice for the same man who thought he had eaten spoiled pork but instead had drunk too much brandy. Ah, and my old friend François Bosseron has made reparations to his billiard table but of such a nature that I nearly failed to beat him, *quoi!*"

"But the town itself! You remember our talk before you left?"

"Ah, a talk so cordial!" Gibault beamed at Clark, at other riders close by, then caught sight of Markham. "Ah, Monsieur Cape! You recall the packet of catnip that you sent after me to the ford when I left? It was received with much pleasure at Vincennes by Bosseron's house-cat, le Père de Lustucru. And behold!" He reached into the distended hood of his robe and fished out a very small, very sleepy and very black kitten. "The son of le Père de Lustucru, who will now make his home with me." He replaced the kitten, very much pleased with himself and with it.

"But the town!" cried Clark. "What's been happening there?"

Gibault looked apologetic. "There is so little that a priest may properly know of matters temporal. I merely go from door to door, I visit the family Gagnon, the families Viaux and Quinette and Valade and Gamelin and many others in the course of my duties. So when Dr. Laffond sits long hours in the blockhouse of Fort Sackville, at the edge of town by the Wabash River, and talks with the leading citizens, their thoughts do not reach me and I do not inquire."

"I know, I know, I know. But — but *what* have you done with Dr. Laffond?" said Clark, obviously swallowing his impatience.

"Ah!" A sunburst of comprehension lit up Gibault's face. "Our good doctor! He rode with me as far as the clearing of Jacques Leroux who was said to be in extremis from a quartan fever, but as he needed medicine more than prayer, I came on alone until your scouts met me and brought me in with them. Ah — I nearly forget —" From the other pouch of his saddlebags he drew a thick packet and handed it to Clark. "From that very doctor to you. It may explain things hidden from me, such as just why the doctor and the others talked so long in the blockhouse; just why the doctor happened to have one of your flags in his kit; just why the drums of Vincennes beat and people swarmed into the *Place* when the doctor and those others raised your flag over Vincennes and —"

Clark caught his sleeve. "What's that? Raised *our* flag?"

"Yes, as I myself noted as I entered the Duval house. Presently many men came to me, asking me what I knew of events in Kaskaskia and Cahokia. You perceive my dilemma? How could a priest gauge matters temporal? I could only assure them that my flock at Kaskaskia and at Cahokia seemed to me as happy and contented since your arrival as mankind may be on this earth. Later I heard much talk, which I cannot explain, about an oath that Dr. Laffond had administered to all the people and of free elections to come. When I left, all Vincennois seemed, like my good people here, happy and content, with one man saying to the other, 'Va! As a citizen of the United States I assure you —' or 'B'en sûr! en ma qualité de citoyen américain je vous dis —' But just *how* and *why* all these things took place, I must plead ignorance." Gibault shook his head sadly at his own shortcomings.

Clark's arms swept high and the sun struck full on his tanned face, glinted on his teeth as he threw back his head. Then his arms dropped to his pommel, and instead of giving a shout of triumph, he said half to himself and half to Gibault, "So our flag flies over Vincennes!"

But others caught the phrase. Virginians shouted, "Vincennes has joined in! They're with us!" The Creoles echoed, "A nous Vincennes! Vivent les Vincennois!" A scarred Virginian with cornsilk hair bright in the sun shouted, "Give a cheer for the little parson. He's done a man's job!" More voices joined in, roaring in French and English.

Then the mouth of Kaskaskia's broad street yawned ahead and the horses went rustling toward it through the tall grasses. The very houses seemed to stir as men and women came running, skipping, limping, lumbering down from the galleries. In shirtsleeves, in frontier leggings, in baggy knee-breeches they came, in bright bodices, in short silvery skirts above long crimson and green and yellow petticoats, in blue and orange and purple kerchiefs they came in a glowing mass to stare and then to swell the uproar.

In the street Clark's horse shied a little at the din and stir, but Gibault's placid broad-back bobbed on as though dragging a

plow down a gentle slope. Markham kept well in the van, vainly
trying to get Clark's attention. Then he heard Gibault call, "You
see, *mon Colonel*, how the whole town rejoices that good fortune
smiles on you!"

Clark shouted with laughter. "Now you're humming me,
Father. They're welcoming one of their own. Watch this!" He
cut sharply behind Gibault's horse, gave it a flick with his crop.
The mount managed to skip, then, nudged heavily by Clark's
horse, headed at a lolloping trot for the little church where someone was sounding the Louis XV bell. The people swerved across
the road and pelted after Gibault. Clark cried again, "See? I was
right. Get a good rest and we'll talk more this afternoon." He
waved his hat at the Creoles. "See that he has a fine dinner and
then make him keep quiet!" A babel of reassurance swept after
Clark as he rode at a sharp trot toward old Fort Gage at the foot
of the street.

Markham overtook him as he was dismounting by the headquarters house, where men of the Detachment ran to take his
horse. Clark stared as they both dismounted. "I thought I spotted
you at the edge of town. What did you come down here for?
Damn it, you must have missed a letter I sent to you at Cahokia!"
He tramped on into the house, his scowl at Markham battling
against his delight at Gibault's news. "Damn and all! This is wonderful." He tossed Laffond's packet onto the table and took his
familiar heavy chair. Then he waved vaguely toward Markham.
"Hope you've got some good reason for being here. See me in
half an hour. I want to look at Laffond's papers."

Markham seated himself opposite Clark and grinned at him.
"Going to court-martial me? Anyway, I did get that letter and
started down here last night. I've got the figures you wanted and
a few thoughts that maybe we'd better weave into something
solid."

"You started down last night? How could you have the figures
then?"

"You go ahead with Laffond. I'll stay right here so you don't get away and make all my ride for nothing. But better send for the Creole merchant you trust most. We might need him."

"What for? Well, all right. I'll get Gabriel Cerré." He went to the door and shouted to one of the men by the gate.

"Cerré?" Markham frowned. "I thought he was hiding out across the river because you had him spotted for stirring up Indians against our settlements. Yes, sure you did. And a guard around his house and his family restricted to the town."

"Don't miss much, do you?" smiled Clark. "Well, a lot happened while you were away. Cerré came in and talked to me. He's clean so far as Indians go. He's thrown in with us, taken the oath and all."

Markham gave a low whistle. "That ties things up for you, doesn't it? First off, you won over Gibault, the biggest moral influence on the Creoles. Now you've got Cerré, biggest trader on the Mississippi and the Missouri, too, for your material influence."

Clark broke Laffond's seals. "Yes. Gibault and Cerré. And they both came to me, not I to them."

Markham stretched out his legs and closed his eyes, dozing a little with the rustle of papers to keep him from quite dropping off. At the end of fifteen minutes the door swung open and a spare, swarthy man whose features seemed carved out of an oak-root entered, was greeted cordially by Clark and introduced to Markham as Gabriel Cerré. He bowed politely to Markham, then seated himself at the end of the table and waited for Clark to finish reading with the air of a man who has infinite resources of patience and strength. Markham noted the controlled passivity of his lined face, the dress rich enough for a city merchant and yet of stout enough material for the frontier. His stockings were obviously silk, though masked high by tough canvas leggings.

At last Clark dropped the final page. "By God! By God Almighty!" His voice rose, only to be steadied by an obvious effort. He spoke again, lower. "It's true, what Father Gibault told us. All true and a lot more!" He went on rapidly. "They all took the oath to the United States. Bosseron called up the militia and garrisoned Fort Sackville under our flag, their flag now, too, it is. Then Laffond met a lot of Indians who wanted to know what was happening and he told 'em — let's see now — told 'em that their old French Father, King Louis, had come back to life and was mad as hell at them for thinking of tying up with his old enemies, the British. There's the magic of that French Alliance again, Markham. So now their French Father tells them to side with us and be damn quick about it. By God, that's a smart man, Laffond!"

Cerré, who had been sitting with heavy-lidded eyes half closed, raised his jutting nose and chin. "I find that valuable," he said in stilted English. "Yes. Now the Indians spread quick word to tribe and to sub-tribe. Yes, matters arrange themselves very well."

"That's what we hope. Well, Mr. Cerré, it was good of you to come here. We've got a business problem which is why Mr. Cape rode down from Cahokia. But he wouldn't act without *your* presence. 'The most trusted man of affairs' was how he put it."

Cerré bowed his acknowledgment while Markham savored Clark's more than free adaptation of his own suggestion that a trusted local merchant be called in.

Clark went on: "It's just that I want to realize the means to go on with some measures that could not have been foreseen a few months ago. I can't wait for help from Virginia, so what we've got to do is turn some assets here into hard money."

Cerré observed quietly, "No doubt reference is made to those goods held in royal Spanish stores."

Clark started angrily. "How the hell did you know about them?"

Markham intervened. "Monsieur Cerré is a trader, Colonel, and I'm sure that some clerks in St. Louis, as well as Arkansas Post and Natchez and New Orleans, enjoy a small retaining fee from him. I used to do the same thing myself, and others, in turn, bribed *my* clerks."

"It is so." Cerré shrugged. "Months ago my St. Louis agent told me of the goods but never could I learn just what they were or find the key to release them. Perhaps one day you will tell me how you managed. But now let us return to our muttons."

Clark, reassured, sprang to his feet. "Good. I've got copies of the inventories locked in that chest.Take them into the room that overlooks the river. No, I'm not coming with you. I'd only be in the way of you two traders." He flung open a heavy iron chest, handed some papers to Markham. "No one'll disturb you." He shook hands with Cerré, clapped Markham on the shoulder and ran out into the sunlight shouting, "Len Helm! Where's Captain Len Helm?"

In the next room, whose plank ceiling shimmered green with reflected light from the Kaskaskia River, Markham found Cerré's keen gray eyes appraising him. "So, Mr. Cape, you are that young man certified by Charcot as riverman? He is not one to waste praises. And I heard other things concerning you before my return to this town. I am content that the Colonel chose you."

Markham bowed as he seated himself across the table. "The approval of Maître Charcot will frank me anywhere along the rivers, that of Gabriel Cerré is a sure passport afloat and ashore. I am honored." He laid his papers among the inkwells and sandboxes. "Shall we go on in French or English?"

"As it pleases you. When we weary of one tongue we may shift to the other, as a man rests himself by shifting to fresh linen. Now do I find myself right in assuming that the Colonel wishes our joint estimates of the value to him in cash of these goods?"

Markham smiled. "He didn't say so, relying, I suppose on our common sense. I have seen all these goods, Monsieur Cerré, except those bargeloads coming in today. I'll show you which they are as we go along. So, for this first item, first sheet, three cases mattock heads —" The two chairs hitched closer as though of their own will.

Time slipped by unnoticed. A Creole came in with plates of beef and lettuce and bread, jugs of coffee and wine. The pair ate absently, a fork or spoon poised forgotten as they debated a point or harked back to precedent. Outside, sleepy-looking canoes idled downstream. Bright birds shot from the treetops to raise silvery showers on the surface of the stream. From the far bank came shouts and irregular *pock-pocks* as unseen experts sent tomahawks spinning through the hot air to lodge in wooden targets. Men of the Detachment, whooping and laughing, rode horses down the bank where the animals sloshed their muzzles about and blew and gurgled.

The sun was dropping below the rim of the horizon and the church's Louis XV bell was sending its high, clear voice down the valley of the Kaskaskia River as Cerré shoved back from the table. "I cannot find agreement with you on these last items," said he wearily.

Markham rubbed his eyes. "Let 'em go. They balance against others where you were high." He rose stiffly. "Come on. Let's go find Clark at the blockhouse."

They left the building together and started across the old parade-ground where darkness made an ever-deepening pool. Fresh smells rose from the river to mix with the tang of dead grass. There was still a glow off in the western sky and all up and down the wide street beyond the stockade candlelight showed in window and on gallery like arrowheads in the nearer houses and bright dots in the distance. A violin wove a thin streamer of notes, strengthened as men's and girl's voices joined in with *"Mon père a fait bâtir maison / Fringue, fringue sur l'aviron — !"* and from the common-lands came, faint but musical, the lazy tonk-tank-a-tonk of cowbells.

The deep calm of the twilight village, added to the past twenty-four strenuous hours, fell heavy and mesmerizing over Markham. He almost tripped over the block of limestone that formed the lowest of the steps of the gallery of the blockhouse, and this trifling near-mishap broke the shell that was forming about him. He squared his shoulders, calling, *"Allons-y"* to Cerré as he ran up the steps toward the great square of orange light that marked the wide door.

Three fat candles stuck to a long plank-shelf shone down on

Clark, Leonard Helm and Will Harrod, who sat at a low table by the east wall. The air held a pleasant mixture of odors that told of fresh bread and roast meats and genial liquors. The Colonel threw up a long arm. "Pull up here and have a drink! You know these two captains, Len Helm and Will Harrod, Mr. Cerré? I thought so. Well, all done with your ciphering, are you?"

"We've got some figures," said Markham, seating himself. "Whether they're the kind you want, I can't say."

Helm pushed forward a stone jug. "Heartener," he said. "Helm's. Never brewed better. Maybe a sup'll let you say the kind of figures George wants to hear. A mug for you, Mr. Serry?"

Cerré raised a hand. "*Merci* — later perhaps." He glanced at Markham. "Shall we begin, Monsieur Cape? I do not wish to hasten matters but my family waits me up the street."

Markham rested his arms on the table. "Monsieur Cerré and I set the total value at ten thousand three hundred dollars for a round figure. Then —" Clark and Harrod started eagerly to their feet, Harrod exclaiming, "By God and by damn that does it!" Markham raised his voice. "That's the *value*, not the price. Figuring what it'd take to ship a lot of this stuff to people who'd want to buy it, figuring on brokers, storage charges, shipping costs and things like that, I'd say — Monsieur Cerré disagrees with me here, but he knows the country and I don't — you'd realize about seven thousand five hundred dollars hard money."

Cerré raised heavy-lidded eyes. "That is quite possible for a speculator, *not* for a trader. I say about six thousand, if for immediate sale. If you wish to wait, then very likely we touch six thousand seven hundred or even seven thousand."

Harrod sank back in his chair. "Mark! You're low, both of you, damned low. You've *got* to be! Otherwise —"

Helm broke in placidly. "Why, yes, I'd kind of admire to hear something that'd skitter round that 'otherwise.' "

Clark sat silent, eyes shifting from Markham to Cerré. Then he reached across the table, one hand on Harrod's shoulder, the other on Helm's. "Look at these two damn squinch-owl faces! All ready to hoot 'Calamity's a-comin'!' " Clark sprang up, paced up and down. "God damn it, if Mr. Cerré'd said nine thousand, you'd squawk that it wasn't ten, and if he said that, you'd egg Markham to say twelve!" He stopped short, hands on his hips. "So, between you I'm middling safe to count on getting something like seven thousand for the Detachment? Wonderful!"

Harrod's chair scraped back. "George! Count up your men! Then there's back pay and how the hell can we get along through the fall and winter? Someone going to drop rations and supplies out the clouds?"

Clark spoke softly. "Will, Will, did you ever know of anyone with me starving or getting shut of powder and no more coming in? Sit by and get your breath, and you, Len. If you two'd ever read a trail the way you're reading me now, both your scalp's be hooped in some Shawnese cabin. Now, Mr. Cerré, you figure we can get around six thousand at a quick sale, but more if we wait. How long might that wait amount to?"

Cerré's face was impassive. "Eight months, eighteen months — who may say? Some of the goods are fit only for the Indian trade along the Great Lakes and up the Missouri. We might even have to deal with Montreal and Quebec. Yes, yes, there are ways, I assure you. Shall we say a full eighteen months might realize — ah — eight thousand dollars, Monsieur Cape?"

"The field is new to me, but I'd say yes. Now for the quick sale. You spoke of people along the river and —"

"Un moment." Cerré turned to face Clark. "There will be no need of them. For a sale of the quickness needed, I say now — at this instant."

"What!" cried Markham while Clark stared at Cerré.

"As I say. Let us divide between the high and the low figure and say not less than seven thousand. If that be acceptable, consider matters arranged as of this moment."

Clark caught the edge of the table in his big hands. "Now? But — but damn it, you've got to get your buyers in, hold a vendue. I know enough about trade for that."

Still impassive, Cerré said, "I, Gabriel Cerré, assume ownership from this moment, and from this moment will honor all drafts endorsed by you up to that amount."

Clark sat down slowly. "You're paying that — or giving credit, which is the same thing?"

"Yes, in my quality of American citizen. I shall have partners of course. With me will be René Auguste Chouteau and —"

"René Chouteau!" cried Markham. "The stepson of Laclède who built St. Louis?"

"The same, and — ah — *tenez* — Charles de Charleville of this town, Georges-Abel LaChance of Cahokia. Possibly two more."

Clark sat silent as though unbelieving. Markham, bewildered, said, "But LaChance went down to Arkansas Post last week and Chouteau's off up the Missouri. They've got to agree and —"

Cerré rose imperturbably. "I agree for them, now, and shall inform them of it later." He bowed to Clark. "And now, *Monsieur le Colonel*, with your permission, I return to that family of mine which expects me since some hours, I having forgotten to send them word." He bowed to the four, settled his hat on his head and walked out of the blockhouse.

The room was very silent after Cerré's departure. In a far corner, a field-mouse gnawed like a tiny saw on a thin board. Up the street a horse kicked dully at the side of its stall and the two sounds, one brittle, one solid, were loud in Markham's ears. Then Harrod shouted, "God damn it, what good does that do us? Just a few thousand dollars to look after a hundred seventy men!"

Helm pushed the pitcher toward him. "Now, Will, when you got *nothing*, a quartern of *something's* mighty big, ain't it, Mark?"

Markham nodded, eyes on Clark, who suddenly shot from immobility like a released spring, his palms swinging together in a pistol-smack. "All right!" The words came swiftly. "Now we're moving. Markham, you missed a lot, being away, but we've been up kind of a tree. A lot of the boys want home, saying their enlistment time's up and they've got families back east. I can't argue against that, so I'm sending Will, here, and John Montgomery with all that ought to go — that's about two companies — down to Corn Island and home from there."

Harrod slapped the table. "No! I said send Joe Mason, not me!"

"I need you bad right here, Will, but home you go." He turned to Helm, who sat immersed in his eternal village-elder-at-rest calm. "Lennie! Bosseron down at Vincennes is hollering for an American officer to take charge there, so away you go with any six men you choose. You'll look after all Indian questions too and I don't know a better man for that west of the Alleghenies."

Helm looked placidly pleased. "That's kindly said, George. I always did admire to see new towns."

"I knew that'd suit you. Now what next — hey! I got it! Will, please light out and tell Alphonse Beaubien that I want to settle my own accounts with him tonight. Find Father Gibault and say I'm sorry I can't eat those bass with him, because I've got to get ready to start for Corn Island come dawn."

Markham and Harrod both shouted, "You're *what?*"

But Helm smiled blandly. "Now George, I ain't thought of that. Yes, it'd be real smart." He tilted his mug with a purring chuckle.

As Harrod left, scowling, Clark called, "Will, make sure a lot of folks hear you talking to Beaubien and Gibault."

Markham rubbed his forehead. "Calm off for a second and tell me what's really happening? It's all moving too fast for me."

The pitcher gurgled as Helm refilled Markham's mug. "It's just George, acting natural, just hitting his stride."

"Stride, hell!" cried Markham. "Are you going to leave two companies stranded here all alone while you hit for the Ohio with the other two?"

But Clark was leaning against the door-jamb shouting orders to Captain Montgomery somewhere out in the dark. Then he was back, crouching over a long list of names under a candle. He was at the door again, bawling for a runner to start for Corn Island at once. "And tell him to keep moving! When he gets to Corn, have him send word so it'll meet me on the trail whether or not there's low water on the north side of the Falls of the Ohio!"

Men began stamping in, filling the room with shouts and the thump of moccasined feet, with a shower of orders and questions that rained on Markham's bewildered mind and glanced harmlessly off Helm's rock-like serenity. Then the moccasins were gone and the clatter of boots ushered in a surge of baggy breeches, bright petticoats and bodices. Kaskaskian voices beat insistently, "Non, non, non! Jamais de la vie! Ah, la misère! Que notre Colonel reste chez eux qui l'aiment, qui se fient à lui!"

Hands folded over his comfortable paunch, Helm observed, "Mark, when George sends someone out to do something, that something's apt to get done proper. And — yup! Here's the parson!" He waved blandly with a genial " 'Evening, Reverend!" as Father Gibault, rusty black robes carefully brushed and new-shaven chin firm as ever, plowed through the press of his parishioners. Clark was on his feet, both hands out. "So you came all the way down here, Father!" He stuttered as though a little embarrassed. "And all my other friends, too! Take this chair, Father." He laughed excitedly. "And Madame Aubain. Brought the new baby to say goodbye to his friend, eh? And Grampa Guérin! Sit right here by Father Gibault and —"

"So, you leave us, Colonel?" Gibault's voice cut in, low but carrying.

Clark laughed rather sheepishly. "Not that I want to, Father, but things are so peaceful here — you understand —"

"We wish them to remain so," began Gibault. The crowd caught at least the sense of his words and a rumbling roar swelled up. Old women and young pressed close, caught at the thrums of Clark's shirt as they cried out in protest. Men pumped their hands up and down as they milled about and added their shouts to the general chaos.

Like a swimmer groping for something solid in a freshet, Markham turned to Helm, who explained in kindly tones, "See, Mark — they ain't wanting George to go."

Two of the candles shivered out in a joyous explosion of voices and in the remaining glow Markham saw Clark and Gibault borne inexorably toward the door and out into the summer night by a whooping, stamping mass of Creoles. A wild burst of song erupted with full voices, reedy voices, high, clear voices mingling. The procession broke into an impromptu dance of rejoicing

as arms were linked and the song roared louder, *"En avant / La
bande joyeuse / Dieu protège / Les bons vivants / En avant —"*

Helm blew out a cloud of smoke from his stubby clay pipe. "See?
George told 'em he ain't going after all," he observed contentedly.

Chanting and shouting sounded in gusts, now blurred, now distinct. Soon Clark came running with his light tread onto the gallery, calling back over his shoulder and waving. As he entered,
Helm chuckled, "So you aim to tarry in Kasky after all!"

Clark laughed, coppery head back and eyes bright. "You've
got second sight, Lennie. What did you think of it all, Markham?"

Markham perched on the edge of the table as Clark leaned by
the mantel. "Couldn't help wondering what you'd have done if
they hadn't raised such a row."

"Oh, I'd have thought of something else." Clark grinned. "As it
is, word will spread mighty quick all through the prairie country
and way beyond that things are so safe here that I can leave just a
few men in Kasky and Cahokia and go back to the Ohio with the
rest. And it'll be said that my Creole friends kicked up such a
din that I let them talk me into staying. The two companies'll
go just the same, of course."

Helm beamed proudly on Clark. "That was mighty cute
stradgetics, George."

Clark eyed Markham, then said, "So *you* figure I'm wrong?"

Markham hesitated, then said slowly, "Knowing just what I do
and no more, I'd clear all my accounts here and take the whole
command way back up the Ohio until I was in close touch with
Virginia. Colonel, you've done everything possible with what
they gave you back home. You stand to lose it all by tarrying."

Clark stood in a familiar pose, hands pushing against the
mantel and one foot on an andiron. After a moment he asked
sharply, "What's the matter with what I've done?"

"I don't say anything is. I just say I'd do differently. The Pollock stuff'll bring enough to clear off your payroll up to now and
all local debts. What next? The Creoles can't support you out of

local funds. You can't live off the country like the old condottieri without having to fight the Creoles. De Leyba's very friendly, but Spain's neutral."

"I've got other resources," said Clark coldly.

Markham dropped from the table. "Your Virginia paper money? That damn well won't do. It'll back up on you when people try to pass it outside these towns. Pretty soon you'll be getting one dollar's worth for ten Virginia, then for twenty, then a hundred. I've seen it happen before in other places. In all common sense you've got to get closer to your real source of support or you'll smash sure as hell."

Clark wheeled about. "God damn your common sense!" His big fist thumped the table. "We'd be chucking everything we've won and never get another chance. Everything we've been scared of would happen. There'd be nothing to beat off the tribes that the British control out of Detroit. Kentucky'd be lost for good. The tribes'd hit east over the mountains into the frontier settlements and then where would Washington's armies get their grain and beef and leather? The frontier'd get rolled east against the seaboard and that'd be the end. We'd be Colonies again and not States and you know what that'd mean."

Markham said doggedly, "Stay here and the best that can happen is that you'll all be absorbed by the Creole towns and not a ripple to show. That is, if Hamilton doesn't send a few hundred Indians to finish you off first."

"No!" Clark shouted. "This is where we can beat Detroit and its Indians. It's worth every risk. Credit against the Pollock funds meets current charges, but I went way beyond that. I had to promise the blue hills of heaven and every God damn golden step leading to 'em to keep the boys who *are* staying. And I promised before I knew about the Pollock values. I had to call on Patrick Henry's secret orders to me to cover myself and they're mighty thin cover. 'Take every possible measure to secure whatever may advantage the State.' I say it's 'advantaging the State' to hold what we've got here and hit out for more. Virginia's going to support us. She's *got* to support us. Damn it, she *will* support us!"

Dead silence followed Clark's outburst, broken only by the whisper of ashes falling in the fireplace and the ceaseless tinkle of crickets outside in the night. Then his manner changed abruptly. He poured a mug of Heartener and grinned over the rim at Markham as he drank. "See how I mean common sense is a luxury? Now we've got a few more things to fix up and you're one of them, Markham. You've done some prime work for us and I'd be damn glad to keep you here. But I promised you'd go east when the first chance came and now it's come."

"East?" cried Markham, and then was aware of a feeling of anticlimax.

"Yes, go on with the two companies and soon or late you'll hit Fort Pitt and an open road from there on. Or you can go to Vincennes with Len and his boys. You'll travel faster, and once on the Wabash you'll find reliable Creole guides to take you on to Pitt."

"Sounds fine!" Markham tried to force excitement into his voice.

Helm beamed on him. "We'll have a heap of fun on the trail, Mark."

Markham rose. "I couldn't ask for better company, Len. Colonel, thanks for all you've done for me. I hope I didn't ruffle you too much, but I had to tell you how I felt about that Virginia paper. I'm still thinking about it. So now I'm off and wishing you luck. But I'm *not* heading east. I'm going to St. Louis to see about passage down the Mississippi to New Orleans!"

Helm stared open-mouth and Clark exclaimed, "To New Orleans? And for months he's been yelling about a chance to go east, Lennie!"

"New Orleans it is," said Markham. "Oliver Pollock's known up and down this river and a good span east and west of it. He's agent for Virginia as well as for the Continental Congress. If he'll back your money, by God, it'll pass freely along the Missouri headwaters or Detroit and Montreal as well as in Illinois. Now good night to you both. I've got some figuring to do!"

XI

River Be Gentle, Lady Be Kind

THE CANOE seemed to hang suspended in a dimensionless opacity that gave no sign of where fog and water joined or where the sky curved upward. Irregular dark bands off each gunwale had the effect of flowing endlessly astern as though the craft lay on a slow treadmill. Guiding by the faint thrill of the current against the bow, by the barely audible voice of the river, Markham handled his paddle cautiously. His fingers on the haft were sensitive as a violinist's to the vibrations that ran up through the wood with their mysterious messages of what lay about and below the blade. A few feet down, the outline of a sunken keelboat showed vaguely and the play of the blackish-silvery light made the old wreck seem to stir as though rocking gently at its riverbed mooring.

He drove his paddle a little more strongly, frowning. "I may have to raise that old keeler yet to get to New Orleans," he thought. "H'm. Wonder where the hell I am. Somewhere north of Fort Chartres and south of Cahokia, headed west. God damn the luck! Everyone I needed to see at Cahokia's off up the Illinois. Joe Bowman told me de Leyba'd left St. Louis to look at fort-sites up the Missouri, and the syndic of the boatmen there's out at the lead mines. If I drop across to Ste. Geneviève, Nieto might know something about a downriver boat." He braked suddenly and swung the canoe about.

He was clear of the fog-bank in a world all blue and gold and green, lying within a yard of a partly submerged tangle of deadly jagged driftwood. Beyond ran a broad avenue of blue water backed by towering limestone cliffs and in the middle distance a keelboat lay anchored, bow to the south.

About a fifty-footer, he reckoned, sharp-bowed and square-sterned like a hundred others. Not quite like. Every plank shone with fresh paint. The deckhouse rose high enough to promise plenty of headroom and was lighted by round glassed ports set in bright brass. A roofed open space amidships could hold twelve rowers easily. The after cabin was rich with red paint and gilding, with carved sliding panels heavy enough to ward off musketry and a hint of glass casements showing behind them. The cabin ended a few feet from the stern, but the roof was carried on to overhang the water and was supported by carved gilded columns, sheltering a sort of private balcony. From the stern, a big Spanish flag stirred to the touch of a rising breeze.

A stocking-capped man stood by the tiller of the vast rudder that ran from the roof to the water astern. Along the treadway, in the bow, over the roof, crewmen ran, getting ready to take advantage of the lifting fog which still lay thick downstream.

Markham, paddle trailing, sat staring, taking in the musketry loopholes in the carved panels, the swathed swivel-guns bow and stern. "San Juan de Ulloa," he read. "And the royal standard. Very official. Where did the Dons keep it hidden up there at St. Louis? I'd never even heard of it." He gripped his paddle tighter, slid carefully past the driftwood, cut into the current and drove on, shouting, "Holà, le chaland! Holà, le patron!" As he swung alongside, two men ran onto the passe-avant or treadway, boat-hooks poised. He cried, "Merci!", then twisted away. The boat-hooks were jabbing at him and the men were yelling that he was not to come aboard, that he was not welcome and, more, if he lingered, people might fiercely enrage themselves.

A sound, piercing as the hiss of a great snake, froze the crewmen. "Pssst! Assez! Assez!" The master had left the helm and now stood at the edge of the roof, glaring down and demanding to know what it was that agitated itself. The crew bawled out the enormity of the intended trespass. The sun struck full on the master's thick, square beard and Markham, with a surge of hope, remembered meeting the man on the Place d'Armes of St. Louis. He shouted, "Ah, c'est vous, Maître Primeau! Quelle chance!"

Primeau stared, then bellowed, *"Par les cloches de Ste. Anne!*
Monsieur Cape!" (He made it "Kepp.") He rushed at his crew
with flapping motions as though shooing hens from a garden,
roaring that even such useless mouths should have recognized
one who had made the killing northern journey with commenda-
tions from the great Charcot himself!

Markham caught the treadway. *"Voyez, Maître Primeau,* I must
get to New Orleans on business of the most pressing for Colonel
Clark and the Western American Army! Have I permission to
board?"

Primeau dropped from the roof. "What? You have not heard?
The British have closed the river south of Natchez, even to our
craft. You of all people, a rebel American, have no hope of going
south."

"Closed the river? They can't do that!" cried Markham.

"No doubt. But they have. It is because of the raids of your
Monsieur Willing at Natchez and Manchac and the like. The
British claim falsely that this Willing was aided by Spain."

Markham suddenly remembered Oliver Pollock's anger at Will-
ing's unauthorized moves, his fear of British counter-measures.
Then he said urgently, "But you're going south. No boat like the
San Juan goes just between St. Louis and Ste. Geneviève."

"Ah, *we* fly the royal standard. They may halt but not stop
us."

"Maître Primeau, I assure you I do not go south to amuse myself. This is vital to all the Illinois country. Smuggle me through!"

The master clapped his hands over his ears. "I will not listen!
Only those in the service of Spain or authorized in writing by
Governor Don Bernardo de Galvez may as much as set foot on
this boat. I beg you, don't keep urging me!"

As he started to turn away, Markham cried hoarsely, "Authorization by Galvez? Oh by God, I've been asleep!" His right hand
shot out and clamped about Primeau's thick, sinewy ankle while
his left fumbled in his shirt. *"Tenez!* No, I do not joke and I do
not release you until —" He reached an oilskin packet up to Primeau. "There! Cut the stitches for yourself. There is Charcot's

certificate and — yes — the parchment with the dangling seals. Deputy Governor Galarmendi directs all servants of the Crown to aid my travels by all means at their disposal!"

Primeau scowled as he toiled through the unfamiliar Spanish. Then he flung out his arms and a great booming laugh rolled down the river. "*Magnifique!* So it is *ordered* that we aid you!" He slapped huge hands on Markham's shoulders and hauled him on board. "So I take you like a press gang. You will sign my crew list, with an X of course, to replace a man who deserted. You will stand watch, man pole, sail or oar, handle musket and swivel-gun if need be. You will draw regular voyage pay of sixty dollars." He handed the papers to Markham and eased himself onto the roof.

Markham stowed the papers away, gathered up his equipment and followed Primeau, panting with relief. "Give my pay to the crew," he called. "If you feel you owe me something, then assign me that state cabin aft."

Primeau's eyes bulged. "That cabin? Ah, for a moment I thought you serious. That is only for high officers of state. In it de Leyba and his family came north. Now the *San Juan*, having been refitted, returns and that cabin is given over to the family of a great factor from Quebec, a Monsieur de Liliac, by order of Governor Galvez. But they do not concern us." He suddenly raced to the edge of the roof roaring orders to the men bringing the canoe on board.

Markham leaned by the varnished mast, frowning. So Madame de Liliac's wait in St. Louis had ended. Under different circumstances the presence of such an attractive young woman might have added piquancy to the trip. But now he had his duties on board as well as his all-important mission. He was probably on her black list anyway, having done nothing, for all his talk, to help in her hunt for clues to her family. There simply had not been time, a fact which she might not appreciate.

Primeau came stamping back as though he had assisted at the mooring of a ship of the line. "*Voilà!* Now Bonnard, my *contre-*

maître, will show you the *San Juan d'Ulloa* and your duties on board her."

Bonnard was a lean, crop-bearded man, river-soaked and sundried, his stocking cap forward on his head so the tassel bobbed and swung endlessly before his eyes. Alternately batting at it or shaking his head, he dove into the forward section, Markham following. There was little new for him to learn as the *San Juan* was only a shorter, showier version of the *Poitou* and the crew were much like those of the upstream voyage. As they emerged from a low door amidships, Primeau leaned from the roof to call that the ladies in the state cabin would be glad to speak to Markham when his duties allowed. Markham pushed back his hat. "With me? How'd they know I was here?"

"Madame said she heard a man speaking French like a Prussian who has been taught by an Englishman and that it could only be you."

"She said what?" began Markham. Then he laughed. "Anyway my Spanish is better than hers. When can I call?"

Before Primeau could answer, the lookout shouted that the fog had vanished downriver, as well as to port. A watchman's rattle set up its imbecile cackle and a rhythmic "Hou-ha-*ha!* Hou-ha-*ha!*" told of anchors being raised. A twisted man with a fiddle under his arm slithered up to the roof like a water rat and the high notes of "*Fringue, fringue sur l'aviron*" sailed out. Bonnard gestured toward the rowers' benches and Markham slid automatically to a portside seat, dragging a long oar from the rack. A bristly man plumped beside him, seized the inner end of the handle. Before they had dropped the blade to the water, other men had filled their bench and the two ahead.

Markham's hands fumbled a little, then he feathered the blade, dipped deep and pulled with a long even stroke that lifted his body from the bench. His seatmate grunted, "*Ah, alors!*" as though satisfied and braced his feet beside Markham's. Along the surface went the blades of the *San Juan*, down deep into the water, up, back smoothly, down —

The normal routine of the boat, an injury to a crewman and a long stretch of difficult navigation kept Markham from answering Madame de Liliac. Like the rest of the crew, he was aware of her presence since the state cabin was so strictly out of bounds that many duties were affected by it. Unlike the rest, who accorded her a sort of exalted status, Markham could recall only too vividly his earlier talks with her in St. Louis, memories accentuated by his present monastic isolation. She rarely emerged from the roofed-in stern, though Primeau had a bench built on the starboard side of the roof with a canvas awning rigged over it. From the *passe-avant* or the bow, Markham caught a few glimpses of her there, reading or sewing, but there was never a chance to speak.

At the end of a watch during which an easy breeze left little for the crew to do, Markham sent word aft by Primeau and was told that Madame de Liliac would be happy to receive him in half an hour. He unpacked his best linsey-woolsey that was all a-swish with long red and yellow thrums in deference to his expected sally into Spanish territory, and went down the narrow companionway that led from roof to the ornate stern. Madame de Liliac, in dove gray touched with scarlet, received him as though he were an old and trusted family counselor. Four-year-old daughter Annette, in a miniature of her mother's dress and looking very like her save for her dark Creole eyes, rose from a taboret and dipped as fine a curtsy as her stubby little legs allowed. A gray silent maid, evidently at least part Huron, knelt by the door into the cabin and watched mother and daughter endlessly.

Conversation started easily enough but Markham found it hard to shake off a feeling of unreality. The carved, painted surroundings, the thick carpets on the deck, the comfortable chairs were alien to all his river experience, as were his hostesses, senior and junior. The setting and its people could not belong to a world of poles and cordelles and oars and dark, rushing water. He had a weird illusion that this elaborate stern was floating downstream alone through a purpling dusk, that if he pushed through the carved doors leading into the state cabin, he would look out on nothing but endless river ahead of him. He glanced across at Madame de Liliac, who had paused in the midst of trying to build her scattered memories into that childhood that had been hers before her seizure by Indians.

Her eyes were closed and she passed her finger tips lightly over her forehead. At last she shook her head. "It is so confusing." (They were speaking English at her request.) "Names, they come and go and end by telling me nothing." She dropped her hands. "It is useless. Just now you spoke of a river of New England, the Merrimack, and I thought it echoed in my memory. No. The echo was the Méramec River below St. Louis, unknown to me until I come here. This wandering through the past! My head splits of it." She smiled at Markham. "But not so much as to blunt my gratitude to you, Mr. Cape, for your thought."

"My thought? But I failed you in St. Louis about this. Here is my chance to redeem myself." He watched her, wondering if he had ever really noticed her smile before, a slow smile with her eyelids dropping slowly as though to meet the upturned corners of her lips and lifting slowly. He went on. "I can at least keep trying."

"That will be —" she hesitated, then finished quickly, "kind of you." She bent to Annette. "But this is all about ourselves, chérie." Annette's black eyes turned up to her, wrinkled in a smile, and then resumed their solemn study of Markham's red and yellow thrums that flowed and rippled with every movement. Her mother continued: "You see, we were wondering, Annette and I, how you come to be on the San Juan and not bound east. Have you given up that thought?"

"Not at all," he began, then hurriedly evaded this undoubtedly pleasant chance to talk about himself. She was a fellow-Yankee by birth but most of her life had been spent among people nearly always at bitter war with his. It would not do for her husband, probably a valued friend of the British in Canada, to learn from his wife that one Markham Cape had come to New Orleans to win support for the rebel George Rogers Clark. Let Primeau explain details that concerned the San Juan to her in case her curiosity was aroused. He said easily, "There seemed little chance of passage east up the Ohio, so I'm trying the sea route from New Orleans."

Her eyes widened. "But the British Navy controls the seas."

He tried to look inscrutably wise. "There are always steps and measures to be taken." He gave a slow wave of his hand that he hoped might seem mysterious. "Currents and implications of events may be read and queried — and used. You understand."

She nodded as though receiving a deep confidence. "But of course. I have often heard men speak so in Quebec and Montreal. I know what you mean." Markham nodded encouragingly and she went on, "You mean — nothing, though you say it with less bombast than most. Do not be chagrined. You have told me most politely that how you leave New Orleans can be no concern of mine, though it might interest such enemies as you and your people may have."

He laughed. "Actually, I was trying to tell you very impressively that I hadn't the least idea of how I'll leave New Orleans."

"That is better yet," she cried, dimples showing in her smooth cheeks. "You should come to the St. Lawrence. By mingling frankness with bombast you'd ruin all our merchants up there, it would be so new to them."

He watched for that slow smile again as he answered, "No, it's only by wrapping undiluted inanities in resonant profundities that merchants can thrive anywhere in the world. Besides, I wouldn't want to change the Mississippi for the St. Lawrence. Not right now, anyway."

She leaned her head back against a carved pillar and looked at him through long lashes. "I see nothing inane in *that*," she began in a lazy teasing voice. Then her manner changed abruptly. "*Mon Dieu,* Annette! The hour!" She said a few swift sentences in French while Markham quietly admired the way the quartering breeze molded her summery dress to her figure. Annette rose, curtsied again, then grasped her nurse's hand and murmured "*Bon soir, Monsieur*" as a half-panel of the carved door slid back.

"*Dormez bien, Mademoiselle,*" said Markham. Then he turned to Madame de Liliac, eager to recapture the teasing, personal tone of their talk. But she rose gracefully and followed Annette and the maid into the cabin. Over her shoulder she said, "We're grateful to you for giving us your leisure. If we do not have a chance to thank you before we reach New Orleans, Monsieur de Liliac will wish to write you in our name. His agent is Henri Dubois, who will be glad to receive word of where you may be found." Then she was gone, the panel closing after her.

Markham went slowly up the companionway. "Before we reach New Orleans — That's encouraging. Does she think I'm plotting an elopement or abduction, to turn so skittish all of a sudden? Oh, damn, the wind's dying. That means oars as long as daylight lasts and my watch'll get the bulk of it!"

Long miles below the junction of the Ohio and the Mississippi, where Markham and Phil Brady had left the *Poitou*, the *San Juan* worked south by the west bank in a channel that edged under eighty-foot cliffs shouldering up from monotonous green flatlands. Dawn was misty and two men stood in the bow, poles ready to fend off bulges in the cliffside while Markham watched from the mast for shadow or riffle telling of underwater hazards.

The sun broke through the mists and all at once the air was alive with twisting, writhing things that looked like lengths of dirty gray-black rope. They fell from the sky itself and spatted into the water. They slapped onto the deck and roof to contort in broken-backed agony. Primeau began bawling that Madame de Liliac close all shutters, *vite, vite!* and hurry her people inside, *vite, vite!* Markham stood frozen as the incredible fall continued, skidding overboard or hanging like wet stockings over the rails. One evil black whiplash gathered into horrible heaped coils a few yards away. Snatching up a boat-hook Markham started toward the hissing, rattling mass, only to be shoved back by Bonnard who, tassel still bouncing before his eyes, led a party armed with long, bright-bladed pikes. A frugal but acid burst of river oaths sent him back to his post, his skin creeping as he thought of what had fallen and was still falling behind him.

A quick glance aloft showed wild-looking, ragged men who

fringed the cliff edge and with forked poles pitched rattlesnakes, still torpid from the dawn mists, out into space. On deck, crewmen screamed curses, shook their fists and popped away with their outranged muskets. Markham looked again. The ragged men were whooping, slapping their knees and capering about. Two of them tramped toward the edge carrying a great canvas bag whose sides were turbulent with what could only have been fully aroused snakes.

Markham stepped back, unslung his rifle and sighted. Men on the cliff saw him, screeched derisively, mimed aiming a musket, bawling, "Boum, boum!" He fired. One man dropped his corner of the bag and seemed to be trying to cram his fist into his mouth. His partner stood transfixed, still holding his end. Then he let go, gave a great spraddling leap into the air, hit the ground and went bounding off out of sight. The rest pelted after him with wide, high steps. Slowly Markham relaxed, leaned against the mast while he primed and reloaded.

Fore and aft the *San Juan* settled itself. Slashed and tattered rattlers were heaved overboard, the last survivor hacked out from under a skiff. The men in the bow grinned at Markham, clapping softly in applause. Then they began chattering among themselves, saying that the people up there were wandering, rootless Frenchmen, Spaniards, a few Englishmen who roamed the west bank, working a little in the lead mines to the north, drifting off on long buffalo hunts or taking piratically to the river. This lot, they agreed, would not bother the *San Juan* again.

A roaring aft made Markham turn his head. Primeau was bellowing praise of Markham's shot, adding that it had earned a reward of thirty Spanish dollars. Markham waved in self-deprecation. But Primeau was not done. A full half of Markham's voyage money was here and now deducted for daring to take his eyes from the river long enough to make that shot. "And two dollars more," stormed Primeau, "for daring to continue to look aft while I tell you all this!"

"*Entendu*," replied Markham, facing obediently about.

The Mississippi bent and twisted, flowed due south, veered wildly to the west, the north, the northwest, east and south again only to repeat its gyrations. High earthen bluffs, flat oozing tangles that seemed to fester under the white rays of the sun, fine grassy meadow-lands slipped past the *San Juan* on either bank. The mouth of the Arkansas was passed and, after several exasperating miles that doubled back on themselves, a fair channel lay ahead.

Primeau called Markham aft and told him to take the tiller for a spell. No special orders. Just follow the channel. Lower sail and order out the oars if the breeze fails.

Markham tucked the tiller under his arm after a quick survey of the river. Aft, the Mississippi seemed to unroll like an endless bolt of green-blue silk. Port and starboard were nothing but shaggy green banks and slow swirling eddies. Forward beyond the lug-sail, the channel opened under the slant of the afternoon sun, lifeless as at the dawn of creation save for a few birds skimming and diving and dipping. The gray-brown of the sail bulged to a quartering breeze and he had only to keep the bow headed into the dark of the channel.

After about an hour the wind died. The sail dropped and men thudded to the rowers' benches. The bent fiddler struck up *"Je Suis des Bords de l'Ohio"* and the words came up muted from below. *"Ma vie est d'être dans mon vaisseau / De le guider avec addresse."*

Through the beat of the voices Markham heard an "Oh!" that was almost a gasp, followed by *"Si j'avais su."* At the head of the companionway stood Madame de Liliac managing to look at once like a truant schoolgirl and an offended marquise. A flimsy blue cloak fluttered in the last of the breeze and blocked the view of the maid who followed, arms full of cushions.

Markham masked a feeling of pleasure by an inward chuckle at seeing her momentarily ruffled. He said, "If you'd prefer a different helmsman, Maître Primeau can arrange it."

Her smile came and went quickly. "Thank you, but it really

makes no difference." She spoke pleasantly enough, following his lead in using English. She nodded to her maid, who spread the canvas awning, plumped the cushions on the bench and scurried away.

A long easy bend in the river allowed Markham to swing the tiller slightly toward her as she settled herself. As she did not look up, he said with mock formality, "I trust that you and Miss Annette have not been put out by this very hot weather."

"Thank you. We both do well. We all of us owe you much for routing *les vilains messieurs* the other day. Clemence told Annette that you routed them by throwing a magic knife at them," she said, as she arranged filmy scarves and opened a painted fan with long ivory sticks.

Markham watched the play of sun and shadow on her slim wrists while waiting for her to go on about herself and Annette. She drew an embroidery hoop from a brocaded bag and frowned prettily over hanks of assorted silks. He tried again. "Miss Annette must hear about my magic knife. I've really built quite a fable around it."

She said with a patient smile, "That was kind of you, Mr. Cape." Her needle winked quickly over the frame. "Perhaps it might be even better if you were to write out your little fable for her." She held up her hoop, bent over it again. "You can't imagine how few things there are to read to a little girl. Just old Monsieur Perrault's tales, 'Le Petit Chaperon Rouge' and 'Le Chat Botté' and the like. But children today are so sharp. They begin at once to ask how Puss can possibly put boots on his feet, shaped as they are, or they see a rotted pumpkin and wonder how a coach can be made out of *that*. As for the little girl and the wolf, well —"

Markham watched her out of the corner of his eye while his attention was on the channel ahead. She talked on pleasantly, rarely looking up from her hoop. She could easily go on and on like this to the end of his watch. He said abruptly, "There's another story that you might take up — why have you been at such trouble to avoid me since our one talk?" He was gratified to see that she had been shaken away from children's books. Her head went back, her eyes widened and she set her hoop on the bench. He met her gaze, adding, "Half a dozen words, written or spoken, might have been better, don't you think?"

She sat forward, elbow on knee and chin on small fist. "You have been out in the world longer than I, Mr. Cape. You have seen more of it than most men whom I have met. How much do I have to explain to you?"

His thoughts seemed to scatter as he met her long-lashed gray eyes, saw the sun in her hair, the rounding of her cheeks and the smooth lift of chin and neck. He managed to say, "You could begin by answering my question. It might answer yours."

Eyes still on his, she said, "I suppose you know that you're a very attractive young man."

Discomfited by her directness he answered, "That's something no one knows about himself. I suppose I am to some, not to others. Which are which I couldn't say." Cloudy water off the port bow was welcome, drawing his attention downstream.

"Be modest if you like — or act so. I have a very clear idea about myself so far as most men are concerned. Hence I probably am to you, particularly with no rivals aboard."

Still looking downstream he said quickly. "That's true, but —"

She made an impatient gesture. "Must I still explain? Very good. You are attractive to me and, I may add, that for you there can be no rivals here." She stopped, then her slow smile threw its magic toward him as he glanced away from the river. She went on, voice low and provocative. "It would be idyllic, would it not? Drifting down this great river, day after day, rocked by it at night, accountable to no one — on board, that is —"

He flushed, "I've never given you the least —"

"Oh, but you have! Without meaning to, I'm sure. Just by being here. And I admit to the idyll. But, like you, I know that we do not drift forever down this river. In three, at most four days, we come to New Orleans. You go looking for that home-bound boat of yours — in which I confess I do not believe very firmly —

while Annette and I are met by Monsieur de Liliac. The idyll, pretty in theory, becomes a teasing memory of something that never took place."

He stole a glance at her, shaking his head. "You're far too pretty a woman to have reasoned that all out and then said it."

Her French accent became more pronounced. "I say I am much too pretty not to say it to a man who is much too handsome not to have it said to him."

He slapped the tiller impatiently. "All you're saying is that you have no confidence in me, which is quite unfair."

She held up the hoop to the light in frowning absorption. "No? Let me say, Mr. Cape, that I have been married nearly ten years, that I have lived in Montreal and Quebec, cities which swarm with elegant, polished, often very handsome young men who are good-hearted enough, if allowed, to do more than pity the fate of young wives whose husbands are rather older and deeply immersed in affairs of commerce or state. I say this to show you that I do not theorize. In you I have faith enough. In myself, a good deal more. I have less in circumstances that sometimes play unexpectedly on people and turn excellent intent into regrettable results." A loop of bright silk rode a chance gust to the deck. Markham tried to duck under the tiller to pick it up but she was on her feet at once and saying *"Ne vous dérangez pas!"* caught up the silk without breaking her step and vanished down the companionway.

The tiller nudged Markham and he was just in time to swing the bow away from a yellowish patch ahead. He held the course steady. Fragments of Madame de Liliac's talk buzzed in the back of his head. But there was no point in analyzing it. Seventy-two hours, if the San Juan's luck held, would bring the great levee of New Orleans into sight. The passengers — mother, daughter, maid — would land and go about their own affairs. The crew, himself included, would then be paid off. He would go at once to Oliver Pollock's counting-house —

He shifted the tiller again. "Funny thing, I don't even know what her first name is," he thought.

Hours, days and nights glided by. The *San Juan* slipped by Natchez in a mist that cloaked both banks. Then it lifted, and the banks on either side unrolled in a slow-changing panorama. Sunset fell on masses of live-oak and magnolia. Sunrise brought cypresses standing in water with their high, sharp knee-roots huddled close like thin men bathing. Cypress yielded to more live-oak and high-reaching lilac. Strangling mistletoe wandered and climbed everywhere, straining up through ladders of dead branches, and on all sides Spanish moss hung draped in hopeless gray mourning.

The river widened to a coffee-colored lake. Broad-galleried houses, standing aloof from slave quarters, appeared with the green and red-gold of orange trees between plantings of indigo. The crew shouted and stared at this new world where life was thick on banks that had been deserted for so many long days and miles.

Close off the port bow the great levee began its long run down to the city. The green embankment was high as the cabin roof, shutting out the countryside beyond. A long, graceful fringe of willows burst from the summit. A farm cart drawn by white oxen, a bright-varnished carriage behind glossy blacks moved across the sky while the gravel of the levee road hissed softly under the wheels. At last a forest-bristle of masts showed like a ragged cloud far down the green wall.

Markham stood in the bow, waiting a call for his next task. He told himself that at that moment Madame de Liliac was seeing to the last details of Annette's clothing while the silent maid bent over curve-top trunks. He thought of offering her assistance in the business of landing, but Bonnard appeared, still tossing and flapping at his tassel, saying that Primeau wanted the two to go ahead in the canoe to deal with various port officials farther down the levee. "*Allons-y!*" shouted Bonnard. The final minutes of the voyage were running out.

It was mid-afternoon before Markham shook hands with Primeau for the last time and went up the steps to the crest. There he looked down on a sea of noncommittal roofs, hot and damp with a heavy, swampy smell of poor drains, poorer sanitation and rotting vegetation hanging over everything. He thought of the clean winds that flowed over thousands of miles of untouched prairie in the north as he tried to orient himself. When he spotted the towers of the Church of St. Louis he went down the stairs, heading for a long stone building flying a Spanish flag where he was to show his papers.

Bored clerks yawned over a form bearing Primeau's signature, pushed a sodden ledger out for Markham to sign, then told him to leave by another door that decanted him into a long stone passage onto which windows opened from inner offices. It finally ended in a blank wall with doors opening right and left. He took the right as the more likely exit and found himself in a windowless, boxlike little room with a door set in an angle at the left. Shrugging, he reached for the latch. The door flew open, closed noiselessly behind Madame de Liliac, cloaked and bonneted in blue.

He could only stammer out his surprise and pleasure as she spoke rapidly in a low, soft tone. "I saw you from the office where I waited. I was afraid we would not meet again. We have only seconds. Can you tell me that for a little while you may think of me, Markham Cape?"

Still shaken by astonishment he nodded, then said hoarsely, "More than a little while. Such thoughts will linger as that slow smile of yours will —"

She raised her hands as though in protest, but there was a catch in her voice as she said, "Now you see how wise I was on the *San Juan* always to be a coward and run from danger. Oh, so wise! But here, where there is no danger, I act oh so bravely — *voyez* —" She was suddenly clinging to him as his arms went about her. Her soft face was turned up to him, her breath was quick on his cheek and her young body firm against his. Then, as though a spring had been touched, she was gone, leaving him with "*Adieu*, Markham Cape!" fading into the soft closing of the door.

Once more he reached for the latch, let his hand drop. "No

help in that. *'Adieu'* let it be!" he muttered, shaking clear of the immediate past and into the instant present. Oliver Pollock's counting-house was only a few blocks off, and he would do well to take a steady head into those high-ceilinged rooms. He made his way out into the street, settling his rifle-sling and other straps.

In the broad Place d'Armes women were scurrying toward the Church of St. Louis, their eyes on the ground and elbows against their ribs as though being in the streets at all were just a little raffish. By the Cabildo, wilted sentries kept apathetic watch. Long market carts jolted past. A string of neat-footed mules, ears and tails flicking to the jingle of their bells, trotted out of a side street.

People seemed inclined to make way for Markham in his frontier clothes and slung rifle. He himself stepped aside for some Spanish officers, then joined a general shift to the pavement at the approach of sooty chimney-sweeps with their great palmetto brushes and their chant of *"R-r-r-ramonez la cheminée du haut en bas!"*

Back on the banquette he slowed again until some Ursuline nuns ahead of him turned in at a high gateway. Then he found a narrow stretch blocked by the leisurely progress of a stocky man in white linens, a long cane in his hand. The man lagged still more, took off a hat of finely woven straw, uncovering a gingery head. He tucked the cane under his arm and passed a silk handkerchief over his hair, the sun flashing on the silver top of his cane.

Markham smothered an exclamation, then stepped down to the street, lengthening his gait to a prairie stride. As he came abreast of the stocky man he said quietly, "Howdy, friend."

The man nearly stumbled, blinked at Markham through little square spectacles, then burst out, "Eh? Oh — God bless my soul! But I mean — Markham Cape! Never thought to see *you* back here! Let's get to my quarters. How can I help you? In any trouble?"

"No trouble at all, Mr. Pollock. I just came down here to talk to you about some friends we have in common."

Pollock's laugh was genially loud. "Pleasure to hear about old Natchez friends." His voice matched his laugh. "Yes indeed, pleasure!" His tone dropped. "By all means, to my quarters. Just keep talking about anything, anything at all."

XII

Message on the Wind from New Orleans

COMPLETELY refreshed by much hot water, a new linen suit and ample cold food and drinks, Markham let himself into Oliver Pollock's private office to await the merchant's return as he had been instructed. Hurricane-shaded candles of aromatic myrtle-wax showed him little change since his first glimpse of the premises. Thick, locked ledgers lay on the carved worktable with its high-backed chairs. The heavy brass ruler which served as pointer, gavel and field-marshal's baton weighted down a neat stack of papers. On the wall behind Pollock's chair glowed the jeweled frames of the miniatures of the bygone Spanish governors with whom he had lived and who had called him friend. There they were, Don Antonio de Ulloa, Don Alejandro O'Reilly and Don Luís de Unzaga. A fourth had been added and Markham stepped closer to peer at the handsome, trim-bearded man in his early thirties with his piercing dark eyes and wide forehead. From his uniform and insignia Markham guessed that the newcomer must be the present governor, Don Bernardo de Galvez. His trader-instinct set him wondering just how much, in actual money, those four miniatures were worth to an American merchant operating in a Spanish colony. Any figure, however you reckoned, would be too low, he thought.

Then the great map on the wall caught his attention and he remembered his bewilderment at his first glimpse of the lands west of the Alleghenies. Now he could look almost casually at the wavering black lines and know that this distance or that was exaggerated or shrunk. But the Great Lakes now told him far more than he could have remotely imagined earlier. They hung like scowling brows over the lands to the south, and that point on the sausage-link of land between Lakes Erie and Huron that was marked with a star and the name "Detroit" now seemed to take on the form of a cannon's mouth ready to blast a deadly charge toward the Alleghenies and the Ohio River. He thought he could almost feel the shock of the fancied detonation that could push the western frontiers of the States east to the very ocean — and oblivion.

He started as the latch of the door clicked and he turned to see Pollock entering, laying hat and silver-headed stick on a table. "Sorry that I had to leave you before we'd had more than a dozen words, Markham," said the merchant. "But I felt it advisable to start moving at once. Now we can make up for my neglect." He seated himself in his high-backed chair, picked up the brass ruler and turned it over and over in his hands. "First of all, about your coming back here. Did the road to the east begin to seem a little long to you?"

"Not at all. In fact I was actually on the point of starting east when I decided I'd better see you first, instead."

"Still given to quick action." Pollock smiled. "I'm anxious to hear just why you decided what you did — but first, while I was out I asked a friend to join us. He ought to be here any moment —" He stepped quickly to the door as a gentle tap sounded, and opened it cautiously. Markham rose as a tall, slim man in a cloak and wide hat glided in. As Pollock closed the door Markham knew that introductions were unnecessary. The small, pointed beard, the piercing dark eyes, the wide forehead might have sailed out of the miniature frame on the wall. Bowing deeply, Markham began, "*Vuestra Excelencia*, such an honor is one to which I could hardly —"

Galvez's eyes swept over him, seemed satisfied with what they saw. "Señor Cape, my family has tried to avoid ceremony ever since my paternal grandfather, bowing to one of higher rank, became entangled in sword and cloak and rolled down the steps of the great hall at Valladolid. Let us dispense with it now. I already know a good deal about you from my officers in the north as well as from my old friend here, Don Oliveros Pollock. So I feel great pleasure in welcoming you to New Orleans — and a greater sorrow in telling you that you must leave at once."

Markham tried to show only courteous interest. "There is some reason for leaving of which I am not aware?"

"There is!" laughed Pollock. "It struck me the instant I saw you in the Place d'Armes. As soon as I had you settled here, I sought out his Excellency and was not surprised that he agreed fully with me."

"So I should have gone east instead after all," said Markham wearily.

Galvez laid a hand on his sleeve. "By no means! Your coming is good fortune for us all. Don Oliveros, will you explain?"

Pollock bounced to his feet, rolled up the map until it showed only the lower Mississippi and rapped the paper with his brass ruler. "Here's Natchez on the east bank, under two hundred miles above us, Markham. You know all about the British and their blockade there. What you must do is to rush back north, see Colonel Clark, then go on to Virginia and see Governor Patrick Henry. They must catch fire from our plan, so listen carefully."

Pollock talked on, clearly and concisely, with Galvez breaking in eagerly from time to time. Markham listened, and a death-like chill stole up his back, settled about his heart. In brief, the plan called for an expedition of some two thousand men ("Or even only fifteen hundred," put in Galvez) to come down the Mississippi under George Rogers Clark, take Natchez from the British, drive east and take Manchac, thus uncovering the three great lakes east of New Orleans that led to the Gulf and the Gulf ports, Mobile and Biloxi and possibly Pensacola. Pollock, face flushed, pointed out how little opposition there would be, how the conquest would assure the United States possession of all the lands east of the Mississippi to the Alleghenies. Galvez, eyes ablaze, whispered that while Spain was neutral, she would view with contentment a friendly nation such as the United States sharing control of river and Gulf with her. In fact, substantial aid might be forthcoming, quite unofficially of course.

Markham's head throbbed, partly from weariness, partly from the prospect of having to make clear to these men the utter impossibility of their wild visions. And then he would have to bring up to the probably resentful Pollock the delicate question of helping Clark maintain himself and his little force in the Illinois country. If he could only unveil for both these men a portrait of Clark, a great, bright canvas conveying the magnetism, the drive, the power of the Virginian, the joyous, blazing daring and courage that shone from him.

He glanced at Pollock, at Galvez and was surprised and a little touched to see in their eyes almost a plea for his approval. He had a wild impulse to sweep away all the papers that lay on the table, to shout that their plans were rooted in profoundest ignorance of actualities.

He ran a hand over his dark hair, stretched out his legs. "I — I can only say that this is tremendous," he said and saw that they were pleased at this vague endorsement. "What I've got to do is to explain all this to Colonel Clark, first of all, as you have to me. Can I do it? If you knew the Colonel, you could advise me just how —"

"That's it! That's it!" they both broke in. Galvez continued, "Perhaps if you could tell us how you first saw him, how he appeared day after day, we could, the three of us, arrive at a proper presentation."

For the first time Markham saw Galvez not as a high Spanish official linked to Pollock by long-standing ties but as a benevolent neutral of the de Leyba-Nieto stamp. He thought, "If I can only bring Clark right into this room," and felt hollow and empty at the thought.

All at once it was easy. The miles and days and nights on the trail stood out in his memory like bright etchings that he was describing to people unable to see them. Clark was on the trail again, urging the column along, plunging into evil swamps with shouts of laughter that pulled the slackest onward. Food ran out, but his voice and presence gave strength to every man. There were no stragglers, because he ranged endlessly up and down the trail and the weakest men drove themselves on, eager not to fail him. And so to Kaskaskia and the night rush of perfectly co-ordinated groups of men who had not eaten in over forty-eight hours. "Still no stragglers, no missing," Markham added casually but watching his audience.

Pollock sat motionless, oblivious to everything, hands folded on a big ledger. Galvez's eyes never left Markham, but his hands, moving as though of their own will, brought out pencil and paper, took swift notes. The pencil raced faster and faster as Markham spoke of Clark's status. He was a Virginia lieutenant colonel, but his commission would not have been worth a strip of charred birchbark had his men not accepted him. They were an unusual lot, Markham said, all volunteers raised for this particular campaign, many of them older than Clark. They accepted him be-cause they trusted him utterly, relied upon him — and because he could do about anything just a little better than anyone else.

Now Markham turned to Clark's handling of the Creoles, from their first demands that he allow them to become American citi-zens to the departure of Father Gibault and Dr. Laffond to cap-ture Vincennes for him. The Governor would know, far better than Markham, about Clark's trip to San Luís and the reception by Don Fernando. Here Markham paused, but the two men sat motionless, attention riveted on him, and he knew that he — or Clark — controlled them. They waited like men listening to ac-counts of the feats of some admired hero, impatient for the un-veiling of his next exploit, which, of course, ushered in the sud-den flood of Indians. Surly, suspicious, if not actively hostile yet, they had come to stare at this new warrior who did not even deign to notice them, let alone try to win them to his side. The scene was sharp in Markham's mind. Clark stood in that packed room and tossed the cherished Indian tokens onto the floor, refused con-temptuously to punish those braves who tried to kidnap him. "One of Clark's men, an old frontier hand, interpreted for me," said Markham. "But you could *feel* their thought: 'Here's a strong man who defies us, all our thousands, and he must have hordes of strong men like him at his back, to talk and act like this.' Everything changed. They couldn't get close enough to him, shaking his hand, slapping his back or just staring in awe at him. They called him 'Gitchi Mokoman,' or 'The Big Knife,' and were ready to promise anything he wanted." Markham paused again, smiling to himself, then went on, "All he wanted, he said, was for them to keep out of this war of the white men. They swore they'd stay neutral and — then he just sent them home, like a crowd of unruly little schoolboys, and like them they went. Of course, it was all mighty risky, seeing that Clark had, purposely, no more than a score of his own men nearer than Kaskaskia, over fifty miles south."

Pollock drew a long breath as though he had been pulled back from staring down a hideous abyss. Galvez sat twirling the end of his little beard into a fish-hook point. Then he said, "So there our Colonel lies, safe in the Illinois country. Tell me, Señor Cape, just why did he do all this?"

Markham started to speak, then stepped to the map, rested his elbow where Detroit lay between Huron and Erie, then let his forearm and hand swing like a pendulum down and to the east. Only a few words were needed to show his listeners how the growing menace of heavy Indian raids against the American western frontiers and the lands that lay behind them could be eliminated by the capture of Detroit. "Every step of Clark's since leaving Virginia has been a step toward Detroit," concluded Markham. "It's all Clark's plan, too."

Galvez dropped his pencil and slapped the arm of his chair with an exultant shout. "There's our man for Natchez, Don Oliveros! He was born to lead it and nothing else! Señor Cape, you must go back at once, explain matters to our Colonel and he'll swim the Mississippi in high flood to join us. A mere note to Governor Henry is all that he needs to write for this. Now just one more thing, you've not said how many men Colonel Clark had with him, those at the Ohio River base as well as those who went on to Illinois. A rough figure will do."

Markham suddenly felt ground crumbling under his feet. He had done too good a job in presenting Clark and now all Galvez could think of was Clark heading an expedition down here. Would the loss of these illusions turn him and Pollock against him? And the question of numbers. That had been a deadly and close-held secret. Could he break the seal? He sat forward in his chair, mind made up. The disappointment of his hosts would have to be faced anyway. As to secrecy, New Orleans was far too distant in time and space to hold any danger to Clark. He said easily, "They thought a thousand men would be ample at first. But when Clark left Fort Pitt, five hundred men seemed about all he'd get."

"Five *hundred?*" Galvez's voice was a thick whisper.

"That wasn't the final total, of course." He let the two enjoy their patent relief, then shattered it. "When Clark's force finally mustered at Corn Island, the Illinois Detachment *and* the Western American Army numbered one hundred seventy-five men — including Clark." His words fell into a dead hush. "Since then, many enlistments have expired, so Detachment *and* Army amounts to, I'd say, eighty-seven men — and George Rogers Clark."

Galvez rose without a word, crossed the room, dropped his notes and some other papers into a deep brass bowl and touched them with a lighted candle. He flicked a hand at the thin smoke that rose. "*Pouf* for Natchez, for Manchac, for Mobile, for Biloxi! *Pouf!*" He resumed his seat.

"Eighty-seven men," stammered Pollock, still dazed.

"Eighty-seven men — and Colonel Clark," added Markham.

"But more may come from Virginia," urged Pollock.

"That's possible."

"More may not come from Virginia," said Galvez wearily.

"That's possible," repeated Markham.

"What if he is attacked?" asked Galvez. "I believe that the British and the Indians have rather more than eighty-seven men, even though they do not have our Colonel."

Markham shook his head. "In theory, any attack by anybody could be fatal. But I've seen Clark refute theory time and again. However, I'm afraid that natural laws may be pushing him nearer to the edge than he realizes."

Pollock hitched his chair closer to the ledger-piled table and picked up his brass ruler as though it might comfort him. "You refer to the laws of economics, Markham?"

"They seem to be his blind spot. He's had two windfalls, the auction of de Rocheblave's property — *spolia opima* of course — when I was in San Luís, and then finding your goods in Don Fernando's care."

"Dribbles and drabbles," snorted Pollock. "They couldn't last long."

"No. So he has to rely on Virginia paper money and drafts drawn on the Virginia treasury. It all passes freely enough in Kaskaskia and Cahokia, but farther out, discounts are heavy and some bills are not honored."

Pollock sighed. "Damnation, that's awkward. Why, this could sweep Clark out of Illinois without waiting for the British or Indians."

"And leaving a political vacuum," observed Markham.

Galvez passed his hands over his forehead. "Our Spinoza says, 'Nature abhors a vacuum.' So does politics, and into this vacuum will rush the British, determined not to be ousted again."

Pollock looked as though he had bitten on a sore tooth. "They'll control the east bank of the Mississippi from the farthest north right down to Natchez. They'll be ten times more suspicious, more belligerent, everywhere. They'll choke off *all* navigation except their own." His voice rose. "New Orleans could be pinched off like a ripe plum! Something's got to be done! If only those Congressional grain-ships would arrive!" At Markham's questioning look he explained that Congress had notified him to expect some shiploads of grain which he was to sell and thus reimburse himself in part for the heavy outlays that he had made on behalf of the United States. "They never have come in," he concluded.

Markham glanced at Galvez, who sat with his legs stretched out, hands clasped across his lean belly and his head thrown back. He seemed indifferent to Pollock's fears but candlelight betrayed a slight flick-flick as the Governor's jaw muscles flexed spasmodically. Then he spoke, as though reciting from an official document. "His

Christian Majesty's Government cannot contemplate with equanimity the presence of an actively hostile power on the east bank
of the Mississippi." He sat up, went on as though apologizing,
"However, my country is legally a friend of England, so I fear that
all we may do is — to continue to fail to contemplate with equanimity."

"Yes," said Pollock quietly. "Just so. H'm. Let's see. There are
my plantations up toward Baton Rouge and the German Coast.
My lands across in the Algiers section." He began to write.

Galvez stirred in his chair. "To change the subject, Don Oliveros, have I informed you that authorization has come in for
extending our fortifications here as well as improving the levees?"

The abrupt lifting of Pollock's head suggested that the Governor
had not changed the subject very radically. The two began a rapid
conversation full of elliptical references, of allusions quite lost on
Markham and he realized that his role had shifted from that of
narrator to mere spectator. He had nothing more to contribute.

He rose, spoke of the fatigues of his journey and begged leave
to retire. Pollock rang for a servant and Markham withdrew to a
chamber on the floor above, borne out on a wave of courteous
goodnights from two men who were obviously itching to plunge
back into their talk that had begun with sweeping plans for
blasting the British from the river and the Gulf and then had zigzagged somehow to projected work on local forts and levees.

Markham breakfasted alone in Pollock's walled garden where a
hint of breeze, left behind by the cool stir of dawn, set up a pat-
ter of dewdrops from broad-leaved trees and lush shrubs. As he
made his way through fruits and fresh rolls and pots of thick,
strong coffee, he reread the note his host had left for him. Markham was to be outfitted with linen clothes, straw hat, proper
shoes and long, silver-headed stick. Then he was to go to the
Cabildo where the enclosed card would admit him.

Half an hour later he was strolling down the Rue de Chartres,
savoring the last full drafts of an evenly burning Havana cigar. As
he came to the Place d'Armes, he stepped down from the *ban-*

quette only to pull up short as two beautifully groomed horses clattered out of a side street drawing a well-sprung open carriage, uniformed driver on the box and two uniformed grooms clinging to perches in the rear.

He was about to shout angrily to the coachman, who should not have taken so sharp a turn. Then the carriage came abreast of him. Riding with his back to the box was a bony-faced, hawk-nosed man, his tight-drawn hair heavily powdered. The French Cross of St. Louis glistened at his wrinkled throat and his mottled hands were impassive on a gold-headed stick. He did not even glance at Markham but the slender occupant of the other seat sat bolt upright. Under a broad hat fringed with blue and white flowers her eyes widened to gray circles and her slim brows sprang up in Moorish arches. Her mouth gathered into a rose button that melted into a delighted smile and a white-gloved hand lifted in a flutter that might have been involuntary.

Then an unholy din arose as two urchins and a slightly hysterical dog drove a column of grunting, shrieking hogs out onto the *Place* and Markham stood knee-deep in a porcine torrent. The carriage rolled on, the old man still immobile, his eyes fixed on the upper stories of the houses opposite.

"I'll be damned!" thought Markham. "So that's de Liliac! '*Ancien regime*' down to his shoe-buckles. If I'd spoken to her, I'd probably have a visit from his seconds by noon. She said Henri Dubois is his agent. I'd better drop cards there. Ah, here's the Cabildo."

While a sentry scurried inside with Markham's card, a de Liliac groom ran up, holding out a note. His master, he said, not knowing Monsieur's address, had been about to inquire at the Cabildo, but the meeting in the *Place* had made that unnecessary. Markham gave him a coin and was about to break the seal when a very fat *teniente* popped out of the Cabildo in a burst of salutes and invitations to enter.

The cool, vaulted interior was just as Markham remembered it. In its echoing dimness, lawyers were voluble with anxious clients. The sandals of brown-robed Capucins went slap-slapping down mysterious passages and messengers with notes tucked into deep cuffs whipped fish-like in and out of doors that were studded with heavy nailheads and bound with iron bands. The *teniente* ushered Markham into a room where Don Julio Galarmendi rose from a vast desk in a joyous flood of histrionics, pouring out a whirl of orotund greeting that made Markham feel at least the single-handed redeemer of a whole Spanish province from the Moors. Then the deputy rushed Markham along like a devoted retainer supporting the sorely wounded messenger who bears the news that will save the hard-pressed monarch, the castle and the whole realm. At last he halted before a very plain door, gave an anti-climactic tap and tiptoed off, motioning Markham to stay where he was.

From within Galvez's voice called and Markham entered, closing the door after him. Galvez and Pollock sat at a wide desk in a monastically bare room, whose walls showed only the arms of Spain and an unrolled map. Heavy coils of tobacco smoke eddied through the high windows. Markham seated himself, noting that both men were red-eyed, unshaven and pallid. Their coats were slung over chairs and their shirtsleeves were elbow-high. A pewter platter by Galvez's elbow was thick with cigar butts. Markham tilted the platter as he looked at Galvez. "You ought to have called me when you found your work would last till morning!"

Galvez rubbed his eyes. "We felt you would be more useful after a good sleep and a calm breakfast."

Markham smiled. "I've heard of regiments being fattened up before a campaign. Is there a resemblance here?"

"We merely refer you to the first suggestion we made you at the start of our talk this — or rather last evening," said Pollock, wheezing in the smoke.

Markham frowned. "But that was to get out of New Orleans quick!"

"And we say it again, Señor Cape," put in Galvez. "Though now we do omit our hare-brained plans for you to lay before our Colonel. Just convey to him our good wishes."

Markham wondered if the strain of the all-night talk was blur-

ring his hosts' minds. He said, "I can assure you that no one's good
wishes could be more highly valued by Colonel Clark. But —" his
patience suddenly ebbed — "damn it all, didn't I make you see
that Clark is only hanging on by —"

Pollock's chair rasped on the stone floor as he sprang up. "Did
you think you were talking to a pair of Houma Indians? When his
Excellency spoke of 'good wishes' he meant just that. Good wishes
for the success of every move that Colonel Clark makes for his
country. You've got to get up there quick as God'll let you and
tell him that all the drafts he draws will be honored by me. And
I'll see it's known along every inch of the river and the Gulf,
along the Great Lakes and, yes, right up to Montreal and, by God,
Quebec!"

Markham rose, completely taken aback. "This — this is the biggest thing that's happened to the Illinois country since Clark
brought his men up the old Massac Trace," he cried, and wondered why his knees felt unsteady.

"Hope it'll help." Pollock sounded almost grumpy. "And I must
say that I expected more questions from an old trader like you."

"One question only. How long can he count on this?"

Pollock hesitated, shot a quick glance at Galvez, who nodded.
The merchant went on. "Just as long as resources are available to
me."

Markham stifled an exclamation. That exchange of glances
could only mean that Galvez, as an individual, would throw his
private means into the plan, would draw other Spanish officials
and trusted Creoles along with him. "His Christian Majesty's
Government" would lose no equanimity due to a hostile east
bank of the Mississippi if Don Bernardo de Galvez could, unofficially, prevent it.

Galvez knocked the ash from his cigar with a hand that still
shook with fatigue. "Now your trip north, Señor Cape, will be
most unlike your first one. As Columbus tried to go east by sailing west, so will you go north by starting south." He plucked a
paper from the stack under Pollock's hand. "You will board a
downriver ship today. Halfway to the sea, a cutter will take you

southwest by sundry bayous to Barataria on the Gulf where you'll find an armed sloop. This sloop will receive written orders from you to go up the Appelansas and land you at a point the master knows." He turned to Pollock, smiled as he saw the merchant's head resting on a stack of papers. "Come, come, Don Oliveros. Señor Cape stands poised on the rail of that sloop ready to leap ashore, but only you know into what he will leap. Does he stay poised forever?"

Pollock's head lifted and his eyes opened slowly but he spoke clearly with his first motion. "At this spot, Markham, you'll meet George Bacon, an agent of mine. He'll find you horses, guides, an armed escort. You'll have a long, hard ride, but you'll wind up at Arkansas Post, well north of any British influence. You'll have no trouble in taking ship for the Illinois country from there. Is this clear?"

"So far. There are a good many details that need filling in, though."

Galvez handed him a thick, sealed packet. "You had better take all this back to your quarters at Don Oliveros's and study it there. It will contain answers to many questions such as where do you find your downriver boat, how do you pay your bills and so on." He smothered a yawn. "I may be able to stay awake perhaps ten more minutes and will spend that time explaining a few steps of your journey. Now the bayou route to Barataria —"

Half an hour later, Markham emerged from the Cabildo, head still buzzing with what he had heard. Clark surely would be able to weather the next three months or so, and at the end of that time he, Markham Cape, would arrive with tidings that would free the Virginian of many of his present difficulties, remove obstacles that might lie under foot later. He felt like kicking up his heels, shouting his exultation to the whole *Place*. He recalled an expression of an old Scots shipmaster, "Aye, ye've braggart in yer step!" Braggart was surely in his step now, and he gloried in it, thinking of those few men clinging to so much up there in the Illinois country.

He stowed Galvez's packet away inside his coat and his fingers met the edge of the note that the de Liliac groom had brought. He drew it out, broke the seal, saw craggy script that looked as if it had been hammered out on the famed Rock of Quebec. Claude Gregoire Lupien de Liliac was sensible of the courteous attention paid to Madame de Liliac on her recent voyage and wished to make suitable acknowledgment. If Monsieur Cape would present himself at Plantation St. Cérisy just beyond the old Ursuline Convent at the east of the city at four o'clock on the afternoon of September 29th, 1778 —

He stuffed it back into his pocket. "I'll be gone two days by then," he thought. "H'm. Old de Liliac wishes to make suitable acknowledgment et cetera, does he? Couldn't be, could it, that he wants to find out, most discreetly, just what one of Clark's men is doing in New Orleans, whom he's been seeing, where he's been staying? Anyway, I'll talk with Galvez before I go and see what he thinks about a proper reply. Two hours to get my new gear together. I'll be going north against the season later on and I'll need heavy stuff." He touched Galvez's packet as it lay in his coat, felt the de Liliac note crackle. "And I still don't know what the hell her first name is."

XIII

"Coon-Cub-Crazy"

"Hamilton's a mighty smart soldier. He knows that no one in God's green earth'd be coon-cub-crazy enough to hit east through a hundred fifty miles of drowned lands in the depth of winter to attack him. So that's just what we're going to do." — G.R.C.

IN DON RAMÓN NIETO's Santa Genoveva quarters, familiar since the mock "arrestation" of the summer before, Markham balanced among inlaid tables, propped himself against armchairs and stepped over rugs as he stripped off his dripping clothes. Nieto, lean-faced and jut-nosed as ever, hooked up the rough garments with a cane and dropped them through the trapdoor that led to Markham's former prison. "In ten moments they shall be parched as two peas," he cried in his wildly fluent English. "In ten more the wife of Sergeant Aspromonte will reparate them as well as new. Take more rum to stop your teeth from clattering. Thick towels are under your hands and dry clothes beside them."

Still stiff with cold, Markham flooded his throat with rum and then plied a towel vigorously. "I'm beginning to thaw a little," he said. "Now how about an answer to the question I asked when you pulled me out of the river?"

"Ah, the question you asked anteriorly? To that I say yes. Captain John Rogers did come to San Luís from the south and then went swiftly to Cahokia."

Markham knew a sudden relief so deep that it was beyond any shout of triumph, and for the first time in weeks he dared breathe easily. "So he got through!" was all he could say. "That's good, damn good!"

"My answer was not displeasing to you? Then I rejoice with you about Rogers, just as I rejoice to see you here not knowing why you come to be here to be rejoiced at. And now, Markham, as old friend, I have right to ask why, oh why did you spring like a great brown frog from *passe-avant* of *Le Cerf* into our river? My guard nearly shot you, taking you for an invasioner, and my Aspromonte, hearing the shot, called out the rest of the guard to make repulsive gestures with pikes as you swam to earth."

Markham moved closer to a glowing brazier and began to dress. "I was in a hurry to leave *Le Cerf*, that's all."

Nieto slammed the trapdoor. "More in a hurry than you are to erode worry from the mind of an old friend who fears evils may have fallen over you while you were doing whatever you were doing in the south?"

"Sorry," said Markham, as he continued dressing, "I was in New Orleans. Your governor Don Bernardo de Galvez helped me to come north through the British blockade."

"Ah!" cried Nieto. "You saw — you *talked* with Don Bernardo himself?"

"I spent several hours with him and an American friend. His good will toward me I attribute to reports received by him from Don Fernando and yourself about the Detachment, those reports including me." Nieto looked thoroughly pleased and Markham went on, "So I was sent north by a very odd route to Arkansas Post. It took longer than we thought and to make things worse I was seized of a fever and the master of the one keeler on which I could have gone as passenger refused to take me. In the meantime, this Captain Rogers and a few others who had been with my compatriot Willing came into the Post by the same route I'd followed. The keeler accepted them, so I gave Rogers most of my news for Colonel Clark."

"I find your waiting tragical," said Nieto, dropping into a chair. "We could have sent down for you."

"I know you would, if you'd heard about me. But at last *Le*

Cerf, a decrepit old keeler, put in and I got a working berth aboard it. That's all!"

"That's all?" echoed Nieto. "But those miles, those months, that great frog-leap into our ice-bitter river?"

"Miles and months always pass. As to the jump, the master refused to release any of his crew till he reached the Illinois River up north there. He knew that I was Kaskaskia-bound and watched the starboard side of the ship. I dove over from the port side and here I am."

Nieto sighed deeply. "How truly simple are the actings of the truly great! So now you will wish to cross to Kaskaskia where your friends will be waiting your adventing with craned necks, did they know about it." Characteristically Nieto did not ask just what news there might be for Clark.

"I'm not stirring until you've fed me as you promised. Oh yes, and please have those old clothes thrown away, they're useless. Now first of all, tell me what's been happening across the river. All serene, I trust."

"The pinnacle of serenity, or so they were two days past when I dined with my so good friends of the Company Bowman, of which I am honorable member. It was at Cahokia and I wore the hunting shirt and great knife which they gave me. But there have been more distant happenings. Do you know Francisco Vigo, the merchant, an Italian who was once a fellow officer to us?"

"I've often heard of him, but I've never met him."

Nieto rose, opened a squat Moorish cabinet of heavy black wood and drew out some papers. "I leave these sheets with you while I go out to arrange food for us. They are most unofficial notings which may prepare you for the craned necks of Kaskaskia."

Sitting close to the brazier's glow, Markham took the pages that were covered with Nieto's neat script and ran an eye along the opening sentences with polite curiosity. Then he sat up in his armchair as though a pistol had been jammed into his spine. He read on, unaware of the slow death of the coals, of Nieto coming softly onto the gallery, glancing at him seated by the brazier and vanishing discreetly. At last he stacked the sheets neatly together, laid them on the arm of his chair and sat staring ahead, fingers drumming on his knee.

Back in December, Francisco Vigo had started east from St. Louis for Vincennes, accompanied by one pack-horse and one clerk. When he had reached the Embarras River, near his goal, he had been jumped by Indians and Canadian French who handled him roughly, looted his packs and rushed him off to Vincennes. There, to his horror, he found the stern British regular, Colonel Henry Hamilton, in possession, backed by men of His Majesty's 8th Foot in their blue facings along with red-pomponed Detroit militia and many Indians.

Incredible as it seemed, Hamilton, on belatedly learning of the loss of Kaskaskia and Vincennes, had set to work at once to recapture them. Gathering supplies, Indians and auxiliaries, he had started out in October on a fantastic march from Detroit. He carried his bateaux where there was no water, dammed little streams until they could float his craft, battered his way south through ice-covered or timber-choked rivers. In mid-December, Vincennes was his, along with its tiny American garrison commanded by Captain Leonard Helm, now a prisoner of war.

Vigo's neutral status had won him fair enough treatment, although Hamilton was reluctant to let him go and did nothing about restoring his horse and goods. At last he freed Vigo on the strict understanding that he would do nothing "to injure the British cause" while en route to St. Louis. Vigo kept his word to the letter. In an old pirogue he had gone via the Wabash, Ohio and Mississippi to St. Louis. At that town, however, he crossed at once to Cahokia and sought out Clark to tell him of doings along the Wabash.

Nieto pushed open the gallery door and came diffidently in. "You have finished?" he inquired.

Markham handed him the sheets. "This is a gay little *novela* that you have written. My thanks. There was no warning of all this?"

"None." Nieto fell back onto Spanish for greater precision. "In December, the fortnightly reports of Captain Helm do not arrive. Mounted scouts go out but are turned back by flooded prairies. The next news is from Francisco Vigo."

"I see," said Markham somberly. "Don Ramón, I should revel in a good dinner and a long talk with you. But I feel that I should start for Kaskaskia at once." He sighed. "Damned if I know how it'll help, but I'd better go."

Nieto nodded vigorously. "Thinking such might be the case, I ordered a canoeman to await you at the wharf. Food, wine and brandy are aboard."

Markham rose stiffly, rubbing his elbows. "I'd better paddle bow and melt some of the ice out of my joints. You'll come too, of course?"

"Ah — I think — you and the Colonel will have so much to talk over — duties pin me here — another time soon — but at least I go to the river with you to point out the canoe and casserole of food."

Kaskaskia lay desolate and somber under the low gray bowl of the sky as Markham mounted the gentle slope that led up from the river. There was almost no snow on the ground but the fences about the wide common-lands sagged in mud and the long narrow fields had turned from green ribbons into grayish paste. The first roofs that showed over the crest were dank and sodden in the wet air and slow thin spirals of yellowish smoke oozed joylessly up from their chimneys.

Slipping in the mud that formed greasy pads under foot he wondered if this sudden disaster on the Wabash had in any way shaken Clark, dimmed his contagious fire, sapped his whirling drive. The thought oppressed him, darkened his mood to match the day, and he found himself repelled by the dank lifelessness of this town that had been his goal since leaving New Orleans. He felt ill at ease, almost lost.

Then the Louis XV bell in the little church began to peal, its notes shimmering out over the wide street and the houses that lined it. He looked up, a little cheered, wondering how he could have forgotten the tone of that bell that had tolled so fearfully in the early hours of last July fifth and so bravely and gaily later. A black cassock stirred in the doorway and Father Gibault was waving and shouting, "*Mais voilà Monsieur Markham qui est revenu!*" The priest's hand was strong on his, but his words of welcome were blurred by the squish and plash of pattens in the mud, by a dozen, a score of voices, men and women crying out that another Kaskaskian had come home from the river. No one detained him, taking it for granted that he would want to see Clark as soon as possible, but all pressed close for at least a word and a handclasp.

Markham hurried on, spurred by the lifting mist which showed him the American flag sailing high over Fort Clark (as it had been called since the summer before). One or two men of the Detachment were moving about inside the stockade and some horses were tied close by the blockhouse. He began to run. A Kaskaskia militiaman tried vainly to bar his entry into the enclosure. An unidentified but obviously Detachment voice bawled, "Where in the name of leaping, roaring hell d'you think—" Markham was already over the threshold of the familiar room with its long table and heavy chairs and Clark was springing up, coppery hair fairly glowing in the misty air, and his voice boomed like a clear gong, "Markham! By God, Markham! Oh, what you did for us down in New Orleans!"

Clark's hands and fists slapped and thumped at Markham until he gasped and through the smoke and mist Clark's voice rang on, presenting the other two men who sat at the table with him. "You've met my cousin Captain John Rogers already, Markham." A heavy-chinned Irishman with blue-black jaws and hair was dragged forward. "Captain Rick McCarthy, who's raised a fine company of militia for us at Cahokia. Now sit down, everyone. Cousin John gave me your message and it was like a breath from a pass in the Blue Ridge on a hot day. Got anything else?"

Markham pulled out a thick oilskin packet and slit the stitches. "This just embroiders what Captain Rogers told you, but I think you'd like to hear Oliver Pollock talking, if only from paper. He's what my father used to call 'an old-time Whiggish sort of man, a man with a zeal in his heart.' I didn't have to tell him a great deal about you. He'd heard so much that for sixpence he'd have come up here to enlist."

Clark caught up the damp sheets and scanned them quickly, pausing to chuckle every now and then. At last he folded the pages, reached out and seized Markham's hand. "By God, I envy you. You saw him and talked with him!" He turned to the others. "He's a real man, Pollock. If we had a dozen like him we'd win the war before next fall's frosts were on the bottom-lands. Listen to this: 'The cause on which we have embarked urges me to strain every nerve toward its glorious and successful conclusion. A number of good friends here in New Orleans have made it possible for me to serve my country. I count myself lucky that you, far in the north, have offered me still another chance.' And this: 'I am determined to share the fate of my countrymen if they should fail and rely on their justice if crowned with success.' Where's the bottle and mugs? March them right out here and we'll drink to the realest kind of man."

There was a splashing and clinking, a general murmur of "To Oliver Pollock!"

Clark went on, "There ought to be another health drunk to Markham. This letter builds a whole book out of the word you brought from Arkansas Post, Cousin John, that message that Pollock'd honor our drafts on him. And he'll do that just because Markham got a wild look in his eye last summer and went down-river to tell Pollock what'd happen here and a lot of other places if our drafts weren't honored and our paper money backed." He shook the pages. "All spelled out here. By God, it's wonderful to see you again, Markham."

"Wonderful to be here. I wasn't too sure I'd find a going concern, even with the Pollock news, after Nieto told me about Vigo's trip east. But from the easy faces I've seen here I guess Don Ramón used more black crape than he needed in the telling."

Clark exchanged glances with the others and began to laugh. "So old Rame made things look bad, did he? Well, he shouldn't have done that, Markham. Things *aren't* bad. They're sheer, knife-edge murder."

Markham, who had known a blessed easing of tension at Clark's first words, felt his face go suddenly tight. He said slowly, like a merchant forcing himself to ask for details of a bankruptcy, "Just how much worse should Nieto have made them sound?"

Clark sat back, eyes on the ceiling and legs stretched out before him. "Let's look at all the pieces without trying to scrape the mud off the bad ones or polish up the good ones — if there are any. Hamilton's at Vincennes, all right." He shook his head in somber admiration. "By God, what a soldier! That march he made was a killer. I don't know as I'd have dared face it, even with my timber-trained boys. He's a wizard, that man. Vigo says he made his Indians lug bateaux and supplies at the hundred and one portages he had to make and no one I ever heard of managed to do that before. So now he's at Vincennes with about eighty-five of the 8th Regiment and some hundred twenty Detroit militia. Doesn't matter how many Indians are with him right now because he can whistle up five hundred any time he wants, tribes that didn't take the oath to me to stay neutral. And he's got his agents out among the tribes south of the Ohio, trying to stir them up."

"The Indians *south* of the Ohio?" asked Markham.

Clark's eyes grew dark. "Yes, and if he can splice up all the tribes north *and* south and supply 'em so they'll stay in the field he'll be ready to do what I've always been scared of — to wipe out the Kentucky settlements and then jam east through the mountains. For that he'll throw all the troops west of Montreal in to join them. And all the tribes that took the oath to us'll forget about that swearing and race east with the pack, hoping for scalps. You've got to remember, Markham, that Indians admire success a lot more than their oath."

"You've got help coming to you from Virginia?" asked Markham, deeply puzzled that these men seemed serious but by no means fearful.

"To be honest, I've heard nothing from Virginia since I left

Corn Island and that was back in June, so I've got to assume they can't do anything for us. Here we are, then. Eighty men of the Detachment, maybe eighty Creole militia. So what do we do?" He tossed his hands in the air. "We're too few to move east to help Kentucky and anyway we'd be scuppered by Indians before we were twenty miles up the Ohio. Hamilton's sitting at Vincennes working on the Indians. The prairies between us and him are part freezing water, part frozen mud. When they dry out in the spring, Hamilton'll move west with his two hundred men and four hundred Indians, pull down our flag and hoist the Union Jack while the Indians are busy harvesting scalps and playing with prisoners. It's all as simple as that, Markham."

Still baffled, Markham said, "So we just sit here till Hamilton comes after us?"

Rogers muttered, "What else is there to do?"

"Then, theoretically, I'd have done better to stay at Arkansas Post."

Clark burst out laughing. "Oh, no, Markham. I'm going to make good on my promise of sending you east."

"East? What in God's name have you hatched up now?"

Bouncing to his feet and slapping his hands together, Clark called, "Time to get to work, boys! Markham, Hamilton's a mighty smart soldier. He knows that no one in God's green earth'd be coon-cub-crazy enough to hit east through a hundred fifty miles of drowned lands in the depth of winter to attack him. So that's just what we're going to do, and at the same time we'll be your escort east. This is February second. We'll start — let's see, yes, on the fifth." He put an arm over McCarthy's shoulders. "Come on, Rick. You and I have got to see about the army. Cousin John, you and Markham get busy on our navy." He whooped with laughter, sweeping the others ahead of him out of the room.

"What in God's name is he talking about now?" asked Markham as he and Rogers crossed the parade ground toward the water-gate.

Rogers grinned. "Sure, George is crazy as hell, always has been, always will be. And we've got a navy."

A fearful din of hammering and sawing and adzing arose as they went through the gate. There by the near bank lay an eighty-foot keeler. Men were swarming all over it, reinforcing the long deckhouse with a facing of oak planks, sawing loop-holes, rigging iron Y-shaped gun mounts to the bulwarks.

"The navy," observed Rogers. "The U.S.S. *Willing*. We'll go down the Kaskaskia and the Mississippi, up the Ohio to the Wabash and up that till we hit the White River, say fifteen miles below Vincennes, and wait for George and his boys hitting overland. We're lugging supplies his men won't have to carry. We've got cannon for the attack on the fort at Vincennes. We're carrying enough arms to beat off any Indian attacks — four swivels and two brass four-pounders."

Markham rested a foot on the gunwale of the *Willing* and ran a hand through his hair. "Look here, Rogers, Clark's splitting what force he has, sending part by land, part by water, and praying that they'll meet. Then he's moving against a strong, trained force in a strong fort. To attack it we've got to make a march that no respectable lunatic would even consider."

"Sure," said Rogers calmly.

"Then why in God's name is everyone here and in the town looking so cheerful? It's damn well unreasonable."

"That's George again. When Vigo came in with his news, people looked like they'd pay someone to shoot 'em. All George did was walk about where he could be seen, grinning to himself and whistling 'La Bande Joyeuse,' or 'Killiecrankie.' Then he got folks raking in supplies. He found this old keeler somewhere and told me to build him a navy. He had the Detachment here and at Cahokia working the day around. It was like the sun busting through clouds. Everyone in the Illinois country set at his job as though wading to the Wabash and pulling Hamilton's queue was kind of a holiday. Does that answer your question?"

Late that afternoon Markham sat on the gunwale of the *Willing*, face streaked with sweat and paint and tar, watching while two silent Creoles settled the bow four-pounder in its carriage. He looked up as a crackling and thrashing sounded overhead and saw Clark wriggling out along a limb that jutted from a sycamore on the east bank. The Colonel gave a heave and dropped lightly beside Markham. "Going to be ready to sail in time?" he asked. "This leaves a day before the overland party, you know."

Markham grinned. "Rogers says it's apt to sail right up the Wabash and take the fort there — Sackville, isn't it — before we sight it."

"Good for Cousin John. 'Course, he won't, though. It's not in the plan. This ship's going to do a lot more than just tote stuff for us. You see, Markham, I'm a bit scared that Hamilton just might get wind of our coming and bolt down the Wabash to the Ohio and then we'd never find him. But the *Willing*, lying a few miles down the Wabash, can block any bateaux Hamilton might try to send down, and it's strong enough to fight off any attacks from the banks. That way, it'll keep Hamilton pinned, if he does try to break away, until the rest of us can come downstream and finish him off. I'm sure we'll nail him right in his fort, but either way, his service is finished."

"That'll be a big thing, Colonel."

"Big?" Clark's voice sank to a whisper. "Have you been able to reckon out just how big? Detroit'll be paralyzed for a long time because the British won't hear of his capture for weeks and then there'll be his successor to choose and all that. But the Indians, Markham, the Indians! They worship success. With Hamilton beaten, the tribes to the south'll lose interest. Those in the north'll be still shyer. It'll be pretty near as good as taking Detroit itself."

Clark's face was alight and his eyes were looking far beyond the tree-tops. His plans were predicated, step by inerrable step, on Hamilton's defeat, without even a pause to consider what to do in case of stalemate or disaster. It was obvious that everyone would be carried along by his unshakable belief that everything would happen as he said it would — as it had so often happened in the past. Markham, caught up in the sweep, said, "I'm almost surprised that you don't hit right for Detroit and to hell with Vincennes."

A darkness clouded Clark's face. Still in a half-whisper he said, "The men! Why in God's name won't Virginia answer me? Markham, I'd gladly bind myself seven years a slave if I could have five hundred men right now. Just five hundred men to finish off the job for good and all, not just fix it for a while."

Then without warning he sprang to his feet, slapped Markham between the shoulders, caught Rogers, who had just appeared in a cabin doorway, by the arm. "Everything's going like a fine clock. Come on, everyone, every man aboard. Back to the blockhouse. I'm going to serve rum out all around and an extra mug to the man who beats me to the door." He scaled the short mast, caught the bough of an oak on the west bank and swung himself into the tree, working along among the bare branches and making for a sycamore close to the stockade.

The workmen downed their tools and went whooping over the short brown grass. Markham and Rogers looked at each other, then Rogers faced east, cupped his hands and shouted, "Hey, Henry Hamilton! Guests coming!"

The misty drizzle of the past days hung like a whitish curtain over Kaskaskia, intensifying the strange hush that had fallen. It was as though the U.S.S. *Willing*, now twenty-four hours gone, had drawn downstream in its wake all other sounds along with the beat of its hammers and the rasp of its saws.

The door of Gabriel Cerré's big house at the head of the street opened and Markham and the merchant stepped out into the milky light. "Of course I didn't need to give you all this about New Orleans." Markham unconsciously lowered his voice in the wet, muted world. "But the Colonel wanted to be sure that you knew everything that had gone on."

"His courtesy never fails," said Cerré. "And I am content that you wrote Monsieur Pollock of the great share of the underwriting of the Colonel which Monsieur Vigo assumed after you left last autumn, so —"

They both looked down the street toward the ghostly outlines of the stockade and blockhouse as a single drumbeat shivered up through the silvery shroud. A vague stir of wind, as though summoned by that lone drum-tap, rose from the river. The mists shifted, parted to show the American flag high above Fort Clark, then fell away from the stockade and its gates. The drum spoke again, a long vibrant roll that climbed and climbed. Markham felt a chill along his spine and Cerré breathed, "*Mais enfin!*" through his teeth.

The drumbeat swelled and the bell in the little church boomed in answer. The gates of the Fort shivered and a dark mass flooded out of the gap with the slant of rifle-barrels pointing the way. In an echoing clatter men, women and children poured out of their houses, across galleries and down to the street, their shouts swelling to a vibrant chorus as the column cleared the fort.

In the van was a loose screen of a dozen scouts, Creole and Virginian, gliding on unconcernedly. Then hands began to reach out from the crowd toward Clark who strode on in the wake of the scouts — toward Clark and the black-robed figure of Father Gibault who marched beside him, lips moving soundlessly.

So they came on, Clark and the stocky priest of Kaskaskia followed by Joe Bowman, second-in-command. The companies took the gentle slope in fair enough formation, guidons bright with the American and Virginian colors at the head of the first two and more brave hues over the Kaskaskians and the Cahokians.

By the church, whose royal bell had fallen silent, the march stopped. The companies broke ranks, melted into a thick semicircle as Clark, sweeping off his hat, escorted Gibault gravely to the church steps. The priest faced about while Clark knelt. The Creoles dropped to one knee, uncovering. The Virginians looked at each other uncertainly, then most of them knelt while all uncovered. Markham, kneeling beside Cerré, could only marvel inwardly, "Some of them Church of England, a lot of Scotchbyterians and Lutherans, kneeling for absolution and meaning it!"

Gibault's voice rang out, strong, dominant in the organ-roll of the sonorous Latin. He held his crucifix high, then slowly lowered it, his eyes on the ground. There was a stir among the companies. Two of McCarthy's Cahokians and two of Charleville's

Kaskaskians moved up toward the priest, holding out their guidon-poles. Gibault touched the four little flags with the fingers of his left hand, intoning richly. The Creoles straightened, crossed themselves and fell back among their fellows.

The single drum, stationed at the head of the Cahokia men, resumed its beat. Markham shook hands with Cerré, caught up his haversack and rifle, and ran off to the flank of Helm's old company. As he took his place he saw a Virginian break ranks and run to Gibault, holding out the national guidon, desperately in earnest and his voice hoarse with respect. "Mind fixing this one up for us, Reverend?"

Gibault looked up quickly and then he smiled, as Markham told himself later, like the sun breaking through a Mississippi fog. The priest touched the red, white and blue folds and there seemed to be an extra warmth in his "*Benedicite.*"

There was a hurried but heartfelt "Thanks, Reverend," and the man scurried back to his company. The bell boomed again. The column headed out toward the prairies. Men looking back saw the floods of color about houses and the street but most of all a stocky black figure standing under the booming bell, one hand still raised in blessing.

XIV

Prairie World *et Puis*

THE PRAIRIE world spread out endlessly from the lone sycamore among whose high branches Markham sat perched.
North, south, east and west it lay before him so flat, so limitless
that he had to fight off the feeling that it was all an optical illusion.
It was hard to believe in monotony on so tremendous a scale.
Color had been leached out, leaving oatmeal grays, sullen browns,
heavier grays that refused to harden into blacks, thicker browns
that never warmed into reds and oranges. A weak sun struggled
through the western clouds to send fleeting waves of pink over the
eastern flatness only to be swallowed up in the rising monotone.

A long procession of neutral-hued dots lay a couple of miles
away to the rear, moving imperceptibly east as though drawn by
an unseen cord toward a thin grove where a few bare-limbed trees
stood huddled like men waiting hopelessly in the rain. Markham
identified the components of the march: Helm's old company
under Edward Worthington, then the pack-horses with Bowman
ranging past them; the head of Charleville's Kaskaskia company
and McCarthy's Cahokians winding past a wide pool of surface water. He noted that on this, the third day of the march to Vincennes,
none of the company commanders was riding. Their mounts
were loaded down with extra equipment, except for Worthington's,
which plodded on, a man limping along on each side with an arm
thrown over the animal's neck.

Markham went still higher, strained east again. Then he called
down, "Phil! Any lakes supposed to be hereabouts? There's a lot
of glitter ahead."

Brady, holding Markham's rifle at the foot of the tree, shouted,

"If there is a lake out there, all I can say is that it's lost as hell. We better get back to the column and tell someone who gets paid more'n we do to worry about lost lakes. Hate to tell you, Mark, but you've spotted the drowned lands two days too soon. Or else they've moved."

"Can't be helped." Markham took another look to the rear, called again, "Hi, here comes the hunting party, John Williams's company and Clark, two-three miles off to the northwest!" He descended carefully, blinking his eyes, as a sullen murk rose to meet him in the lower levels. He dropped to the ground, took rifle and equipment from Brady. "Damn and all, looks a lot darker down here than up there." The two started out at an easy lope and Markham went on, "Phil, were you humming me about those drowned lands?"

"Wish I was, but a glitter like that around here means floods and nothing else."

Markham heard the squish and plosh as their four moccasins struck into what looked to him like firm ground. "Maybe you're telling the truth for once, Phil, but if you are, what the hell are we running over *now?* Doesn't feel or sound like sand to me, even if it doesn't show much."

Brady snorted. "When the ground gets like this at home, we haul out our fiddles and the gals put on their silk slippers and we dance the night out. This is nothing but a dew-fall. When the water gets so high that a man on horseback can't see his horse's ears, then we allow it's close to flood time."

At the end of a half hour's trotting, they both shouted in relief as fires ahead of them spouted through the dusk, faded, swelled to a steady glow. As they came nearer, they caught a joyous chatter, then Clark's voice, deep, resonant, cheery, somewhere beyond the glow. "Sure, sure! All the fires you want. Shoot anything you've got a mind to shoot. Blast off a cannon if you've got one in your pouches. We hit north a good eight leagues and there's nothing hostile that can't be eaten. We know there's nothing south of us since yesterday's scout. Poke up those fires. We've got buffalo, venison, duck, teal and goose and a mess of little truck. Stay in your squares and John Williams's boys'll bring your vittles. Cahokia company hunts tomorrow and the rest of us are its guests."

Markham jumped as a man materialized close by out of the dusky flatness where no cover existed, only to vanish with a shout of, "All right! Just Phil and Mark comin' in."

As it had done since the end of the very first march on the night of February fifth, the column had gone into camp by halting the leading company and bringing the others abreast of it. Then each command formed a forty-foot hollow square some twenty yards from its nearest neighbor, with pack-horses and singlemounts staked out in the center and their loads of powder and provisions piled out of reach of tooth and hoof. Each square maintained its own interior guard while scouts picked by Clark himself patrolled a three-mile circle outside.

Guided by the fires, Markham and Brady headed for the end of the line where Williams's company was setting itself on the left of the Kaskaskians. The hunters must have done some butchering in the field, for men were trotting to other squares carrying shapeless loads that gave off a rank, meaty smell or long poles from which wildfowl dangled like overripe fruits.

Markham called, "There's the Colonel!" and headed toward a new fire in Williams's square. Clark was rubbing blood-stained hands on a hot, wet cloth while talking with his company commanders and Bowman. "Herd of about three hundred buffalo," he was saying. "They're drifting east, no wolves trailing them. We shot what we needed and they didn't panic. Of course, the meat's poor this time of year except for tongues and humps and that's what we took. They ought to stay in our range for another day or so." He turned to Charleville. "Your turn tomorrow, Frank. Get all you can without scaring 'em. Hi, here's Phil and Markham! Joe Bowman told me about chasing you two out ahead of the column. See anything new?"

Dropping his voice a little, Markham reported briefly that the prairies seemed empty of all life except the column. Then he added, still lower, "There's an awful lot of water just this side of the eastern horizon. I caught the glint very clearly. Phil says there's no lake in these parts." Although Markham had purposely kept his voice pitched below normal, no one crowded closer to the little group, no one left the other squares to edge nearer in hope of news. Yet he had a strong impression that every car and mind on the prairie was turned toward him, not so much for the news itself as for its effect on Clark.

The report was received calmly enough. Bowman asked quietly, "You saw real enough water, Mark?"

"All I saw was the glint, Joe," he replied.

McCarthy, rubbing his cheeks that sprang black an hour after shaving, broke in, "He saw the shine, all right. But look, I've seen this — you take flat, wet ground and a low gray sky. Well, that ground'll kind of reflect back the shine of the clouds, see? Like a mirror. I've hit it in the flats west of Lake Superior. Mark could have seen something like that."

All the squares kept up a steady buzz of undisturbed life, apparently oblivious to the report and its meaning, yet more than ever Markham was conscious of a sharp tension, a waiting to see how Clark reacted. Charleville began, "But that reflection, I find it quite possible, and that could be very —"

Clark drowned out his words in a burst of laughter and slapped him on the shoulder. "Not worth worrying about either way, Frank, because it all plays into our hands. If it stays dry ahead, why, we just keep on. If some of it's flooded, all the better. We make the damn water work *for* us! There are enough groves hereabouts to build canoes and rafts. We'll load the stores on them, float them ahead and swim the horses. And there's enough roll to the country so we'll find little ridges shouldering up every few miles. We'll camp on the best of the ridges and push on to the next." His voice rose, clear and contagiously cheerful. "Why, we'll be able to make twice the usual distance each day with half the effort." A random swirl of smoke wrapped the group in a rich smell of roasting meats and fine, thick drippings. Clark sprang up from his seat on a bale of goods. "By God, all this makes me hungry. I'm going over and eat with the Cahokia boys. Joe, you see that Phil and Markham get two fat mallards apiece because, by God, they've earned them."

He left the square at a light trot, calling greetings to half-seen figures right and left.

Markham was sure that there was no difference in the sounds that came from the companies yet he knew that tension was gone. In the Kaskaskia lines a fiddle began to scrape and voices took up the dismal "*Complainte de Cadieux*," sure sign that the singers were unquenchably cheerful. The ominous words sailed out to the wet sky, "*Pensant toujours à mes si chers amis / Qui me dira? Ah, sont-ils tous noyés? / Les Shawnese les auraient-ils tués?*"

A drum sounded among the Cahokians, that same lone snare drum that had beaten the Detachment past Father Gibault's church and the last houses of the town. It held a rhythm that sent cold shivers down Markham's spine as he recalled the endless boomings that had swelled from the Indian villages when the tribes had come to Cahokia. The tone was thinner but the beat was the same — Tat, tat, tarataty-tatatery, tat-a-tat-ta-tat! Someone whooped like an Indian, another answered far off on the left. Men began a slow drift through the fire-streaked darkness. Now the drummer was beating with the palm of his hand. The tone flattened out and the meter raced faster — pam, pa-pam, pam-pera-pam-pam-pam!

A slab of clean bark piled with turkey and buffalo tongue was thrust into Markham's hands, another was passed back to Phil Brady, who clutched his slab, rose suddenly and darted off toward the din. Markham sat on a log watching the high-springing flames of the Cahokia square. Silhouetted against the blaze, a long line of swift-moving men went bending, crouching, leaping, twisting, bending again in a widening circle, whooping as the Winnebagos had whooped down by the Rigolet. More men came running to join the firelit frenzy of the dance while the drum yelled out its pam, pamter-am-pam-ta-pam-pam!

Markham turned away to toss a turkey-bone into the nearest fire and saw Joe Bowman close by, writing calmly in a sodden notebook. Bowman nodded to him. "Here's the tally, near's I can figure it. Today, February seven, we covered twenty-one miles, Mark. Got to do better than that!" He stowed away the book and looked

WhaTaFuck! Spider was Here.

the speaker who drawled, "Reckon most everywhere must 'a' looked something like this round about Creation-time. I'd not wanted to 'a' been there much."

"You mean Flood-time, not Creation-time," he was corrected by the familiar voice of Joe Simmonds. "Ask Mark back there."

Markham grunted as he stepped into a hole that brought water up above his knees. "What's that? I was too young for the Flood, but I did see Creation. Quite a sight too. Better ask someone who saw both."

Markham felt his feet strike a slope, found sand, then grass under them, and the water leveled off knee-deep. So that was a submerged brook! He began to wonder what would happen if they struck a drowned river, a steep-banked drowned river. The first men entering it wouldn't have much chance, weighted down with their rifles and pouches and haversacks.

Twice he slipped, then caught hold of a dangling rope on the pack-horse's load. It was easier, much easier, to be towed along like this and it added nothing to the horse's burden. The cold, wet boots that he had imagined on his legs grew heavier, seemed to stretch, reach higher and higher until they were more like breeches than boots. When he stepped on a sharp stone, it was like watching gunfire at a long distance where you first saw the puff of smoke and then, after a pause, heard the report of the shot. He knew the stone was underfoot, but it took what seemed a good second for the aching stab to dart into his consciousness.

The horse wallowed on impassively. In water that was only ankle-deep, Joe Bowman ordered the column to halt for a rest that had to be brief, else cold and wet would begin to take a toll. Leaning against the horse, Markham worried a slab of dried beef out of his haversack, sliced off a chunk with his long knife and worked the meat about in his mouth to soften it. He started to shiver and began raising his feet in high-kneed steps like an awkward clockwork toy held off the ground. He kept time and was sure that warmth and suppleness were returning. The beef began to soften in his mouth and he worked away at it, pleased by an unexpected tang of garlic and herbs.

The column lurched on again, Markham clinging to his bit of rope and busy with his dried meat. The feeling of heavy, cold wrappings about feet and legs ebbed, was replaced by spreading warmth over soles and insteps, and for a moment he believed that he was becoming acclimated. The warmth increased. Not acclimated. Foot-scald. If there were only some rock or stump exposed where he could sit and strip off his moccasins and massage his soles. But on all sides the grayish plain stretched away, broken only by the brown eddies churned up by horse and man.

He thought again of the morning jesting and felt now that the flood-lands must be very like the early days of Creation. Those must have been uncomfortable times before the waters ebbed from the earth. A man would have had to learn to live standing or crouching. No sitting, probably. Certainly not lying down. If a man had a bit of fish or meat or a weapon in his hand, there would have been no place to set them down.

He must have dozed while walking, despite the growing burn of his feet, for all at once it was darker. There were shouts and whoopings ahead, a long, straggly grove of trees and the glow of starting fires. The pack-train halted. Beyond the far left end of the trees a sort of surf was rolling, whipped up by McCarthy's Caho-kians returning from the hunt. They had had good luck and the men were draped with wildfowl, rabbits and squirrels. The six pack-horses detailed to the hunt tramped on, clumsy under chunks of butchered meat, under deer-carcasses and dismembered buffalo. The thought of food did for Mark, and his feet suddenly became too painful for walking.

All at once he found himself flat on a mass of soft boughs with George Rogers Clark pushing a mug of rum at him while John Saunders and Joe Simmonds stripped off his moccasins and rigged them on a twig frame near a fire. Then Saunders uncorked the sawed-off tip of a cow-horn slung about his neck and smeared black gummy stuff on Markham's soles.

Markham suddenly gagged and choked, sputtering, "Get that hell-brewed stench away from me!"

Simmonds pushed him back. "Sure, Mark, it stinks like the

NOW THIS IS GOINING

TO FAR.

Well before dark the head of the column was across and pushing east again. The other companies and the pack-train followed its trail over an interminable plain where feet sank deeper and deeper in watery mud. The last squad to leave the west bank stripped the ropes from the makeshift bridge, catwalked perilously to the other side and then sent the logs pitching and lurching into the current. No one was pursuing, of course. No one could possibly be pursuing. But extra-careful men were apt to live extra-long in the wilderness.

Camp that night was in a sodden tangle of overgrown bushes that failed to look like trees even in the uncertain light of small fires lighting against swirls of thick mist. The men were not pleased and cursed what they termed a scurvy God damn half-dead briar patch that, by God, back home wouldn't house so much as a runty stink-bug. The hunters came sloughing in to rejoin the column. Their horses were heavily laden, but chiefly with firewood, for the party had been able to come up with no buffalo, deer were scarce and even when found were stringy and ragged. A good haul of waterfowl was brought in but, it seemed, there should have been many more. A vast pond, literally paved with birds, had been found, but as the hunters came toward it against the wind, some prairie beast, species unknown, had made a wild rush from the shore, sending the birds aloft in screaming hundreds to lance away across the sky in search of less troubled spots.

Despite the poor yield of that day's hunt, the boggy ground and the twisted caricatures of trees that could hardly be called a grove, the squares were formed as methodically as ever, the fresh rations were carefully shared out, to be supplemented from the men's pouches, and details squabbled fairly amiably over the dry wood brought in on the horses. The rain increased, but before the last bone had been gnawed the drum started its clatter and the fiddle took up its whining refrain.

In Worthington's square, Markham scraped dead leaves from a patch of reasonably dry, hard ground near a fire. Then he hauled from the slack of his shirt a soft, thick roll as long as his arm and tossed it onto the cleared spot where it gave out a rich, rank smell of wood-smoke and greasy cooked meats. A voice from the darkness called, "Hey! What you got there, Mark?"

"Hi, Phil. Just some old leather I got off Henry De Witt for that set of awls I brought up from Arkansas Post."

Brady dropped to his knees and spread out the roll in the firelight. Through deep-grained smoke-stains a pattern of blues and reds and ochres and whites still glowed faintly. Brady whistled softly. "I know Henry De Witt, big sergeant in Williams's company. Only man in the Detachment tall enough to look down and tell George if he's got a bald spot coming. And you took *this* off him for those little stickers? Mark, he ought to have the law on you."

"So? Think awls like those are easy to come by?"

"Jesus, try and get more elk-skin like this. It's from near the peak of an Ojibway tepee, so it's got naturally sun-dried and smoked and greased until it's cured proper."

"That's what I figured, Phil. Let's straighten it out flat. Now I sink this peg here and here, then here and here on your side. Look pretty square?"

"Couldn't have ruled it much truer. Two feet by 'bout three."

"Good. Hold up your side the short way. Watch out. I'm starting to cut." His knife hissed along the fold toward Brady's hard fingers. "Now the other short side."

"Neat," said Brady approvingly. "Wait — better start trimming from here."

"Right. Holler if I'm getting off the line." With the point of his knife he scored out a long tongue of leather, then sliced it free save at its base where it extended the main body of the sheet. Then he stripped off one moccasin, placed his bare foot on the leather, gathered it up about his Achilles tendon, pulled the long, broad tongue up along his instep and ankle, and closed the two side flaps over the tongue. "How does it look, Phil?"

Brady grinned. "Damned if you could have done that back when we left old Charcot, Mark. Yep, that'll do."

Markham pulled an awl from his pouch and punched two holes

It was still raining and Markham, with Clark and McCarthy, was standing at the edge of a thick grove of trees looking northeast over a chilling expanse of water. The surface was wrinkled a hundred yards ahead by weary bush-tops straining above the flood. In the middle distance trees showed, a double line of them, with a noticeable gap between those lines and, off in the distance, more trees.

"You've covered this trail before, Rick," said Clark. "Tell us about it."

"I'm diddled," said McCarthy in his hoarse voice. "What you got here — and I'm guessing when I tell you — is the Lower and Upper Forks of the Little Wabash, all flowed together. It's got to be, 'less we've strayed off the map and hit into Krim Tartary. Yes, sir, the two's one stream and so help me God I never did see 'em wedded like this before."

"This isn't Krim Tartary," said Clark with a grin. "It smells and tastes and feels like something north of the Ohio, west of the Wabash. Look, Markham, let's call these bushes down here the near bank of the Lower Fork, and the first row of trees yonder its far bank. Then the trees beyond them are the near bank of the Upper Fork and those standing tippy-toe away off've got to be the Upper's far bank."

"A lot of water," said McCarthy, chewing his underlip. "Call it five-six miles from us to the yonderest tree of the Upper. Why not strike downstream along this fork, Colonel? We might strike a better crossing below."

Clark made an impatient gesture. "That's shivery. You go always moving. Always hoping for something better. First thing you know you're on the Wabash miles below where you ought to be."

Clark rose as though he had heard something. Markham looked back through the trees toward the open prairies beyond but they were lifeless as ever and gave no hint of an approaching column. Then the Colonel turned quickly to Markham. "Didn't you tell me you helped build a pirogue at Arkansas Post?"

"No. I used to see them in the Canaries, though, brought in tow from the African coast. The men who really know pirogues are

Louis Gendron of Rick's company and the Frechette twins of Charleville's."

"Fine! Now Rick and I want to prowl this shore a bit upstream. I want you to go through this grove and find a trunk long enough and thick enough for a pirogue. Come on, Rick."

After a long search Markham found a healthy cedar with a good thirty feet of straight trunk. As he blazed it with his hatchet a distant shout from upstream told him that Clark and McCarthy had sighted the column coming east across the prairie. He squatted at the foot of his tree and waited patiently while light rain sifted down onto his hat-brim and shoulders.

In another five minutes the whole grove was flooded with men and pack-horses, the latter willing to trot the last few yards that stood between them and a feed. Then Clark came running toward Markham followed by Gendron and the Frechettes, one of whom dragged a reluctant pack-horse after him.

Markham rose as Clark shouted, "I knew you'd find one, Markham." Gendron intoned, "Ah-ah-ah! Le bel arbre!" while the Frechettes fell upon the pack-horse, flung off a sheaf of handles and a heavy sack that spilled out adze-heads as it hit the ground.

"There you are!" cried Clark. "I'm sending some axe-men to drop that tree for you. You start hollowing it out into something that'll float a heavy load. I'll send men to spell you in relays. Compree?"

Within half an hour the tree was down and trimmed. The three adzes made careful, muted, steady snick-snick-snick which went on until dark. By dawn they were going again. For the first time Gendron and the Frechettes allowed picked men to spell them while they watched the deepening trough-like scoop along the trunk, as though a hairline shaving too much or too little would ruin the work which they had started.

In the camp the men hung about, uneasy at the unwonted leisure that was so suddenly thrust upon them. Uneasiness turned to uncertainty, to suspicion over nothing at all. Squabbles broke out that could develop into serious brawls.

Then Markham saw Clark drifting with apparent aimlessness

the march across what was supposed to be shallower water to the near bank of the Upper Fork. How would he carry that out and what would happen when that near bank was reached?

Someone came sloshing and puffing behind him and he turned to see Joe Bowman churning along waist-deep. "What happens at this next bank, Joe?" called Markham.

Bowman waved Markham and the others on. "Get there and you'll find out. You've staked enough of a trail. Bottom's beginning to shelve up already. Not far to shore now."

Markham stuck the rest of his poles upright in the muddy bottom as a signal, and he and Bowman sloshed towards the shore, perhaps a quarter of a mile away, where a grove of saplings grew. Bowman said, "Now here's what I want you to do. Cut us a couple of dozen forked stakes about six feet long and drive them into the ground in a square, about five feet across. Then cut a couple of dozen stakes to lay across the forks, to make a platform above the ground where George can stow what's in that pirogue until it's loaded back on the horses again. Better hop to it — George will be along with that pirogue in no time." Then he turned back to direct the lead men in the column, floundering along leading the horses.

As the first men came scrambling onto the bank, Mark, Hodges and Beaubien set them straight to work. Within twenty minutes a tough platform of stakes stood a good two feet above the level of the water; and when the pirogue, its trough-like interior crammed to the limit of safety with bales and bundles from the horses' backs, dug its clumsy nose into the shore, all was ready. Clark, heaving at the stern of the pirogue, was still panting as he emerged from the water. "Wonderful, Mark," he shouted. "Just what I wanted! Now everyone help unload the pirogue onto that platform. And you men leading horses, bring 'em up to the platform one at a time. When your horse is loaded, lead it over into that clearing and have the pack-men stand to head." The pirogue was emptied in no time. Clark whistled up his crew, pushed off for the other shore.

The last two horses were being led up to the platform as Bowman shouted that Clark was halfway across with the final load. "Do we pitch camp on the platform now, Joe?"

"George knows. Wait long enough and the rest of us'll find out."

The pirogue butted ashore once more, was unloaded. As the last load went on the last horse, Clark leaned against the platform — a man quite at ease, not a spent, weary one. The four companies stood knee-deep and more in water, as patiently as though on the parade-ground of Fort Clark, back there at Kaskaskia. Clark began to grin, wiping his forehead and fanning himself with his hat. "Now when I sighted this spell of water on —" he turned to Bowman — "when was it, Joe?"

"Thirteenth," answered Bowman, "unless my diary's wrong."

"Thirteenth," said Clark. "Thanks, Joc. Well when I saw it, I felt real bad. It was worse than I'd ever figured on." He ran his fingers through his coppery hair. "Don't mind admitting it looked *too* big. Then I started totting up and it came to me there's one thing it ain't bigger than." He pointed a finger, swept it across the group. "That was *you* — all of you. By God, I was right and here we are, we've bit off the first tough chunk and I've been kicking myself for having a doubt for even a second." He began to laugh softly.

Clark paused and Markham noted that everyone was unconsciously puffing out his chest, standing straighter in the biting water, preening himself a little. Markham found himself shouting something, he was not quite sure what, was drowned out by a score of other voices. The Colonel rode easily over the din, his words booming out. "Anyway we're here now and there are two things I want like hell to do. One's to hurry the horses right across those three miles to the Upper Fork, build another thingumbob like this, load the pirogue from it and get across to the far bank. The other's to build a lot more scaffolds like this so we can all lie on 'em and get some rest. We don't know what it'll be like over there, but by God, there we'll be, bag and baggage, ready for the Embarras."

Markham moved with the rest in a great sweep of spray as more than two hundred feet beat like dashers into the muddy water. The last of the loading detail stood by Joe Bowman's second platform and looked up at the sky in unbelief. A pearly light was spread-

The horses were gone and the column left its muddy ridge to plunge into shallowing water. Sometimes Markham's moccasins were pressing onto solid, fairly dry earth for a hundred yards or so before another sheet of water less than knee-deep would spread before him and the others. A sluggish stream, which Phil Brady identified as the Fox River, cut across the line of march, its banks actually above the flooded plains. Without waiting for orders, men threw heavy brush into the channel, felled a few meager-trunked trees and were across before the center of the column was aware of any obstacle.

Markham with the towering Henry De Witt, to whom he had given his set of awls for the spread of well-smoked elk-skin, and one-eyed Sergeant Harrison, to whom he owed his first knife, were sent out far in advance of the column after the Fox was passed. The trio plashed on the next day through more level plains, found a sparse-treed ridge, crossed it and hit on, still bearing northeast.

The ground rose during the morning, sloped away from them, rose once or twice but never to its former level. Markham was carrying his rifle like a yoke across his shoulders, was forced to shift it still higher as random gusts of wind splashed water dangerously close to muzzle or lock. Sergeant Harrison, squinting and twisting his scarred face like the sculptured demons Markham had seen in old Italian churches, held his rifle well above his head. Even De Witt, tall enough to look down on Clark, was balancing his piece carefully. Suddenly he began to slide downward. Markham snatched his rifle from him while Harrison caught his powder-horn, and both halted on the edge of a slope. De Witt went on as though drawn by some unseen hand until the water was around his armpits. Then he stopped abruptly.

"Right smart little run you're paddlin' in," said Harrison. "Me, I'd be dipping my ears was I along of you."

"How wide?" asked Markham.

De Witt went ahead a few cautious steps. The water fell away from him until his chest was well above the surface. "So wide," he said.

Harrison spat disgustedly. "And by Jeze, there's more 'n that. See, half-mile ahead where the water's all kind of pimpled out with drowned bushes pushing up to the air?"

"By that dark streak?" asked Markham. "Sure, I see it now."

"Well, that's telling me something," said Harrison, squinting more horribly than ever. "It's telling me that Little Wabashes is overflowed and that we knowed already. It tells me that Embarras is overflowed and likely the God damn big Wabash, too."

De Witt rubbed his rain-wet face. "You can be wrong, and I'll be wrong right along with you. But if we're both right, then we're standing in one son of a bitch of a big lake and Vincennes and its fort are setting on an island somewhere in it off there. So what do we do, Mark?"

Markham shuffled carefully about until he was headed in the direction from which they had come. "I'd say the next move is to get back and tell the Colonel about this lake."

De Witt sloshed in the water and called out, "I'd not contrary you. Let's get back and tell George."

The three, rifles still high, worked their way west until they saw the heads of the advance party topping a low bare ridge. Harrison prodded Markham with his elbow. "George is out to front. You do the telling."

Clark pushed on toward them as they halted. His eyes scanned the three faces carefully but his tone, when he hailed, was as easy and confident as ever. "What's fretting you, boys? Get tired of a little walking?"

Harrison nodded. "Plumb shriveled up on you like three curly God damn caterpillars."

"Might have known it!" shouted Clark, laughing. He casually turned his back on the advancing column so his expression would not be seen if the news were bad and he allowed himself to show it.

"Henry and I figure from the drift of the water that all rivers around here have joined up," said Markham.

"All of 'em?" Clark asked pleasantly.

"They've maybe left a chunk of land sticking out here and yon," put in Harrison. "Say enough for half a Kaintuck' corn-patch."

were lit and, spoiled or not, rations were cooked. In all squares the same excited talk of the night before swept on, but now the fall of Vincennes was treated as a stale matter and a dozen plans were launched for a swift march straight up against Detroit.

As Markham fell asleep the rocks under his back felt like feather beds, and soon he was having his first dream of Boston in a very long time, finding himself in the family pew at King's Chapel watching, with no surprise, Madame de Liliac across the aisle looking very lovely in a rose colored bonnet. Then he woke. "Idiot!" he said to the distress of De Witt. "Why didn't you ask her first name!"

"Don't want to know it! Shut up!" replied De Witt. "Get some sleep!"

Peering through trees as though through a high picket fence, Markham saw more water, stretching north and north again. It seemed to stretch at least two miles ahead to the east, to a thin line of trees and bushes in the distance. After the luxury of the night before, it had seemed like nothing to wade all day in water that never rose as high as the knees. But now, in what must have been a burned-over tract, young saplings bristled like endless rows of coachmen's whips set upright in the ooze. Markham was wading to his thighs, and his face stung from the lash and snap of the branches.

Phil Brady sloshed up to him. Behind them, in the trees, the column was halted, standing in grim fatigue, the realization of their plight beginning to steal across their faces. Now a scouting-party floundered into the grove from the north, and Markham and Brady followed the party until it reached Clark. It was growing dark.

"There's only one explanation that I can see," said Markham as he pushed a sapling aside. "These rivers run parallel to each other like the fingers on a hand; but with this warm wet winter they've all overflowed their banks, as though the fingers had swelled up."

"That's it, I guess," admitted Brady. "We've been able to cross them all so far; but the Embarras looks too deep for that; and judging from the sour expressions on the scouts' faces, I guess we're going to have to swim or else take the long way around."

The leader of the scouts was finishing his report as Markham and Phil came up; and every man's face was angry, disappointed, fatigued except Clark's whose clear voice rang out from the dusk. "Fine! Wonderful! You've done a great job! Now we know for sure that it's all right to keep on south to the junction with the Wabash. We'll cross the Wabash there and strike upstream for Vincennes, as soon as the *Willing* arrives. That way we'll be marching on full stomachs. Now all we have to do is to find a place to bed down tonight!" And he began giving orders to the captains.

As darkness deepened Markham plodded along, chewing stolidly at a handful of dried corn-kernels, wondering if his pleasure in the faint, nutty taste was real or just due to the generally dismal surroundings. Though he could pick a dozen flaws in Clark's summation, he felt somehow cheered and lifted by it. Night grew clammier, thicker, colder. It was several hours past sunset before a stretch big enough for a camp was found, a miserable mud-shelf that shouldered up out of water like a tidal bar. The men waded onto it, hauling the weak, the sick, and the lame with them. Markham, every joint and muscle aching, stripped off his now tattered moccasins and pitched them into the water. Then he drew from his shirt the next-to-last pair of new ones. As he laced them about his ankles he smiled to himself, noticing that the men coming out of the water onto this most hopeless of campsites, unhesitatingly stumbled or fell into proper square formation without an order being given or a word spoken. He shook his head, "By God, I wonder how many men there are in the world who'd be able to do that after such a day. Hell, how many are there who'd be able to stick this far on a march like ours?" He did a little mental arithmetic. "Who'd have believed it? Just fourteen days ago we left Kasky and not a man's fallen out!" The thought somehow braced him. He accepted as a matter of course the order that no fires be lit and spread his blankets on the driest ground he could find and was asleep almost at once.

XVI

"Good News Quick and Frequent"

THE FIRST bewildered milling about by the banks of the Wabash gradually gave way to more concerted activity. Some men raced to the southerly edge of firm ground, peering downstream, hoping for a glimpse of the *Willing*. Their shouts rose. "By Christ, she could be waiting just below that there bend." "This is where she's supposed to meet us, she can't be far away." A higher voice, a man pointing. "*Voilà. Qu'est-ce que c'est que ça? A gauche! Parmi ces arbres-là!*" Another, higher still, "By God, I think Louis is right! Ain't that her, loaded and headin' this way? By the willows there." Then a dull groan. "Naw, just a God damn ol' log."

Other men, more practically minded, ripped down thin saplings, trimmed them and moved to the water's edge, prodding and sounding. Sergeant Henry De Witt tossed his pole away after a minute or two. "The true bank's a good five foot under. God knows how much deeper the channel is! Well, no chance of running aground anyway."

Impervious to all the turmoil, Clark stood with Joe Bowman and the four company commanders, McCarthy, Charleville, Worthington, and Williams. They were looking east at the huge lake that held, hidden somewhere in its depths, the east bank of the Wabash and the trail to Vincennes. Then the group scattered, and Clark called, "Joe Hitchens and Zeb Mason! Remember that raft you built up by the Great Kanawha last year? We want another like it and right away. Everyone else! Report to your company commanders and show them any sacks or pouches that've lugged food. Strip off your shirts and make sure you've got nothing stowed away to chew on in a shady spot!" Markham thought he caught a murmur as though in protest. Clark went on. "Hell, I know no one's hiding rations, but if we can get a pinch of meal here and a corn kernel there or a sausage end or a knob of smoked meat we'll be able to mix something up for the boys that are weakest. Come on, Markham. Show me your haversack and rip your shirt off. Then you go over my gear."

Pouches and sacks were turned inside out, the seams brushed and scraped, shirts were flapped and beaten. To his surprise a few odds and ends were actually collected and turned over to Joe Bowman for distribution. Under the trees, Hitchens and Mason and a few others chopped and trimmed and measured their timber, then bound the components together with a fearsome rig of tough ropes, cords and supple vines. As they dragged the raft to the water's edge close to dusk, Clark gave orders to the launching party. "Joe and Zeb! Who's with you? Zack Tyler and Caleb Best? Right! Head upstream and be on the lookout for the first farms or plantations. I don't want them to see you. All we want's for you to find out if a canoe or two won't kind of shake loose from the banks. If they do, you grab them and hustle them right back to us." The raft moved slowly north under paddle and pole, its crew miserably awash on the slippery surface.

Relative calm settled over that odd little peninsula which in normal times must have been a pleasant wooded hillock overlooking the meadow-lands that edged the Wabash-Embarras junction. Evening came on with the command making itself as comfortable as it could in its squares, and another night crept in through the ragged shadows of evening.

Rain arrived with the dawn, and the raft was missing with its four men. Markham got creakily to his feet, saw John Saunders and tall De Witt standing like bent old men, blinking and rubbing their joints. He managed to lengthen his stride, broke in between them from behind, caught each by an elbow and forced them to match his pace up and down the sodden ground. From somewhere in the rear he heard Joe Bowman call, "Quit chattering like crones in an almshouse. Look at Mark Cape there and John Saunders and Hank De Witt! That's better than hot rum and buffalo tongue."

downstream, Markham felt a gradual easing of mind. In this drowned tangled country anything might happen; but each stroke southward diminished the feeling that he and the other two were invading British territory on their own. He pulled the sash of his shirt tighter, rather relieved to find that the preliminary hunger-cramps were lessening. If the symptoms ran true to form, a period would follow in which the crushing weakness would remain, but all desire for food would be gone. He hoped that it would stay away for a long time. Things were easier that way.

The other canoe came as a complete surprise to him and to McCarthy and Benoit as well. It slid out of a stretch of open water that slanted off to the east among the trees and harsh scrub growth, and entered the stream just ahead of them. It was a large canoe and there were five Creole men in it, all armed with thick-barreled muskets and so intent on scanning the drowned growth on both sides of the river that they had not noticed the craft just upstream.

McCarthy gave no command, but drove his canoe ahead with a silent, powerful stroke. Markham caught up his rifle, grateful for dry priming and fresh charge. Benoit shipped his paddle, reached out a long, sinewy arm. His hand dropped on the stern of the other canoe, checking its progress.

The strange craft rocked as five heads swiveled about abruptly, and, to Markham's surprise, rattled out questions like bird-shot. Had McCarthy's canoe been far upstream? Was there any sign of *canard* or duck? For hours, *ventre de dieu!* the five had waded through marshes, poled through underbrush without seeing as much as a *mésange*, a chickadee, and now they were far from Vincennes.

McCarthy growled, "*Allez-y, Raoul!*"

Benoit politely requested the Creoles to come downstream and meet a friend. They answered that it was impossible. That they had been departed from Vincennes an incalculable number of hours. One could conceive that their families would be all that there was of the most *distrait*. Benoit repeated his invitation, but in a different tone. Markham wondered why the Vincennois bothered to argue. With their five fowling pieces they could have blown the smaller canoe out of the water. Then he saw that Benoit's free hand held a long knife against the thin hull of the other canoe, that his own muzzle was poised to rake it from the stern up, and that McCarthy was covering the water line. The three strangers might be put out of action but the Vincennois would be left in mid-current with two sinking canoes. Few Creoles could swim. There were five shrugs, the five grunted, "*Il n'y a rien à faire!*" and the two craft ran in seeming amity downstream.

There was no doubt that the Vincennes Creoles were impressed by the group of worn, lean but alert and lively men with their well-kept rifles and long knives. Clark greeted them as welcome guests on whom no demands would be made. Soon all five were talking eagerly with him, Bowman and Charleville while the carefree life of the camp went on unchecked about them.

Not long afterward, the group broke up, with Clark and his officers strolling away casually as though stopping at all had been mere routine politeness. The Vincennois soon found cousins and uncles and friends among the Illinois people and were swallowed up in swirls of greetings and reminiscences.

Clark beckoned to McCarthy and Benoit and Markham. "Why'd you hang back? Figure I was mad at you or something?"

McCarthy answered quickly, "Thought they'd talk easier this way."

Clark moved over to Markham. "Right. That hadn't hit me at all. Well, you got a fine haul. They talked. Ample. The Hairbuyer hasn't got the least notion we're not in Kasky. No one has." He grinned boyishly. "When the floods are gone, Hamilton's going to march his soldiers into Illinois and finish us up for good. Yep, he sure is. Oh, and Len Helm's all right. Shares the Hair-buyer's quarters, wins shillings off him at cards and brews that damned Heartener for both of 'em. Now we've still got daylight left. Let's use it." He strode off, shouting for Captain Worthington.

In a few moments that officer and two of his men paddled back up the Wabash in quest of two canoes that the Vincennois said they had seen adrift in that quarter. McCarthy's canoe, staffed by two of his best paddlers, vanished downstream on some unexplained mission.

Left to himself, Markham moved toward the western edge of the bare land, tugging at old roots, ripping up bulb-like clusters from the rank black bottom. Others were out ahead of him, pushing over dead trees, thumping on their hollow sides in never-dying hope of flushing game no matter how small. But darkness fell on this strange hunt before Markham had come on an edible root or the dead trees had yielded as much as a grub. Worthington and his men came in from their upstream trip, towing one medium-size canoe. There had been no trace of the other reported by the Vincennois.

Somehow the sight of this one pitiable, leaky *"spolia opima"* sent a wave of excitement through the camp, now arranged in its proper squares. Men came to stare and point at this rare treasure which they had not brought with them, which they had not had to build or win from the floods. It was a glittering bonus, almost too good to be believed in.

Later the whole camp, except for the usual guards, slept deeply. Few besides Markham heard the silent return of the canoe that had gone south, the reluctant report to Clark: "Tell you, George, we hit down a good ten mile, mebbe more, always in the current. High nor low they ain't no sign of the *Willing* nor of Johnny Rogers."

But dozens heard Clark's shout, "Hear that, Joe? Not a damn thing to wait for, to hold us back! We'll start crossing at first light!"

One man kicked another awake. Someone sprang from a deep sleep yelling, "Chris' sake, don't leave me behind!" The cry "Worthington's men this way!" mingled with *"Cahokia! Rangez-vous par ici!"* The squares melted into long thin columns under the trees. The half-seen Wabash began to blur as the first canoes were joined by others that Clark had had built.

Few orders were given. One by one the canoes were loaded

and sent out onto the black floor of the river. The men left behind silently reckoned ten men to a load, calculated when their turn would come and sat patiently in place while time, with nothing to mark its passage, stood still under the dripping boughs.

Markham huddled his knees to his chest, thankful that the sharp hunger-pangs were giving way to a dull, empty feeling. As he waited he heard the light scrape of paddles, the faint slap of the current against the hulls. Then came a long, whispering rustle mingled with a few cutting slaps. The canoes were going through the tree tops of the east bank. Those sounds gave way to intermittent scratching. He said to himself, "They're in among drowned bushes, probably on a flooded slope."

Someone nearby exclaimed, "They're ashore!" and a gust of laughter swept over the gaunt, waiting men. They coughed and sputtered and slapped their knees, crowing, "By shot, ain't that cute? *Ashore* in four foot of God damn water!"

The canoes returned, were filled silently, pushed out again, moving still more quietly since the paddlers learned to avoid the worst of branches and menacing snags that thrust dagger-like from the flood. The sky was graying when Markham's turn came and he was halfway to the east shore when the sunrise gun of Fort Sackville thudded, off to the north. His canoe and the one just ahead drove faster at the sound. Markham, flinching inwardly, was sure that that shot was routine. Just the same, warning might have reached Hamilton and the redcoats of the 8th Foot and the white of the Detroit militia might be swarming from the sally-port at that very moment.

Drowned bushes beat a steady tattoo beneath. A canoe to port was heaved up by some hidden bough, pitching almost to the capsizing point. A trailing bough rocked him and he saw the glint of shipped water inside his canoe, but the paddlers worked on steadily.

More woods were wading to meet them, more and scratchier bushes until a nearly submerged hilltop, with a few good trees and a huddle of waiting men, showed close ahead. As he landed, Markham remembered that the Vincennois in describing this terrain had called the drowned hill La Mamelle, winking and making curving gestures as they spoke. Its mate, all that there was of the most perfect and *pimpante* in form, lay three miles north.

Scrambling ashore onto a muddy, tree-capped reef covered with muddy men, Markham pushed his way through to the northern edge and looked out, hoping somehow that the other rounded hill might live up to the Vincennois description. All he saw was oily gray-brown water between wide-spaced trees, dripping bush-tops and little spouts rising everywhere to the touch of a thin, drilling rain.

Clark came bursting through with his company commanders and Joe Bowman. "There!" he cried. "Look at that. You agree with what Joe said, you four? With all those bushes and trees out there we'd be two days ferrying the command across to the Upper Mamelle. Ferry? Hell, you'd have to push the canoes every inch of the way."

Charleville said slowly, "It will not be amusing to take weary men over there. *Quand même —*" he shrugged. "It must be done."

"Charleville's right," said Williams. "Tough, but we got to get there."

Clark went on. "Then what's keeping us? Just one damn short league across there. Joe, start the boys coming, any order you like. Hello, Markham! Didn't see you. Stand by with Joe. Come on, you others, let's give 'em the lead." One arm about a shoulder of the two nearest officers, he strode into the flood. "You know, this is going to be a sight easier than it looks — for some of the boys."

The first men came up over the little crest — John Saunders, Joe Simmonds, Dick Brashears, Phil Brady. They walked heavy-lidded, with stubbly gray faces, and they breathed through parted, caked lips. But their arms swung free and easy and their stride flowed on as it had on the open prairies and their heads were still high. They nodded to Markham and stepped out into the drowned lands again.

The Vincennois, who had been brought in the night before,

followed, shouting in protest. Even such an army as Colonel Clark's could never get to the Upper Mamelle and let alone beyond it. Impossible! In all friendship, they cried, a tactful word to the Colonel — The long column streamed on, disregarding the wails of *"Ah, les pauvres!"*

Bowman called, "Start any time you want, Mark!"

Markham waved in acknowledgment and tramped in behind one of the Grenier twins. He was not conscious of wet or cold, just a heaviness about his legs that slowed his pace. The bushes seemed to reach out, catch him with brambly arms, pass him on to the next rank growth. He grabbed the least spiky branches and went on, hand over hand in Grenier's wake, trying to move in before the displaced branches snapped back at him. The Creole kept up a high, thin humming, *"Sur le pont d'Avignon — madondaine —"* Markham began to echo the refrain almost unconsciously, while wondering irritably why the Creole didn't complete the verse.

The bushes were thicker now with more trees scattered among them and he thought of Clark's words that this stretch would be easier. Easier for whom? He heard panting and thrashing close by and looked about. The water, waist-deep for him, was nearly shoulder-high for stocky little Aubain of Cahokia, who clung gasping to a young hickory. Markham moved toward him but Aubain grinned. He did himself very well, he said, so long as the trees, resting places, set for him by *le bon Dieu*, held out. A moment to breathe and he would flounder on to the young oak *là-haut.*

A little farther on, something butted Markham's shoulder, pushing him forward. A canoe was being half hauled, half floated on through the underbrush and he looked down into a waxy face, wiry with red stubble and closed, swollen lids. Someone had given in to bone-cracking fever and another man with a bandaged leg lay beyond him. Two men tugged the canoe past Markham who made way for them. Stumbling over unseen roots and branches, he wondered how far he had come. Three miles between the Mamelles, so if — His reckoning was broken by a shout from behind. Geoffrion of McCarthy's was holding the little drummer, complete with drum, toward Markham and growling, "*Alors, prend cela!*" while nodding ahead.

Markham took the wiry little body, looked down at the hollow temples, the high cheek-bones blued with cold and grunted an encouraging, "*Ça marche, hein?*" The round cropped head nodded silently and Markham was relieved to see that towering Henry De Witt was now in front of him. He called, "De Witt! Pass him up the column!"

De Witt turned, held out his long arms. "*Allons!*" cried Markham, glancing down as he shifted his grip. One swollen, reddened eye met his, flicked in a wink. The drummer whispered hoarsely, "*Merci, mon brave!*"

Markham laughed as De Witt took his burden. "'*Mon brave*' be damned! Henry, if he calls *you* 'my good fellow,' let the brat swim!" Then he slipped on a slick root, nearly fell and devoted himself to his own progress.

There were more scattered trees, a wide zone of bushes that stood wall-solid before yielding grudgingly. The water was knee-deep, then ankle-deep. Markham knew a weird sense of lightness and cold from waist to foot and thumped his feet on firm, muddy ground.

He hooked an arm about a sapling and looked dazedly around him. He had reached the Upper Mamelle, a long three, even four miles from the Wabash. He felt a sort of unsteady elation and knew it for a further symptom of too much exertion and too little food. Other men, seized with the same uneasy excitement, clambered up near him, peering and huffling. Ed Bulger of Williams's company stared sourly. "All I got to say is, they ain't named these hills after no gal in Kasky or Cahoky, not that *I* seen!"

De Witt said reasonably, "You got to admit these two hills is *alike*, Ed. It's just that there ain't much to 'em."

Markham put in, "Bet they're Indian mounds, like Monk's mound at Cahokia."

Bulger looked dubious. "Wish I'd paid more heed to them Indian gals in camp that time. They's *something* here that ain't just right."

De Witt sat down with his back against a tree. "Hell with 'em. All I want's to sleep a hundred and ten and a half hours and then eat for two hundred and twenty and two halves."

Others grumbled in weary agreement. No one made any move to form squares. No one gave an order. A heavy slackness, deepening as more men came up, spread over the crest. Markham saw them as a crowd of spent men who had gone about as far as they could.

Then, as though some single slow impulse had run over the island, men began sorting themselves out, forming their squares. The moving and shifting ended and in the last flurries Clark and Ed Worthington waded ashore unexpectedly off the east end. Clark stopped, swept the squares with a swift glance. In Williams's company a man who was wringing out his shirt with a friend looked up rather guiltily. "Well, hell, George, didn't any orders come so we kind of figured —"

Clark laughed. "Figured you'd use your wits even if no one else did? You were right!" He raised his voice. "Dry out. Build little fires. No one's going to look for us, not in the fog that's coming in. Now the Vincennes boys tell me the next land's a league north, a place they use for sugar camps when the maple-sap's running, so there are sure to be huts of some kind for the sick and lame. We'll go there tomorrow." He began to grin. "The Vincenners say we'll never make it, but, hell, they said we'd never cross the Wabash and when we'd done that they said we'd never get to the Upper Mamelle here. Reckon they don't understand how you boys tear into rough travel."

Before he could say any more, men in all the squares were shrugging into dripping shirts, slapping wet moccasins onto their feet. Someone shouted, "What the hell are we waiting for? Me, I crave a corner of one of them huts." Others joined in. Markham levered himself to his feet and hitched at his rifle-sling. A dull, rhythmic tapping sounded as the drummer strove manfully to draw stirring tones from his sodden drum-head.

Clark dropped to a rock with a helpless gesture. "I knew you were tough but I never thought I'd find you tougher than *I* am. My legs are hollering 'No!' But go on. Take the canoes. This time, though, you'll leave me behind."

Someone muttered, "By God, George is smart at that, more smart than tuckered!" Everywhere, soaking shirts were being peeled off again, interrupted tasks resumed with elaborate casualness as though men were trying to hide their covert relief. Here and there flint snicked against steel over heaps of dead leaves and twigs. Markham moved away, looking for John Saunders and his horn of foul black muck. Not that he could detect any real return of foot-scald but his left sole itched and this would be a good chance for a treatment. From the depths of his shirt he worried out some new, dry thongs. The last time Markham had seen John, the latter's moccasins were bound at the ankle with twists of vine. These strips ought to be welcome.

The next day's sunrise-gun from Fort Sackville sounded as remote and unreal as had that very first report heard near the junction of the Embarras and the Wabash two days before, as distant as though no progress had been made. The thought unreasonably depressed Markham as he went with McCarthy toward the north side of the island on unsteady legs. He nearly collided with Joe Bowman and François Charleville by an alder-clump but Bowman waved away his apologies. "Everybody walks slew-foot on an empty belly, Mark. If I'd kept on where I was heading when I first got up, I'd have ended back on the first Mamelle."

"Such is hunger, *mes amis*," observed Charleville.

"Yup, and something's got to be done," growled McCarthy looking through the mist. "My boys are willing enough but the day'll come soon when they'll just shiver apart like thin ice. Where's George?"

"Out to the north looking for a good passage to the sugar camps," answered Bowman. "Here he comes wading in now."

Clark's tall frame slashed on toward shore, and, as though animated by a single cord, the men of the Detachment began mov-

ing shoreward, step by slow step, their eyes on him. Markham gave
Bowman a warning jab, flicking his eyes toward the silent drift of
men. Bowman muttered, "Thanks, Mark," then shouted jovially,
"George, I got a bet that says you found us a spot where we could
cross in silk stockings."

Markham, McCarthy and Charleville managed noisy laughs
while Bowman reached out and pulled Clark to the center of the
group, slapping his shoulder. They then laughed louder than ever,
even while they noticed his dulled eyes, drawn-down mouth and
the listless set to his head.

Clark rested a hand on Markham's shoulder, another on Charleville's as though to steady himself. Without looking up he muttered
hoarsely, "I don't know — I just don't know. There are currents
out there and the water's deep as hell, muddy and cold as ice, running strong. Joe, it's bad. I'm scared we'll lose a lot of the boys.
And we've only got two good canoes left. If we ferry, it'll take
two days, maybe three, and even one's more than we can gamble
on. Let me get my breath. Maybe I can think of something."

The five kept up their screen of carefree clamor, but over it
swept an ominous murmur from the rest of the men. No one word
stood out, but the low rumbling tones meant that hope was fading
from the Detachment. Men were ripping down branches, dragging
them into heaps as though gathering material for rafts, dragging
them on to the *south* side of the hilltop as though common instinct
were telling them that in retreat lay salvation, that if Clark had lost
hope, there was no hope left for anyone.

Markham and Charleville gave simultaneous shouts as Clark's
big fingers bit into their shoulders. Then Clark began speaking
in swift, low tones that tumbled out with hot urgency.

"Stupid bastard! I let them read me! Maybe we can cheer them
up. All of you do just what I do — everything. No questions!" He
seized his powder flask, shook a little black heap into his wet
hand, worked the stuff into a paste and smeared it over his face.
He gave a piercing whoop, straightened in a leap that carried him
high off the ground and, hatchet in one hand, knife in the other,
bounded off in a wide arc, now crouching, now leaping.

Quickly Markham and the other three men imitated him, twisting their blackened faces as they uttered yells and high, thin cries and followed closely his weird dance. Through all his acting, Markham was aware that the drift to the south edge had stopped, that men were dropping their hastily gathered branches and staring. Someone bawled, "George, you got the Ottawa ghost dance mixed with the Sauk buffalo dance." Laughter broke out, more shouts. "Ever see the Maumee Elk-spirit dance? . . . God, but George had me fooled just now. Look at him and Joe go at it! Hi, damn, this is how to start a march!"

In single file the four leaping, yelling men followed Clark into the water. Under cover of shouts and splashes he snapped, "Don't look around! Keep going! Even if we have to make the sugar camps alone, we'll make it alone. At least we'll be there!"

The tumult ashore swelled. A voice called, "Get the canoes over this side!" There was an almost continuous sound of men taking the water, whooping as Clark whooped. Markham still did not look back but presently heavy ripples overtook him and he knew that the march north had started.

The going was as bad as Clark had warned, with muddy, icy water and strong cross currents as though swollen tributaries of the Wabash were running under the flood. The depth increased slowly and steadily. Out of the corner of his eye Markham saw a canoe push forward. It was dangerously loaded and men clung to bow and stern and sides. Shouts for help echoed in the rear. He wondered numbly how long all this could go on.

It would always be a matter of dispute who found it first. Markham was sure that he had but others were as firm in their claims. He was wading uncertainly over drowned grasses four feet down on a mucky bottom. Then he shouted as he felt firm ground under foot, smooth, level ground. He followed it for a few steps, lost it, found it again. His knees were out of water, sometimes even his ankles, and the footing stayed firm. Other men were crying out of their own discovery — and his.

They had hit an old submerged path, perhaps an ancient one, part of an Indian trail or buffalo-run, and the men moved along almost as though on dry ground. Hoarse cries sounded under the iron-gray curve of the sky and wide wedges of duck wheeled and circled lower and lower to drop out of sight somewhere in the north. Men licked their lips and fingered the carefully wrapped rifle locks. *If* those duck were within range from the sugar camps, just if —

The old drowned trail held its course, firm and broad, running submerged toward a maple grove ahead. The nearer boles seemed to be wading in water but there was no tell-tale glint of flood beyond them. Markham splashed along near the head of the column, noting almost impersonally that prolonged fasting had now brought the expected utter lack of interest in the thought of food. He was sure that the flights of duck were settling far beyond the island. That probably meant at least twelve more starving hours and a return of waves of nausea, if the remembered pattern ran true.

All at once he was clear of the water and stood with half a dozen others on a half-acre of muddy ground where rotting lean-to's and a sagging cabin with planks missing from its sides lay among the maples. The sight of structures which they themselves had not built seemed to bewilder the men. Someone muttered, "The hand of the Lord's with us, God damn me if it ain't. Look at the roofs!" Then they all shied away from the old shelters as though they were too fine to be touched and began forming their squares well away from them. Overhead, more duck set up their clattering chorus as the rest of the command waded ashore.

Markham woke during the night from an uneasy sleep. The camp was silent save for the faintest of patterings that told of guards making their rounds. He got to his feet and wove toward the northern shore. One of the Vincennes men had said that from this camp the town and fort ought to be in plain view and he had a vague feeling that just a glimpse of the common goal would somehow make growing hunger and fatigue weigh a little less, might ease the miles that still lay ahead. He pushed on toward an alder-clump that hung over the water.

One sharp exclamation was swallowed up in the night-hush. He was looking out over eternal floods and the lights that he saw were not reflections of the candlelit windows of Vincennes but only the mirrored shimmer of the cold hard stars breaking through the clouds overhead. For another long minute he clung to the alders. Something low and black and solid showed off to the right front. Another island.

Over the drowned lands came a harsh, chill wind. Another island, and tomorrow would be like all the other days of the march, with deep waters, and perhaps knife-sharp ice-sheets, to battle until another muddy island was reached. It would be reached, of course. Clark's men always reached the next island. And what would the island beyond that next one be like? He pushed away from the clump and made his way back to his blankets.

The ice lying a good half-inch thick close to shore had been bad enough at the start from the sugar camps, but half a mile out the bottom turned slick and treacherous. At least it was knee-deep and Markham could not see any more blood on the water about Clark's legs or Phil Brady's or Ebenezer Severns's. The bitter water had checked the bleeding and stifled the smart of the ice-slashes across knee-caps and tendons. Markham's own legs felt numb from ankle to waist and his torso seemed to wobble uncertainly at each step as though it rested on an unsure base. He watched Phil, then Clark, then Severns. It might have been the shimmer of the water but it seemed to him that they too were having trouble, even Clark the tireless. Henry De Witt splashed into sight. He didn't hail and his cheeks kept puffing out about his rounded mouth with each breath.

Suddenly Clark halted, turned and faced the rear. He cupped his hands and Markham knew a bracing of spirit as the Colonel's voice rang out, clear and cheery as ever. "You canoe-men! Paddle ahead quick, dump your loads on the island. Then get back and pick up any man that's in trouble and rush him ahead. Keep shuttling!" He threw one hand high. "Joe! Joe Bowman! Close the rear with your squad! Now for the rest of us — keep going. Get to those trees ahead if you can and hang onto them until you're picked up by the canoes. If you can't get that far, stay where you are and they'll get you just the same! Understand, everyone? All right! Come on!" His voice soared still higher. "NO ONE FALLS OUT OR TURNS BACK! NO ONE!"

With the others of the advance, Markham looked automatically shoreward, saw the canoes shoot ahead. Bowman was closing in on the rear with a score or more of men strung out like a cordon. "What's that for, Phil?" asked Markham.

"You were still asleep this morning. George got Joe and those boys together, made sure their rifles were primed and loaded." Brady passed his hands over a face that looked sickly white under his dark beard. "Yep, loaded. Orders to shoot to kill if anyone breaks column for the rear. George's taking no chances. Christ, my mouth and tongue are stiff. Can't even handle slippery elm bark now or — Hey! George is hollering at us."

Still facing the rear Clark waited until a dozen men were gathered about him. Then he spoke quickly. "You're about the tallest men I've got and here's your job. String way out ahead. Keep moving. And keep hollering, 'It's getting shallower!' Understand?" Clark's knees sagged for an instant but he straightened up. "Just that — 'It's getting shallower!' — I don't give a God damn and you don't either if it's *not* getting shallower. The boys behind have got to have good news to feed on, good news quick and frequent. You'll get it for 'em. Even if your mouth's under water, still holler that it's better, better, holler, 'Land! Land!' " He swayed back, caught himself. "Hi! Swing that canoe in close to me. Henry De Witt, stand by!" The bow of a canoe slid in from the right and Markham stepped out of the way as Clark, reaching over, plucked from the craft the wizened little drummer whose sticks were thrust through his hat and whose arms were clinging to the drum. "Henry!" shouted Clark and swung the drummer over onto De Witt's shoulders. "There you go! Now grab your sticks and beat the charge or a rat-a-plan or whatever you call it. Slam it out! We're Vincennes bound!"

The canoe shot off ahead. The drum-head was in foul condition but somehow the strokes rattled out into the air. Clark waved the towering De Witt and his burden on and the others closed in after him. Eyes half-closed, Markham waded along. One canoe was out of sight behind the nearest trees and the other, fantastically loaded, was laboring on abreast of him.

The drum snapped on. From behind, Clark's shout came hotly, "How's the going ahead there? I told you to report." From waist-deep water Markham called, "Getting shallower, damned if it isn't!" Brady almost slipped as he cried, "Footing's fine, George!"

The water was knee-deep, it was chest-deep, it was waist-deep. Markham and Brady and Severns and De Witt and other men whom he could not see kept up their shouts. The attempt at deception seemed hopeless until Markham remembered how uncertain anything sighted along the surface of the water can be. To the men following well behind, the difference between ankle-deep and waist-deep could scarcely be detected.

They were among drowned trees still shouting, "Getting shallower!" or "Land's just ahead!" The drummer was swaying on De Witt's shoulders, sticks clutched in one hand. The water was chest-deep, pressing against Markham so that breathing was more difficult. He hauled himself along by branches and once or twice his feet floated clear of the ground. He saw Phil Brady clinging to a thick bough, head buried in the crook of his arm and chest heaving. Markham reached him, tugged at him, shouting hoarsely, "Shallows just ahead, Phil!" Brady shook loose, swung forward from his bough with a cry of "Rocks! Under my feet."

The trees seemed interminable. Clark came ranging up on the right, went chin-deep, rose again. "Get a song going! Anything!" A man behind Markham began to croak out the old refrain, "Nippin' round, around, around, nippin' round around!" Somehow the senseless words and monotonous air caught hold. The drummer picked up the rhythm and beat out a soggy accompaniment. Clark, his voice stronger than ever, roared approval, "Nippin' round, around! Keep those legs moving! Not far now." Markham managed to swivel his head stiffly to the rear, saw that some of the weaker or shorter men had reached the trees, were clinging to the boles and shouting for the canoe.

The drummer kept beating round, around, around, and men were floundering and shouting right, left and front, shouting in encouragement of others, in the very ecstasy of desperate effort, in the panic-thought of being left behind. Everything became mechanical. Markham hauled on one branch, let go, seized another — haul, seize, hand over hand, let go, seize again. Muscles ached and sagged but somehow kept doing what they were supposed to do. Someone was clinging to his shoulder, reaching a dripping arm past his face to clutch a bough that gave under their combined weights. Whoever it was shook clear, lurched ahead and, amazingly, brought up against a bank that rose steeply from the water.

More men had reached that bank with all its trees. They were half in, half out of the water, struggling with futile little leaps to spring clear of the flood. By an odd trick of memory Markham recalled a lot of young frogs that had fallen into a smooth basin at home. They, too, had kept leaping with ceaseless and hopeless persistence to jump free of a predicament.

Someone butted Markham from behind. He was pushed, shoved, boosted blindly, shoulders, knees and elbows rasped by bole and rock. He was on the bank with Grenier slapping his back and pointing down to the water with shouts of "*Vas-y, vas-y!*" Markham reached down and seized an arm whose soaking thrums flapped like oily fish-tails. He felt his own grip suddenly harden. He hauled, found that he was dragging Joe Simmonds onto the bank. As Grenier had done with him, Markham slapped Simmonds roughly, shouting, "Drag 'em out!" as he moved on to the next struggling figure. One of the canoes towed in Bowman and some of his rear-guard who clung to the thwarts and held their rifles high above the surface. Clark, far down the bank, was shouting, "Frog-march 'em, you men who can stand! It's worth a dozen fires."

None the less, fires blazed high and past them went a reeling procession of exhausted men, blue-lipped and ice-handed, who were hurried up and down the firm turf between two less spent men. Markham and a Grenier twin, each with an arm about Simmonds's shoulders and a hand clutching the seat of his breeches, kept him walking, walking, no matter how much his knees sagged or his head rolled. Constantly young Grenier murmured, *"Pas mal — tout au contraire!"* When Simmonds began to curse and struggle and fight, they dropped him, caught up another collapsed figure from the flood's edge. Markham could only think, "Don't know why it's not me, damned if I do." Off by a rock the drummer beat on and on, "Nippin' round, around, around. Nippin' round, around."

One by one the men who had been barely able to stagger up onto the island were hauled and pushed and shoved up and down, up and down. It seemed hours of haul and push, but Markham knew that the work had been completed when he and John Saunders seized a kneeling man only to have him thrash and struggle in their grasp, flailing his arms and bawling, "God damn it, let me go! I been marching men around the island since George started hollering and so help me Christ, John, you were the first I laid hold to. Let me go!"

The man slipped away and Saunders blinked at Markham. "Wonder when I teamed up with you, Mark," he panted. "Think George'll let us rest a spell here before we hit the next island? Man, man, that was a killing route here."

"Didn't hear him or Joe Bowman say anything about stopping long here," answered Markham, bending to press water from the legs of his breeches. "We'll sure stay past noon, though. What's ahead can't be as bad as this last stretch was, can't be —" The words died away as he saw men crowding toward the northern edge of the island. He broke into a stumbling trot, Saunders at his elbow, and wedged in by Phil Brady. "What is it, Phil? What's out there?"

Brady could only shake his head and point through a gap in a thick clump of bushes. The unexpectedness of what he saw came almost as a physical shock to Markham. There was the edge of the island, a great flooded plain — not really flooded, but covered with broad pools that threw back the unaccustomed blue of the sky. Many pools were black with duck. A few men on horseback, heavy with muskets and game-bags, were threading along on the grassy bands between the ponds. Beyond them — Markham passed unsteady hands over his face before he dared look again. Jagged against the sky across a good stretch of land and broad pools lay the steep roofs and wide galleries of what Markham had come to recognize as a Creole town ever since his first glimpse of Kaskaskia the July before. The houses presented fences and gardens to the same wide main street and off to the east lay seemingly endless fenced common-lands with the eternal forests of the wilderness world dark on the horizon far beyond. At the north end of the town stood a little church with a tiny cross-topped belfry and he knew a quick glow of recognition. Father Gibault's church, opened for worship when that quiet, devoted priest made his seasonal swings to the eastern end of his broad parish.

Rising high above church belfry and town roofs, a palisaded wall ran what a good guess could call two hundred feet, then bent sharply to run toward the west. Square, pointed-roofed towers crowned each of the four corners with shuttered gun-ports, and in the middle of the great enclosure a blockhouse, pierced for artillery like the towers, shouldered high above the encircling wall. Fort Sackville, Hamilton's headquarters.

Smoke came from a dozen chimneys of the town, from hidden barracks behind the stockade, but there was no other sign of life except for the riders circling the duck-pools with musket and game-bag. Then a small gate opened in the palisade-face nearest the island and two men stepped out. They seemed to be examining a stockade upright, and one of them swung a maul against it. They stood there for a moment, then went back into the fort and closed the gate. At that moment the sun pushed aside a small cloud to light up fully both the town and the fort.

Someone nearby breathed, "So them's the fellers we come all

this way to say 'howdy' to!" Another muttered, *"Sales Anglais!"* Markham, still staring, said, "Phil, did you really think we'd see the day when we'd be looking at Fort Sackville?"

Brady's face creased in doubt behind its thick mantle of black bristles, but before he could speak, someone farther along said in mild surprise, "Who's asking? Hell, 'course we were coming here. Ain't George said so?" There was a muted chorus of "He did! He sure did!"

Markham leaned on a young maple. He suddenly felt very cold; the glow brought on by running had ebbed away. He felt empty too, despite the revulsion at the very thought of food. The men about him looked as dulled as he, almost as though the knowledge that no more long wading lay ahead of them had made them go slack and weary.

A great shouting and splashing broke out far to the left along the shore. Deep voices cried out, and higher, shriller tones soared above them. Markham joined a general rush toward the sound and saw that one of the canoes had intercepted a long bark craft paddled by a hunched, bundled-up squaw. Amidships and in the bow, three Indian children watched with stolid, beady eyes. One of the five Vincennois captured in the canoe had come down to the water, was talking partly in some harsh, clattery dialect, partly in signs, with the woman. She nodded woodenly. The man laid the back of his hand over his mouth, pointed to the town, then moved both hands rapidly and she nodded again. One of Clark's men dropped to the water, lifted a good half-side of buffalo, some bulging sacks, a few whitish slabs, and four good-sized kettles. Clark's face showed between two saplings, grinning. He winked broadly at the squaw, said a few Indian words, then leaned out, eyes pathetically wide and mouth curved in a timid, placating smile. The squaw stared at him, then broke into a high, cackling crescendo of laughter, made a sweeping motion with her hand toward him, "For all the world as if she were saying, 'Fie, fie, sir,' " thought Markham, then paddled off, still cackling like a tree full of crows.

Clark caught up two of the kettles and ran to the nearest fire, others following with the rest of the supplies. Joe Bowman slammed the buffalo quarter onto a flat rock and sliced at it, tossing the meat into the kettles. The sacks were split open and corn slid out in a rustling golden stream. The white slabs of solid fat were whittled into the water in the kettles with the meat, bones and corn.

As men crowded up in a thickening circle Clark called, "Not a hell of a lot for a hundred thirty men. Company commanders, tell off the weakest of your men. The rest'll take what's left!"

The very fact that there was *something* to eat lifted a cloud from the little island. Heads were carried higher and shoulders were very nearly square. Markham was reminded of a print in the family copy of *The Pilgrim's Progress*, showing the burden falling from Christian's shoulders. For himself he found that he could only gnaw an end of stringy meat and gulp down a few kernels of soggy corn. The rest he turned back for reissue and settled himself in the lee of a fire. His shirts and breeches felt so warm to the touch that they were as good as dry — nearly. A hungry man could always sleep and he reckoned that he might wake with his clothes no worse than sodden.

XVII

"Full Stride and a Clear Trail Ahead"

BUT THERE was no rest for Clark. Things began to happen in quick succession as though seizing those wretched scraps had touched off a long fuse. First, the Colonel sent one of the Vincennois off to town with a letter to the inhabitants, after reading it aloud to the command. It was short but important, saying that he was about to attack Fort Sackville with his whole army; that all Vincennois who wished to hold to the oath to the United States that Father Gibault had administered should remain indoors; those who opted for the Crown should get into the fort at once, since anyone found out of doors and under arms would be assumed to be hostile. As the envoy was embarking, Bowman added ominously that the stroke would be swift, as this part of Colonel Clark's force was anxious to secure a firm base for the second and third sections which followed just a few hours behind. The Creole's eyes widened as he took in the warning of the larger force to come.

No sooner had the canoe left than two Cahokians, whom Clark had sent out earlier, brought in a captured duck-hunter. Dumb with indignation at first, the hunter suddenly dropped from his horse and erupted in shouts and high-pitched squeals of delight as he recognized four Kaskaskia cousins and a Cahokia nephew, who smothered him in wild embraces. Then, facing Clark, he orated at length. Not a soul in town or fort — this he would swear on the holiest of relics — had the remotest idea that an enemy was in the area. Many of Hamilton's Indians had gone home. The townsfolk? Ah, everyone, even including the women and little children, would welcome the sweeping away, the obliterating of the whole force that had come down from Detroit!

Markham must have drifted off through several outbursts of activity after this, for he was plagued by a dream in which Clark embarked everyone on a keelboat for a blow at Detroit itself. Hands aching from the memory of his own long hours of poling, he woke to see men running past him carrying long, fresh-cut saplings. Poles? But the keelboat was a dream, must have been a dream — He sat up, shook his head violently to clear his wits, then rolled to his feet, sweeping up his belongings and pushing his arm through his rifle-sling, and started off after the poles.

Through slow-fading daylight the pole-bearers made for a hollow in the east end of the island where others were pulling long, dank cloth panels from pouches and haversacks. Slanting sun from the west lit up patches of blue and red and green and buff, somehow unfaded by seeping water over three long weeks.

The flags, the banners and guidons! The companies had carried them up the Kaskaskia street and Father Gibault had blessed them all impartially from the steps of his church while the Louis XV bell sang in the little belfry. They had vanished at the first hasty camp, but now they reappeared as though to mark that start of another chapter in the history of the Illinois Detachment, Western American Army. Markham speeded his pace, spurred on by what he saw.

Men were already standing in line along a broad flat space beyond the funnel and more were running to join them, emerging from hidden paths or pouring on over open ground. Color-bearers were spacing themselves right and left and the late-comers were flocking to them, weaving in and out as they sorted themselves by companies. A final rush of men came out onto the flats. The little drummer raced to the right flank of the Cahokia company while others sought out their proper places. Towering De Witt and John Bayley with the cornsilk hair made a place for Markham in Worthington's company. Remembering that Bayley was a lieutenant, Markham asked, "I don't see any of the Vincenners and wonder — did the Colonel send them back?"

"Sure. They'll tell all the townsfolk what George wants told. They incline to us, and they'll be sure to pass on to the garrison anything George figures *they* ought to know. Jesus, don't George and the rest look like a mess of hell-roaring cavalry, like in books!"

Clark and Bowman and the four captains — McCarthy, Charleville, Williams, and Worthington — their worn, fringed clothes flapping about their shaggy mounts, moved slowly down toward the center of the line, then wheeled about with Clark a little ahead of the others. Mark had no idea where Clark had shanghaied the horses — unless more duck-hunters had been found.

Clark leaned his forearms on the ewe-neck of his nag as though leaning on a mantel or bar or fence-top and surveyed the Detachment calmly. Then he spoke. He did not raise his voice but Markham shivered as he noticed a new sharpness to it.

"We're going to do what we came a sight of miles to do." He nodded, swung his horse's head toward the right of the line, raised his arm, dropped it. "Here we go. Full stride and a clear trail ahead."

Markham faced right with the others and took up the old swinging frontier gait, Henry De Witt behind him and John Bayley ahead of him. High over the swinging column of broad-brimmed hats and round fur caps, over the swaying brown or gray or drab shoulders rode the guidons on their new-cut poles. Up by the head of the Cahokia men, drumsticks rapped out a brittle warning, paused, then swung into a swift-flowing quick-step. Phil Brady went racing along the column, rifle and pouches and flasks tossing, his right hand holding a crudely whittled fife. As he ran he shouted, "Gautier! 'Phonse Gautier! Here's your God damn whistle. Get up there with Al Le Moine and do some piping!"

The drum rattled on. Two fearfully off-key fifes picked up the beat, valiantly essayed a tortured, racking melody that Markham remembered hearing years ago in Europe. "*Malbrouck s'en va-t-en guerre . . . Ne sais quand reviendra! Ne sais quand reviendra! . . .*" No one tried to keep step but somehow the undaunted attempt at field-music drew the whole column together, reaffirmed its purpose. On went the hush-hush-hush sound of moccasins on dry turf, while along the left flank hoofs slapped briskly.

They struck water again after marching a few yards, but since it was barely ankle-deep so far, few noticed it. Rising ground in the west cut off all sight of town and towered fort by the Wabash, and to Markham it seemed as though the present line of march were bearing widely away from their objectives. He called to Bayley, "Where are we going now, John?"

Without looking back the latter answered tersely, "With George."

A few months before, Markham might have taken the reply for sarcasm and gone on with more questions. Now he merely grunted in acknowledgment of the two words that told him that no fresh orders had been issued and that anything new would be passed to the companies by their respective commanders, now riding along the left flank on their woefully unkempt horses. George Rogers Clark was, as always, improvising, sure in the knowledge that necessary changes in direction or intention would be instantly carried out by the men, in obedience to long-standing shared confidence rather than to drill or formal discipline.

There was high ground right and left now and the column seemed to be heading along the bottom of an extensive furrow scooped out of the earth as though by some gigantic plow. The furrow was dry under foot at first, then gave way to ankle-deep, to calf-deep, to knee-deep water. It was hard to gauge direction now, but Markham had a feeling that their course was slanting gradually back toward the Wabash. Then he saw a break in the furrow's west wall beyond the leading man of McCarthy's Cahokians, and the ground was dry again. They would be out in clear country where a man could see.

It was only a gap in the furrow wall, which went on slanting obliquely toward the east bank of the Wabash, perhaps due to long-forgotten natural upheavals or to the work of mysterious tribes centuries gone.

All at once there was activity along the line of march. The four captains trotted ahead, formed two lines of three riders each, with Clark and Bowman, the latter carrying a long-poled guidon like some medieval champion. After riding ahead for some twenty yards, the six dismounted and raced back toward the column, dragging their mounts after them. Clark waved the head of the Cahokians on, shouting, "Let's hear those fifes and the drum. Everyone shoulder his rifle. Color-bearers, hoist those poles up till they get all tangled in the clouds! That's it!"

Markham nearly dropped his rifle. He was opposite what he had thought to be a gap in the west bank of the furrow. It was a dip, rather than a gap, and sank no lower than the level of his shoulder. But through this open space he looked west across flooded fields to the town. From this angle the fort would not be seen; it was hidden behind houses. The wide main street was deserted. But at the south end of that street, a dense mass of Creoles were gathered, staring and pointing. Now they were waving and faint high-pitched cheers rolled over the flood toward the furrows. Markham was past the dip but, as the Vincennois saw the setting sun light up more and more banners, more rifles, hats and even a few heads and shoulders sliding past the deep wide "V," their shouts increased. "Fine!" thought Markham. "But Clark's giving them — and Hamilton — a damn good chance to count us and why the hell —"

The head of the Cahokia company was doubling back on its course, the men running crouching past the dip, all rifles and banners carried so that no trace could be seen by the distant watchers. Worthington's men in turn followed the Cahokians. Well past the dip, Joe Bowman reached out, caught the Cahokia drummer, whisked him into place among Charleville's men who had somehow been pushed and coaxed into a column of fours. The boy grinned and thumped out a heavily accented march as he passed beyond Markham's sight. Two horsemen, riding stiffly abreast, followed the Kaskaskians and after them came Williams's company, the men moving with their heads thrust forward, their arms and shoulders partly turned to the rear and their arms behind them as though they were tugging at something wheeled and heavy — something perhaps like a cannon.

McCarthy and Worthington were diving in among their men, butting them into a long, wide-spaced single file and turning them back into their original line of march. McCarthy called, "Ready, George."

Clark materialized close to Markham. "Where are the rest of the flags, Rick? That's it. Keep 'em low till you get near the space, then stick 'em up into the sun. Who's this? Phil Brady? Take this banner. Start off. Henry De Witt's next. Here's your flag. Let Phil get a good thirty paces ahead. Now — follow after him. Where's that drum?" It was getting dusky in the deep furrow, but expert hands far up ahead had snatched the drum from the little Cahokia boy, and tossed it in a series of long, low arcs past the gap and on to where Clark stood. "Here we are. Take it, Andy Selden. Beat out anything. Just anything. Keep about five paces behind Tim Carey and his flag. Make all the racket you can. John Bayley, a flag for you. Ten to fifteen paces behind Andy. Now Mark, hoist this way up and trail after John." Clark swung his hands together, laughing. "There we go. Just a line of flags and let whoever's watching try to guess what's between them. Just try!"

Markham started on after John Bayley, thinking, "Good thing I'm used to Clark. God, what a rary-show! The Vincennes people must have counted treble our real number already, not to mention the cannon that Williams's boys *must* have been hauling." He began to laugh as the Cahokia drummer, snatching his instrument away from Selden, went pelting to the rear to take his place. Then he himself turned, ran back with his long flagpole carried low. When he was some twenty feet beyond the dip, François Charleville caught him, turned him about. "*Un moment! Le Colonel veut —*"

But Clark had been touched off by still another idea. "Just the thing, Joe," he called. "Yes, I saw one too, at Fort Pitt. Six horses were hitched, two abreast, and a man rode each nigh horse and drove the off horse. Let's start while it's still light. Claude Prévost, take the first pair, Phil Brady the next and Raoul Tessier the other. Mount up! Keep the nags digging as if they were hauling something pretty damned important. Remember, you're all supposed to be in the same hitch, so don't space out too far!"

Relieved of his impromptu flagstaff, Markham leaned on his rifle by the inner wall of the natural furrow as darkness arrived and wished that he had kept those few scraps of buffalo-meat and corn back on the island. Just a few shreds would have helped quiet the quick cramps that kept plucking at his belly. His legs felt very weak, and his breeches, drenched again by the wading, were heavy and cold, made his legs feel as though he were standing in soft deep snow. He wondered what the next move would be.

Clark had endowed his force with a great many new companies, with artillery and even a little cavalry — for the benefit of the watchers in town and fort. Very likely he would return to the island, under cover of night, and then open negotiations with Hamilton for the surrender of the fort. Why not? Markham had seen him gamble even more desperately in the past. A brisk march back to Warriors' Island might warm the blood a little and there might be enough of the buffalo and corn left over to issue more rations.

"Sure God is getting dark in here," Markham muttered to himself. "I can hear a sight of moving around but —" He broke off, as a hand fell on his wrist. "Come along," John Bayley's voice said. "We're starting. Keep close to me and you won't get strayed in this hole."

Markham followed Bayley. He knew that someone was behind him and had a feeling that more men were moving in column a few feet to the left. He found that he could just see Bayley's broad hat bobbing before him and that was all. That was enough. The hat would lead him back to the island, a fire and perhaps — who could tell — a scrap or two of buffalo-meat. He started as he saw, dim against the western sky, that same dip on the funnel past which Clark's whole Falstaffian army had marched. So the same pattern was being followed, even in the dark — march past the dip, countermarch back to the starting point and, this time, keep right on to the old camp.

Eyes half closed, holding to a long cord that dangled from Bayley's haversack, he marched on with a hundred and twenty-nine other men bearing once-deadly rifles and horns of useless powder.

All at once he heard a great splashing and floundering with Clark's voice ringing out, "This way! Men with special orders, stay with your leaders. The rest bear after Joe Bowman."

"Makes it easy for me," thought Markham. "My last order was from John Bayley to stay with him." Then his breath went out from him as he stepped into knee-deep, then waist-deep water. It was very dark ahead, but there was enough shine in the sky to show him that somehow he and the others had worked free of the funnel and were moving into open, flooded country.

Water splashed across his face as an anonymous horseman floundered past him. Somehow his vision sharpened. The evening skyline ahead was broken by steep-pitched roofs and, now for the first time, over them rose the towers and stockaded walls of Fort Sackville, black, powerful and menacing.

Other men were running now, and Markham let himself be carried along in the rush through the darkness. He was beyond speculating, beyond questioning this wild assault by a handful of hunger-weakened men bearing useless weapons on their bony shoulders. It was enough to make sure that he kept his footing in these drowned lands that were now ankle-deep, now breast-deep.

The steep roofs were off a little to the right, and the water was shallower, always shallower. In the immediate foreground a few horsemen loomed vaguely while at ground level, beyond them, a weird mass of wild forms rose and fell to a piercing ululation. The riders were tumbling from their horses into a yelling, cheering mob.

Bayley called tersely, "Stay by me, Mark! The others'll trail you." Then, more loudly, "That you, Major Bosseron!"

A deep voice by a mass of crimson and black embers answered,

"*Bosseron ici!* My men, they pass among yours. A guide will take you along!"

"I know about Bosseron!" thought Markham. "He commands the Vincennes militia. Father Gibault plays billiards with him and he's got a cat!" Recognition somehow warmed the dark confusion on all sides, gave Markham a welcome scrap of assurance.

Men were moving out from beyond the embers, reaching toward him, toward Henry De Witt and other shapes behind the huge man. A Creole voice cried, "*V'la. De la poudre!*" and looped the long cord of a powder-horn about Markham's neck. He heard a muttered "Thanks, stranger!" from De Witt as he kept moving on after Bayley.

At a featureless black but mercifully dry spot Bayley called, "Stop here! Charge up." Markham unslung his rifle, stripped off the oiled and waxed covers from lock and muzzle, snapped up the pan and primed. When he loaded, the rammer forced the linen patch and ball down the barrel with just enough resistance. He rapped the butt a couple of times on the ground to settle the charge, saying to Bayley, "You sure polished up this bore for me while I was asleep. Slick as silk."

"Didn't polish a thing," muttered Bayley. "Just pried off the muzzle-cover and squinted down toward the vent. Saw it was clean and that's all I wanted to know."

"Why choose mine to look at? And where are we trailing off with you? What are we supposed to be doing?"

"You'll guess when we get there." He peered past Markham. "Henry De Witt, you and the rest charged up? Then let's start. There's a guide out beyond me. We follow him."

They went on through the dark at a brisk trot and Markham figured that he could hear at least a score of men padding on behind him. Ahead there was only John Bayley, and the half-seen guide beyond him and the eternal black wall of the night.

They wheeled to the right, and then Markham gave a low cry of surprise, and a dozen other muffled exclamations echoed the sound behind him, shocked out of silence by the abrupt change around the little column. It had been one thing to peer across a

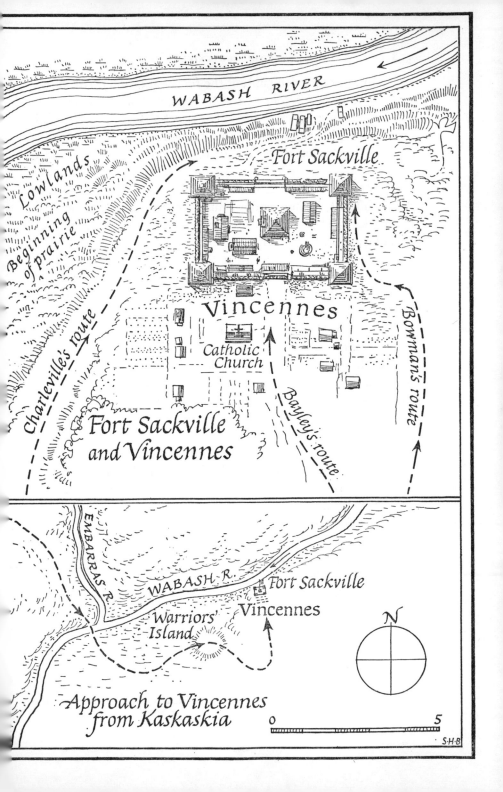

WABASH RIVER

Lowlands

Beginning of prairie

Fort Sackville

Vincennes

Catholic Church

Charleville's route

Bayley's route

Bowman's route

Fort Sackville
and Vincennes

EMBARRAS R.

WABASH R.

Fort Sackville

Vincennes

Warriors' Island

Approach to Vincennes
from Kaskaskia

N

0   5

S·H·B

mile or more of flooded lands at the fences and windows and roofs
and chimneys of Vincennes, but to burst without warning out of
the night into a peaceful, inhabited street — Garden gates, walls,
windows, high roofs sprang up as though out of the ground on
both sides. Candles shone out of open doorways at the head of
high steps. Markham could have tossed a pebble into a lighted
window where a thick-set woman was leaning out to watch them
pass, while a baby in a cradle behind her waved its arms and legs
in erratic, gleeful arcs. In the next room, a white-haired man,
smoking a short gnarled pipe, was making fast the shutters. Farther
on, a woman stirring a great kettle looked over her shoulder at
the hurrying steps out in the street. Setting down her ladle, she
came to the door and hissed into the darkness, "Vivent les Bastonnais!"

Markham rubbed a wet sleeve across his forehead. What was in-
congruous, the rush of a score of drenched, famished, bone-weary
men or the peaceful bedtime Creole street which might have been
in Kaskaskia or Ste. Geneviève? And why the rush down this street
where bars of red-gold light fell from door and window? Probably
another act of George Rogers Clark's never-ending, never futile
pantomime.

Markham's breath went out suddenly. There, just ahead, unexpectedly, incredibly, lay the end of the long journey from Kaskaskia with the high-shouldered bulk of the Church of St. Francis Xavier lifting up in the night and, fifty yards beyond it, the
log stockade and high corner towers of Fort Sackville. Somewhere, just a few yards from the far western wall, the swollen Wabash muttered along on its way south to the far Ohio.

Now the guide waved ahead toward the church and Bayley
called softly to Markham and the others, "See it? Long high bank
runs at right angles to the church. Push up against it. It's as good
a breastwork as was ever dug for you. Spread along it and wait my
word!"

Markham flattened himself against a steep, grassy slope and
peered out uncomfortably at the fort. Why the devil were he and
the others here? No artillery to batter down those walls of heavy

uprights, no bayonets to storm a breach if one were made or a weak point if one were found. Fort Sackville could sit there by the Wabash and laugh down at a force treble their strength.

Someone touched his right arm and a voice that was a mere rustle of air asked, "Who's that? Oh, Mark? John Saunders. Hell, I didn't know you were supposed to be with us. Phil Brady's along left and Joe Simmonds."

"All I know is that John Bayley said, 'Come along,' so here I am. At least I'm out of the drowned lands and off Warriors' Island."

"That's so, ain't it? God, Mark, honest did you ever expect to see that fort there?"

The question seemed familiar. Markham answered slowly, "Why, I guess I did. No reason to — except the Colonel said so."

"Reckon that's it. He said we'd keep going, so we did."

Saunders was again silent and Markham studied the black mass ahead. He had heard that the walls were formed of uprights as high as twelve feet. The corner towers, peak-roofed, seemed to be poised for a leap to the ground and their gun-port eyes were sealed by heavy wood panels. A great two-leafed gate broke the south wall that the group faced. Everything was still, but an odd sort of glow hung over the walls like the glow of live coals in the bottom of a kettle. As his eyes adapted to the night, Markham saw the huge blockhouse rearing up in the heart of the enclosure.

There was something horribly menacing in the size and stillness of Fort Sackville. And yet — an observation of Clark's back on Warriors' Island — it was hard to link the Colonel Henry Hamilton who had made that fantastic winter march down from Detroit, who had such command of his big expedition that he was able to make Indians do navvy work and stay with him, with the passive Colonel Hamilton who now sat back of those walls without as much as a patrol roaming the countryside or even circling walls and town.

Markham raised his head. Voices were audible behind the dark stockade. Men were moving closer to the main gate just opposite the church, for lights showed between surprisingly wide gaps in the uprights. A haunting feeling of menace hit Markham and he

felt anything could happen, a fire or an explosion. Anything!
Once or twice he was quite sure that he saw someone pass between
him and the source of that light. Now men were calling out, laughing, and the menace thinned a little. A hoarse voice, uncertain
on most of the notes, was singing, "She was going to Salisbury,
Sir / With butter and eggs to sell / So we jogged along together
/ Tiddy fer-aye fer-roo fer-ell!"

Someone was talking with Bayley. Markham looked about but
the other speaker was gone and Bayley was walking quickly to the
bank. When he came to Markham and Saunders he whispered,
"We're opening up. Soon's I fire, Phil Brady and Adam Page over
next the church'll let go, then the next pair, then the next, see?
You two plug at the shutters of this corner tower. Find out how
thick the shutters are. You can see a light back of 'em. Try and
snuff it through the gaps in the uprights."

Markham began to sweat in the February night. This would be
no night rush into a town like Kaskaskia whose sleeping Creoles
were only too glad to be conquered. When the crack of Bayley's
rifle came, it might well loose a hard-driving mass of His Majesty's
8th Regiment in a lightning sortie. Other parties might even be
poised waiting to close in on the far end of the town where Clark's
men had left the drowned lands. The cannon in the towers would
have no target, other than the roofs of the innocent town, and so
need not be feared until daylight, but just the same —

He flinched as Bayley's rifle ripped the air and a clear, tiny
"tock" sounded somewhere in the compound, from the blockhouse
Markham guessed. The echoes of the shot died, only to be picked
up again as Brady and Page fired in quick succession just by the
church. Two more shots, with bullets rap-rapping against walls
and towers. Markham heard Henry De Witt croak, "Mine!" and a
cracking flash lit up the earth close by. He raised his own piece,
nudged John Saunders, who grunted acknowledgment. Then
Markham set the front sight of his rifle against a thin orange line
on the near tower. The butt kicked hard against his shoulder. Saunders fired, and two, four, six shots blazed out beyond him. The
double gates seemed to shiver and Markham tensed once more,

then felt his neck growing hot as he realized that the illusion had been caused by barely visible powder-smoke drifting across from the right. Utterly disdainful or utterly insensitive, or unaware, the fort still crouched there in the night as though no march of one hundred seventy miles had ever been made over the drowned lands of Illinois to the Wabash. Someone beyond De Witt growled, "Well, John, we're wasting powder."

Bayley answered, "It's what George wants. Any questions?"

The voice grumbled, "Suits me, if George wants it."

"Then bend to it and get that rifle barrel glowing. Start 'em up, Brady and Page!" Rifles cracked again from the left, worked on toward the center, while bullets rapped crisply against hard wood. Markham thought he heard a distinct splitting sound when he hit the high shutter but John Saunders elicited a deep metallic clang. Then someone else must have hit a water-butt, for a spasmodic splashing was clearly heard and was muffled suddenly as though a plug of some sort had been jammed against it. Another shot —

From behind a shutter in the eastern tower, a furious voice stormed, "Ah, ye feckless, drunken red-skinned devils! G'wan back to your stinkin' tents and let Christian men sleep in peace!" Someone else joined in from the enclosure, "Hell roast that divil of a commissary that was after givin' unwatered rum to ye painted Haythin! Give over with yer shootin' or we'll be comin' out after ye!" A higher-pitched, aggrieved tone cut in, "You, out there! Stow your blazing off near the fort. Here, Mister La Porte, can you talk to them? Well, better find someone who can. God damn it, that last shot hit Sergeant Pumphrey on a jacket-button and drove the wind clean from him!"

Markham held his breath with the others, listened first in amazement, then in sheer delight as the meaning of the shouts from behind the stockade became clear. Bayley hauled Henry De Witt away from the hillock. "Get you back to George, quick, or find someone who can get to him. Tell him that the Hair-buyer's boys think we're just a mess of drunken Indians. Cut away, now!" De Witt went racing away up the street. "Keep firing, you others. God help me, but they're a mole-deaf lot in that fort! Mistaking the sound of our powder for the weak stuff they sell the Indians! Hi! What's this?"

Markham was already aware of a fabulously rich aroma that spread a regal splendor through the dark. Saunders cried, "Food!" and Phil Brady yelped, "Gals!" Turning, Markham saw bent forms scuttling off up the broad street in a swish of skirts. Someone muttered, "Kettles! Thick pea soup!"

"There's tin cups stacked here if you've lost your own," Bayley called in a low voice. "Come down one at a time from the church end. The rest keep up your fire till I call you."

In his turn, Markham knelt by the second kettle, his hand shaking with eagerness as his cup clinked against a ham-bone. A voice close behind him said, "Take it easy, Mark. Plenty of time for you." He looked up to find Joe Bowman kneeling by him. Bowman went on, "Halt your fire, John. We're ready for what we talked about with George at Warriors'." Bayley nodded and trotted off to the bank where the others leaned with poised rifles.

"Something happening?" asked Markham, fearful lest some new order whisk away the kettles and send him and the others back into the floods.

"Eat up and say nothing." Bowman sounded quite at ease as usual, so nothing could be read from his manner. Markham merely gave thanks for whatever respite there might be and emptied his cup, filled it again. The soup was so thick that it flowed slowly and was heavy with the flavor of split peas and ham-bone and herbs and the bits of real ham and diced fried bread that floated on its surface. At Warriors' Island there had been much time and no appetite for the merest scrap of food. Now there was keen appetite, much food and, for the moment, much time.

The others came crowding back from their posts and attacked the kettles. There was little talk above the clink and rattle of cups. Once Bayley whispered, "Getting close to time, Joe?" Bowman merely answered, "Time's always close, John." Markham dipped his cup again.

Interruption came with shattering suddenness. Away off on the right front, a rippling flash of light ushered in a prolonged burst of rifle-fire that was followed by scattering shots. Someone yelled, "It's a sortie! They're coming out!" Others dropped their cups without a word and raced for the breastwork. Markham started with them, but saw that Joe Bowman and Bayley still sat calmly by the kettles. "This what you were talking about, Joe?" asked Markham.

"Part of what some of us were talking about. Set quiet," answered Bowman. Then as the others returned somewhat sheepishly, he added. "That was just some of Ed Worthington's boys off there. George wanted it so." Silence fell over the rough ground about the church. The fort was mute under the halo of subdued light that glowed somewhere within the enclosure. The little town of Vincennes gave off a soft hum, like any country town settling down for the night a little later than usual. There was hardly a start when an outburst of firing ripped the air — far to the left, this time. Bowman hummed to himself, then announced to the nearest kettle, "Frankie Charleville's Kasky-boys off yonder, near the Wabash."

There was a further wait, then Bowman rose, dusted off his hands as though a job had been finished. "Get your boys back by the church, John. You know what to do." He went ambling off into the dark.

There was a volley from the bank by the church, then each man fired a couple of shots at will. Leaning against the crude parapet on whose crest feathery dried weeds waved in the dark, Markham warmed his hands on the hot barrel of his piece and wondered how these bursts of firing would have sounded from the fort.

Bayley was speaking in a low tone just behind the firing line. "Charge your pieces. Pick your targets. Steady, now!" Then off on the right Worthington's company opened up and Bayley's command "Fire!" cut through its first echoes, and his own volley set off a fresh outburst from Charleville off on the left.

Markham rubbed his sleeve across his forehead. He felt almost sympathetic with Henry Hamilton, whose "single mobile band" outside the walls had suddenly changed into three fixed bodies whose size would be hard to estimate in the echoing darkness.

Henry De Witt came back from the town with news gleaned from friendly Indians, who reported that a scouting party under Captains La Mothe and Maisonville — names that seemed grimly familiar to most of Bayley's men — had left the fort that very afternoon. Captain John Williams had gone out with a group to intercept them. There might, De Witt reckoned, be sort of a fight when the two bands met up. The talk turned back to La Mothe and Maisonville and wandered on into Kentucky's early days, courageous settlers and many tragedies.

Markham forgot De Witt and his news as he saw a bar of light brighten on the face of the southwest tower. It flickered, burned steady, flickered, steadied. He leaned forward, caught a dull rumbling, a muffled thumping, a clear boyish voice calling, "Now, lads!" a hoarse, "Stand clear of the breech, you mucky slink!" The rumbling again, louder. Markham stood frozen, trying to interpret rumbles and thumpings. Then he remembered the sound of cannon, perhaps a twelve-pounder, being loaded and run forward on its wheeled carriage on shipboard. He whipped up his rifle, covered the shuttered gun-port of the tower and shouted, "Stand by!" just as the shutter was rolled back with a halting clatter. There was a high-hung lantern, a group of men tugging at heavy ropes, a final rumble as the broad muzzle of the piece thrust out into the night. The crew sprang clear. Someone in the rear raised a lighted linstock, started to drop it onto the breech.

Every rifle around the church seemed to blaze off in answer to the pull of Markham's trigger. The lantern slung from the peaked ceiling clattered to the floor. The half-seen man holding the linstock spun on his heels, dropped the glowing stick. Frantic hands tried to roll the shutter across the port without first hauling the piece back into place, and the shutter jammed. Markham reloaded and fired again, aiming for the wide space between sill and shutter. Other shots cracked out ahead of him, behind him. The lantern must have been knocked into spilled powder, for there was a quick, white, hissing flare, yells of warning. A voice wailed, "Darby Mc-Cune! Hell's fires are searin' me guts, Darby! Help!" Then the squat twelve-pounder backed into the tower as though self-propelled, and the shutter was slammed to.

A buckskin-clad figure leaped up by Markham's side to the top of the bank, and began screeching in a voice that was edged with fury. "Can't take a powder-burn? How'd you like to be made to watch your wife and babies burn in a sealed cabin, you dirty British bastard!" Another figure jumped to the top of the bank and yelled, "Don't worry about a few powder-burns! Watch your hair, Redcoat! Nobody needs to pay us to take it; we'll scalp you for free!" A third voice, farther away, shouted, "Where are La Mothe and Maisonville? We want La Mothe and Maisonville. They won't worry about powder-burns when we're through with them!"

Then cannon thundered from the northeast and southwest blockhouses, and the men jumped down. Markham thought he could catch the hiss of the shot before it crashed into some building by the end of the town.

The dying echoes blurred in with the sound of hoofs coming on from the left, and Clark's voice called, "That's it, John Bayley. Keep whacking at the gun-ports and we'll choke back every shot they try. Had any trouble?"

Bayley reported no casualties and plenty of targets. "Just like you planned on the island, George."

"Good. By the way, I didn't hear any cannon-shot from this tower."

"Mark, here, spotted a shutter being shoved back and fired. We all joined in. They went away."

"That's fine!" Clark loomed huge in the darkness as he leaned from the saddle. "But keep watching. English don't discourage easy. They'll start again soon's they get patched up. And listen. Frankie Charleville's moved closer this way. He's going to have half his men watching your tower. You keep half yours watching his. See? Get a nice cross-fire that way. Clear?"

"Sure. Sure."

"Now where's Markham Cape? That you, Markham? God damn it, you weren't supposed to be here. I sent someone after you before we left the deep furrows back there. They couldn't find you. Why'd you come here?"

"No one told me different. Where should I have been?"

"Been? Out of it! Hell, I told you back at Kasky that we'd be your escort east as far as Vincennes. You've no call now to get your big nose shot off in the Wabash swamps. Go into town and find a place to sleep."

The air shivered and the earth shook as another cannon roared from the southwest tower, followed by the same crash of boards. Markham laughed shortly. "If I go back to town where those are landing, I'm likely to get more shot off than my nose."

"Never thought, did you, of the tower gunners dipping their muzzles so's to pitch shot right down here?" asked Clark curtly.

"I heard that piece up there rumble when they tried to run it forward. It's on a navy mount; big block of wood with four little wheels no bigger than your fist. I'd say that it was depressed maximum right now. The closest shot they can make is way over our heads."

Clark's saddle creaked as he leaned farther forward. "You're sure of that?"

"Ought to be. I've been around enough navy mounts to know that sound."

Clark turned to Bayley. "John, you keep Markham right here. Shoot him if he tries to get away. I thought he'd come to the end of his usefulness a while back, but he keeps seeing and hearing things. I'm going over to see Ed Worthington's company on the right. Spell your boys two to three at a time so they can get some sleep. Colonel Le Gras says he'll send down some more hot rations later. Good night, all." He gathered his mount and rode off into the night.

Bayley called, "George wants two-three of you to sleep. Who's going to?"

Markham found that relief at being on dry ground, the excitement of the rush through town and the firing had more than offset the soporific effects of accumulated fatigue and the hot soup. The others along the high bank seemed to feel as he did. Bayley

snapped his fingers impatiently. "Come on. You heard George."
There was another long pause. "Christ, do you call this discipline? All right then, this is an order. You — you — you and you!
Lie down there under the bank. That's more like it. Now, God
damn it, *sleep!*"

The count had ended with Markham and he settled himself half
reclining with his back to the bank. He was still startled by the
savagery of the response of the men who had jumped onto the top
of the bank to scream at the doubtless frightened young Royal Ar-
tilleryman up there in the tower. He remembered the background
of most of Clark's men, had heard a few tight-lipped reminiscences
of Indian raids with their wanton bloodshed and burning and torture. Yet until this moment, they had all kept those memories and
the resultant hatred tight-leashed, held well below the surface.
They had endured a horrible, killing, mid-winter march, but outwardly they had faced it just as grimly determined men, rather
than as a vengeance-bound band driven on by hideous, ineradi-
cable memories. Now the men of his group stood above him,
keenly alert, fingers on triggers, once more calmly efficient frontiersmen.

He drifted off into uneasy sleep, from which he was awakened
once by a burst of fire all about him, apparently brought on by an
attempt to roll out that tower piece again. Then more rifles cracked
on the left as the gunners opposite Charleville's men managed to
send another round smashing into sheds and men in the town.
Then Hamilton apparently tried to man the musketry loopholes
flanking the main gate, but Clark's men held their fire and there
were no targets for the garrison who aimed blindly in the dark
for a half-hearted minute and then were still.

Now even the tower guns were mute and the night was unbroken save for an occasional shot loosed off by the besiegers just
to keep the garrison wakeful. Markham leaned back again, feeling
real sleep settling over him. Then he was on his feet in an instant,
rifle steady in his hands, staring at the black curtain of night off to
the right.

At least three of Bayley's men had left their posts and were racing off towards a reeling, struggling knot of men who rolled unsteadily along. The noise was so utterly mad that for a moment he thought that too liberal a rum ration had been issued. Then words came to him.

"I say he's ours, God blast you!" . . . "I claim that murdering son of a bitch! *I* got the *right* to him!" . . . "Maisonville! Do you see me? Do you know me? By God, you're going to, if you don't! What about them four gals you and your gang lifted from the spring below Carly's Fort?" There was the sound of a blow. A voice, strangled but seemingly unafraid, croaked, "You cannot do so to me! I am *officier*, yes, of the Crown! I demand —" Another voice cut in, "Officer of the Crown, officer of the God damn bloody scalp! Did you listen to them old men you pinned in the cabin off Harrod's Run?"

Maisonville! One of the Canadian officers leading the scouting party that had left Sackville that afternoon. Now he had been caught and — Markham jumped down from the bank, sickened by this sudden wave of mob violence. He shouted, "Stand clear! He's a prisoner of war!" Bayley moved in beside Markham, yelling, "George won't like this for a damn! Turn that man over to me! I'm in command here."

The milling group about Maisonville frayed out and a dark mass of shouting men engulfed Markham and Bayley. Markham's arms were pinned, his rifle ripped from his hands. A voice that sounded like Henry De Witt's roared, "Keep out of this, John Bayley, or so help me Christ I'll club you down!" A knife-blade pressed against Markham's ribs and a man growled, "You've stood with us good, but you ain't one of us! Easy now! Once I start cutting you're apt to stay cut!"

In the darkness beyond, Maisonville was being hustled along, shrieking, "*L'assassins ici! L'assassins! A moi, à moi!*" Now they all seemed to be moving faster and a thick voice was shouting, "Stand him up like he stood up old Garth!" while confused scuffling, hacking sounds came from beyond the church and Maisonville sharpened his "*L'assassins!*"

There was silence for a moment and the men who held Markham and Bayley moved toward the church, keeping their prisoners close. As they cleared the far end of the building, fresh shouts echoed from the men who held Maisonville. They seemed to be working closer to the fort. "All right, you bloody bastards, we'll come closer so we are in range of your God damn muskets. See? Now we're equal! Go on and hit us — if you can! Christ, call yourselves soldiers! There ain't a fair shot in the lot of you!" A musket flashed somewhere along the stockade and a long, jeering laugh answered it. "Try bows and arrows! Chuck rocks!" Another shot. "See? What did we tell you? You ain't men enough even with all the odds with you!"

Markham and Bayley both shouted in angry protest, but hard hands were clamped over their mouths and they could only stare at the half-seen figure of Maisonville, bound to a post well up the slope toward the fort gate. A half dozen or more riflemen crouched about him, weapons poised expectantly while they kept up a steady flow of taunts and insults to the garrison. Suddenly one of the riflemen fired. A man yelled hoarsely from a loophole. More muskets spatted out. "How'd you like that, Maisonville? Your tame Shawnees stuck lighted splinters under Dave Garth's nails while they kept him tied up like you're tied now and —"

A sudden rush of men burst through the group that held Markham and Bayley, scattered their captors. Joe Bowman's voice was booming, "What the hell's all this? By God, you've sunk lower than Shawnees, the whole lot of you. Don't cross me, Kit, nor you, Hi! Out of the way! Eph! Carl! You others! Drive 'em away! Any man that disobeys will face me, man to man and knife to knife!"

Everyone fell back, leaving Bowman and Maisonville alone on the slope. It struck Markham that for an ordinarily placid, workaday body, Joe Bowman was showing a good deal of fire and dash. A musket or two blazed from the walls but Bowman went on, methodically cutting Maisonville's bonds and paying no attention to the shots. When the last coil fell away, Maisonville gave a bound as if to race for the walls, but Bowman's big hand snapped on him like a trap, hauled him back by the collar.

"No, you don't, Maisonville!" he growled, pushing the prisoner ahead of him as he returned from the post. "You just act proper and not a hell of a lot'll happen to you, maybe." He straightened his arm, sent the Canadian stumbling into a group of men who pounced on him. "Now you take him to Colonel Le Gras's house. George is going to want to talk to him. Don't mess him up."

A pleading voice said, "Just his scalp, Joe, just his scalp! George can still talk to him."

"None of that!" snapped Bowman. "George wouldn't — Oh, well, nick just a nubbin off. Reckon that'd be all right. But no bigger'n my thumbnail or I'll take the same off you." He laughed. "No, two nicks. Maybe Hamilton'll pay you a guinea for the pair. Rush him off now. But those men who've been on duty, get the hell back to your posts."

There was a gradual drifting away through the night. Bayley herded his men back to the bank by the church, and Markham followed slowly after them.

Bowman said quietly to Bayley, "No fault of yours, John. The boys were a mite eager. I was scared I'd have to call for George to get Maisonville away from them. Yep, you did all right. How are you, Mark? Middling sane?"

"Just middling," said Markham dryly.

Bowman lowered his voice. "Middling's enough. Take this. I'm going to be stirring about and I wouldn't want to drop it accidental for the boys to see." He shoved something into Markham's shirt-front. "I snuck this off Maisonville before anyone saw it. The boys would have slivered him." He moved off, calling to Bayley.

Markham felt inside his shirt, gave a convulsive start as his fingers met a soft, silky mass. Bowman was right. The sight of that woman's scalp with its long, flowing hair might well have stung the men into a wild, howling rush at the stockades that could have had only one end.

A rustle of softly moving men came from the town. Dark forms were gliding up and Markham recognized the low voices of Captain McCarthy, of one-eyed Sergeant Harrison, now seemingly quite cured of his fever, one of the Gendrons, Creoles, Virginians all mixed together. He gathered that some of them had been out looking for the La Mothe-Maisonville patrol, and cursed the fact that all but Maisonville had eluded them somehow in the darkness and had holed up somewhere outside the fort. The hunt would start again before sunrise, a man said.

Bowman moved in among the newcomers. "Men who were out after La Mothe, get some rest! Same for Bayley's men. But stay close! You in the center, close up to this bank by the church. Rick McCarthy, take that other bunch over to Ed Worthington. Just keep bearing right. He's watching for you." A Creole voice joined in, directing another group down where Charleville had taken post.

More men moved up through the night, staggering under clumsy loads that turned out to be buffalo-robes, brought out by Vincennois. These were dealt out lavishly, then with a quick *"Mais avec plaisir,"* the townsmen vanished off to the right, unslinging muskets and rifles.

Dropping into a hollow behind the church, Markham rolled himself in his robe, found John Bayley settling himself just beyond. "Damn, but it's good to wrap up in something that doesn't ooze, John," he said as he stretched out luxuriously. "What happens now?"

As though in answer to his question, a great din broke out down by Charleville's post. Shovels and mattocks rasped and chunked into the earth. Axes snicked into wood. Heavy carts sent a long stab of ungreased axles into the night. Men were bawling in French and English that the ground was too soft to support heavy mortars unless strong gun-platforms could be built. They shouted that the reserve ammunition must be stacked down by the gun-park and *not* left on the barges. They roared angrily that the field-pieces belonged away over on the right, *not* down by the river. And all the while the shovels and mattocks and axes worked on, horses dragged vast loads from somewhere to somewhere, and men found loud fault with whatever was being done. Markham, easing his hip away from a sharp rock, was quite willing to believe that, out of nothing, Clark *had* managed to assemble an ample siege-train, ready to blast away at Fort Sackville at the sun's first rays.

Rifle-fire sprang up again, knitting a wide arc of sound and darting light. "Hey!" cried Markham. "We'll be burning the last of our powder if someone doesn't watch out!"

Bayley grunted. "We got enough to take Sackville and then Detroit with Niagara thrown in."

"We can't have!" exclaimed Markham incredulously.

"Didn't you hear the Vincennes boys talking at Warriors'? Well, when Hamilton took this town, he tried to seize all the powder there was, except a little for hunting. But Le Gras and Bosseron got warning and buried a sight of powder kegs under the houses. Then they gave the Hair-buyer just enough to make a showing. You see, from what Reverend Gibault told them, they figured George'd be sure to come over from Kasky pretty soon and they wanted to be ready for him."

Markham mumbled vague agreement, as sleep closed over him.

XVIII

Negotiations

IT WAS still dark when Markham woke, his face itching from
the touch of the hairy buffalo-robe. He tried to settle himself
for more sleep, but the accumulated fatigues and tensions of the
long, drenched march still kept him fidgeting and shifting. At last
he sat up and tossed his covers aside, noting that John Bayley's
place was vacant as well as the two beyond him. Others too had
had difficulty in sleeping, then.

For the moment the night was still, save for an occasional far-
off rifle-shot or the mushy plop of a musket from some other face
of the fort. Markham got to his feet, slung his rifle across his back
and started for the nearest houses whose soft lights threw bars of
gold across fenced gardens and rutted street. Evidently not all
the townspeople could sleep either. Fascinating smells came to
him, strange after long days and nights of nothing but the reek of
wet buckskin and cloth, crowded bodies washed only by tumbles
in rank floods, rotting boughs and leaves and sour, deep-trodden
mud. Here was a tang of new-sawn wood, of myrtle-wax candles,
of simmering meats and fresh-broached wine-casks.

A voice hailed him and he turned. "No luck sleeping?" asked
Joe Bowman falling into step.

"Damn little. The same with eating, too. All this starving shrinks
your gut until you couldn't swallow a chipmunk's ration."

"That's so," sighed Bowman. "There was a right youngerly-
looking woman in the next street with a kettle of fine stew and
maybe a barrel of coffee and the boys were just walking past her
saying, 'Thank you kindly, ma'am,' or 'Mercy,' like the Creoles
say. You doing anything?"

"John Bayley turned me loose, so I won't know until you tell me."

"Then take a run up to the north face of the fort. Swing a mite wide so's the boys'll know you ain't just slipped out the stockade. Find George and tell him we've talked to Maisonville." Bowman paused, blew out his cheeks. "He's a hard, ruthless man, but this time he's scared, so scared he's all coming apart. You just tell George that Maisonville talked a lot but didn't tell us a thing we didn't know or else had guessed."

"Nothing really new from Maisonville? Right." Markham shivered a little. "I'd have been scared if I'd been in Maisonville's place. What made the boys go after him in particular, so heavy?"

Bowman growled. "That bastard's led raids down into Kentucky. We know it. He knows we know it. It's going to be hard to protect him. Yep. Then there's La Mothe, still out there with his scout-party. The boys'd love to have *him* off some place where it's nice and quiet for a minute or two. Oh — and here's one more thing for George. Charleville got some of his company right up to the walls of the fort on the river side and heard the men inside the fort talking. He says they all swear we come down the Ohio. They don't believe George is here or that he or anyone could have hit out from Kasky in flood-time."

Markham gave a short laugh. "Don't know that I believe it either. So this means Hamilton'd know just about how many men Clark could have brought out of the west, but anywhere between a hundred or a thousand might have come out of the east down the Ohio. That it?"

"That's pretty close." Bowman's tight smile distinctly carried approval. "Better get moving, now. Day'll be soon a-bornin'."

Markham made his careful way through a stretch of soft ground where the dead vines of last fall's harvest flicked about his ankles. It didn't seem that dawn had crawled an inch nearer since his wakening, yet objects were beginning to stand out. A barrow showed its wheel and handles instead of remaining a dark blob. A black line ahead became a row of vague sheds and he knew that he was nearing the field of fire of the northeast tower, for he could distinguish walls and roofs smashed by cannon-balls that had sailed harmlessly over the heads of whatever riflemen had been in the area. He crouched a little in walking and caught the crest of the stockade and its near tower black against the dark sky.

After a few more rods he turned west to parallel the north wall. He was, he reckoned, more than a hundred yards away from the stockade and he moved with increased caution, expecting at any moment to come upon a squad of riflemen resting on their weapons. In a shallow gully, well masked from the fort by bushes, an ideal spot for marksmen to shelter, he stumbled over a buffalo-robe and called in a low tone, "Captain Williams's men here?" A faint stir of air in the bushes was the only answer. He muttered, "I'll be damned. Ought to have hit *some*one by now."

Still cautiously, he worked along a line closer to the fort. He was sure that a faint tang of rank Creole tobacco lingered in one little hollow but beyond that found nothing. He was about to wriggle on up to a little knoll when he realized that it was quite bare and that the ragged line of the stockade, capped by the distant northwest tower, was standing out plainly. He froze where he was, more and more bewildered. Light was coming in strongly from the eastern flatlands toward the fort and he was positive that none of Clark's men were covering the north face of the fort or a good span of the east side. All at once he felt horribly alone, horribly naked and defenseless, one man against Hamilton's whole command. What had happened? Whatever it was, not even Joe Bowman had known of it.

Markham was about to break back for town to alert the second-in-command when his eye caught quick motion at the edge of some trees perhaps a quarter of a mile to the north. Flattening himself against the ground, he could see one dim figure creeping on hands and knees, another following, a third, a fourth. Then movement ceased as the crawlers froze.

They moved again. More figures followed them, fifteen, perhaps twenty men. They were too far to identify properly but Markham was sure that they did *not* belong to the Western American Army, Illinois Detachment. He stared harder and was more sure than ever, for the man in the lead wore a dingy white jacket, a battered cocked hat and what seemed like Indian leggings. Those that followed him could only be Indians.

"Who the devil?" muttered Markham, scowling as the furtive column of men worked, step by step, breath by breath, toward the north wall of the stockade. It was La Mothe's detachment, sneaking through the lines! He was about to leap to his feet, roaring a warning, when a sudden burst of yelling sounded from the same woods to the north. They sprang up in unison and sprinted for the fort, the man in the white coat raising a thin cry of "*Sauve qui peut!*"

Markham could only hold his rifle and stare. There was something almost daft in the mad churning of arms and legs that beat on toward the fort. Someone stumbled, fell, squealing like a terrified horse, got to his feet and thrashed on.

From among the trees erupted an irregular line of hunting-shirted men carrying long rifles, men who whooped and fired without pausing to aim. Markham was up again, waving them on, shouting, "You can nail 'em if you hurry!" But the men ran with odd, high-kneed steps that covered surprisingly little ground, and when they fired, their muzzles jetted smoke straight up into the air.

The fugitives were close to the stockade now. Men of the garrison were urging them on, propping ladders from the top to the ground outside. White-coat and his companions milled frantically about, tried to scale the walls with their bare hands, swarmed at the ladders, got in each other's way, overturned two ladders. At last, by climbing and boosting and shoving, the last man was hauled up to safety.

Markham suddenly leaned on his rifle resignedly. The pursuers had halted just out of reach of the short-range muskets on the wall and whooped and roared with laughter, slapped their knees, pounded each other's backs, pointed at the walls. He made out tall Henry De Witt, John Saunders, Joe Simmonds, Phil Brady among the nearer ones, saw a couple of blanket-coats that told of Creoles from the Kaskaskia or Cahokia companies. And a little in the rear a tall, wide-shouldered man took off his hat and the dawn twilight glinted on his copper-red hair. He laughed with the others as the men on the stockade roared in frustration, fired their outranged muskets and shook helpless fists. "Oh, for God's sake," Markham muttered to himself, "I might have known it was one of Clark's tricky enterprises. But why did he let them through?"

Markham strolled over to him. "Good morning, Colonel," he said dryly.

Clark started. "Eh? What brings you out here?"

"Message from Joe Bowman. He says Maisonville's talked a lot but said nothing new. Charleville reports that the garrison all think you came down the Ohio from the east just because no one could ever come overland from the west, out of Kasky. So you're not Colonel George Rogers Clark, so far as they're concerned. Look, that was La Mothe and his party, wasn't it? Why didn't you grab them?"

Clark whistled softly. "*Grab* them? Oh, no, no. I was scared as hell that La Mothe might get discouraged about being cut off from Sackville. Then he'd probably have hit north up the Wabash to the Wea towns, Quaenon and Chillicothe. La Mothe's good with Indians and he'd have come back here with a few hundred of them and caught us between him and the fort. We'd have been holding a wasp's nest stuffed with hell's fire. Or if just one of his party had gone north, it'd have been the same. So I pulled back all our men on this side, showed La Mothe a clear run to the fort. He took it and we gave him a couple of nudges to be sure he'd keep going. And now they're all back where they can't hurt us." He stretched his big arms. "So they think we came out of the east? We can't keep 'em thinking that forever, but it'll help for a while. Come on back to town with me." He raised his voice. "Thanks for a good job, boys! Take your old posts and keep alert."

At an easy open-country trot, Markham followed Clark along a deep-worn trail that swung away from fort and town to cross a hillock before curving back toward the houses of Vincennes. As he neared the crest Markham had the odd feeling of looking down into the stockade, now a good hundred yards to the west. Actually he was only a few feet above the endless spread of the plains and probably owed the illusion to seeing the whole enclosure of Fort Sackville for the first time.

The near southeast angle, topped by its tower, pointed directly at him like the prow of some misshapen ship whose long starboard side ended at the southwest tower overlooking the flow of the Wabash, and whose short port side was capped by the northeast tower. Inside the walls, the blockhouse reared up like a high quarterdeck hiding the junction of the short west and long north sides and their northwest tower. The stockade itself looked less solid than by night. Markham thought that a couple of rounds from the light cannon of the U.S.S. *Willing* could have toppled whole sections of it. Odd that no one had mentioned the *Willing* since the crossing of the Wabash. Had she been given up for lost?

Movement on the open lands about the fort caught his eye and he took in the long chain of detached posts ringing the fort where Clark's men had taken advantage of any cover, natural or artificial, during the night. They lay back of rocks, in shallow gullies, behind overturned carts or among sheds smashed by cannon-fire. They were sleeping or stamping about to shake off the dawn chill or cleaning their rifles.

All at once a bright new Union Jack burst like a blue and red bomb from the blockhouse flagstaff. Drums rattled on the unseen parade and the flat thud of a saluting piece made the new day official. Markham called to Clark but the latter had already halted on the trail and was watching the fort and his own lines through narrowed eyes. Markham started to speak but Clark only shook his head impatiently.

A drum tatted out "Assembly" in Vincennes, was joined by others. From behind a mass of wreckage, Joe Bowman strolled out toward the little church and stood looking about him casually, fists on hips. The Sackville drums began again, were answered from the town as though in mockery.

Then a new sound beat into the warming air and Markham and Clark caught it at the same instant — the rumbling, rattling sound that had preceded enemy action the night before. The gun-ports of the three visible towers jarred open, showing like black gaps from which the ugly muzzles of six-pounders were thrust out. A bar of bright sunlight fell full on the port of the nearest, the southeast, tower, lighting up the dark interior. Markham caught a confused glimpse of the gun-crew in faded blue and red swarming about the thick barrel. A blue arm held high the bright spark of a linstock, ready to drop it at the command to fire.

Down by the church Bowman still stood in seeming unconcern. Then Markham saw him raise a short roll of bark to his lips and a spooky gobbling bubbled out, liquid and carrying. As though triggered by the sound, every post under Markham's eye erupted in stinging bursts of rifle-fire. In the near tower, the crew lurched and pitched over their piece. The linstock spark vanished and the gaping black muzzle stayed mute. A heavy, coughing explosion told that another tower had managed to get off a round. Smoke gushed from the southwest tower far down by the Wabash and a few seconds later a cloud of dirt sprang up in the open stretches near the bank.

Rifle-fire still rang out from the posts below and Markham saw bright wood and splinters fly from the three visible towers as flights of bullets bored in.

"You're still sure Hamilton can't depress those guns enough to damage us?" asked Clark suddenly.

"Only by hauling them out of the towers and setting them up on the ground. He'd need a trained man-o'-war's crew and a first-rate bos'n to do it, too," replied Markham.

"Maybe the Hair-buyer doesn't know we know he can't. Or maybe he figures the great big boom-booms'll scare us the way they do Indians. Seems to me we've been telling him he's wrong for quite a spell now."

The southwest tower pounded out its charge again. Without looking in its direction, Bowman blew his ghastly call. Rifle-fire increased in intensity, the men who had been covering the southeast tower shifted their aim to the southwest corner whose timbers quivered as they oozed a faint dust-cloud. From inside the stockade, a powerful ringing voice reached the hillock, faint but distinct. "God damn it, Mr. Bourne, can't you keep those bloody gunners to their duty?" As though in answer, rifle-fire raged still heavier.

Clark exhaled slowly. "That Joe Bowman! He figured this out last night and told me about it. I said try it and he told the company commanders what he'd figured. Works slicker'n a greased eel, doesn't it?"

"Probably, but just what is it that's working?"

"Don't you see it? Joe told off twenty rifles to cover each tower and smother it if it showed signs of life, blasting in through the gun-ports and crevices. Then that twenty would shift its fire to the next that's making trouble." Bowman gobbled out his call again. A dozen men rose from posts by the northeast tower and doubled off toward the river. "See that, Markham? Charleville wants help on the northwest, so Rick McCarthy sends a few of his boys to him. Damn it, that's a remarkable man, Joe Bowman. Doubt if we'd ever got as far as the Embarras without him." He shook himself. "We can't loll here watching. There are things to do in town. Did you meet Bosseron last night? No? We'll soon fix that. Let's go."

They followed the trail along the crest and down the far slope. Markham shivered as he saw the hard dazzle of sun on water to the east and southeast and southwest where the Wabash had spilled over its banks. "Jesus!" he thought. "Did we really come through all that?"

The trail leveled off, swung between high-fenced back gardens of the town. Markham shied as he caught sight of some Indians, armed and painted, gliding down an alley to the left. Clark called back, laughing, "They're all right. I spent a bit of time with them early this morning. They came in with Tobacco's Son, the one the Indians call the Grand Gate to the Wabash, because he keeps all the tribes of the Wabash Valley in order. They all wanted to join us against the Hair-buyer, but I told the Grand Gate we'd be better off alone." There were no Indians in sight now but Markham was sure that coppery faces were pressed close to cracks in the fence and twice he caught guttural whispers of *"Mitchi malsé."* He found himself wondering if less skilled hands than Clark's might not have found dealing with Tobacco's Son rather more difficult than the Colonel's casual tone suggested.

They turned into the main street. Markham picked out Bosseron's house easily. It was no bigger, no more ornate than any other in Vincennes, but it somehow stood out as tighter, more solid, more self-assured. And the aquiline-faced, wiry, taut-jawed Creole who stood at the head of the broad steps was cut to much the same pattern as Cerré, a man who could bow himself into the presence of General Guy Carleton in the Château of Quebec or skipper a canoe-load of voyageurs and Indians along the wild shoreline of Lake Superior. For this day Major François Bosseron had put on his worn militia uniform with its faded blue trim, and a gold-hilted sword was thrust through a frog at his side.

He saluted Clark, then lost all formality as the Colonel presented Markham. But of course one knew of Monsieur Cape from the esteemed Father Gibault. And it was Monsieur Cape who had seen to it that the Father brought a fine *cadeau* of catnip for the Major's cat, Le Père de Lustucru. Then the trio settled themselves in the wide front room that served as Bosseron's office, most incongruously furnished with a towering carved secretary, looming above bales of fur, a scarred pine table with slender-legged chairs about it and, over by the far window, the green-topped bulk of a billiard table with a tight cue-rack on the wall. Markham felt somehow warmed by the thought of Father Gibault, cue in hand and rusty soutane chalk-smudged, pondering a difficult shot.

As they seated themselves, the Major spoke first. "So, the *impasse* is reached, eh?"

Clark grinned. "Anything that's been reached has been reached by us. Which reaching did you have in mind?"

Bosseron shrugged. "Hamilton, he cannot harm you from his fort. Nor will he attempt a sortie against your rifles across thirty *toises* of open ground. And you cannot harm him behind his walls, since you have no cannon to make a breach. You have no bayonets for an attack by *escalade*, by scaling his walls, which would be madness anyway."

Clark rubbed his coppery head. "I'd say that was summed up right pretty, Major."

"So you and this Hamilton will now sit and watch, each the other?"

Markham felt an inward start of anger at the almost taunting words. Then he realized that the Major was struggling to express himself in a not too familiar tongue at a critical time to a man who had been a complete stranger up till a few hours ago. And it seemed clear that Bosseron had committed himself solidly on Clark's side.

Clark was silent, seemed to be listening when the sound of musket fire came from outside. Then he answered almost negligently, "Oh, I reckon the next thing to do is, well — ah — to write the Hair-buyer a letter. I was chewing on that as Markham and I were coming over here."

Bosseron's carved-oak face was impassive. He said, "Ah, a letter? *Mais pourqoui pas?*" He brought from the high secretary some sheets of heavy foolscap, a massive silver ink-pot and sand-box with a sheaf of quills in a leather cup stiff with Indian beadwork. As he arranged all these on the table, he said calmly, "As you will now write officially, it is best that I leave you."

Clark looked up in protest. "No, no, Major. We'll need you — if you don't mind taking the time. Really, we'll simmer this up between us." Bosseron inclined his head politely, but Markham was sure that he was gratified. Clark went on, "Markham's folks sent him to a writing school in Boston, and his script's real pretty, so we'll let *him* get his fingers inky. How'll we start? To Colonel Henry Hamilton —"

Markham put in, "Maybe 'Governor' would be better. He's got political as well as military power, I've heard. Address him in the higher office and he can't claim later he was speaking only as commander of troops."

Bosseron nodded. "The young man is right, Colonel."

Clark's palm smacked on the table. "That's the sort of help I want. Fine! Now we're going to summon him to surrender. Let's say, 'In order to save yourself from the impending storm that threatens you —' "

Line by line the demand took form, warning Hamilton against rejection: "for by Heavens if you do, there shall be no mercy shown you!" Markham read the text aloud and with the last words started to question the extreme severity of language and terms, with Bosseron urging at the same instant, "*Il vaudrait mieux, peut-être —*"

Clark reacted violently. "No, by God, and no for all eternity! You haven't lived in Kentucky, you haven't seen these deliberate waves of murder and torture and dragging off into slavery — you don't know the arson and pillage and rape that's gone on there. *Why* has it? Because it's all been planned by one man, Henry Hamilton. And he's probably brewing bigger and bigger Indian raids against *all* the frontiers, given the chance."

The muskets and rifles continued to rattle in the distance, but no more angrily than before. Markham was already sanding the unamended draft while Bosseron silently produced red sealing wax, lit a fat candle of greenish myrtle-wax and stood ready for Clark to sign the summons. The signature was sanded and the sheet sealed by hot wax pressed down by the boss of his long knife. Then Clark pushed back from the table.

"Now for delivering it. First we have our drummer beat a 'cease-fire.' When our boys quiet down, he'll beat for a parley. Reckon the Hair-buyer'll be glad of an excuse to quit for a while, so he'll start *his* drummer working. When all firing stops, we'll give this letter to —" He paused, then turned to Bosseron. "Major, want to lend me one of your militia officers to act for me? Someone Hamilton's garrison is apt to know?"

Bosseron looked surprised, "An officer of Vincennes? By chance, Captain Nicolas Cardinal is in uniform today, a man of the most reliable. If you wish, I send for him at once." He tramped out onto the gallery, calling.

Markham, puzzled at first, smiled as he realized what Clark was up to. At Cahokia, Clark had paraded Nieto and Trottier before the Indians to show that Spanish and French were his allies. Now all eyes in Fort Sackville were to witness a Vincennes Creole officer acting as emissary for the Virginians. Would the effect be the same?

Under the brittle prompting of the drums, a hush settled reluctantly over fort and town. Clark, Bosseron, and Markham stood in the wide street before the Major's house and looked down toward the upright timbers of the little church, the sixty yards of bare ground and then the great double gate in the rambling south wall of the fort. Off-duty Virginians and Creoles of the Detachment leaned on their rifles up and down the street, eyeing the expanse of stockade warily. On galleries and broad stairs, in the street itself, the women and girls of Vincennes formed a vivid fringe to the drab of buckskin and linsey-woolsey. Markham, glancing about him, saw crimson and green and sky-blue bodices laced over the whitest of white linen. There were demure silvery-gray skirts that ended just below the knee to show orange or purple or cerise petticoats. After his drab weeks on the Mississippi and drabber days on the trail he found this blending of color and femininity dizzying as well as cheering. Provocative, too. Those bodices, laced tightly or loosely, were equally —

Clark muttered, "There he goes!" and brought Markham back to the siege. Captain Nicolas Cardinal, erect and taller than most Creoles, appeared past the church and walked steadily toward the double gates. As he raised his sword-hilt to rap on the uprights, a slide in a little wicket-gate just at his left opened. A hand reached out, took the letter. The slide snapped shut and silence fell heavier over fort and town.

In the street, people shifted from one foot to another with a soft rustling sound. The men in the visible posts were quiet, but their rifle-barrels were covering the stockade around Cardinal, who stood by the wicket-gate at attention, waiting. Clark muttered as though to himself, "Wonder what they'll answer." The slide snapped open again, thrust a square of paper at Cardinal, clicked shut.

The Captain returned at a brisk trot and uncovered in salute as he handed the paper to Clark. Markham's own fingers jerked toward the sheet and he caught a similar unconscious move on Bosseron's part. Clark, who must have been shaking inwardly with impatience, thanked Cardinal courteously, turning the note slowly over and over as though it were some routine matter. Then he broke the seal casually, saying, "Well, let's see what the Hairbuyer's got to say to us."

It must have made an interesting picture, Markham thought, framed in the spyglass lenses which were surely trained on the street, from the fort. Clark was shaking out the paper while two senior officers of Vincennes militia stood close by. The fort could not have heard Clark's tones, but the poorest glass must have caught the thrown-back head, the flash of teeth as he read out the few lines. "Governor Hamilton begs leave to acquaint Colonel Clark that he and his garrison are not to be awed into an action unworthy of British subjects." Rocking with laughter, he handed the sheet to Bosseron who, with Markham, joined in a delighted outburst up and down the street until all Vincennes seemed to be roaring with the Colonel over Hamilton's reply.

"All right," said Markham when the laughter, feigned or real, had died a little. "What do we do now?"

"The Major's got coffee and rum and fixings for us. We'll tell Joe Bowman to get on with his war and we'll eat while we wait."

Markham looked inquiringly at him. Bosseron gave a tight smile. "Yes. Wait. Hamilton is of a famous Scots family and will soon feel that la politesse demands a fuller answer from him." He bowed, pointing to his house. "In the meantime, Messieurs —"

The bright February morning, now nine and one-half hours old by Bosseron's bulbous watch, had turned clangorous again with rifle and musket and futile cannon as Bowman opened fire and the fort answered. The fine china and silver in the neat little room across the house from Bosseron's office vibrated and chattered to the sound as the Major's guests sat themselves about a polished table. Almost at once a band of pretty Vincennoises bearing jugs and bottles and trays and loaves and crocks battled one another for priority. Gratefully appreciative of Bosseron's hospitality, Clark and Markham sipped, relished, emptied their wineglasses as the beaming black-haired girls came on, black-eyed with red lips and cheeks to match the most scarlet autumn maple in Illinois. As they served the Americans, the girls paused for a word, a smile, a kindly look. For the first time, as course followed course, Markham felt himself beginning to relax.

But not for long. Presently more than the mere sounds of the siege sought out George Rogers Clark. Virginians, Kaskaskians, Cahokians and Vincennois, singly and in small groups, began to push through the narrow door to plead with their Colonel. They told him that they had found a dozen weak spots in the stockade. They begged that every ladder and hook and rope in town be used in a sudden rush at the walls of Fort Sackville, for the rush, they said, could end only in triumpth.

Bosseron's house, like all Creole dwellings, had no doors between rooms, and the sole entry to any was from the gallery. While the mud-stained men in tattered shirts and breeches milled around to talk to the Colonel, the Vincennes girls with their banquet in progress ducked under buckskinned arms, twisted and wedged their way between voluble six-footers. While a Virginian pawed Markham's shoulder, begging him to give "a message to George, George'll listen to you," a warm cheek brushed Markham's on the other side, and a slender white arm pushed a coffeepot past him onto the table. "S'il vous plaît, Monsieur le Bastonnais?"

The confusion grew, until finally Clark leaped to his feet, shouting, "Outside! Into the street. We haven't got room to think in here."

As though giant hands had squeezed the walls of the house, men and women were slowly ejected onto the gallery, down the wide stairs and into the street, Clark, Bosseron, Cardinal and Markham bringing up the rear. By some inscrutable magic of their own, the women and girls had managed to cluster about

Clark, a worshipful bodyguard whose shiny black heads were a foot
or more below his. Their eyes were on him, even the eyes of two
girls whom Markham had been sure were smiling *just* for him
back in the room.

Clark held up his big arms. "Now wait a minute! Just listen to
me! For God's sake don't even *think* of trying to scale the walls of
Sackville! The Hair-buyer's got good Canadian troops there and
about a hundred tough British regulars. If you get within reach of
them — well, that's all you'll get, except a couple of bullets in your
face! So forget it! For good!" Clark stared down any mumblers in
the crowd, then turned back toward Bosseron's house. But he did
not reach the door, for silence fell unexpectedly on street, town,
fort and encircling posts. A white flag fluttered from a crude staff
by the main gate, an unseen drum beating for a parley was answered by Clark's own drummer down by the church. Bosseron's
voice sounded loud in the sudden hush. "So Hamilton, he has
written so soon his little *billet doux, hein?*"

The Colonel's face cleared. He hitched at his rifle, pushed his
hat brim a little higher. "Reckon I'd better get over there. Major,
I'd be glad of your company along of Markham's."

They struck out down the street at a brisk stride. The last houses
were passed, then the little church, looking forlorn and apologetic
in the high sun for all the rubble about it. Joe Bowman detached
himself from the shelter and said calmly, "Figured you'd be coming, George. The boys have got you covered in case the Hair-
buyer tries anything cute."

"Thanks, Joe," answered Clark. "We're not worrying."

When they were some twenty yards away from the main gate,
Clark said, "This is close enough. We're not waiting to be bidden
in."

As they halted, the little wicket-gate that had taken in Clark's
first message opened jerkily. A bulky man in snow-white buckskins
with long, multi-colored thrums and broad hat backed carefully
out. Then he turned and came forward. Under one arm was a
heavy jug.

Clark cried, "Len Helm! We've been spoiling bad for the sight of you!" He caught Helm by the arms, shook him gently. "How'd you get out? Are you on parole or still prisoner?"

Helm could only stare at Clark, his lined face working and his big features unsteady. His voice wavered a little, but he looked healthy enough. "Reckon I'm kind of glad to see you, George, you and the boys." He gave an uncertain smile, nodded to the others. "You're looking good, Mark. Major, my duty to you. Now — Oh, yes. George, I'm still kind of a prisoner. Got a message from Colonel Hamilton. Seems he'd like to talk terms with you."

Clark stiffened. "The Hair-buyer's got nothing to say to me but 'I surrender.' I'll do any other talking that's needed."

Helm looked distressed. "Now, George, the Colonel didn't send those raids out because he *wanted* to. He *had* to. Orders from London. Don't glower like that! I tell you, I'd give a sight if you and him and maybe me could set down together and you two get to know each other over a mug of Heartener . . ." A grin spread and spread over his broad face. "I brought this jug out to you, George. I never did brew a finer mess than this. Try it." And his big, thick-fingered hands began fumbling with the cork.

Clark smiled as he laid a restraining hand on Helm's arm. "God love you, Len, if you sat down with the devil himself and a jug of Heartener, you'd be ready to take him home to meet the family within half an hour. And by Jesus, so would I. Put that cork back."

Helm sighed. "I figured Hamilton's message would come a hell of a lot easier with a toothful of this all around. Well, here it is. He wants to talk to you right away. In the fort if you'll come. Otherwise he'll come out as far as this gate."

Clark's eyes narrowed. "He's telling *me* where we'll meet? Who does he think is doing the surrendering around here?" He was speaking rapidly now, biting out his words. "Now here's what I want you to tell the Hair-buyer, Len Helm. Sure, I'll talk to him, but tell him it'll be right out there at the door of that church, not in the fort or in front of the gate. Tell him I don't like to be kept waiting. Tell him that the boys are getting restless out there." His voice softened a little. "And when it's all over, Len, you and I and the Major and Markham'll hunker down to a whole jeroboam of Heartener."

Helm sighed, hugged his treasured jug more tightly. "I'll do just like you told me, George," he said wistfully, then trotted back to the wicket-gate that closed behind him.

"Eh, voilà!" cried Bosseron. "So now it is time, and not hair, that he wishes to buy. Have you any to sell him?"

"Didn't happen to hear of such," replied Clark. "Let's get over to the church."

The little high-shouldered building looked just as it had on the trip out, Markham thought. So did the town, with its fringes and wreaths of Vincennois up and down the main street. But in the lines themselves, where every soul on duty had been carefully sheltered, each post, each bit of crude earthwork now bristled with gaunt, ragged men who raked the stockade with sunken eyes while their long rifles lay balanced and ready in skilled, leathery hands. "Hell and death!" muttered Markham. "They're apt to scare Hamilton so he'll barricade himself in his high blockhouse."

Clark shook his head. "He's got a name of not scaring at all good." He waved the gaunt men back under cover. Then he raised his voice. "Thanks, boys. The Major and Markham and I are all right. Rest while you can. No telling what's going to happen." Clark gave a quick smile as they vanished as though drawn down by a single cord.

A drum began to mutter somewhere behind the stockade and Markham, with the others, turned quickly from the church. For an instant he was blinded by a stabbing glare as the sun's rays were reflected back toward him from a rotting rowboat, filled with rainwater, lying near the church door. His vision cleared and he saw the shabby wicket-gate quiver uncertainly, then spring inward with a crash as though a firm hand had ripped it from a more timid grasp. The gap was filled for an instant with a dazzle of scarlet and white and blue as a tall rawboned man, dress sword at his side and a gold-laced cocked hat solidly planted on a powdered head, stood framed there. Markham exclaimed, "Here's Hamilton!" as the newcomer strode resolutely forward, followed by another British officer in a green coat.

As they came on Markham saw that the bright scarlet was faded to a dead-leaf color, the blue facings milky and the white breeches and waistcoat patched under their coating of pipe-clay. The nap of the hat was mangy and the gold braid faded and frayed. But the original impression stayed. In full-dress or rags, Hamilton stood out as a leader, just as Clark always did.

The aide too was striking in his own way. The worn green coat was merely something to cover immensely wide shoulders and long, dangling arms, and its major's knot looked like some tawdry gaud added by whim, rather than a badge of rank. In place of breeches the major wore long Indian leggings on short, grotesquely bowed legs and moccasins instead of boots.

Now features showed more clearly. Hamilton had a strong, bony Scots face, gingery eyebrows, a snub nose and a tough obstinate chin. Markham felt a warming glow as he caught the level gaze of the gray-blue eyes and thought, "There's a man we could work with! No wonder Lennie Helm likes and respects him." Then he remembered why George Rogers Clark had sent for Henry Hamilton, and the warmth died. Clark seemed to have been touched by the same conflict, for he muttered under his breath, "Why the hell does he have to look like *this!* Well, it'll do him no good."

There was no such struggle so far as the tubby major was concerned. He scowled at nothing in particular, very likely had been born scowling. Fountains of coarse black hair shaded his eyes, burst from his ears and struggled up from under his worn collar. A broken nose pushed down toward a heavy pugnacious jaw.

The two halted before Clark, with Markham and Bosseron falling a pace behind the Colonel. There was a moment's hush. Then from the nearest post toward the river, a voice crackling with fury rang out, "I seen that bandy-foot son of a bitch when they burned out Embry's on Buckhorn Creek near the Big Sandy!" Hamilton and the green-coated major gave no sign that they had heard, and stood, correct and military, waiting for Clark to speak.

Clark, hands clasped behind him, surveyed the two officers coldly. Then Hamilton raised his hat. "Your servant, Colonel Clark."

Clark barely moved his lips to answer, "Yours, sir."

Hamilton flushed a little as Clark added nothing to those two curt words, but his tone was calm as he went on. "This, sir, is Major Jehu Hay, His Majesty's Indian Agent in and for the District of Detroit." He smiled politely. "Through your Captain Helm I have been able to understand the deep loyalties that you inspire in your command."

Still on the same icy level, Clark said, "You are very good, sir. As to Hay, I know of many of his feats —" he paused, looked first at Hay then at Hamilton — "feats carried out under your orders." Markham noted that as Clark spoke on, his words and accent were losing their frontier flavor, were showing the influence of earlier years in long-established Virginia surroundings.

Hamilton answered evenly, "You and I are both soldiers, Colonel Clark. I appreciate your recognizing that the Major loyally carries out my orders, just as I execute those imposed on me by my superiors — just as your subordinates carry out those dictated to you by those of still higher rank than yourself."

Markham exchanged glances with Bosseron, who nodded in understanding. Hamilton was telling Clark plainly that he, Hamilton, was assuming responsibility for anything that Jehu Hay might have done in the past. He found himself unconsciously urging Hamilton to keep on saying what would touch Clark's softest spots, to come to amicable terms with him. He fought against such half-formed thoughts. It was partly in disappointment, but more in relief, that he heard Clark set matters on a strictly formal basis.

"I was under the impression, Colonel Hamilton, that you had certain proposals to lay before me. What were they? The day is wearing on and my men grow restless."

If Hamilton, professional soldier, resented this thinly veiled rebuke from a buckskinned frontier fighter, he gave no sign of it.

"Thank you for recalling me to my duty, Colonel Clark. The men must come first. So I have ventured to draw up a set of suggestions, an agenda. Major Hay has the papers." He half turned as though to ask Hay for them, but something in Clark's look or tone seemed to change his intent. "And to save us both time, and spare our men this trying wait, may I sum the points up for you verbally?"

"If it be understood that I in no way commit myself by listening," said Clark.

"My word on it — It is understood. I first urge a three-day truce, binding on both sides. In that time, I shall carry on no military activities other than routine. You will equally bind yourself." Hamilton's gray-blue eyes were fixed on Clark's impassive face as though hoping for a softening, a yielding. He went on. "Details of all these points I have expanded in the papers that Major Hay has. Now while this truce holds, you and I must meet at frequent intervals, seeking some way by which this present unfortunate situation may be honorably terminated and peace restored. What have you to say to that, sir?"

Clark's voice remained at the same impersonal level. "That last is impossible. You, Colonel Hamilton, have not carried on one day of honorable warfare since hostilities began. I deny you the right to ask for honorable terms — or to expect them. What have you to say to that, sir?"

Harsh, actually insulting as Clark's words were, Hamilton remained admirably calm, at least outwardly. Markham wondered just what seething turmoil must be going on under the tough Scots exterior. He saw a muscle twitching along one weather-beaten cheek and prepared himself for an outburst. He was also oddly touched to note, on close examination, that the Colonel had been forced to use ration flour to whiten his hair instead of the usual powder.

When Hamilton did speak, he sounded puzzled, rather than angry. "If I understand you correctly, Colonel Clark, you are telling me that I have no choice save to surrender at discretion?"

"At my discretion."

Hamilton turned a slow brick-red. "So I must accept your demand for unconditional surrender or go on fighting?"

Clark nodded coolly, then turned his head back toward his own lines and raised one hand shoulder-high, as though ready to give a signal.

Jehu Hay's voice broke in unexpectedly and harshly. "No ye don't!" And Markham realized that he had overlooked the bow-legged major in his absorption with Clark and Hamilton.

"Steady, Major!" Hamilton called sharply, then said to Clark, "You offer a hard choice, Colonel."

"You offered none to the settlers on the Kentucky and the Licking."

Hamilton, obviously controlling himself with difficulty, said, "In any event you must, in all fairness, allow me to consult with my officers. Will you extend our truce by a half-hour?"

"One half-hour." Clark raised his stained, battered hat. "Until then, I wish you a good day, Colonel Hamilton."

The group broke up, Markham and Clark and Bosseron walking on toward the Church of St. Francis Xavier, while Hamilton and Hay started for the wicket-gate. Then Hamilton called unexpectedly, "Colonel Clark, may I beg another moment of you?"

The trio turned. Hamilton, with Jehu Hay still at his elbow, came toward them, an almost pleading expression on his bony face. "It will help me with my officers if I know just why you insist on your own terms."

Clark gave him a long look. "I think you know why, but if you want me to say it, I don't mind." He hooked his thumbs through his belt and narrowed his eyes. "I know that most of your Indian partisans, your whites who lead the Indians off on those Kentucky raids and often go with them, are in the fort. My aim from the start has been to stop those raids and to dispose of those partisan leaders."

Hamilton's face hardened. "They are honorable men, acting under my orders, men who've given a lifetime in the service of —"

Clark cut him off shortly. "Men who've built careers on the torture and maiming and slaughter of helpless settlers, often only women, children and old men. If you really want to expose your garrison to massacre just to protect those skulking raiders —"

"Massacre!" exclaimed Hamilton, and Markham thought he looked really shaken, though not for himself.

"There's not a man in my lines, Colonel, whose family or close friends haven't been burned out or tortured or dragged off to the Lakes by your partisans and their Indians. Some were captured by your men and escaped. They could tell you tales that would age you twenty years in the hearing."

Hamilton's face suddenly cleared, became somehow easier. "Then we have the solution, Colonel Clark. Let the garrison and the partisans go back to Detroit on parole or to Pensacola. I say again that every raid went out under *my* orders and I stand ready to answer for them to you and to your men, individually or as a body."

Clark studied him for a moment, "Yes. You'd sacrifice yourself. I haven't the least doubt. But it wouldn't do, even if I accepted. Your partisans should never have left survivors in the settlements they raided, nor let people escape on the Canada trail. A score, perhaps two score of my men have actually *seen* Maisonville and La Mothe, to name only two, raiding with Indians." He turned abruptly on Hay, "Jehu Hay, would *you* dare walk through my lines, armed and under my protection?" He stared at Hay, who turned a muddy gray under his weathered skin. "No? You're wise. Your arms wouldn't help you and not even I could save you. You burned out Culver's Station — after you'd nailed up the cabins. There are at least four men from Culver's, men who survived somehow, within a hundred yards of you. There are men from other places here in my lines." He paused as though out of breath, then went on in a calmer tone. "I think you see, Colonel Hamilton, why I say that surrender must be on my terms."

Hamilton answered bleakly, "You're saying, 'Surrender or fight'!"

Clark inclined his head. "And you have one half-hour to make ready to do one or the other. Whatever your choice, you'd better make it whole-heartedly." He raised his hat again. "Until then, Colonel Hamilton —"

On the way past the church, Markham looked back over his shoulder. Hamilton, his bearing as erect and easy as though he had merely been out for a stroll, was just passing through the wicket, raising a finger to his hat as he returned some unseen sentry's salute. Jehu Hay padded on after him, seemingly anxious to keep close to his Colonel.

Markham caught up with Clark and Bosseron as they skirted a sheltered slope where half a dozen men slept happily in the sun, rifles clutched in powder-blackened hands. Joe Bowman sprang up from a broken wheelbarrow that he had somehow fashioned into an armchair a few yards back of the nearest post. "You did just fine, George," he called. "I was watching. You hold the high cards and Hair-buyer knows it. Now listen. I didn't want to break in on you, but —"

Clark sat down on the handle of the barrow, rubbing his fists across his forehead. "God Almighty, that took more sap out of me than the whole march from Kasky. Look, Joe, I want to tell you everything that was said. The Major and Mark'll nudge me if I forget. I need your opinion bad, Joe. We've only got a half-hour."

"But George, before we start on that —"

Clark waved a weary hand. "This comes first. Hair-buyer came out there with Jehu Hay and —"

Bowman bent lower, shouted almost in his ear. "Something's happened, George. No, don't push me off. Listen. God damn it, George. *Indians! Ottawas! The Hair-buyer sent them on a raid toward Corn Island three weeks ago.* And now they're heading back to Sackville!"

XIX

A Jeroboam of Heartener

CLARK was on his feet in a flash, fatigue gone. "Indians? Where are they now?"

"Let's say a mile and half, maybe only a mile to the north, George. Tobacco's Son's sister's navvy was out scouting by himself, picked up their trail, hung onto it and got word to us. I alerted the companies and sent John Williams and some of his boys out to meet them." He rubbed a knuckle across his broad chin. "I wouldn't be a mite surprised if John was getting close to 'em about now."

"You did just right, Joe. Where can we get a look at things?"

"I am sure that Father Gibault would offer the use of his church in such a cause," said Bosseron as he tugged a battered, muddy ladder out of a heap of lumber. "With your permission, Colonel, Monsieur Cape and I will hold this firm for you."

In a moment the four men lay on the west slope of the church roof, clinging to the ridgepole as they stared off to the northeast. Markham, wedged in between Bosseron and Bowman, made out an old trail, faint against the dead grasses, leading away from the fort to a high, tree-covered mound about a mile away where the Wabash swung east before heading north again. Along that trail a dozen brownish-gray shapes moved steadily on toward the mound. They were obviously John Williams's men. But the Indians? Their presence in that quarter puzzled him.

"Why would a raiding party from the Ohio come in from the north?" he whispered to Bosseron.

"And why not? They make wide detour to avoid the lands

where you and the Colonel and the others wet your feet to arrive here." Then Bosseron's voice shot up and Clark and Bowman shouted with him, a good second or more before Markham spotted that first returning Indian under the trees at the mound's crest.

He came on at a lithe, tireless trot that Markham envied. When he sighted Williams's party down below, he stopped, stared, then held his musket high over his head and fired blindly into the air. Then he gave a great leap, beating his chest and loosing a series of ghastly whoops. More flat musket-shots echoed from the depths of the trees and more Indians appeared, leaping and whooping in imitation of their fellow raider.

Clark made a rattling in his throat. "That's it, God damn it, that's their scalp-halloo!"

Williams's men, coming up the slope, began acting oddly. Some of them, too, fired in the air. They leaped and sprang about, thumping their chests and answering the bellowing from the crest. Suddenly Markham took in the whole scene as it must have appeared to the Indians. There was the British flag still flying over Fort Sackville. They had no reason to suspect any hostile presence, so Williams's party seemed to them merely men of the Detroit militia or Vincennois coming out to welcome them. And on they came.

It was impossible to see from the roof just what made the raiders scent something amiss. Whatever it was, the first Indian suddenly froze, threw his arms high and gave a warning shout, much too late.

The leading man on the trail slung his rifle over his shoulder and sprang at the raider. The two thudded together, were motionless for an instant. Then something flashed above the Indian's head, the pair collapsed to the trail and the rifleman stepped clear, wiping his long knife on his sleeve.

The rest of the party had already fanned out, those with loaded rifles covering the few who had joined in the Indians' victory fusillade. Then they all vanished among the trees in a steady crackle of rifle-fire. Markham could not detect any answering musketry.

Bosseron remarked with the detachment of a man watching a billiard match, "The point is yours, Colonel, and prettily played."

Eyes on the grove of trees which oozed smoke, Clark replied tersely, "Yes — ours. We better go down, Major. There's no more firing off yonder."

A few minutes later, six Indians stood in a resigned circle, facing inward on the open space a dozen yards from the main gate of Fort Sackville, guarded by their captors. Those of Clark's command who were within eyeshot crouched tense at their posts, heads and shoulders and rifle-barrels showing. To Markham, standing by the church with Bosseron and Joe Bowman, the crouching men seemed to be waiting for some signal that would free them to set upon the Indians. Clark stood at one side, an elbow slung across a knee, one foot resting on the soggy hull of the rowboat.

A prisoner began to howl. A guard jammed a rifle-butt into his ribs but the howls only rose louder and higher. The guard grinned, stepped back a pace. Other Indians joined in the yelling that swelled in an unholy, clanging din. At least some of it was understood inside the fort, for heads were showing all along the top of the stockade. Markham could hear shouts which sounded like angry orders, but the heads stayed up, staring.

Joe Bowman gnawed off a bit of black, twisted tobacco and frowned judicially. "I'm not scholared in Indian tongues, Major, but I'd say these fellers ain't liking the Hair-buyer much."

"At least they are not amused," said Bosseron. "They say now — ah — un moment — they say that the Hair-buyer is a liar, for he had told them many times how their Great White Father in England would always protect them. If so, why are they now prisoners and before the Hair-buyer's very eyes? They call the Hair-buyer a squaw, fit only to chew deerskins for fighting men."

Markham watched and listened reflectively. A good many Piankashaws and Kickapoos were gathered near the edge of the town. They could see and hear. They would unfailingly spread word of their observations. Tribes far up and down the Wabash and the Ohio would hear in detail how the arm of the Great White

English Father was too weak to protect his red children from the least of dangers.

A change had come over the flat ground by the gates of the fort. The Indians had stopped jeering and were looking at Clark, who still stood motionless by the boat. No heads showed now over the stockade top or at the gun-ports. Then from the posts out of sight along the river-wall two of Clark's men came running, jaws set and eyes hot.

"That's a good pick," observed Bowman calmly. "Abel Trent and Zeke Rankin. Ain't two men amongst us who's lost more close kin than them two."

Now Captain McCarthy stormed around the east corner of the fort and made for Clark. "Hold on, George! Word was passed to me! Let me in here! Got to be sure —"

Clark nodded in silence and McCarthy plunged in among the Indians, twisting a chin this way, pushing a head that way. Then he let out an excited whoop and dragged an Ottawa from the circle and began slashing at his cords, calling, "It's him, George! Poor old drunken Pontiac's son. Pontiac, he saved my life in the old wars. That was before rum bit him. The boy's mine, George, under any laws!"

Once more Clark nodded without speaking as McCarthy threw an arm over the Indian's shoulder and led him off. An approving murmur ran through the watching men. The remaining Indians uttered little barking cries as if in applause. Markham felt an odd sense of relief as McCarthy and the Ottawa vanished round the corner of the stockade. But all easement vanished as Clark straightened up and said a few harsh words in an Indian tongue. The prisoners spaced themselves carefully, widened their circle and knelt, facing inward. One of them began a long wailing chant. The others joined in, bowing their heads. There was sorrow in the set of their heads but no fear. Trent and Rankin unslung their hatchets, tested the edges with tough fingers and moved closer to the circle.

Markham turned away abruptly. He remembered the two kneeling Indians in the crowded room at Cahokia. But this time there was no play-acting, no sudden reprieving gesture of amity. He walked on to Father Gibault's church, pushed the door gently and stepped onto the packed dirt floor inside.

There was a hard bar of light slanting in from the entrance, but the rest of the interior was dim. At the far end he saw a chancel of planks, the mass of a rude altar beyond. He took off his hat and stood facing the chancel, head bowed. Outside the Indians wailed on, the volume undiminished — so far.

In a few minutes it was still outside, oppressively still, save for a few shouts that seemed to trail off toward the river.

Markham braced himself and walked out into the sunshine. Now, where the Indians and their guards had stood, there was nothing save a wide, sullen, reddish puddle. Joe Bowman had gone back to his wheelbarrow armchair and the men on duty had sunk into their improvised rifle-pits. More men were moving in little groups on the path that led down to the Wabash. Those making for the river stepped cautiously along as though carrying heavy, awkward burdens. Those returning scrubbed at hands and arms with bunches of grass. As Markham watched, there was a dull, muted splash as the last slaughtered Indian was consigned to the river. Then another group began its journey back. There was no sign of life from the fort itself.

Bosseron cried, "Hé! Regarde-moi ça!" and pointed toward the stockade.

The wicket-gate whined on its hinges and swung slowly wide. Colonel Hamilton strode resolutely out, a British officer and one of the Detroit militia close behind him. With strong Scots chin set, his cane tucked firmly under his arm and his sword swinging to his brisk gait, he did not strike Markham as a man about to surrender.

Bosseron muttered, "Ah, ça! Perhaps we have not yet witnessed the last act."

"You don't know Clark," said Markham. "Any play is apt to end only when he says so. Let's get up closer." He moved on toward the gate confidently enough, yet troubled in spite of himself by Hamilton's bearing.

The British colonel had stopped, obviously looking about for Clark. If he was aware of the wide, murky pool soaking slowly into the ground, he gave no sign of it. His eye lit on Markham and Bosseron. His head went back as though he were about to call to them, but he seemed to think better of it and stood waiting, erect, silent and commanding.

From the river path a deep voice called, "Have you an answer for me, Colonel Hamilton?"

Hamilton turned quickly and some of the rigidity left him. His back and shoulders seemed to sag a little and his two officers drew closer together as though unconsciously. Markham felt that he could even sympathize with them and he caught a muffled, "*Mais enfin!*" from Bosseron. Then he saw Clark.

Clark was hurrying up the path from the river. His hands, his arms bare to elbow, the front of his hunting-shirt, his leggings were daubed with blood, and his moccasins left bloody pads on the worn grass. He said again, "You've an answer for me? I hope so, because my boys are getting harder to hold back."

Hamilton had recovered himself quite well, Markham thought, but he was still silent as he stared at Clark's arms and clothes.

Clark kept coming on, head forward expectantly. Then, as though just aware of his own appearance, he checked himself abruptly. "My apologies, Colonel. I didn't realize — with your permission —" He stepped to the side of the rain-filled boat, plunged his hands and arms into the tepid water and splashed about vigorously, churning up a pale red froth. "A bad state to get into, Colonel Hamilton, but at times there's no choice." He straightened up, shook water from his still stained arms and hands. "There, that's about all I can do right now."

Markham was sure that Clark had not raised his own hand against any of the Indian captives. He was equally sure that there had been plenty of men on hand to carry the dead Indians down to the Wabash. Clark had, however, carried or helped to carry one or more of the slain, had exposed himself to every spurt or gout of blood solely to present to Hamilton something of the raw essence of those raids that could hardly have been evident to a commander ordering them from barracks in Detroit. And Clark's casual ablutions in stagnant water had been one more harsh touch.

Now Clark was repeating his question. His arms and hands were paler but his whole effect was still gory. "Have you made your choice, Colonel Hamilton?" he asked, more sharply.

Shaken though he might be, Hamilton managed to assume a coldly formal mask. His voice was level as he said, "A counter-proposal, Colonel Clark, that I and my command be paroled and allowed to proceed by boat to the Ohio and thence, via the Mississippi, to Natchez. You will perceive —"

Clark kept his voice low as he interrupted. "I perceive that you forget that I gave you just two choices. Surrender on my terms or — fight it out." His tone suddenly snapped like a whiplash. "Which?"

Now Hamilton's voice was low, and Markham had to lean forward to catch the words. "My own men of the 8th, they'd stick to me close as the shirt to my back. But you brought too many Creoles in your ranks, and too many Creoles have joined you since. The Detroit militia won't fight against their own kin. God above, I've no choice. I surrender." Hamilton could say nothing more. He bowed his head, and his mouth worked, then tightened. His right hand slowly moved to his left side and unwillingly fumbled there until it lifted his sword from its gilt scabbard, reversed it. Then Hamilton raised his head and, looking Clark straight in the eye, proffered his sword.

There was a silence from the men all around as they watched Hamilton's slow gesture, as Clark raised his left hand to accept the sword. Then Clark stepped back two paces and with all the formality of a parade-ground snapped his right hand up in a salute. With that the cheers broke out, in French and English, crashing so loud that Markham, standing next to Clark, could only see Hamilton's lips moving, only just hear his words.

"Colonel Clark, I, Henry Hamilton, Colonel in His Majesty's Army and by His Majesty's grace Lieutenant Governor of Detroit and Superintendent of Fort Sackville, do surrender myself and my men to your discretion." His eyes fell to Clark's bloody feet and leggings.

Clark's head was high as he responded, and the cheers were silent now. "I, George Rogers Clark, Lieutenant Colonel, Commonwealth of Virginia, do accept your surrender. You will deliver up Fort Sackville as it is at present with all the stores and provisions in it. Your garrison will deliver themselves up as prisoners of war and will march out with their arms and equipment at ten o'clock tomorrow morning. You will have three days in which to settle your accounts with the traders and inhabitants of Vincennes."

Hamilton nodded grimly. "And my officers? What is to become of them?"

"You will be informed of that in good time."

Hamilton saluted once more, wheeled about smartly, and marched back into the fort. As Clark watched him go, his face relaxed, and as the gate closed behind Hamilton, suddenly Joe Bowman, then one man after another, rushed forward to throw his arms around Clark. The pulling and hauling almost knocked Markham off his feet. All at once the entire crowd reeled back as if struck by a blow. Pushing larger men aside as though they were children was the barrel-shaped figure of Leonard Helm, a huge jug under each arm. "George, bless you, here it is. Here's that jeroboam of Heartener I promised you."

It was much later, and the cold of the February night seemed somehow a long way off as Markham, Len Helm, Joe Bowman, and half a dozen others sat in the kitchen of Bosseron's house, watching a huge fire swim cheerfully before their eyes.

"Now tell me, Len," said Bowman, "When did you first get wind of our coming? Did you know we were here before the Hair-buyer did? Didn't anybody in the town tip you off to us?"

"Boys, I was so unsuspecting I could have gone on all winter; but I had a wee hunch that George wouldn't sit around in Kaskaskia once he knew that Hamilton had jumped me over here. I was telling George a while ago that when Hair-buyer and his men showed up out of the woods there wasn't a solitary soul in the fort but me, Jim Pickett, John Gartleby, and Bob Carter, so all I could do was make the surrender as formal as I knew how. I tell you, when I came a-walking out of the wicket-gate with my white flag I wasn't sure how long I'd be breathing God's air, especially with that pack of Indians Hamilton had with him. But by and by Hamilton got a snifter of Heartener, and before long I figured he needed me more than I needed him. So he taught me to play pee-kay (that's one of your tony English card games, you know), and we used to swap stories something dreadful.

"Well anyway, the other night we was sitting there and I was shopping him pretty bad at pee-kay while he was telling me about the Highlanders in Scotland and how they ain't so different from our Indians as you might think. I had a mug of apple toddy sitting on the hearth just the way I always did at Bouvier's in Kaskaskia — you know, just to keep the cold out and all — and then we hear some rifle-shots. Hamilton says those must be the party of Indians coming back from the Falls. Well, the gunfire kept up and I knew right away it wasn't muskets but American rifles, but I wasn't going to upset the Hair-buyer. Then one of you damn rascals — who was it anyway? — shot at the chimney and a big chunk of mortar come crashing down into the fireplace and knocked over my jug of Heartener. Well that shook me. 'Colonel,' I says to him, 'That ain't Indians. That's George Rogers Clark, and by God he must of had to swim all the way from Kaskaskia to get here. And let me tell you, the next time we play a game of pee-kay it'll be you who's the prisoner and me who's the superintendent.' Well, he didn't like that much and he frowns fit to kill and jumps up and runs out to see what's going on. But boys, boys, why did you have to ruin that apple toddy? Why I had me a batch of good strong apples, just right. Then I took a good splash of Heartener and water, and nutmeg, and sugar and . . ." Len's face was beginning to screw up at the terrible thought of that ruined toddy when the door burst open and there, stamping his shoes dry, was George Rogers Clark.

The Colonel was aglow with the enthusiasm familiar to every man in the room. The lines of fatigue that had cut furrows into his face on the long march across the drowned lands had eased now. He was dressed in clean buckskins. He took the cup of Heartener that Len Helm reached out to him, and he sat down on a settle by the fire. "Len," he said, "you're looking a little plump compared to the rest of us. Better work some of that off. I want you to take a group of men upriver right after the surrender tomorrow. Lord knows where the *Willing* is. We haven't heard a peep out of Rogers. But stores in the fort are running low. Len, I want you to round up that party of British that you tell me was sent upriver last week. Get them before they return here and find us in charge. If we wait a day longer the word of Hamilton's surrender is bound to get to them, and they'll go flying back to Detroit. I was going to send the *Willing* after them, but I don't dare wait. If she doesn't arrive tomorrow, take the swivel-guns from the fort and as many canoes and pirogues as you need."

Len Helm, garrulity vanished, leaped to his feet and rushed from the room. One second later his head was back in the door. "Bless you, George, I didn't know if you'd ever give me a command again." And he was gone before Clark could smile or demur.

"Len Helm did everything he could to keep Hamilton away," Clark said to the men in the room. "He did right to surrender. He did us a lot more good as a prisoner than he would have dead." He mused for a moment. Markham knew that Clark had more to say, that there was still much to be settled.

"Colonel, what are you going to do about Hamilton after the surrender is official?" Markham asked. "Some of the boys have been talking about lifting his scalp."

Clark's mouth set sternly. "There'll be none of that. Hamilton was carrying out his orders — to harass the American settlements by every means within his power, and that meant Indians. Len told me earlier that London sent Hamilton thousands and thousands of pounds to spend in bounty for white prisoners. The trouble was that the Indians kept getting carried away and never brought the prisoners in alive. Oh yes, Hamilton was supplying the Indians when they took scalps; but he set his bounty on captives. He wanted us alive, not dead.

"No, Mark, I've decided that the only way to treat Hamilton and his officers is as formal prisoners of war. I'm going to send them back to Williamsburg under guard, and the more settlements they pass through along the way, the better. When the tribes see their Great White Father being carried helplessly under guard through every post along the Ohio and in Kentucky and Virginia, they'll spread the word fast. The Indian threat to Kentucky will fade away. The Indians have no hankering to be on the losing side in this fracas. They'll be here in Vincennes — you'll see — within two weeks, wanting to make peace with us and telling me how the Great White Father Hamilton has let them down. And when the Indians come over to our side, then I'll be able to tell Governor Henry and Mr. Jefferson that this part of our task is done."

"*This* part of our task? What do you mean, George?" asked Joe Bowman. "What more do we have to do than that? We've cleared the British out of Illinois. Aren't we ever going to go home? We've already been out here for six months longer than we signed up for. Can't you garrison Fort Sackville and let it go at that? I don't know about you, but I'm about ready to go find myself some nice land in Kentucky and settle in."

"Settle in?" Clark's eyes were flashing brighter than ever. "Settle in to what? To a country which could be just as hostile next summer as it was last summer? To a country threatened again from the north? As long as Detroit's there, and in English hands, and there's a war on and there are Indians for hire, there won't be any safety for Kentucky *or* Virginia. No, boys, if we're ever going to take Detroit, now's the time to do it, while we have the advantage! If only we had more men!" And with those words Clark rose, suddenly a thousand miles away from the group around the fire, paced back and forth twice while the men watched, puzzled and amazed. Then without looking at them again he walked to the door and went out, closing it behind him with a sharp slam.

"Oh oh," said Phil Brady. "Watch out. George isn't finished with this campaign yet."

"But we can't go any farther now," said Joe Bowman, wearily setting his cup of Heartener down on the hearth. "We've just marched hundreds of miles. The men are fagged out. We've got to garrison this town, and beef up the garrisons for Kaskaskia and Cahokia. We don't know where the *Willing* is, nor the forty men aboard her. We have to keep some men in reserve for counter-attack or Indian raids. Where does George think the men are going to come from to make a winter attack on Detroit? From Paris, France?"

Markham said nothing. He looked down at the ragged knees of his buckskins, at the stiffened and tattered moccasins. He felt the ache in his bones and muscles, the weakness in his limbs that persisted despite the venison and cornbread that had been pressed on Clark's men the last few days by the amiable Vincennois. He looked back to the long, cold, grim, sloshing tramp through the drowned lands, the sodden misery of the last month. Yet, beyond all that he remembered the flash in Clark's eyes, the shout of "Shallows just ahead!" and the sight of that tall copper-haired figure. And despite everything he felt the leaping surge of pride that came from following such a man. He got up. He wanted to be alone.

"I don't know about you boys," he said, "but this sorefoot is ready for some sleep."

XX
A Salute

THERE wasn't much sleep for Markham that night after all. When he finally dropped off, his dreams were of marching men, and the British moving in a surrender parade across the Boston Common. He was awake long before dawn, despite the relaxation of knowing that the end was near at Vincennes. This morning Hamilton would surrender formally, and Fort Sackville would fly the American flag once more. The road to Detroit was open, if Virginia could supply Clark with enough provisions and enough men to take it. The Illinois, with its vast prairies and rich lands, was to be part of the United States. Clark, with his vision and energy, had done his work well.

But hadn't Markham Cape done enough? First he had gone along to Kaskaskia without complaining, though hardly as a volunteer. Then the long journey downriver to Pollock and back again; and finally, stirred by Clark's leadership, he had joined the march to Vincennes. Now at last he was near enough to his goal. Wasn't this the time to cut loose and head east? Visions of a half-remembered Boston flitted through his thoughts; dreams of the life of a city merchant, where you slept in a feather bed and ate meals off pewter plates, the lovely chatelaine — perhaps — a charmer with a slow smile and eyelids dropping slowly. Maybe, someday, Madame de Liliac would be free and . . . Surely he had been a wanderer long enough. Later, after the formal surrender, he would talk to George about it. If only he could resist Clark's appeal this time . . .

He was walking, limping slightly, through the town toward the parade-ground when Phil Brady hailed him. "George wants to see

you, Mark. Has a job that'll keep you off your feet." Markham
turned towards Bosseron's house and found Clark in the kitchen
in a close conference with Leonard Helm.

"Oh, Mark, good to see you. We've got to find out for sure where
the *Willing* is. If she doesn't arrive today, Len will take a party of
men upriver to capture the express from Detroit. I want you to
take a canoe with Phil Brady and drop downriver as far as the
Ohio. If you don't find John Rogers and the *Willing* before the
Ohio, come back. The boys may have run afoul of a raiding party
or come to grief in the flood waters. Do you mind missing the
surrender?"

"Well, Colonel, I had kind of looked forward to it, but if you
think there's no time to lose . . ."

"All right. Get your gear and be ready to move in twenty
minutes."

Markham chuckled as he limped back to his billet. George
Clark would never change. When Markham had walked into that
room, it had been with the firm intention of talking to Clark
about his future role with the Virginia militia. Well, that could
wait — but not forever.

The next morning, February 26, Phil Brady and Markham
watched from the bushes along the Wabash as the dawn slowly
grew gray. It had been raining ever since they left the fort, and
the previous day they had made their way downriver, careful to
avoid floating logs or cakes of ice that might punch a hole in the
canoe. Careful, too, to keep an eye out for any trace of the
Willing and her men. Expecting to see the keelboat perhaps lying
in wait at the fork of the Wabash and the Embarras, they had
been disappointed. As they drifted with the current, paddling
slowly but steadily, they had waved now and then to a Vincennois
out duck-hunting. By nightfall they estimated they were a third of
the way to the Ohio. They had tied up to a thicket at the downstream end of a small island, where they could hardly avoid
hearing the sounds of a riverboat being poled upstream, even at
night. Then they had munched their pemmican and stretched

out in the bottom of the canoe, "like a pair of lizards side by side," as Phil put it.

Now in the drizzly gray of early morning they were about to shove off when they both spotted the heavy, glistening bulk of the keeler a quarter of a mile downstream, slowly making her way towards them. The men on her decks were filing back and forth with their poles, and Phil and Markham saw them before they were seen. With a whoop they cast off, and it was the work of only a few minutes before their canoe was sliding along the oaken side of the *Willing*, which was crowded with grinning faces. "It's Phil Brady!" "And Mark Cape! Out for a paddle, are ye, boys?"

"Where have you been keeping yourselves?" shouted Brady as he tossed their sack of provisions over the side of the keelboat. Eager hands helped Brady and Cape aboard and pulled their canoe after them. "We thought you boys had decided to pole straight on up the Ohio," Markham jested.

"We came closer than you might think," said John Rogers, as he passed the rum-bottle to Brady. "The fork of the Wabash and Ohio was swelled up so high we thought we must have come on Lake Erie unsuspected. It took us two days to find the real channel. But quick, what's the news from Vincennes? Have you made it already? You must have, we're so late."

"Oh yes," said Markham, settling himself on the cabin roof while the men gathered around. "We made it, though we could have used this boat of yours once or twice, and the guns." Markham was going on, but a look around him showed haggard faces, the gauntness of fatigue. What's more, a bandaged head here, an arm there, showed that Rogers's men had not been on a pleasure cruise. Markham swallowed the words he had been about to speak.

Phil Brady, who had been using his eyes too, cut in, "Tell you right off: Vincennes surrendered yesterday morning. The Hair-buyer and all his partisans are in the lock-up. It worked, boys, it worked. They didn't expect us any sooner than our Governor Patrick Henry coming by for tea. It was so pretty that George is even beginning to talk about taking a stroll to Detroit."

There was a cackle of voices all at once: "Surrendered already?"
"Jesus Christ! George done it." "Anybody kilt from our boys?"
"How did the Frenchies do? Could they keep up?"

"All right, all right," shouted Brady. "One at a time. No, it
wasn't hardly easy, but thanks to George we kept going, every
man jack of us. And, yes, we lost a man or two. I'll tell you all
about it. But what about you? I can tell you, you boys have been
on our minds plenty."

John Rogers said, "Well, you can right-about-face that for us
too. We've been cursing our luck for the past three weeks, and I
can tell you, this news of yours is the best relief we could have
thought up. We didn't have any trouble till we started up the
Ohio. Then near everything you can think of went wrong. The
channels were all altered on account of the flooding, and we kept
running aground where we thought we had twenty feet of water,
out in the middle of nowhere, where we didn't have a tree to cordelle from. We had to pull her off with canoes, or by swimming
under and digging her out. Then we hit a great pack of ice, all
jammed together where the floods had brought it down. After
that there wasn't wind enough to sail, mostly. Then a bunch of
Indians tried to ambush us — right there, you know, near old
Fort Massac — and they might have got away with it too if Abner
Byrd, here, hadn't kept his brains about him."

Rogers pointed to a heavy man, both of whose hands were
roughly bandaged. He grinned. "Yep, Phil, I was awake for once.
The devils snuck out in their canoes and heaved a pot of coals
aboard before anyone seen 'em. Willie Bennett managed to put
holes in two of their canoes before they got away; but they got
Willie while they were at it, and he died next day. Anyway, we
had a pretty warm fire here before we got it out." He gestured
with a bandaged hand toward the stern, where charred timbers
and a charred mast showed black.

"That did for our sails and rigging," Rogers put in. "So we had
to pole and paddle the rest of the way. Except for having a hellish time finding the mouth of the Wabash, we came on pretty
steady since. But it was slow going, I can tell you. Well, now, is

George expecting us? We picked up William Myers, here, down on the Ohio, with news from Williamsburg."

"Yes," put in a lean, leathery man. "Colonel Clark doesn't know yet that he ain't a Lootenant Colonel no longer. And Joe Bowman is promoted to Major. I've got some secret papers as well, from the Governor."

"That's what George is waiting for," Markham said, briskly. "He's been waiting to hear from Patrick Henry for nearly a year. John, let's not waste any more time. Let's move along."

"All right, men! Heave your poles, heave your poles! Let's go! Send her along! That's the way! Now, Mark, tell me how you got to Vincennes before we did. . . ."

It was a week later. Ever since the *Willing* had been welcomed to Vincennes, Markham had been trying to get a word with Clark alone, but it had been out of the question. "Not now, Mark, I'm working out these supply lists." "Not now, Mark, I've got to talk to Rick McCarthy about a powwow with the Chippewas." Mark began to get angry over this indifference to his problem. What the hell, hadn't he followed Clark as loyally as any Kentuckian, when this fight was none of his affair?

So went his inner complaint, until Lennie Helm and his men returned, swaggering and triumphant from their errand up the Wabash, having rounded up an entire British supply column, including seven boatloads of supplies. They had captured, too, De Jean, the Grand Judge of Detroit, who was on his way south to see Colonel Hamilton with a plea from the citizens of Detroit for Hamilton to return to their midst before spring came and that madman Clark should descend on their city. Markham was told off to make an inventory of the supplies, and, borrowing an empty barn, he set to work. The next day, he was finishing the job with the help of a Kentuckian named Simon Linn, when without warning George Rogers Clark walked in. He strolled over to a bale of shirts that Linn was counting. "Whoo-eee, George," said Simon. "What my old woman wouldn't say if she could get the feel of these shirts. Why these are smooth as slippery elm. Don't suppose they'd keep out the cold the way linsey-woolsey does, though."

Clark smiled. "Good for summer wearing, Simon," he said. "Mark, it's lucky for us you've had experience with goods. How's your count coming?"

"Very well, Colonel," Markham said, adding a figure to his inventory. "I reckon about six tons of Indian goods, as well as general supplies for the relief of Fort Sackville."

"You mean Fort Patrick Henry," said Clark jocularly.

"The supplies which were *meant* for Fort Sackville," Mark answered. He could hear the fatigue in his voice and knew that Clark must hear it too. But Clark kept right on smiling, reached down for Mark's papers.

"You probably can't read those rough figures," said Markham. "I reckon the total value of this stuff is about fifty thousand dollars." Clark's eyebrows went up. "There are about five hundred shirts, uniforms for forty-two men, including coats, vests, trousers, caps. Also some fancy stuff for Colonel Hamilton: two pairs of white silk stockings, mind you; three pairs of white silk pants, a new scarlet coat (bet he wished he'd had it for the surrender, then maybe he wouldn't be feeling so undignified right now), six shirts, eight towels, eight handkerchiefs (help to take snuff with, I guess). Over there in the corner under those hides I've put eight gallons of fine brandy just in case anyone developed an overpowering thirst. And then . . ."

"That's enough, Mark. I get the idea. I want you to take all the trade goods, everything we don't actually immediately need for supplying the fort, and divide it up into shares of equal value for the men. Just make sure the value is equal. It doesn't matter whether the share is knives or handkerchiefs. The men can trade among themselves. Then make out a list . . ."

Mark could hold himself in no longer. "Now just a minute, *Colonel*," he said. "You seem to forget that I'm a civilian. I put myself under your orders voluntarily, and I can remove myself voluntarily. If you want a commissary to do your work for you, appoint one. As for me, I don't happen to give a good God damn whether you throw all this stuff in the river."

Simon Linn knew when he wasn't wanted. "Mark, I got some hauling to do from the last boatload. Be back after a while." And he padded out of the door, his face expressionless.

He had no sooner disappeared than George Clark burst into a loud laugh. He laughed louder and louder, took off his fur cap, threw it on the ground, and kept guffawing until he collapsed on the bale of shirts. Mark stared at him, nonplused.

"Markham Cape," Clark finally said when he had recovered his breath, "if you aren't an honest-to-God New Englander after all. I just can't help laughing when you get on your high horse that way. Of course you're a civilian volunteer, and don't think I'm not grateful." His voice grew serious. "Mark, I said we'd give you an escort on your journey east, and I meant it. But you've done better than even I expected of you. You've been a Virginian among Virginians, and there isn't a man under my command who doesn't know it." He stood up, held out his hand. "I want to thank you for your effort and, yes, damn it, your courage. I've known all along I could count on you for a cool head and a steady eye."

It was almost too much for Mark. How could anyone resist a man like this? His pique vanished in an instant. If Clark had asked him at that moment, Markham would have gone along with him to Quebec, if he had to walk barefoot. But Clark went on.

"You're free to leave this minute if you want to, and you'll take my blessings with you. But if you don't mind waiting until tomorrow, you might find your trip east a little more comfortable — along with Captain Williams and John Rogers and the escort that's taking Hamilton and the other prisoners to Williamsburg. You can do what you like, of course. Leave them at Pittsburgh and make your own way back to Boston from there, or else tag along with the party to Williamsburg. Think it over and let me know before you go. If you want to string along to Williamsburg, and if you wouldn't mind giving me a little help . . ."

Markham was tumbling over himself now. "Well, Colonel, I

didn't mean it that way. I mean, yes, well, I wouldn't mind getting on my way, but if there's anything I can do for you before I finally go home, I mean, surely I'll be glad to do anything for you in Williamsburg. It won't be much out of my way, not after all these years."

"Good." Clark was all seriousness now, entirely the commander. "Here's the situation. Keep it to yourself, since I haven't talked about it to anyone else. That packet from Williamsburg brought important news. If only I could be sure it was true! Detroit, Mark! We've got to take Detroit." Clark's jaw set, and he slammed one fist into the palm of his hand. "But I can't do it without help. I have almost as many prisoners as I do men at this moment. The only way I can get free is to send the prisoners downriver — that is, the important ones. That's why I'm sending twenty-five men, tomorrow, along with Hamilton, at least as far as the Falls of the Ohio. The French militia who fought with Hamilton I'm sending home."

"You're letting them go?" asked Markham incredulously.

"Yes, Mark. They'll be more good to us in Detroit than they will here. Their Detroit folk probably haven't been allowed to hear of the French Alliance yet, and once their friends and families hear that the Vincennois are happy with our treatment of them, that they've taken loyalty oaths to us, those I've sent back will convert their friends in Detroit. When the great day comes, the British won't be able to count on anyone but themselves. No French, no Indians."

"No Indians?"

"No. Not if things work out the way I expect them to. Once the word gets out that Hamilton is being taken to Virginia as a prisoner, along with Jehu Hay, La Mothe, the Grand Judge of Detroit, Hamilton's partisans, and all the rest, the tribes will draw back. I want you and the escort party — if you really mean it about wanting to go along — to make as big a noise as you can wherever you go. I've got to send twenty-five men to keep Hay and the others from being scalped. They aren't exactly popular in Kentucky, as you've noticed. But I expect that the Indians will fall away and come to treat with us. I've already had messengers from the Piankashaws, the Chippewas, the Miamis, Wyandottes, Ojibways, and the Potawatomies. You can help. Now if only Patrick Henry . . ."

Clark was silent for a moment. When he spoke again his voice was an excited whisper. "That message, Mark. I'm promised seven hundred men. Seven hundred men! John Montgomery is bringing a regiment of five hundred, and Joe's brother John Bowman another two hundred. If they get here before the middle of summer, Detroit is ours. Just like that." Clark's two hands made the motion of breaking a stick in half, and throwing away the pieces.

"I was dreaming of making the move right away, while Detroit was still weak. Their fortifications aren't finished yet, and, with Hamilton taken, they must be demoralized. But I just don't have the men, Mark, and I can't ask these boys to march again unless I'm certain of victory. God knows they're willing. But if I marched now, I'd be leaving Kaskaskia without a garrison, Vincennes almost naked, Cahokia helpless, and staking everything on about one hundred men, who would have to make it upriver against these floods. Yes, it's March, but we can't expect the weather to stay warm forever. One good blizzard, and there we are out in the wilderness and helpless. You know me, Mark. Valor is the better part of discretion as far as I'm concerned. But I can't play the part of a madman. If you can get to the Falls of the Ohio and carry the message on to Williamsburg from there for me! See Henry. Tell him how close Detroit is. Get him and the House of Burgesses to send money, send men, send supplies. Mark, the American flag will wave over hundreds of thousands of square miles of the most beautiful country in the world!"

Clark's eyes were ablaze. What a man this is, Markham thought. "Colonel, when you talk like that I feel as though I could get on my sore feet this minute and take Detroit single-handed. Of course I'll go to Williamsburg for you. You have my word."

Clark reached out his hand and shook Mark's in a grip that would have squeezed the juice out of an oak.

"Damn it, George," Mark said, laughing. "It looks as though you've got yourself a permanent volunteer — on a personal basis."

Hamilton by courtesy of Clark had the new uniforms that Helm's party had captured. He sat now, dressed in the fresh scarlet, the pure white breeches, looking for all the world like a prize package. He shone out, a brilliant spot of color under a cloudy sky. His face was calm, but etched into it were lines of shame and mortification. Markham, sitting beside him in the lead boat, knew that his expression would grow grimmer as their long journey progressed.

Their five boats were moored by the side of Fort Patrick Henry, as the stockade was now called; and the last of the British prisoners were being led down the steep slope. Jehu Hay, his face as dark and malevolent as ever, came down the slope with his bandy-legged stride, a Kentuckian on either side of him. He and his guards stepped aboard into the last boat. Hay shook off the restraining arm of one of his captors and was cuffed alongside the head for his pains.

"Sweet-tempered fellow, ain't he?" said John Rogers, standing in the bottom of the boat next to Markham and Hamilton. "Well, that's the load. Everything ready. We'll push off and moor below the fort. All right there! Let the lines go! Follow me!"

The five laden boats pushed out into the current, and Rogers's lead boat drifted a hundred yards downstream, then headed into the bank again. The bank was lower here, and the passengers could see over it to the parade-ground. While they had been loading up they had seen nothing of the preparations that had been made for this departure. Drawn up on the parade-ground was every man of the garrison, in as close military order as George Rogers Clark's forces had ever known. Here in the center were the Virginia companies: on the left, Leonard Helm stood like a barrel at the head of his men; next came Ed Worthington, pale, but drawn to his full lean height with his company behind him. The thrums on their buckskins, as clean as Markham could remember having seen them, fluttered slightly. Behind them stood Charleville with the Kaskaskia company, dressed in linsey-woolsey and buckskin — a confused mixture of rough cloth and smooth hide. Beyond them, with Rick McCarthy at their head, were drawn up the Cahokia company, with a banner, it seemed, for every five or ten men. Farther still beyond the main body stood the Vincennes militia with Nicolas Cardinal.

In the town itself every window had been thrown open, and from dormers and upper stories, women waved handkerchiefs and gaily colored tablecloths. Over the church the flag of St. Vincent flew, and before its main door stood Bosseron, holding another pennant on a long staff. Cries and cheers in French rose from the townspeople. "*Vive la Virginie! Vivent les Etats Unis! Vivent les Bastonnais!*"

Off to one side, motionless and impassive, stood a band of half a hundred Piankashaws. The colors of their feathers, their tawny skins, their robes, made a solid contrast to the brighter colors of the town.

At the head of all this panoply stood the towering, leathery figure of George Rogers Clark, dressed now in a worn uniform of Virginia militia. A sword hung at his left side, a long knife at his right. His head was bare and his long coppery hair shone bright. Before him stood, proud as a pouter pigeon, Al Lemoine, the little drummer, and Alphonse Gautier with his battered fife, as well as two Virginians, one with fife and one with drum.

There was a sudden silence as Clark drew his sword, held it before him in a salute. With one accord, every banner raised aloft — French, Virginian. Over the blockhouse the Stars and Stripes fluttered briskly. The drum began to beat slowly, the fifes took up a tune. Markham didn't recognize it at first, but as the fifes continued, he remembered it from watching a parade somewhere, long ago. Yes, that was it, wasn't it? "The World Turned Upside Down"?

The boats slowly cast loose from their moorings and began to slide downriver. Markham was on his feet, though he didn't remember rising. By his side, he noticed now, stood the stalwart Scot, Henry Hamilton, his eyes full, his craggy face set, his hand raised in the salute of a conquered adversary.

Historical Epilogue

TODAY few have heard of George Rogers Clark, and, sad to say, most of those who have are prone to confuse him with his younger brother William, who accompanied Meriwether Lewis to the Pacific in 1804-1805. Clark flashed across the scene, for a few short years played a vital part in the history of the West, and then dropped back into obscurity. Yet, had it not been for his activities, Pittsburgh today might well be part of Canada.

The great Appalachian chain of mountains extends from Maine to northern Georgia. In colonial days it effectively cut the coastal colonies off from the Ohio Valley and the West, forming a barrier difficult to penetrate. During the last of the French and Indian Wars, which had ended in 1760, French posts in the West, shielded by the great mountain chain, had spewed forth raiding parties of bloodthirsty Indians, who had carried torch and tomahawk to the scattered settlers along the colonial frontiers. The peace of 1763 brought an end to this long-looming threat from beyond the mountains, and all eastern North America became British.

By the time the Revolution broke out the Appalachians had been breached here and there by settlements along the Mohawk Valley in New York, at the forks of the Ohio, today's Pittsburgh, and barely over the mountains into eastern Tennessee. From Pittsburgh, the Ohio River extends south and westward, an invitation to further advance, and soon word was brought east of the wondrous lands along that river and to its south. It was a region conducive to land speculation, and young Clark's earliest activities were in exploring, surveying and commencing the development of tracts in the Ohio country. He soon became prominent, a leader among the dwellers in the new lands. Friction between Indian and encroaching white man had led to Lord Dunmore's War in 1774, and for the moment stalled further settlement in the Ohio Valley. Clark's first military experience was won in this war as captain of Virginia militia.

The end of Dunmore's War saw the start of a migration into the Bluegrass lands of Kentucky. There was constant conflict with the Indians, who greatly resented this intrusion into their hunting grounds. Despite Indian resistance, the immigration continued. In December of 1776 Kentucky was formally made a Virginia county, and soon Clark, as major of Virginia militia, took command of troops raised for the defense of the western limits of that state.

By the summer of 1777 a great change had taken place. The British commander at Detroit, acting under orders from London, commenced to equip the Indians and urge them to war against the frontiers of the young American states. They needed little urging, and Kentucky soon felt the brunt of their savage attacks. Clark, military commander on this most western frontier, quickly decided that to sit on the defensive was to await disaster. The only effective protection for the settlements would be to destroy Britain's offensive capabilities by the capture of Detroit, the most important post in the northwest. He appreciated, however, that before he could operate against this major target, he must be master of the other posts in the region: Kaskaskia, Cahokia and Vincennes. It is at this point that Bruce Lancaster takes up the thread of Clark's campaigns.

The story ends with the second capture of Vincennes and of Lieutenant Governor Hamilton, and this was the apex of Clark's career. He never won Detroit, but he held the Kentucky country throughout the Revolution with his puny force. In 1781 Yorktown saw an end to active warfare in the East, but the British continued to supply and encourage the Indians to keep up their raids on Kentucky for another two years. During this period Clark, with only a handful of troops and a minimum of supplies, conducted an active defense of the Ohio country and neutralized all attempts to drive the Americans from the Ohio. The peace treaty of 1783 assigned all the northwest territory to the United States, but despite this the British showed a fierce determination to hold the trading posts in that region. Acting under one pretext or another they continued to occupy Detroit until 1796, thirteen years after they had agreed to give up the place.

Clark's actions in the Ohio region during the Revolution were vital to the ultimate success of the American cause. His initial move against Kaskaskia caught the British just as they were preparing an assault on Pittsburgh. The attempt was abandoned. Furthermore, his active presence west of the Alleghenies furnished a most effective screen to counter British moves against the undefended back country of the coastal colonies. Think of the havoc and confusion that would have resulted from even a relatively small enemy raid into Pennsylvania made in the spring of 1780 when Washington, his army disheartened, mutinous and less than four thousand in number, faced General Clinton in New Jersey!

Clark's operations in the Ohio guarded the vulnerable rear of the southern and central regions of our country throughout the last difficult years of the war. But they also made our occupancy of the Ohio country an accomplished fact, a fact that could not be denied at the peace table. Small as was our hold, we nevertheless retained it, and Britain could boast only Detroit. Though Clark himself, let down by Virginia's unwillingness or inability to support his activities, retired into a private life dogged by disillusion and ill-health, he nevertheless had won and held for the new United States the land that was to become Ohio, Indiana and Kentucky. His country has almost forgotten him. It is to be hoped that Bruce Lancaster's last novel may help restore George Rogers Clark to the memory and the veneration of his countrymen.

EDWARD P. HAMILTON
Boston
January, 1964

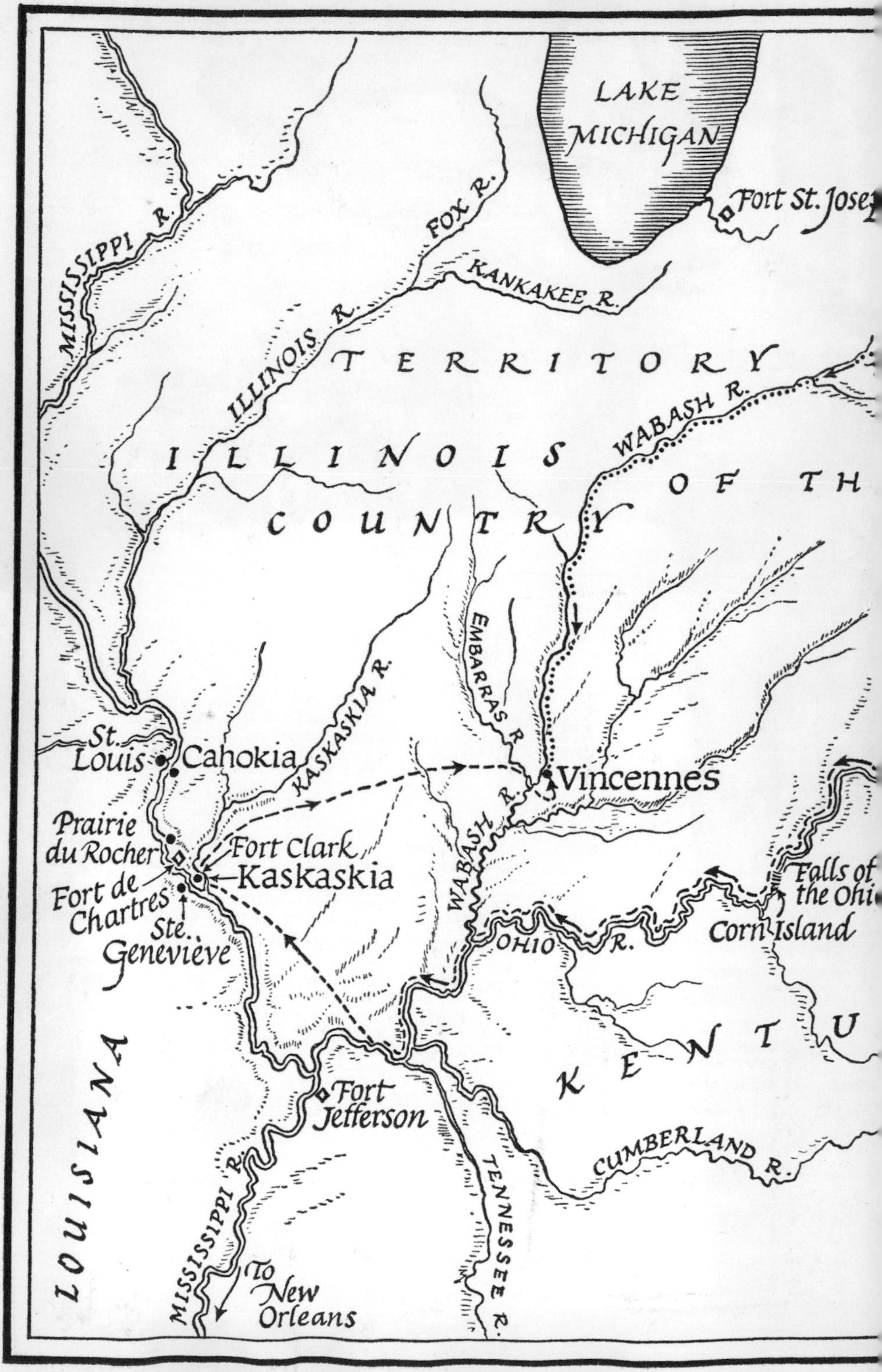
LAKE
MICHIGAN
Fort St. Jose
MISSISSIPPI R.
FOX R.
KANKAKEE R.
ILLINOIS R.
TERRITORY
WABASH R.
ILLINOIS
OF TH
COUNTRY
EMBARRAS R.
KASKASKIA R.
St. Louis
Cahokia
Vincennes
WABASH R.
Prairie du Rocher
Fort Clark
Kaskaskia
Fort de Chartres
Ste. Geneviève
Falls of the Ohi
OHIO R.
Corn Island
KENTU
LOUISIANA
Fort Jefferson
CUMBERLAND R.
TENNESSEE R.
MISSISSIPPI R.
To New Orleans